T0116800

American Mercenaries

Jake Dunn

iUniverse, Inc.
Bloomington

iUniverse books may be ordered through booksellers or by contacting:

iUniverse
1663 Liberty Drive
Bloomington, IN 47403
www.iuniverse.com
1-800-Authors (1-800-288-4677)

ISBN: 978-1-4620-1367-8 (sc)
ISBN: 978-1-4620-1365-4 (hc)
ISBN: 978-1-4620-1366-1 (ebook)

Printed in the United States of America

iUniverse rev. date: 06/27/2011

Book One

Life at a Deep South Military Academy

Chapter One

★   ★

8:10 am, August 19, 1968
Fairhaven High School
Fairhaven, Alabama

On being summoned to the principal's office at Fairhaven High, JD Volt glanced through the glass top of the door and slowly backed away when he saw his father, Big Jake Volt, Melanie a rather small, blond, pretty majorette with a figure that belonged in Playboy. They had been having unbridled carnal relations, morning, noon and night for the entire summer vacation. She along with her father and Big Jake were facing across the principle's desk with their backs to JD as he quietly shut the door.

The night before, Melanie's father a tall hard man, reputed brewer of white lightning in Citronelle Al. that JD knew kept a shotgun and other assorted weaponry in his Olds 98 had caught JD and Melanie making passionate love in the back seat of JD's car. It was a Morris Minor and undoubtedly one of the slowest vehicles in the world with acceleration to sixty mph somewhere in the two minute range and a top speed of seventy down hill, a fast cyclist would have been a challenge. Big Jake had bought it for JD so he wouldn't have to worry about drag races, etc. His thought to flee in the car was quickly rejected in favor of a running dive and swim across a nearby river for an escape through a dense, swampy, wooded area.

He got to the beach for the last few miles home after a long nights trek through the forest avoiding the highway in case Melanie's father was looking for him. Arriving with just enough time for a quick shower, he got dressed and caught a ride to school with a friend before Big Jake woke up. He knew the Morris, if it wasn't already destroyed was at extreme risk, and a shit storm was going to descend on him within an hour or so.

Uh oh I'm in deep shit, he thought then slowly backed away from the door with a strong urge to run. Ms. Stuart, the principal's secretary who every student at F.H.S knew really ran the school glanced up from her desk to berate him.

"JD Volt you have been a ve very bad boy. I've already informed the principal of your presence so you get in there and face the music before your father has to run you down. Knowing Big Jake, I doubt that would be pretty.

JD reluctantly entered the office and the pervasive moldy odor of old books stacked on shelves around the entire room lent an air of impending doom. JD figured he might em emit a similar odor after Melanie's old man got through killing him. As the door clicked shut, Melanie, her father and Big Jake all swung around to glare at him. He glanced at Melanie hoping for some sympathy and received none. Man! It looks like her old man is ready to skin my ass alive. Why was I dumb enough to be screwing in her back yard? There aint a guy in school who wouldn't run ten miles and jack off twice if he thought he had a chance with her. Come to think of it, why does she have her panties in a wad. She sure wasn't complaining about what we were doing. JD thought.

Melanie was petite, fair with sky blue eyes framed by lovely all American girl features. Her golden blond hair cascaded around her shoulders to the front of her bodice accenting perfectly shaped breasts that seemed on the verge of breaking free of bra and blouse. With all the curves in the right places down to beautifully shaped legs she was what every male teen the world over prayed would move next door. JD thought she was the sexiest girl on the planet in her short gold majorette skirt, tasseled white boots and blue bodice that enhanced her perfect breasts.

JD's Father, Jake Volt's moniker 'Big' was an apt description. He couldn't be called huge or immense…just 'Big,' From lean muscular, broad shoulders, he stood well over six feet tall and tipped the scales at a hard two hundred and fifty pounds or so. With a face seemingly chiseled from granite ending at a somewhat prominent cleft chin and a slightly off kilter Roman nose. JD figured he'd acquired from some past bar-room brawl. His steel gray eyes seemed to glint if he had a mad on and during his preteen years, JD was sure they were capable of emitting lightning bolts and was always ready to dive for cover when some offense on his part earned a burning glare from Big Jake.

He'd outrun Jake on the beach in front of their house at parties Jake threw for his employees. But, thinking about it, he figured Jake might have let him win just to sucker him into running when he knew he shouldn't. The thought of big, lean, mean running his ass down wasn't anything JD wanted to deal with. He had inherited his progenitors broad shoulders, muscular build, brown hair, dark complexion, hard jaw sans cleft chin although his eye's were dark almost black. He was resigned, but felt a little cheated that he would never attain his father's massive size. At eighteen he stood five eleven, 'six feet with the right shoes on', and weighed in at a hard hundred and ninety pounds.

Melanie's old man stood and shot looks that would melt diamonds at JD. Damn he looks like he definitely wants to kill my ass, JD thought. He glanced at his progenitor and was the recipient of an angry scowl. Shit! I'm fucked! Jake is more than a little pissed himself.

Big Jake glowered at his son for a few moments, It's gonna be hard, but I got to act real mad, he thought, then had to struggle to suppress a smile when he looked at the comely lass the boy had been dallying with. The only reason for me to be upset is I sure as hell never got a shot at a prime filly like this one when I was in high school. He forced himself to continue frowning and then growled at JD. "Son, you been carrying on in ways you shouldn't have. Just stand there and keep your mouth shut." JD moved aside as the principal rose and headed for the door.

"Folks, since this isn't a school problem, I'm going to excuse myself and let you hash it out among yourselves."

JD glanced back at Melanie hoping for any sign of mercy, again received none. As the door closed her old man stared him as if the reincarnation of Jack the ripper had just entered the room. Shit! Melanie got in so much trouble she probably wants to cuts my nuts off too. He quickly shifted his eye's back to Big Jake.

"Uh…yes sir, what's up?" *It aint like I don't know*, he thought, desperately wishing he could melt back through the door. It became apparent that Melanie had confided in a girlfriend. She had relayed the info to her mama who had burned the phone, lines, poles and the ground they were sitting in passing the good news on to Melanie's mama who then called in her gun toting husband.

A heavy long pause ensued until Melanie's father rose cursing JD and the ground he walked on, demanding at a minimum castration as the appropriate punishment for his villainy. Big Jake listened sympathetically until the idea of neutering his first son came up, then stood and interrupted in a harsh tone.

"You're gonna` need to settle down if we're going to be able to work this situation out without any violence." It appeared to JD that he was about to see Big Jake in action after years of hearing what a bad ass he was when Melanie's old man bowed up and it looked like war was about to be declared.

Melanie's father being well aware of Jake's reputation as a tough hard man that if he felt an individual or individuals were being unreasonable was capable of extreme violence, caused him to have second thoughts about his demands for a bloodletting. With that in mind he sat back down mumbling curses and threats of legal action. Jake waited until the mutterings died, then in a quieter tone continued.

"If you're considering a law suit. And that is the only road you can take since this lovely girl is certainly at the age of consent. There aint much I can do but refer you to Sam. But…if it were my daughter, I'd think twice before going down that road. A long drawn-out court case wouldn't do anything but sully this young ladies reputation."

They all knew Jake's lawyer, Sam was the sharpest mouthpiece in the county. He'd kept Jake relatively unscathed from a few legal problems over the years, and the mental picture of him grilling Melanie about her sexual conduct with JD was too onerous for her father to contemplate. Jake let the oppressive images solidify before continuing, "on occasion, I've been tempted to skin the boy alive myself, but his mama dearly loves him so there's not going be any cuttin`." He waited as the grumbling began anew then held his palm up for quiet.

"The sapient solution to our problem is to get the miscreant out of the area for the next few years so this beautiful young lady and you sir, can hopefully forget he ever showed up on your doorstep disguised as a nice young man. `Jake was always using the latest big word he'd picked up from it pays to increase your word power in the Readers Digest. JD had a good idea what a miscreant was and figured he sure fit the bill in this instance, but he didn't have the slightest inkling what the hell sapient meant. Jake continued, "I don't know where we went wrong raisin' him, but I intend to do my level best to mend the mistakes we've made right now."

JD was a little worried about what, 'out of the area' meant but knew there was another girl he'd worked into his schedule the prior two weeks and she got wind of what was going on, the consequences of her daddy, a hard scrabble fisherman, known to be more than proficient with knives was pretty scary to think about. With that in mind, he turned to Big Jake.

"So, when we going to leave Daddy?"

They drove North ninety miles up Highway forty-three in Jake's Fleetwood Cadillac with a set of longhorns adorning the hood...Jake had spent some time during his younger years in the Texas oil fields and liked the way they decorated their Cadillac's.'

JD finally got the nerve up to inquire about his destination and for how long the sentence was as they motored through Jackson, Alabama. Shit! Now I've really pissed him off. I shoulda kept my stupid mouth shut, he thought as Jake turned and fixed a baleful glare on him. He eased a hand over to the doorknob, fully prepared to bail out even though they were clocking up the highway at around eighty mph. Jake, seeing his scion's hand on the knob relaxed his scowl slightly.

"Son...Mama and I have tried everything we can think of to straighten your ass out and nothings worked. Now, this last bit 'a tomfoolery has finally convinced her that the only chance we've got to keep you alive and out of jail is to stick you in military school for the next few years" He waited for JD's reaction, got nothing but a blank look and continued. "If it had been up to me, you would 'a been sent off years ago so the answer to your question is Martin Military Institute, and you'll be wearing a uniform for the next few years."

Yeah you grumpy old bastard, you were smart enough to kidnap my ass before I knew what was up and had a chance to work on Mama. If I'd had a couple a days with her, she'd a been convinced that it really wasn't my fault since I inherited the bad blood from you, then she would have made your life a living hell until you changed your mind about haulin̄ my ass off to a high falutin jail. JD thought.

The further North they drove, the more JD got depressed as they passed through Grove Hill, Thomasville, North to Pine Hill and he hadn't seen a movie theatre much less any honky-tonks. There might have been some off the main drag, but it didn't look like there was anything but corn fields and cow pastures outside of those little towns.

Jake stopped for gas just north of Thomasville in the little town of Pine Hill. Downtown consisted of one old two story clapboard building serving as general store, post office and gas station. It had been painted red in the past but had faded to a splotchy russet brown. The planked front porch still had two hitching posts on either side of the front steps and was covered by a sagging rusty tin roof supported by six four by fours cracked and peeling from age. There was a railroad siding directly across the two lane highway with hundreds of saw logs stacked for shipment to lumber mills in Mobile or Birmingham. Damn! I can't believe people are still ridin̄ horses to the store around here, JD thought when he saw the hitching rails then glancing up, realized the second floor was probably the owners living quarters as there was a wizened old woman propped on her elbows puffing on a corn cob pipe in a window gazing down at the big dusty black Cadillac with long horns for a hood ornament. Two gaunt old geezers with it appeared two or three days growth of gray whiskers dressed in worn bib overalls, no undershirts, brogans and sweat stained Red Man caps were seated in weathered wooden rocking chairs on the porch. Both were missing a few teeth and chomping away on what JD assumed were chaws of tobacco. Jake braked to a stop at two nineteen thirties vintage gas pumps with glass tubes on top where little bubbles spun around when the pumps were in use. He unfolded out of the car, stretched, then leaned back in the window. "Fill 'er up, son," he said, "I'm gonna̔ get me a cold drink." JD got out muttering to himself, "Yeah ya big butthole, you wouldn't dream of gittin̄ me one." Jake cocked an ear and stopped with one boot on the porch then turned to frown at JD. "What was that boy?"

"Uh…I was just wondering which one a̔ these is high test Daddy?" Big Jake scowled at him for a moment.

"It sure didn't sound like that to me," he grunted then stepped all the way up on the porch and shot back over his shoulder, "The one that cost the most dummy." JD got frustrated trying to figure how the pump worked and swore under his breath until one of the old geezers spit a brown wad at a spittoon, missed completely and spoke up.

"Boy, you got to turn that little whirly-gig on 'a side 'afore that thar pump is goner' let loose 'a any gas," he said. JD felt like asking the old goat just what the hell a whirly-gig was, but knew if he did and Jake heard, he'd swat him for not showing proper respect to his elders. He finally located a little handle on the side and spun it until a bell sounded and fuel started to flow. He had almost filled the tank when Jake stepped out of the store and tossed a soft drink to JD, then propped a snakeskin boot up on the porch and shoved his Stetson back. 'In addition to how they decorated their Cadillac's Jake liked the way they dressed in Texas.' One of the old coots glanced up at what he figured was a real big Texan and launched another gob off to the side to make sure he didn't offend the big man, totally missing the spittoon again.

"Howdy, neighbor," he said. "That your boy?" Jake swallowed the last of his drink and glanced over at JD.

"Yes sir, sorry to say he is." The old man noticing JD had figured out how to operate the pump opined.

"Well, he aint total dumb is he?"

"No, once in a while we get a faint glimmer he might be worth claimin' someday," Jake grunted as he glanced over to make sure JD wasn't screwing something up. The old man eyed the horns on the Cadillac's hood. "You aint from Alabama are you?" Jake swung his attention back.

"Yes, I am, but I spent a few years in Texas wild-cattin' and took a likin' how they decorate their cars. Fact is, I grew up around Forkland, and Boligee, which aint but about sixty or so miles from here." The old man spit again and actually scored.

"I figured you was from Texas, what with that setta' longhorns on that thar Cadillac," he said, paused spit and rang up another one. "I aint never seen no long horns 'afore, but have always had a hankering to." He nodded at the other old coot. "Billy Joe swears they got some over ta' Monroe, Louisiana, but he's been known to stretch the truth and I don't put much stock in it. Far as I know aint neither one of us been west of the Alabamer, Missippi' line." The other old geezer frowned and spoke for the first time.

"Whut you don't know would fill up a whole libary`, Joe Bob. Why don't you jist shut yer trap." Joe Bob ignored him and continued, "I've had a hankerin` to see if them long horns were as big as they look at the pitcher` show," he said. "I'm right happy you showed up with such a fine set on that thar Cadillac autermobile

JD finished pumping the gas and got back in the car. There the big palooka is with his Stetson kicked back happy as a hog in slop and I'm so edgy about how long I'm gonna` be stuck in military school you could drive a ten penny nail up my ass. And where the hell did this old geezer find a movie around here?

He figured his situation had progressed from dire to dismal when they arrived at Martin Military Institute's guard-house and he discovered that the Commandant was none other than Colonel Bull Stier, U.S. Air Force retired. He was JD's uncle by marriage being wedded to Big Jake's younger sister, JD's aunt Zodie. Him being commandant confirmed JD's thought that his time at military school was going to be anything but enjoyable. The colonel was the most aptly named individual JD had ever known being a shade below average height and built along the lines of an English bulldog, including bow legs, jowls, massive neck and a rough bark in perfect harmony with his appearance. He and Big Jake were in complete agreement on almost everything. Their politics ranged about two steps to the right of Attila the Hun and in their opinion liberal Democrats were either dumb as stumps or Communists in disguise. A certain amount of Scotch whiskey on a regular basis was necessary to keep a man in balance. Friendly women were the only reason most men went to war, wanted to get rich, etc, etc, etc. And last but not least… young JD was hardly worth the price of a small caliber bullet, but they knew they had to try to straighten his ass out since anything short of arson, rape, or pillage, his mama and aunt Zodie always came down on his side. He and Jake spent a few minutes commiserating about what a sorry individual JD was, then the colonel turned to him.

"JD, if you ever address me as anything other than 'Colonel', or anybody at this Institution or in Perry County finds out you're related to me or your aunt Zodie…I'll see to it that your time here which is probably going to be long is a miserable living hell and you will undoubtedly set new records on the bullring." JD didn't have any idea what the bullring was, but it didn't take but a few days for him to become well acquainted with it since Martin Institute had so many rules and regulations it would 'a been hard for Jesus to keep his butt out of trouble.

He spent the first night in a barracks with other newly arrived cadets, then awoke at 05:30 the next morning to the sounds of reveille blaring over loud-speakers and a cadet sergeant running up and down the hall pounding on doors hollering.

"Get your ass outta' that rack, you got thirty minutes to shit, shower, shave and be in formation for inspection!" JD understood the three-esses but hesitated before getting dressed. I wonder what they're gonna" inspect? Aint nobody told me which one a" these uniforms I'm supposed to wear. He rummaged through his footlocker and decided since it was August the light khaki trousers, shirt, black tie and hard billed hat would probably be about right. Strolling out of the barracks thirty minutes later he was startled when the same loud mouthed sergeant met him as he came down the steps and loudly braced him.

"Fall in stupid...we aint got all day, I know you're used to Mama powdering your sweet little ass, pinching your rosy cheeks and feeding you breakfast with a spoon. All 'a those little love gestures are history now, so fall your ass in and we can all proceed to the mess-hall for breakfast like real grown up men." JD realized the loudmouth was at least three inches shorter, thirty or so pounds lighter, and was considering popping the little shit in the mouth when a restraining hand grabbed his arm and jerked him in formation. After lining up he looked to see who had pulled him away from the obnoxious sergeant and saw the grinning countenance of a young man approximately his age.

"It aint a good idea to go whipping up on your platoon sergeant the first day you're here," the young man muttered out the side of his mouth. JD was trying to keep his mad going, but couldn't help being affected by the cadet's infectious grin and was smiling as the Platoon leader screamed, "Ten hut!"

The Platoon, including all newcomers assigned to it came to a semblance of attention for inspection. JD discovered they were inspecting for things like polished brass, clean starched uniform, spit shined shoes, properly tied ties which reached but did not cover the belt buckle, clean shaves and a proper haircut. He didn't pass muster on all of them, but there were a few new arrivals less informed so he wasn't singled out for a whole lot of ridicule.

There was one rule he had never dreamed of…Martin Institute hated nose and ear hair and JD having both gave a little cadet Lieutenant an excuse to stop in front of him and question what kind of missing link was in his ancestry to cause such a hirsute problem while he was still in high school. JD's temper was beginning to boil again. *Damn I guess you got to be a little twerp to get any rank around here,* he thought. A bugle sounded, signaling it was time for the battalion to march to the mess hall which interrupted his thought to punch the little twerp in the nose. On further thought he decided it would cause undue trouble to strike a superior officer anyhow.

After they finished breakfast, JD and the other new arrivals were marched to the auditorium for orientation and assigned faculty advisors. He wasn't surprised when he found his advisor, Major Vader had in addition to his transcripts from Fairhaven High some special notes from Colonel Stier. His course of study was laid out and the major informed him he was assigned to Easy company and would be rooming with Cadet Squad Sergeant Mickey Dix.

"Sergeant Dix, is a senior in high school," the major stated. "He's been here since his sophomore year, is a fine young man, an exemplary cadet and will help you keep on the straight and narrow during your training here." *Shit! it's gittin worse! This dude has got to be a total asshole to have spent years here and liking it enough to get promoted.*

Chapter Two

13:00 hours, August 20, 1968
South barracks, Martin Military Institute
Martin, Alabama

JD lugged his footlocker up to the second floor of South Barracks on granite steps worn to the last inch of thickness in the middle by untold numbers of personnel trudging up or down the steps. It was a two story red brick structure erected before the civil war with thick concrete walls supporting the brick veneer. The builders were likely worried about the damn Yankees rolling up with artillery. I heard this place was run by the confederates during the war but didn't believe it. I wonder how many people and years it takes to almost wear through seven inches of granite.

Upon reaching the room he was surprised to find Sergeant Mickey Dix was the cadet who'd kept him from punching the platoon sergeant at breakfast formation. Despite JD's prior thoughts, Mickey turned out to be a divine gift. He knew every trick in or out of the book on ways to get around Martin Institutes myriad system of rules and regulations. He was from Monroeville, Alabama about eighty miles Northeast of Fairhaven. He was an inch or so taller than JD, with a lean sinewy build, fair complexion and ice-blue eyes set in a sharp aquiline countenance.

JD was surprised to find Mickey had been banished to Martin for approximately the same transgressions as he had. He just got caught a little quicker. After he'd unpacked and hung his uniforms in his wall locker, he turned to Mickey and asked him three things he'd been worried about since arriving. "What do you do for entertainment? Where are the girls? And how do you get away from here?"

"There aint any girls except over at Judson," Mickey replied. "That's a Baptist girl's college the other side 'a town. It aint really worth the trouble to try to hook up with one of them since there's a bunch of old biddies that keep 'em under lock and key. If you want to get away from here for any time at all, you need to try out for anything that travels. You got the build to be an athlete?"

"I've played some ball," JD replied.

Good, we'll head over to the field-house tomorrow afternoon and sign you up for football. "The team makes three or four good trips a year to play other high schools and most of 'em are overnight trips. The coaches are more worried about winning than all 'a Martin's rules so they'll usually let us go to town after the game. You got a lot better chance of meetin' some girls in those towns than around here. It aint much, but it's better than being stuck on post the whole semester."

"That sounds fine to me," JD said, "but what do we do after football season?" Mickey chuckled.

"Hold your horses, the next question is, are you gonna' be here for Junior college next year?"

"I'm stuck through my sophomore year," JD muttered.

"Then we'll go out for the Junior college team this spring. They make a lot more trips than the high school to play a lot of major college freshman teams. You aint ever seen girls like the ones wandering down sorority row at the University of Alabama. The only problem is you got to survive the game, those guys take their football real serious and they usually beat the shit outta' us.

JD was beginning to see a small ray of hope and really felt better when Mickey added, "there are two other teams that travel; the Rifle team and the White Knights, that's the drill team. I'm on it and we go to New Orleans and Mobile every year for a few days during Mardi Gras, and almost every year to Pensacola for the Fiesta of Five-Flags Parade."

"Who do I see about signing up for them?" JD asked.

"Me," Mickey replied. "Howard Kurt, our company commander is the White Knights platoon leader and a friend of mine. Soon as you get unpacked we'll go see if he's checked in yet. Then, I'll get you together with another buddy of mine, Mike Saliba. He's the best at close order and rifle drill and can help you get ready for the tryouts next week."

"What about the rifle team?" JD asked.

"That's the best of all, it makes four or five trips a year usually for two or three days competing against other schools. According to how we do in competition against them, if we do well, we get to compete with the regular army team and that's a week long competition," Mickey replied. "You ever fired a rifle before?"

"You better believe it. My old man taught me how to shoot when I was six years old. I can take a hair outta' a gnats ass at two hundred yards," JD replied.

JD spent an hour a day for the next week with Saliba being tutored in close order drill and rifle handling. He learned how to make his rifle snap sharply, even how to execute the Queen Anne salute, a maneuver with the entire platoon lined up in a straight row with each man on first sighting movement from the man next to him, pitching the butt of his rifle up over the muzzle, then catching it as he knelt with a knee and rifle butt resting on the ground at the same instant. After a week of tryouts with Saliba's coaching and Mickey's influence with Cadet Captain Kurt, JD made the team.

chapter Three

★　　　　　　　　　　　　　　　　　　　　　　　　　　　　　★

16:00 hours November 10, 1968
Parade grounds, Martin Institute

Captain Parker, Professor of military science and tactics, a stocky, average height, regular army officer in charge of the drill team looked on as the platoon practiced for an upcoming Veterans Day parade in Birmingham. He waited until Cadet Captain Kurt formed the platoon in front of him, returned his salute, then stepped forward to address the platoon.

"I am not here to enforce all of Martin Institute's regulations and don't particularly care if some of them get a little bent," he barked. "There are four simple rules, hereinafter to be classified as 'Parker's Law' and they will be adhered to, and strictly enforced."

"Number one. If the team is due to depart the same day as a given exhibition, you better be back at the bus on time."

"Number two. When the team is scheduled for an overnight stay, bed check is at twenty-four hundred and you better be in your rack when Cadet Captain Kurt or I check. If you can't find what you're looking for before then, you sure as hell aren't going to find it on the street later and not risk catching a social disease. That will not be tolerated while I am in charge."

"Number three. Do not get arrested, a lot of locals tend to get a tad irritable when you show up in fancy uniforms and try to move in on what they consider their women folk." He paused a moment. "I know it's not reasonable, but you better believe it and keep it in mind when you decide to cut one out of the herd."

"Number four, be advised that I've heard every lie or excuse any cadet ever dreamed up to explain how he didn't start the fight or any other trouble he might've stirred up. If any of you think you can come up with a story good enough for me to sympathize with, know this, you cannot!!!

Most exhibitions, parades or functions the team was scheduled for were usually over by mid-afternoon leaving the cadets adequate time to seek out members of the fair sex. And, if one believes Jason was a little obsessed with the Golden Fleece, it's doubtful that he was anywhere near as obsessed as a full platoon of eighteen to twenty year old young men locked up in all male barracks for several months were with finding girls. That obsession led to one near disaster, coupled with another that almost got JD and Mickey dismissed from the team.

The White Knights had been picked as one of the top drill teams in the country the prior year and as such were chosen to give an exhibition for President Nixon at the end of the Veterans Day Parade in Birmingham with the Queen Anne salute being executed in front of the reviewing stand as the grand finale. The exhibition went to perfection until the Queen Anne, and JD missed his rifle on the way down, then was horrified at the racket an M1 rifle made as it clattered to the pavement. Muttering curses as he scrambled to pick the damn thing up, he glanced at the reviewing stand and saw the President staring right at him. To make matters worse, Captain Parker was standing behind Mr. Nixon and it looked like he was about to come uncorked.

During ensuing years, JD was a little confused why there was always someone on television claiming that President Nixon was a terrible unscrupulous evil man. He for one considered him one of the best men he'd ever met, but he was probably a little biased. After the platoon formed for dismissal and JD was standing at attention, waiting for Captain Parker to get around to taking a huge chunk out of his ass the President came down from the reviewing stand surrounded by secret service agents glaring at anyone in the general vicinity with Captain Parker bringing up the rear. He wasn't glaring at anyone, but JD.

The President walked directly to JD, glanced at his name tag and smiled. "Cadet Volt, I know you feel bad about dropping your rifle but you don't need to. I've seen a rifle dropped during that maneuver by the best team in the world, the U.S. Marine Corps drill team." He chuckled and added, "I am kind of happy it wasn't loaded since it was pointing at the reviewing stand when it landed." Captain Parker immediately volunteered that the team was never allowed to carry loaded weapons and the President glanced over his shoulder at him.

"Damn, Captain that was a joke, didn't you think it was funny?" Then, without giving the Captain a chance to reply he turned back to JD. "What about you Cadet, did you think it was?"

"Yes sir, I thought it was extremely funny," JD replied. "But, I've already embarrassed the platoon and have to curb my natural inclination to laugh, it isn't allowed in ranks." The President chuckled, and turned back to Captain Parker. "Captain, this cadet is a prime example of what we need more of in this country," he said. "Any young man who can come up with a good story that fast after screwing up ought to be rewarded not punished and I would appreciate it if you would see to that." JD decided on the spot if the president asked, he'd descend into hell and take on old Beelzebub with a rusty pocket knife. After inspecting the platoon Mr. Nixon left, Cadet Captain Kurt ordered, "At ease." Then Captain Parker marched to JD's front and braced him.

"Divine intervention has altered my plans to strangle you," he growled. "But...if you ever drop that rifle again, you better bend over and open real wide, 'cause I'm going jam it up your ass sideways."

Mickey caused the next near disaster. His having been on the Drill team the prior year and to the metropolis of Birmingham for several exhibitions they decided, since the team wasn't going to be staying over night and check-in time was 23:30 hours for the bus ride back to post. They wouldn't have time after the parade was over until check-in to find members of the fair sex of a non-professional nature. Mickey, with his knowledge of the city and because he claimed to know of a good whorehouse was put in charge of getting them both laid. Since Academy rules forbade a cadet receiving more than ten dollars a week to spend on things like movies, snacks, etc., a rule Big Jake was more than happy to comply with. They had forgone all of those for an extended time before the trip to save money for their visit to the bawdy house.

After dismissal, they decided to take a cab to give them more time at the house to experience the pleasures Mickey had been describing for weeks before departure. JD was literally licking his chops thinking about it. The taxi fare was twelve dollars and JD was worried they wouldn't have enough cash to get both of them laid until they exited the cab in front of the house North of the city in Irondale. He was halfway up the steps before Mickey caught up and stopped him. "Since we're in uniform and kinda` young looking, give me the money and I'll go in and set up the deal," he said. "The Madam knows me and knows I won't make any trouble." JD grudgingly handed over his cash.

"How long is it gonna` take?"

"Don't worry, I'll come get you in a few minutes," Mickey assured him. JD waited outside for over an hour, intermittently banging on the front door to no avail until a huge black man came out and barked at him.

"Boy, yo` hit this hyar doo one mo` time, An Ahm gonna come out heya and turn yo` ass inside out. JD waited, extremely frustrated another thirty minutes until Mickey finally emerged. "When I got inside," he mumbled. "I found out the prices have gone up since last year and started to come back out and head back to town to see if we could round up some coeds. But a girl came out that anybody would be proud to take home to Mama and I couldn't help spending every dime on her." JD seriously considered killing him on the spot, but knew Captain Parker would pitch a hell of a fit if he brought him back dead or even severely bent up. He also needed to conserve his energy as it was a four mile hike back to the bus and Mickey had spent their cab fare too. The track coach would have tried to sign them up if he'd timed them for that four miles. They made it with a minute to spare even with JD almost carrying Mickey the last block. The girl had evidently drained him dry.

Captain Parker was standing by the bus door checking cadets off as they arrived and heard JD cursing Mickey for the last block. He gave them a black look as they arrived.

"Get on the bus," he ordered. "I don't want to even think about what you two have been up to. And I don't want to hear a sound out of either one of you until class tomorrow."

To avoid listening to his room-mate bitch, Mickey sat up front next to the captain when JD headed to the back to sit with a couple of other cadets who sympathized with him about the serious misdeed Mickey had perpetrated. They spent an hour trying to come up with an adequate punishment to fit the crime, and agreed an everyday ass whipping wasn't sufficient.

"Besides," one of the plotters said. "Mickey is one tough sum-bitch and I really don't want to get on his bad side. There aint any doubt the three of us could whip his ass, but he's mean enough to hold a grudge and look us up one at a time. I don't know about you JD, but that aint something I'd look forward to."

They spent the better part of the trip back to post trying to decide on something. Then, considering his fellow plotters reluctance to do anything to really piss Mickey off, JD gave up and ceded him a pass. Damn! It's amazing how some guys seem to skate by on every dumb ass thing they do. If I'm standing on the fifty yard line during the national anthem and scratch my balls, some asshole is bound to snap a picture and send home to the local paper. One of the other cadets brought up what they'd done to an over-zealous Corporal in A company the prior year when he got carried away with the honor system and turned in two long-timers for passing answers on a chemistry exam.

They had trussed him up with a gunny-sack over his head, then hung him by his feet on the flagpole a half hour before reveille. They were lucky the officer of-the-day found the Corporal before he got severely screwed up as they heard later it could have caused brain damage for him to hang head down for an extended time.

Everyone, but the Commandant ended up happy. The over zealous Corporal was, because when they heard about it, his parents took him home. Then during the ensuing Investigation, the real honor system took effect. The Corporal didn't know who the villains were since his head was in the gunny-sack, and Colonel Stier couldn't find another soul who could recall seeing who had committed the dastardly deed. He tried to pin it on the two cadets the Corporal had turned in, but they'd been on guard-duty that night and the officer of-the-day vouched for them.

Chapter Four

One month later
South Barracks
Martin Institute

Martin Institute had regulations to control just about every facet of a cadet's life. It was against the rules for him to be in his rack between seventeen-hundred and twenty three hundred when taps sounded. That time was supposed to be spent at his study desk. If caught in his rack or not putting the desired effort into his books, he would be assessed five demerits. Cadets were also assessed demerits for myriads of other offences, unshined shoes, unpolished brass, wall lockers not being squared away with all buttons properly fastened, rack not being properly made up to the desired, tautness so the inspecting officer could make a quarter bounce etc., etc.

The biggest problem JD had receiving demerits was daily-room inspection by Colonel Morse a retired marine who reputedly had three balls, hence his moniker, 'Three-Ball.' JD never having seen them wasn't sure he had them but assumed the number was correct as almost the entire battalion referred to the colonel that way. He seemed to stick JD with two or three demerits every day for little things like not having a button fastened properly on a shirt or a shoe or boot not being polished to a glossy spit shine. There were an ungodly number of nit-picking things the colonel could stick a cadet with if he felt like it and said cadet had arrived on his shit list. JD didn't know how he'd made the list, but had a sneaking suspicion it was at the behest of Col. Stier.

For each demerit exceeding ten, during any one week a cadet was assigned one penalty tour. That was a half-hour spent on the bullring, a large concrete square in front of the Chapel and administrative offices marching in full field gear which included his M1 rifle, helmet liner, back-pack with all gear and rations for three days, web belt, canteen and all other gear and equipment necessary for day and night operations. All of which added up to around forty pounds. In addition to the pain of having to walk the tours, he was confined to post until all penalty tours were expunged.

One week, JD had collected ten penalty tours by Wednesday morning and since five hours on the bullring in addition to class and other scheduled activities in three days, he was looking at the possibility of being confined to post over the weekend. Even praying for divine intervention and the colonel contracting a debilitating illness for the rest of the week there was the distinct possibility he would add to the total Thursday and Friday.

With that in mind JD got the bright idea of reporting to the commandant to discuss the full field gear requirement then marched directly in Colonel Stier's office, saluted and stood at attention until the colonel returned his salute and growled, "What the hell do you want?"

"Sir, on several occasions I have seen movies about West Point and they walk penalty tours in the uniform of-the-day," JD said. "Since West Point is certainly a more up to date institution than Martin, I think it is only proper that we conform with them and drop the full field gear requirement." Colonel Stier glared at him for a few seconds.

"Cadet Volt," he snapped. "The next time you walk in this office with the idea that you can in some way influence how discipline is to be administered here, you better be ready to face some real misery. I wish we could still flog the likes a' you." Then he bellowed, "Now…get your ass outta' my sight before I double your tours!"

After spending two hours on the Bullring that afternoon, JD slouched in the barracks and found Mickey lounging on his rack.

"Three-Ball stuck me for one damn button in my wall locker," he groused. Mickey waited until JD finished stowing his gear, then opened his wall locker to reveal a fold out Playboy pin-up. "If you want him to lighten up, tape a good pin-up in your locker," he said. "Keep an up-to-date Playboy girl and he'll spend more time looking at it instead 'a things to stick you with. He's an old fart but he's got to be the horniest old fart in the world. You'll need to change it at least once a month or he'll get bored and go back to checking for buttons and so forth." JD spent a few moments enjoying the playmate of the year.

"Well shit! Asshole why didn't you tell me?" he grumped. Mickey nodded at the pin up.

"I figured you had to have seen her and couldn't figure out why you didn't have one in your locker; why don't you?"

"I thought you probably took it down every morning before Three-Ball came around, then came up here between classes to jack off in private." JD replied.

"It aint none of your business when I jack off," Mickey snapped. "She's hanging there mainly to keep him off 'a my ass." He waited for JD to absorb that, then continued, "There's one other thing you ought to know about the old goat. If you ever get a good looking girl to come up for one of our military balls, you'll need to keep her out of his sight. Otherwise, the horny old bastard will be trailing you all night like a hound on the trail of a boar hog."

That wasn't a problem for JD since his girl connections at home were in dire straits.

He might have come up with a good enough lie to convince a girl to come up for a weekend. But he knew the girls he had in mind parents would rather have their daughter take up residence in a Sheik's harem than have her squired around all weekend by JD Volt. They knew, even though visiting girls were housed in a Judson college dormitory under lock and key. A conniving rounder like JD would undoubtedly come up with a way to get the girl off by himself. That being the case, he had to spend the remaining time until Christmas vacation with nothing to look forward to but wet dreams and two out of three of those, Mickey would get up to take a piss and wake him up at the best part.

JD became more depressed and decided to try to round up some local talent at Judson when Mickey told him he had a girl coming up for the next weekend. He spent Monday through Friday every afternoon following class and extracurricular activities stationed outside the front gate of Judson and finally connected with a likely prospect late Friday afternoon. Then, he found out it was an exercise in futility as Judson girls weren't allowed to stray off the street leading from the campus gate two blocks to Main Street and a half block to the movie theater, the only entertainment available in Martin, Alabama.

Once inside, there were always two crusty old ladies from Judson patrolling the aisles to make sure nobody was grabbing anything beside coke and popcorn.

A few days before Christmas vacation, Big Jake called and gave JD the bad news that since he'd given his word JD wasn't going to be in the area for quite a spell. He was going to have to spend Christmas vacation with his aunt Zodie or in the barracks with some of the foreign cadets whose parents were too miserly to pay for their round-trip air fares home. JD dearly loved Aunt Zodie. But, he'd rather have spent two weeks in the Perry County Jail than with Colonel Stier. So, after swearing he wouldn't even think about sneaking into Fairhaven to try and connect with the girl he'd caused so much trouble for, Jake agreed to let him spend Christmas with Mickey in Monroeville. He and Mr. Dix had become well acquainted commiserating about problems they had raising sons, who seemed to be a little short on ambition and long on testosterone and Jake figured Mr. Dix would keep them on a short leash.

Big Jake wouldn't own up to it, but he must have been feeling a little guilty for not letting JD come home. He didn't protest much, when JD's mama took the phone to tell him how much she missed him and told him she was going to put a check in the mail so he could get something nice for Christmas. *That's fine. A check is probably better than anything the grumpy old bastard had planned on to make my eye's light up Christmas morning. He's so tight he could squeeze the buffalo off a nickle and he aint real happy about how much it cost to put me in this high falutin jail.* JD thought. When his mama handed the phone to Big Jake, JD heard her snap at him.

"Jake Volt! If you don't get back on this phone and say something nice to your son, I'm going to make you regret it." *Go Mama! I hope he don't have enough sense to do it.*

"Merry Christmas JD," Jake groused. "But it will be a relief to not worry about the phone ringing at two in the morning to get you out of trouble." JD knew that particular complaint was a big exaggeration on

Jake's part. If, in the past he had on occasion run afoul of the law for fighting or some other transgression it was safer in the towns two cell jail. Big Jake was ornery enough regular without someone waking him up before he was ready. In later years Big Jake admitted he had known about almost every incident and admired how JD had the gumption to get himself out of trouble instead of whining to him or worse, to his mama. JD knew it wasn't gumption, but strictly the lesser of two evils. One, bustin' his butt unloading brick at the local hardware store to pay fines and any damages or ask Jake for help, then have to face whatever punishment he had in mind and have to work twice as long to pay him back. When Jake finished talking, he gave the phone back to Mama.

"Baby, I sure do feel bad about not spending Christmas with you," she said. "I'm going to make Jake come up for Government day weekend. We'll be able to spend some time with you then and maybe drive over to Prattville to visit your uncle Bill. It's been a couple of years since we've seen him and I'm always hopeful the two of them will try to get along better." JD could never understand why his mama never gave up hope that all the relatives in Jake's decidedly cantankerous contentious family would all see the light and love one another. And he didn't particularly look forward to spending any weekend with Jake and Uncle Bill. Within an hour after they got together they'd usually be in a raging argument about something or other and on the verge of coming to blows. The thought of his mama yelling at him for two days to intercede every time they bowed up at each other wasn't something JD wanted to do. Uncle Bill was just as big and mean as Big Jake, and why his mama thought him jumping between the two of them would stop anything they decided on, JD had never understood. On the few occasions he'd been dumb enough to try they'd promptly bounced his ass off the nearest wall.

Chapter Five

★   **Chapter Five**   ★

March 10, 1968
Martin Institute

There were three cadets rooming two doors down the hall from Mickey and JD who got together at the onset of their senior year in high school because they were all in JD's opinion, weird.

The first of the trio was Sean Green from Gadsden, Alabama. He had an extreme case of nervous tics and was constantly worried, someone was going to sneak up behind to scare him. When word of that got out it led to him being trailed during class changes by one jokester or another darting behind columns and bushes trying to slip up on him.

Everyone figured any cadet who could sneak up on Sean had to be part Indian since he kept a constant check on his ass. Another favorite was for a cadet to tell Sean he'd heard that someone else was planning on setting his alarm to get up in the early morning hours to frighten him. Sean would sit up all night with a baseball bat awaiting the mythical intruder.

One Saturday after morning inspection, the whole Platoon on Mickey and JD's floor were changing into class A uniforms preparing to go to town when someone set a stick of dynamite off in the back yard of a grouchy old mans that abutted the fence behind the barracks. He had lodged several complaints about noise levels emanating from the barracks at night and cadets running around in various stages of undress. He'd also reported a cadet mooning him on one occasion. That report caused the entire platoon to be confined to post the following weekend since nobody would tell the Commandant who the guilty party was. Everyone knew it had to be Davis Maye, the second of the weird trio. Davis would drop his drawers and moon anybody whenever he got a little wasted. And he was prone to get slammed frequently as he kept a quart of pure grain alcohol mixed with yellow food coloring in a vitalis bottle. A couple of shots of that concoction mixed with orange juice and Davis would be wiped out within minutes.

JD figured Davis was the only one crazy enough to set off a stick of dynamite. It blew a hell of a hole in the old grouch's back yard and scared everybody shitless except Davis. After the blast he was running around hollering.

"Has anybody seen Sean? He was knotting his tie when it went off and just disappeared!!!" JD and Mickey finally found Sean in the back of his wall locker nearly choked to death. He had yanked the knot for his tie so hard that he couldn't get it undone and was turning blue by the time Mickey cut it off with a pocket knife.

The third, and weirdest of the trio was Harry Penkey. He was a doctor's son and a tad confused about his parentage since he had a brother fifty years old by supposedly the same parents. Taking into account the difference in Harry and his brothers age that medical miracle should rank right up there with holy conception. His brother also being a practicing physician and old enough to be his father, served to addle Harry a bit.

That trio, precipitated an incident that got JD and Mickey unjustly accused and punished a few weeks after Government day. The week had ended with a full dress parade for local notables, military brass, politicians and Martin cadre giving speeches to the assembled Battalion and their parents. The main theme being they were all gratified to be associated with Martin Military Institute, a school dedicated to educating and training the future military leaders of America. Hearing the first of those speeches, JD glanced around thinking, *Jeez! If this group ˜a misfits and juvenile delinquents are the future military leaders of America, the country is in deep shit.*

Government day's evening meal and its consequences gave JD and Mickey many chuckles over the next few years. The mess hall staff had gone all out preparing the food for the Battalion and all of the dignitaries with stuffed roast beef being served as the main course. That meal was the only time a lot of parents, faculty, cadre, visiting military brass, the President of Martin, along with politicians and even the old ladies in charge of Judson ate in the mess hall. Faculty and cadre normally avoided it like the plague since the food was usually healthy but tasteless. Either the roast or the stuffing was tainted, and everyone who ate it woke up in the early morning hours with huge lower tract problems.

It hit JD and Mickey at 0:200 and they ran into each other trying to get out the door and down the hall to the latrine. JD finally squeezed through first and charged for the latrine until he slid to a stop behind a long line of cadets, all grabbing their ass in an effort to hold back the imminent explosion. Mickey galloped right on by and down the stairs, hollering," Hit the bushes!!!" There wasn't any greenery on campus needing fertilizing for quite a spell after that night. Cadets were scattering in every direction desperately looking for any unoccupied bush or shrub until the wee hours of the morning. JD and Mickey showered and finally got back in their racks at 0:430 then Mickey chuckled.

"You know everybody that ate in the mess hall has got it and I wonder what it looks like over at Judson with all 'a them old biddies gittin' the shits at once." That brought on uncontrolled laughter, another attack and one more trip outside.

They took another shower and were back in their racks next to the window at 06:00, which confirmed that everybody was sick since reveille hadn't sounded. Looking out the window, they saw Colonel Stier trot down the steps of his residence on the far side of the parade ground for the three hundred yard walk to his office in the rear of the guard house.

The Colonel, being built along the lines of an English bulldog with short bow-legs wasn't very fleet of foot and they fell out of their racks laughing when after the first fifty yards he broke into a fast trot and was sprinting like an antelope with a lion on his ass before he made it halfway across. Mickey was screaming like an idiot out the window between guffaws, "Hit the bushes Fool!!" They were lucky the colonel was in to big a hurry to stop and figure out who the nut was screaming at him.

One other positive, other than reminiscing about the colonel's run was the discovery that if they were careful and didn't use the excuse to often it was possible to avoid some onerous duty like a cross-country hike in full field gear if they charged in the dispensary hollering, "Miz Milly! I got the runs." Miz Milly was the little old lady who ran the dispensary and she, being a kind soul and believing none of her boys would ever lie about such things would give them a dose of kaopectate, then put them to bed for a few hours to make sure it was going to work. They used that ploy for almost a month until a few other cadets got wise to the idea which caused the dispensary to be filled to overflowing whenever a cross-country was scheduled until Mickey opined that the idea was doomed.

"Colonel Stier is gonna' figure this out," he said. "And we better not be in the dispensary when he does."

Everyone in on the scam, was passing enough gas to run a Greyhound bus trans- continental, which led Sean, Davis and Harry to decide they'd have a fart-lighting contest. They felt it was wasteful to expend all of those flatulents for no good reason.

JD and Mickey happened by the room as the competition ensued, heard several loud farts, strolled in to see what was going on and found those three with butts in the air firing them off. About that time, Penkey made the mistake of lighting a slow-bleeder and damned if it didn't blow up and singe the hell outta' his ass. JD and Mickey weren't in on the story they invented to explain Penkey's burnt butt to his doctor-daddy, but it had to be a world class lie to fly. The incident got both of them in trouble. Colonel Stier figured since Mickey ran out to snatch a fire extinguisher in the hall to foam Harry's ass the whole idiotic idea was probably theirs. No amount of oath taking could persuade him they had just wandered in about the time Penkey lit off that slow-bleeder. They got stuck with penalty tours and confined to post until, as the Colonel put it,

"Penkey can take a dump without a jump."

Six weeks before summer vacation, Mickey told JD about a ruse he'd used the prior year to get a weeks' leave. He'd been dating the same girl from Monroeville for over a year and had reported to the commandant that she called to tell him she was three weeks late and thought she might be pregnant. The colonel gave him a weeks' leave to go home and handle the situation.

JD was stupid enough to think, if Mickey could get away with it he could too, then marched in the Colonel's office and told him a girl from Fairhaven who'd been up for a military ball the month before thought she might be in the family way and he felt it was only right that he go home to face the music like a man.

To say the shit hit the fan is putting it mildly. Colonel Stier called Jake. That was bad enough, but to make matters worse, Jake called the girl's daddy, he called the preacher and they all got together at the girls parent's house for praying and confessions.

While the session was in full swing, a couple 'a deacons got wind of it and joined in with their wives. They were all there in the living room, Big Jake, the preacher, the deacons, their wives and the girl, who didn't have the faintest idea what was going on, her daddy and mama. Jake was more than likely just standing around. He wasn't much into a lot of praying and certainly not confessing since he was for sure the biggest sinner in the group.

After they prayed for awhile and the confessing started. The women got fired up and the girl's mama owned up to having an occasional afternoon tryst with the preacher. When she owned up to that, one 'a the deacon's wives got mad. It turned out she'd been doing the same thing a couple of times a week in the morning and the preacher had sworn she was the only one. The preacher's wife was doing one of the deacons, whose wife was doing the preacher and so forth. It amazed JD that Big Jake had missed all of 'em. He for once must have felt real righteous.

JD had to hold the phone away from his ear when Big Jake called until his father got through cussing and calmed down.

"I hope, you're happy now that you've caused the biggest sex scandal to hit the Eastern shore in decades," Jake growled. "If that girl is pregnant you're even dumber than I thought since I been giving you an extra fifty cents to buy protection ever since you started going out with girls. Even when you had a job and could buy rubbers yourself, I still wanted to make damn sure that fifty cents went to the right cause." JD admitted she wasn't. He'd just been trying to get a week's leave. That disastrous idea cost him a summertime girl friend and two weeks out of summer vacation to walk off the penalty tours he got stuck with for gross lying. Anytime, a cadet got stuck with some offense, be it for badly shined shoes, no haircut, sloppy uniform or whatever, the penalty was doubled if they hung the word gross in front of the charge. In later years, when JD wondered if his record for penalty tours accumulated during one semester was broken. Mickey said, "No way, JD you're still the biggest fuckup in Martin Military Institute's history."

Chapter Six

Parade Ground Martin
Military Institute
15:00 Hours, May 15, 1971

After dismissal from the graduation day parade, Mickey & JD were heading back to barracks to hang up their dress blues and relax until they had to don them again for the ceremonies to receive their junior college diplomas that evening.

JD glanced back at the reviewing stand to see where all the brass and notables were headed and saw a regular army major right behind them, came to attention and snapped ten hut before saluting. Mickey failing to see the major glanced at JD.

"What the fucks 'a matter with you? we're about to get outta' here and finally start acting like normal people." Then catching sight of the major he came to attention and saluted.

"Sorry sir I didn't see you."

The major returned their salute, ordered, "at ease," then introduced himself as Major Jack Gordon, U.S. Army Special Forces. He was a tad above medium height, with a barrel chest and a strong jutting chin that appeared it could take a blow from a good sized sledge hammer. His custom fitted uniform could not conceal massive shoulders, arms and thighs. These attributes along with battle-ship gray eyes that brought to mind a soaring eagle scanning the ground for prey and buzz cut hair gave JD the certain knowledge that this was one tough as nails veteran warrior. Looking at the major's tunic they could see row upon row upon row of theater, battle, and decorations for bravery arrayed under combat infantry-mans and airborne parachutist badges. At one time or another during his service the major had received every decoration the military gave other than the congressional medal of honor.

"At ease," the major ordered. "I'm with special operations group and we've been tracking you two since the all army rifle competition this year. It was a little embarrassing to some of our top sniper teams when Cadet Volt scored higher than most of them And Cadet Dix did a helluva' job as spotter." He paused a moment then continued, " I don't want to take a lot of your time since you'll probably be headed down to Gulf Shores to seek out warm bodies in a certainly a more target rich environment in the morning."

"Yes sir, you got that right," JD said.

"Selma is not but five miles out of your way," the major stated. I'd appreciate it if you would stop by the Parrish hotel and let me treat you to a steak and egg breakfast at 0:900.

"Yes sir," JD said. We'll be happy to, then came back to attention to salute.

"I'll be looking forward to seeing you in the morning," the major said, returned the salute and headed back toward the reviewing stand.

Clad in class A uniforms, JD and Mickey strode through the lobby of the hotel at 08:50 the next morning. Mickey had bitched about JD agreeing to have breakfast with some hot-rod army officer for the entire fifteen minute drive to Selma.

"Shit! We been saluting every swingin' dick with a set a bars or oak leaves for years and I'm about ready to get in some civvies and act like I don't even see the next officer we meet." The class A's were his next bitch. "Why the fuck we got to wear these damn things?" he carped. "Maybe you forgot but we graduated yesterday and are officially out of here."

"Yeah, I guess you want to put on some cut-offs, flip flops and a tank top to go sit down with the major, who by the way is probably tough enough to turn both our butts inside out," JD replied mildly.

"Like I said, why'd you agree to it in the first place?" Mickey grunted.

"I guess I missed you turning into a deaf mute yesterday," JD said. "If you were so dead set on a soggy hamburger at some drive in instead of letting the major buy us a steak breakfast, why didn't you say so? It don't make any difference anyhow 'cause we're going so how bout shuttin' the fuck up," he said flatly. Mickey glared at him for a few moments muttered a few curses then seemed to relax.

"You're right JD," he said. "It has been a while since I had a good steak."

They found the major seated at the back of the dining room sipping on a cup of black coffee. He rose to return their salute and said, "Sit." He paused until they were seated and indicated a carafe of coffee, "Coffee?"

"Thank you sir," Mickey said before JD could open his mouth. JD glanced at him in disbelief then reached for the coffee.

"I ordered the biggest porter house on the menu, some grits and three scrambled eggs apiece so I hope you men are hungry," the major said as he nodded at a nearby waiter.

"Damn! That was the best breakfast we've had in years," JD said as the waiter cleared the table and left."

"I guess you men are a little curious about what this is all about," the major said. They both nodded, and he continued. "Have you been keeping up with the war in Southeast Asia?"

"Yes sir," JD said. "But it's kind of hard to follow it closely because we weren't allowed to have a radio in our room. The commandant figured we should be spending' our time studying or keeping our gear in order while in barracks." The major nodded.

"I mentioned yesterday that I'm in special operations group and in going over your records, have decided to offer both of you the opportunity to enlist for special training to get you ready to become members of the unit."

"Thanks, but we've decided to head on up to the U of A next fall," JD said. "We're kind of lookin' forward to going to school with girls for a change." The major frowned.

"I'm going to be blunt. Neither one of you is going anywhere but the army and it'll be thirty days from now instead of the fall. I've seen your records and grades neither one of you rates any kind of deferment. You got two choices, one get with the program, go into an eighteen month training regimen and be a part of one of the elite units in the world, or two get drafted and be in a forward LZ in Vietnam as common every day grunts inside of four months."

"You can't do that," JD protested.

"Try me," The major snapped.

JD glanced at Mickey and could see a blank look then he slowly nodded. JD didn't know what Mickey was thinking about but thought he wanted to take what the major was offering. He turned his attention back to the major.

"I reckon we'll enlist," he said.

"Good!" The major said as he rose. Report to the induction center at the Federal building in Mobile at 0:800 in thirty days. The recruiting sergeant will be waiting for you and I'll be looking forward to watching the progress of your training."

JD and Mickey stood and saluted. The major returned their salute then he walked out and Mickey groused, "JD how the fuck did that asshole find us?"

"I don't know, but we're well and truly fucked There is a bright side though" JD replied

"Please tell me where there is anything bright about what we just got ourselves into," Mickey grumped.

"Well, he said it was going to take at least eighteen months of training and that aint a real big country so the damn war will probably be about over by the time we get over there and we'll just get in on the clean up. Besides he didn't say for sure that was where we'd be assigned."

"If you don't know that's exactly where we'll wind up, you're dumber than I thought" Mickey said.

"You're probably right, but it ought to` be about over before we go and we can come back, go to the university on the GI bill and not have to worry about keeping Big Jake or your old man happy. And the girls up there will go nuts over a couple `a heroes like us."

It was a decision they didn't have a lot of control over but one they would live to regret over the next twenty years.

Chapter Seven

January, 1972
Houng Hoa
Republic of South Vietnam

They spent the next eighteen months in basic, advanced infantry, airborne, ranger and sniper training, then boarded a commercial charter flight to Saigon. After a week of orientation they boarded a Bell UH 1 helicopter commonly referred to as a Huey and were dropped off at a Fire-base near Houng Hoa, a village about thirty clicks east of the Laotian border. They spent one tour and most of another as their C.O., Captain Pete Bradley put it.

"Not in the official sphere of combat operations." Right before he said, "do not get captured and if you are, do not admit you're anything but lost."

"How the hell do you think anybody will believe we just wandered over to Laos by mistake?" JD asked incredulously.

"Don't worry," the captain grunted. "The NVA won't take time to interrogate a couple 'a dumb looking assholes like you two before they nail you up to the nearest tree with your dicks jammed down your throat."

Boarding a Huey for their first mission, Mickey elbowed JD and muttered, "Fuck him! If it looks like it'll help keep our dicks attached, I'll tell 'em we were shipped direct from Washington by the President `hisself." JD agreed except for using the presidents name. He'd had a warm place in his heart for President Nixon since the incident at the Veterans day parade in Birmingham. They settled on the Chairman of the Joint Chiefs of staff until JD asked, "who the fuck is the Chairman?"

"How the hell should I know, you got the stripes and two rockers and are the shooter so you're supposed to be the smart one," Mickey snapped. JD didn't recall anyone telling them, just because he was a better shot that it made him smarter and in charge of all the fuck-ups. But he knew getting in that argument with Mickey was a losing proposition.

Since neither of them could remember a General who had the juice to keep their, dick's in the right place, it was decided they'd just have to avoid capture. It was common knowledge the NVA usually tortured snipers to death anyway.

Their normal mission was to locate three staggered firing positions approximately two kilometers apart South to North along the Ho Chi Minh trail. Set up at the first, wait for an NVA unit which was usually twelve to fifteen men to come by packing gear and equipment, take out as many as possible, then move North to the next position and repeat the process. The reasoning behind hitting at the Southernmost point and moving North was they figured if there were enough enemy left to start searching for them, they'd figure they were headed South toward safety on the other side of the border.

They never stayed around to see how long they delayed those units. JD put as many down as possible without getting their position pin-pointed, then moved to the next position to set up to repeat the process when another unit came by. Mickey would try to point out the leader or officer for JD to take out first, then any others lightly loaded as they were probably well trained troops and might start looking for he and JD instead of ducking for cover.

When the occasional large force came by, Mickey waited as long as possible to identify the officer in charge, then JD would take him out and one or two in the middle of the column before they retreated further back from the trail before calling coordinates in for an air strike or artillery fire. Then they'd head North to the next station. Two or three kills didn't really do a lot of damage to a platoon or company sized force, but seeing the unit commander and a couple more troops brains blown out from a soundless unseen source tended to send the whole unit into panic, drop whatever they were carrying and scramble into the nearby jungle. The time it took for the next in command to get the troops out of cover, get organized and start searching for JD and Mickey or continue their trek South was usually enough for either air or artillery to arrive.

JD was armed with a Hecklor and Koch G3 sniper rifle, chambered for special .308 subsonic ammunition, a sound suppressor and a standard issue 45 automatic. He'd turned the 45 in to supply and bought a Ruger 357 Magnum six shot revolver to replace it when one day he'd forgotten to take the automatic off safety and an NVA stumbled over him and sliced a gash in his left cheek trying to slit his throat. The only thing that saved JD was he caught a whiff the Dink's rotten fish breath as he slid in behind. The sense of smell was key to life and death in Vietnam. Grunts in the bush knew not to bath in any kind of scented soap and JD realized why the army issued blocks of dull tan lye soap; it didn't smell. The down side was it took real effort to work up a lather. Use of deodorant or smoking was a sure way to let Charley or the NVA know where you were. They could smell a man smoking hundreds of yards away. JD fended the knife off with his left arm, threw the small man to the side and finally snapped the safety off and blew him away.

Mickey on first seeing the Ruger snorted.

"Why don't ya' get some cowboy boots, a Stetson and a tin star to go with that thing? What you gonna' do when more'n six git after your ass?"

"Well, if they're four to six hundred meters away they'll be dead in the first fifty and I reckon you can take 'em out inside 'a hundred. Then if they're closer you can use the fifteen rounds in that ugly plastic pistol you tote around," JD replied.

Mickey was armed with an H&K PDW MP-5 for targets inside of one to two hundred meters, a fifteen round Glock nine millimeter with one in the pipe for close in fighting and his ever present Bowie knife for real up close and personal.

The Ruger, being a six shooter was a little limited, but using hot, notched, magnum loads, if that didn't stop a man, JD figured fifteen nine millimeters wouldn't either and their next option was to haul their ass out of the area.

The first time they sighted an NVA unit, Mickey nudged JD.

"These little shits have gotta` be some kind `a dedicated!" he exclaimed. "They're all toting at least seventy or eighty pounds, none of `em look like they weigh over a hundred and it's a long fuckin` way back to North Vietnam."

JD and Mickey, along with other teams slowed some of the supplies coming down the trail, but after a few missions battling a seemingly unending supply of the persistent little bastards toting all the gear as far as they had, they both realized it was probably a lost cause.

"There aint anyway in hell we're gonna` be able to stop the tenacious little shits,"

Mickey complained. "With Hanoi Jane parading her silly ass all over North Vietnam, guarding the dikes to make sure they won't be bombed and maybe starve the bastards into submission. And the dumb-ass, chicken-shit politicians making damn sure the military can't go on the offensive up north and win the fucking war, there aint a chance in hell we're going to do anything but drag it out until the liberal media and hippies convince the public it's time to throw in the towel."

"You're probably right," JD muttered. "It sure as hell aint goin` exactly the way Major Gordon told us is it? And it looks like we're going to end up making a career out of this, aint either one of us is going to be able to go back to civilian society and not risk killin` some loud mouth liberal dickhead."

"I told you that asshole was blowin` smoke," Mickey growled accusingly.

"That's bullshit," JD snapped back. "You never said a fuckin` word.

Depending on how far they were in and how long a hump back to an extraction point. They usually spent seven days along the trail, or up to ten days when the mission was to take out some high ranking NVA or a village chief who was supplying the enemy. The high command didn't seem to worry about risking a Huey inserting a team over a border, but preferred the team move back across before sending a slick or boat to pick it up.

After two tours in, Vietnam, service in Granada, Desert storm and various covert operations, Mickey and JD decided to retire when the draft dodging, President who'd been elected Commander in chief in

1992 decided to make gay rights an issue in the military. His next step was to strip the Military of everything down to and including ammunition in the ensuing years calling it the peace dividend to fund his feel good failed programs for no other purpose than to buy votes for his reelection.

"The next thing you know," Mickey said in disgust. "They'll be ordering us to sign up for sensitivity training in case we happen to run across a limp wrist in the unit."

An elderly gentleman leaning against a standard government issue Ford Crown Vic, puffing on a briarwood pipe was waiting for them in the separation companies parking lot at Fort Bragg after they finished signing their discharge papers and stopped by the barracks to pick up their gear. He was a small graying man clad in a three-piece slightly rumpled worsted suit that reminded, JD of the benevolent God, George Burns had played in a couple of movies. He introduced himself as Charles F. Smith and handed them a card identifying himself as director of Control Associates, listing offices in New Orleans La. and Arlington Va., with two phone numbers, one in the 504 area and another in the 202.

They spent a few moments discussing the disarray the military was in commanded by a draft dodger and his minions before he abruptly changed the subject.

"After you boys blow it out for a while," he said. "And start thinking about what you're going to do to augment your retirement pay. If you can't come up with anything that turns your crank give me a call. Our organization has a place for individuals with your talents at significantly higher pay rates than the Army." He then got in the Ford, backed out of the parking lot and left.

"You think he knows the only thing we do with any real skill is kill people from long distances?" Mickey muttered.

"I wouldn't be surprised if he knows our entire life history," JD replied. "But, what we're going to do in the future is cause for concern. I don't think we'll fit into civilian society very well. We've gone from being in some hell-hole waiting to pop some asshole somebody had a hard on for, to living it up in the closest whorehouse for so long we'll both go nuts inside `a six months trying to fit in on the Eastern shore or Monroeville.

They spent two weeks carousing, traveling South with stops in Atlanta and Jacksonville, finally ending up in Miami with two airline stewardesses they'd been living it up with at the Marriot hotel and assorted bars and restaurants. When the two young ladies had to leave to catch a flight, they checked their finances and it looked like their separation money was going to run out before their next retirement check was due and knew it wasn't going to be enough to keep up their desired standard of living.

"We aint got the slightest idea what a decent living is," JD said. "And I don't think we're going to like bein` civilized in the first place. If you've still got Mr. Smiths card, I reckon we ought to give him a call." JD called the New Orleans number and got a recording stating, Mr. Smith was being paged and their call would be returned in ten minutes. Precisely ten minutes later the phone rang.

"Good day JD," Smith said. "I hope you're calling to express an interest in our offer."

"Yes sir," JD replied. "One question, is what we'll be doing legal?" After a slight pause Mr. Smith replied, "that is a tough question."

Mickey grew impatient with JD's diplomatic tone and grabbed the phone.

"Mr. Smith, do you know the only thing we do really well is shoot people from long distance?" he snapped. "The last time I checked, that's illegal in the civilian world."

"I understand your concern," Mr. Smith said. "While Control Associates is in no way connected with the federal government. We are on a contract basis with several different agencies to carry out covert operations that at times aren't quite legal. But, all of our operations are carried out on foreign soil. If I'm correct, you have operated in areas not quite kosher during your military careers and if you are taken by the targets we'll be assigning, they can't possibly be any worse than some you've successfully terminated for the military." He paused waiting for Mickey to pose another question, then continued, "Take a little time to think about it and call me back in a day or so." Mickey hung up and told JD what Smith had said.

"Makes sense," JD said. "I still got a mental picture of us nailed to a tree with our dicks jammed down our throats."

"Call him back," Mickey said.. "Tell him we'll be at the New Orleans at the Royal Sonesta in seven days."

They spent two days at JD's home on the Eastern shore then two more visiting Mickey's family, told both they were taking a classified government job and headed for New Orleans. Mister Dix and Big Jake having become more respectable over the years were happy to see them, and Mickey and JD could tell they weren't completely unhappy to see 'em heading out of town.

Arriving in New Orleans two days early, blowing more money drinking and looking for love in their favorite combination bar and bawdy house, 'Lucky Pierre's', they waited until Mr. Smith and a narrow shouldered soft looking man met them in the hotel lobby.

Smith introduced the pudgy man as his associate Don Mayer then asked if they would be interested in a mission in Colombia S.A. that shouldn't take more than ten days to two weeks. When he mentioned their fee. Mickey exclaimed.

"Jesus! How many people we got to kill?"

"Just one," Mr. Smith replied. "But there might be a few residual problems." JD and Mickey were well aware of what residual problems were, but still accepted the mission with the proviso that they would approve weaponry, plans for insertion, extraction and be provided with a realistic breakdown of likely opposition. Mr. Smith gave JD a complete file on their target and explained he was a drug lord the Colombian, as well as the United States governments desperately wanted out of circulation.

"The Colombians are scared to arrest him as reprisals against government officials would be deadly," Smith said. "Their only option is for an outside party to take him out with no one being aware of exactly who did it." Mickey and JD understood the situation, and having solved that same type of problem on prior occasions, agreed with confidence that they could do it again. Mr. Smith gave them passports, driver's licenses, credit cards using aliases, and ten thousand dollars for expense and bribe money, then nodded at his associate.

"Don will act as your mission control. He will accompany you during insertion then extraction and will take care of any unforeseen requirements. Mickey scanned the documents and then glanced at JD.

"Damn, these are all valid," he said. "We make it back to the

states we won't have to worry about somebody wantin' to hang us."
That made him happy, thinking about the money made JD happy. He
accepted the target's profile and intel on his location. And not being
aware of what was going through Mayer's mind, he shook Smiths hand,
handed him an account number at Whitney National for himself and
another for Mickey.

"These are the account numbers to wire our fees to be divided
equally."

Book Two

Danger on Foreign Soil

Chapter Eight

★   ★

Panama City, Florida
Bay Point Marriot Hotel
14:30 Hours, April 5, 1993

"Good afternoon ladies," the doorman said, after two young women parked a late model Chrysler convertible with the top down in front of the lobby entrance. The driver was a stunning blond accompanied by an equally attractive auburn haired beauty. He pulled a baggage cart next to the car thinking, College girls, must be the first of the spring holiday crowd. They are usually a pain in the ass but if all of ˜em were as beautiful as these two, I would love it. Unfortunately girls always have a bunch ˜a horny college boys trailing along behind. The girls stood by while he loaded their luggage, then the driver handed him the car keys. "Be sure to put the top up and lock it," she said as the doorman handed them to a valet and then they followed their bags into the lobby.

The desk clerk whistled softly as the girls walked across the lobby to check in.

Man what a couple of babes, they must be here for Spring holidays. I'd like to know what school they're from; there sure as hell aren't any girls like them over at community college. He openly ogled the blond as she approached the desk. With the face of an angel, she's about medium height and that's great since I'm not but five seven. Her rich lustrous hair glistens like spun gold and is cut to perfection as it falls to her shoulders and curls around the neck line of her bodice. He thought then moved his eyes down to drink in the rest of her and took in great tits, small petite waist, shapely legs down to perfectly turned ankles. Man I'd do anything for a chance to get to know her.

Her eyes rested on him as she approached the counter and to keep her from noticing he was blatantly ogling, switched his eyes to her companion and felt the onset of an erection. Oh mama sex exudes from her like sweet perfume. She was a couple of inches taller with long auburn hair and a few more pounds just added an extra aura of sex to her voluptuous figure. Jeez! She's the kind you want to drag in a cave for wet, wild, screaming sex. When they reached the desk. The blond handed him a credit card and he noticed her eyes were deep greenish blue, contrasting perfectly with her angelic face and his heart fluttered when she spoke.

"I'm Susan Dyer and this is Josephine Mcpherson," she said. "We have reservations for a Gulf view room with two queen beds for tonight through Sunday." He slid two registration cards across the desk and scanned the reservation list thinking, I don't care whether you have reservations or not. I'd bump the President to get a couple `a gorgeous babes like you in the hotel for the next four day's. He motioned for a bellboy, waited for them to fill the registration cards out then said, "I'm Bobby, if you need anything just call the desk. I'll take care of it personally. I'm on duty until eleven," His heart skipped another beat as they slid the cards back and Susan smiled.

"Thank you Bobby," she said softly. "We'll be sure to remember that." He gazed in awe as they strolled across the lobby toward the elevator bank. I knew it! Two more perfect asses have never been seen by man nor beast. He sighed then muttered to himself, Shit! I shoulda` told them there was a really good band coming in at nine to replace the afternoon Combo. Maybe I'll get a chance to talk 'em into staying here tonight when they come back to the lobby and I'll get a chance to have a drink with them when I clock out at eleven. Fuck!" he muttered, as the girls neared the elevator bank and two wealthy looking, South American men who'd checked in a few minutes before and had stopped in the lounge for a drink saw the girls as they walked by the lounge entrance, threw money on the bar to settle their tab and hurried to catch them as they stepped on an elevator. Bobby sighed and thought, that blows any chance I have. Those two rich assholes are gonna` put a move on them.

As they stood waiting for the elevator doors to close, Josephine nudged Susan. "It was sure cute the way Bobby was staring at you. For a moment I thought he might crawl over the counter and bathe your feet with tears or something." Susan laughed. "Uh huh, but when he caught sight of you, it looked like he was going to strip to a loin cloth and start looking for a club and a cave."

"That might be fun if he'd promise not to use the club," Josephine said. We don't have any plans for this evening; why don't we hang around here. There was a sign in the lobby advertising a rock band and I just might make his dreams come true."

"Dammit, Jo," Susan exclaimed. "He was cute, but you've got to quit jumping in the sack with every nice looking guy you meet."

"You gotta admit he wasn't just cute, he was really, really cute."

"If you don't grow up you're going to make a complete mess of your life," Susan said. The world has a way of stepping on beautiful women who think they can get away with one night stands with any attractive man who wanders by."

As the doors began to close, two men rushed to hold them and stepped inside. Susan was a little startled. She looked at Josephine and saw she was grinning from ear to ear, then glanced at the two men. Well, it sure didn't take long for her to forget about really cute Bobby, but I have to admit these guys could sure be called tall dark and handsome. The first man turned to his companion.

"Juan, why didn't you tell me a beauty contest was being held at this hotel !?" he exclaimed, then turned back and startled Susan with his intense gaze.

"Uh, there isn't one as far as I know," she stammered.

"Well, that's good as any judges panel would find it impossible to chose between you lovely ladies." Susan blushed. And thought, Lord if you described latin lovers these two would sure fit. Both men appeared to be in their mid thirties, with slender builds, finely chiseled features, generous full lips, dark brown eyes and their perfectly tailored Armani suits gave the impression of moneyed success." Susan took a moment to recover her composure.

"Thank you, but no, we're not in a contest," she said. "It's Spring break and we're here to relax, get a little sun and remove some of the cobwebs we've acquired over the past few months of study at the university."

"Oh, I apologize," he said. "But we should have one, so you lovely ladies could dazzle the world instead of just two lonely Brazilian businessmen." He paused and laid a hand on his companion's shoulder. "This is my friend and business associate, Juan Balboa, and I am Jose de Jesus Diego. Susan glanced at Josephine and saw the same silly grin and thought, *They are probably descendents of the Conquistadores and he sure has a gift for passing out compliments, but they are still too foreign for my taste.* Jose waited a moment, sensed her reticence and quickly continued, "We would be ecstatic, if in an hour or so you lovely ladies could join us in the lounge for a cocktail." Susan looked at Josephine and she nodded. "Well, I don't suppose there's any harm in having a cocktail," she said, then introduced Josephine and herself. Both men bowed politely and shook their hands. Then, Juan spoke for the first time.

"We feel the Lord was smiling when he gave us the good fortune to stumble across such beautiful and refined ladies," he said. "The minutes will drag by like years, but we will persevere with our thoughts of again gazing upon pure radiance." The elevator doors slid open at the girl's floor. "In an hour then?" Jose said, then bowed as they stepped off the elevator.

The bellhop was waiting at the door as they approached the room. He ogled, then showed them the rooms amenities and muttered, "thanks" as he quickly palmed a five dollar bill Susan handed him. He added in a slightly louder and more distinct tone, "my names Mike and if you need anything, anything at all just gimme` a call and I'll be here quicker'n Jack Rabbit" he said as Susan started to shut the door. After the door closed, Josephine whistled.

"Damn there must be a shortage of girls around here the desk clerk and that bell hop were almost slobbering and have you ever seen two more gorgeous examples of Latin lovers?"

"Only in the movies," Susan said.

"You think it would be bad form, if we didn't wait an hour?" Susan laughed at her.

"Very bad form, we're not going anywhere for at least an hour and fifteen minutes."

Josephine started unpacking and glanced at Susan. "How about wearing cocktail dresses?"

"Are you crazy?" Susan snapped. "They'll get the impression we want to spend the entire evening with them."

"Well dummy, I don't know about you, but that's exactly what I'd like to do. They were so elegant in those exquisite suits I think we'd look drab in anything less," she added petulantly. Susan sighed.

"Well okay, but I still think its being a little obvious. Don't you think it would be a good idea to play a little hard to get?"

"Uh huh, but if we don't get a move on, there are gonna` be a couple of hundred coeds down there drooling all over them," Josephine said, as she started undressing, grabbed her make-up case and headed for the bathroom. Susan followed her.

"What about Andy and Gary? You know they'll be here in the morning expecting to spend the next three days with us."

"To hell with those law school nerds, spending the next three days fighting them off aint exactly my idea of fun," Josephine replied as she stepped in the shower. Susan started out of the bathroom, then raised her voice over the sound of running water.

"These Latin types aren't gonna` be satisfied with a peck on the cheek, you know."

"I hope not," Josephine replied loudly in a carefree tone of voice. Susan shut the door. *Damn Andy is head over hells in love with her and she acts like little miss goody two shoes with him then jumps in the sack with any good looking stranger she runs across. If she expects me to hop in bed with one of those guys, I am going to put my foot down and leave the silly twit by herself.*

Bobby's heart sank when he saw the girls get out of an elevator dressed for the evening and entered the lounge to join the two business men.

Josephine glanced around the room to find the men, then swept in front of Susan.

"Jo, try to cool it for pity's sake," Susan hissed. The men smiled as they approached, rose and pulled chairs out to seat them. After they were settled, Jose sat next to Susan.

"You were dazzling before, now you are absolutely ravishing," he said. "Are all of the young men at this university you attend, eunuchs?

Juan and I were afraid there would be a large entourage of eager suitors trailing behind two such lovely ladies."

"Oh there are a couple of guys coming down in the morning, who will be looking for us," Susan said lightly to let them know she and Jo weren't completely alone. Jose chose to ignore the warning.

"Wonderful, that gives us the whole evening to steal you away since they were foolish enough to let you wander beyond their sight." Susan was embarrassed as instead of waiting for the men to order Josephine raised her voice to an approaching waiter and said loudly, "I'll have a Canadian and Ginger.

"Jo don't you think it would be a good idea to go easy this early?" Susan said peevishly.

"Lighten up Suzy, remember we're supposed to be relaxing," Josephine snapped.

"I think you'll be a lot more relaxed if you don't get blasted before the sun sets," Susan retorted sharply.

Jose edged his chair even closer to Susan's. This one is in charge and she is going prove very difficult, he thought. "I agree with you, Mon Cherie," he said softly. "I certainly want to savor you without my vision being clouded by alcohol."

"Do you speak French?"

"Parles voux Francais?" he replied. She thought a moment, then realized he'd repeated her question in French.

"Uh no, I don't speak French but I have taken two semesters of Spanish."

"I can certainly help you conquer the nuances of my native tongue if you will allow me the time," he said. " Would you like to continue our conversation in Spanish?"

"Uh...no, I'm not that fluent," she said. My Spanish would sound stupid to you. Do you speak other languages?" The waiter interrupted their conversation.

"What would you like Mon Cherie?" Jose asked, keeping his eyes focused on her.

"A white wine spritzer," Susan replied. I need to take it slow, if I'm going to have a chance of talking this one into what we have in mind, Jose thought, then nodded at Juan to let him know to go slow.

"We'll have the same," he said, then turned his attention back to

Susan. "To answer your question, I speak fluent French, Italian and can get by in Arabic."

"How impressive," she said. "I've never met an internationalist like you before." He laid his arm across her shoulders, but noticed the intimate touch seemed to make her nervous and pulled back. *She is like a frightened faun in the glade, one wrong move and she will be gone in the blink of an eye.*

"Ah, but it's not necessary for you Americans to speak other languages," he said.

"After all, the world beats a constant path to your shores either to buy from or, sell something to you rich Americans."

"What brings you gentlemen to our shores, as you put it?" She asked lightly

"Nothing very interesting," Jose replied. "I own a tractor and farm implement manufacturing company. We were on our way to Chicago to meet with our main import distributor tomorrow afternoon, landed here to refuel and when we saw the beautiful waterfront on approach we decided to stay overnight.

"Isn't it kind of hard to get a flight to Chicago from Panama City?

"No, we're flying a corporate jet," Jose replied smiling. *You don't know it but you and your silly friend will be on that plane within the next few hours and will provide Juan and I a few days of diversion. Those pilots are going to be in real trouble if they haven't offloaded the shipment to our buyer by the time we are ready to leave.* He did own a small farm tractor and implement manufacturing company in Brazil. It wasn't very profitable but served as great cover for the really high dollar return in cocaine distribution to the U.S. from Colombia. He and Juan had made a last minute decision to make this flight to let their employees know they were on top of things and weren't afraid to take a few risks themselves although negligible as the flight connection and destination into Chicago with a stop in Panama City to refuel was legitimate. Offloading the drugs to their associate working at the airport in Panama City in a hangar owned by Jose had proven very successful for the last two years.

"It must be nice to just fly anywhere on a whim," Susan said. "What kind is it?"

"A Lear," he replied. Josephine interrupted.

"That's a good one!" she blurted. "I've heard the Lear would out perform our military aircraft under ten thousand feet a few years ago. And it was illegal to sell them out of the country when it first came on the market." Jose glanced at her and thought. I wonder how she knew that. She is nothing but a silly puta.

"Quite true, but that restriction was removed many years ago," he said mildly.

The afternoon Combo came on as their cocktails arrived and played a perfect rendition of Moon glow, the theme song from an early sixties movie.

"My father has that on tape," Susan said. "When he plays it, mother always accuses him of being in love with Kim Novak." Jose leaned close to her.

"It is quite a lovely tune," he whispered. "Would you care to dance, Mon Cherie?"

"Oh yes, but I hope you ate your Wheaties because I love to dance."

"Wheaties?"

"Uh, it's an American colloquialism about a cereal."

Jo and Juan joined them on the floor and the four of them thoroughly enjoyed the next hour or so, as both men were accomplished dancers. The music flowed from one tune to another barely giving them time to catch their breath between songs until they all sat down to rest.

"We should fly down to Nassau for some gaming and really fine entertainment," Jose suggested after they were seated.

"That sounds great, Jose," Josephine said, slightly slurring her words.

"I don't think it's such a good idea, Jo," Susan said, raising her voice a decibel. "If we aren't here in the morning, you know Andy and Gary will be on the phone with our parents trying to find out where we are."

"I think you've gotten the wrong impression, Mon Cherie," Jose said softly. "I didn't mean to suggest an overnight stay." He held his diamond encrusted Rolex up to let them see, it was six o'clock.

"Oh that's a beautiful watch," Josephine exclaimed. "Are the diamonds real?"

"Oh yes, it was a legacy from my late father," he replied thinking, this one is stupid. It will be a pleasure to watch Juan slap her into submission. He turned back to Susan.

"We can take off and be in Nassau in two hours. As Josphine said, the Lear is a very high performance aircraft." He could see from her expression that she wasn't convinced, and quickly added, "I personally guarantee we will be back here no later than three in the morning. We do have to be in Chicago tomorrow afternoon. Business must come first, if a man is to afford the finer things in life." Josephine rose and interrupted.

"I need to powder my nose, come with me Suzy." she demanded.

As they walked to the ladies room Susan wasn't surprised when she noticed Josephine was a little unsteady then was startled when Josephine turned to her.

"Quit being such a party poop Suzy!" she snapped in a strident tone of voice. "These guys are obviously refined wealthy businessmen and they're sure a lot more polished and debonair than Gary and Andy will ever be. Will you just once let your hair down and have a good time!"

"It sounds like a lot of fun," Susan replied. "But we just met these guys and really don't know anything about them. They appear to be perfect gentlemen, but it seems a little foolish to get on a plane with a couple of foreigners we just met," she added nervously.

"Damn it Suzy! You know they're okay," Josephine said passionately. "Besides, I've never been to Nassau or on a Lear jet either and they promised to have us back by three." Her fervid demand startled Susan. Maybe she's right, I seem to be the one who "always throws a damper on things and if I refuse to go she'll pout for the whole weekend. She sighed and grudgingly agreed.

"It's against my better judgment, I'll go. I hope we don't live to regret it.

★ **Chapter Nine** ★

03:45 April 12, 1993
Gulf of Mexico, off the coast of
Colombia, South America

United States Army Air Corps Chief warrant officer Guy Dost, veteran of Vietnam, Granada and the Gulf war, prepared an unmarked black Vietnam era Bell UH 1 helicopter for lift off from a helicopter carrier cruising a hundred miles off the coast of Colombia, South America. His sun-bronzed face was creased around the eyes from the accumulated tension of two tours attached to Special operations group as a helicopter insertion pilot during the Vietnam war, duty with Air Cavalry through the Gulf war, then as a flight instructor, interspersed with covert missions for several clandestine branches of the government. He climbed in the command seat, reached to start the engines thinking, Six months to go for thirty years and here I am tree hopping a couple ˜a hundred miles into fucking Colombia. Knowing my luck We'll get shot down by drug traffickers. I would sure liked to know who the asshole is at operations that decided to shit on me. He had complained bitterly when the order came down but the C.O said, "It aint my idea Guy you were requested by somebody way above my pay grade. As the rotors began to turn he resigned himself to the injustice of it all, nudged his copilot and pointed out two hard-bitten men clad

in full black battle-dress, accompanied by a Washington staff type as they approached and prepared to board.

"I sure as hell wouldn't want to be who-ever these guys are going after," he grunted. Then was amazed as the first man climbed aboard and Guy recognized him and the other as one of the more infamous deep insertion sniper teams he'd ferried out of Bin Long during the Vietnam war, rumored to have terminated over twenty-five high level NVA and VC officers and an unknown number of NVA troops as they moved men and supplies down the Ho Chi Minh trail. He climbed out of the command seat, stepped back to the cargo bay and shouted over the rotor noise, "I'll be damned if it aint JD Volt and Mickey Dix! I figured somebody would have killed you two by now." Mickey looked closely at him and elbowed JD.

"I'll be dipped in shit.! How's the most fucked-up pilot that ever lied and cheated his way through Army flight school." JD peered at Guy and grinned broadly. "Now I reckon you know who requested you for this mission. How the hell you been, black clapp? Who would believe all of us could 'a survived all the shit we been through over the years." Guy frowned slightly at JD's use of a nick name he'd hung him with the morning he had set down for the first time at a fire base just west of Huong hoa then found JD and Mickey along with other members of Special operations group in a bunker drinking beer. He couldn't believe it when he saw Mickey blowing some vile smelling weed through the barrel of an M16 into a gas mask JD had on. It's been years and I forgot he was the one that hung that moniker on me and it stuck when he asked if Dost stood for a good old red blooded dose of Southeast Asian Clapp that seemed to thrive on antibiotics. He slapped JD on the back, and yelled over the mounting noise of the Huey's rotors.

"Through superior skill, intelligence and a little luck, I've survived. But I could have done without this shit. Hell, JD, I aint got but a few months before I have thirty years in. You're probably gonna' get me shot up by a bunch 'a druggies. And the reason you two have lived this long is old Beelzebub probably looked over the record and figured he didn't need a couple of trouble making fuckups like you down in hell. By the way, who is the unlucky 'sumbitch who warrants a visit from 'ya'll?" JD smiled and threw an arm around Guy's shoulders. "Can't say," he said. "Crank this bird up we'll do our duty for God, Country and you'll hear about it when you extract us if we don't get killed."

As they approached the coast of Colombia forty-five minutes later, Guy descended to a hundred feet then flew at tree-top level into the jungle covered mountain region until they arrived at a predetermined landing zone Mayer had selected. He hoped the long trek into the target area would give him enough time to get word to the Narcotics cartel about the shooters and get them killed so he could uncover the covert operation for the congressman from Massachusetts he had met at a gay party one of his aides held a few months before. He could envision the headlines and the television interviews as he and the congressman would be front page news and held in high regard as the two gay men who had uncovered a far right wing conspiracy in contravention of the law against assassinations. He couldn't figure out how as the Pilot and Copilot were both watching him suspiciously and had refused to let him use any communications equipment, stating it was a mission requirement. He didn't believe that but the Pilot seemed to be a vicious killer just like the two he knew were.

JD jumped as they hovered a few feet over the LZ, then slipped on the damp grass, landed on his back and gasped for breath. While he was struggling for air Mickey stepped on the Huey's runner, tripped as the helicopter lurched forward and fell on top of him.

"Damn Mickey, you gone blind?" JD grunted, "Git your ass off 'a me!" Mickey pushed himself up, reached down to help JD, then stepped around to swat debris off his back.

"No, I aint blind. I just figured you'd get off your butt a little quicker'n' 'a old lady," he groused. "What the hells the matter? You been acting like a crabby old goat ever since we turned forty last year." JD glared at him.

"We are getting a little old for this shit and it sure don't help when you drop on top 'a me to avoid hittin' the dirt."

"I didn't jump on you," Mickey snapped. "Guy jerked the damn bird and I tripped. And…if I remember correctly, you were the one who let us get talked into the army and this line 'a work in the first place."

"Shit! You sure didn't raise any objections when the alternative was a line unit in the Nam. I'd appreciate it if you'd shut the fuck up about it.

They spent four days steadily cursing Mayer, when they discovered he'd picked a landing zone at least ten clicks further from the objective than necessary causing them to endure a long slog through dense jungle for an extra day before finally sighting the target's jungle redoubt.

It was a very large three-story Southern style red brick mansion with six large white fluted Doric columns facing South located on the floor of a valley, surrounded by a three hundred meter clear cut field with gentle hills on the East and West sides with the valleys floor running North and South. There were single-story wings with smaller porches on the east and West sides with four smaller columns. An Olympic size pool and tennis courts cut into the eastern slope with another red brick poolside cabana with more columns. The front entrance door was a large ornate u shape, edged in white marble with a key over heavy arched double doors. All the windows of the main building and cabana were trimmed with the same white marble with keys and lentils and all corners were adorned with white marble quoins. The entire complex was completely enclosed within a hexagonal red brick wall capped by the same white marble with a spiked iron fence adding another meter.

Slowly circleing the perimeter looking for outposts inside the jungle's edge that seemed on the verge of recapturing the land from human habitation they found only one. It was situated on the West side just inside the undergrowth overlooking the complex and a rutted track descending from the East down to a spiked iron gate at the South end of the compound. A concrete drive led from the gate to a circled parking area at the front entrance of the mansion and it's attached six stall garage on the West side of the building.

"The asshole must think he's some kind 'a Southern gentleman," Mickey muttered. "That fuckin' place ought to be in Natchez Mississippi, I'm surprised there aint any moss covered oaks transplanted around."

"I wouldn't be shocked to see the shit-head and his entourage sittin' around the front porch sippin' on mint juleps. But I don't think anyone in Natchez has the bad taste to overdo all those columns and windows," JD said. Mickey leading as they circled back West hand signaled, opposition when he discovered the out post then crawled back to JD and pointed out some bushes twenty meters to their front.

"There's an OP behind that brush ," he murmured.

"How many?" JD whispered.

"Three, with Aks and a radio." JD checked his watch, then thought for a few moments.

"Okay, its 17:30, we'll move back uphill, and check out the rotation until 0:600." He crawled twenty meters back up hill then turned to provide cover as Mickey retreated to his position.

"There's a thicket about twenty meters to our left," JD muttered as Mickey reached his side. "It should give us a good view of both the outpost and compound." They alternated the watch every four hours and timed the guard-rotation at six hour intervals, 18:00, 24:00 and 0:600 which in JD's opinion was stupid, there was no way a sentry could stay alert for six hours.

Mickey nudged JD awake, after the 0:600 rotation arrived.

"I can't figure out what they're so interested in down at the house," he muttered. "They've had binoculars on it the whole watch. I swear, we could stroll up and slit their throats, they aint looked this way one time." JD sat up, took a swig from his canteen and splashed some water on his face.

"I noticed the same thing," he grunted. "I guess they figure aint anybody dumb enough to hump this far through a fucking jungle." He paused. "We'll ease back down and wait for the relief to settle in, then take 'em out and set up for the shot."

Mayer had informed them that Intel had confirmed the target usually got up around 0:730 for breakfast. Then his normal routine was to take a stroll around the compound before his morning constitutional. When JD heard that bit of news, he'd looked Mayer in the eye.

"Considering the expenses of the operation, and the hefty fee we're being paid. If you have somebody close enough to know when he takes a dump every morning, why don't whoever that is do the job?"

Mayer had harumphed and then replied snidely.

"It's not my job to explain how our operatives get their information or within your purview to question why we choose to handle the situation in a particular way. You men are being highly paid for this mission, and we expect results within the planned time frame." Mickey glared at him for a moment and then turned to JD.

"How 'bout I take this little twerp's fancy cellophane covered operations booklet and shove it up his ass?"

" Uh uh, Smith wouldn't like that." JD replied smiling, then turned back to Mayer.

"I find out you're holding back information about anything that could cause a problem," he said in a soft deadly tone. "I'll personally survive long enough to come back and rip your fucking head off. Then if I'm really pissed I'll let him take care of your ass," he added, nodding at Mickey. "He picked up a few pointers from the NVA on how to spend days killing anybody they had a hard-on for. One of their favorite tricks was to strip a man and nail him up to a tree with his dick jammed down his throat and let the ants feed on his ass." Mayer looked nervously from one to the other and saw nothing but deadly resolve. MY lord! What kind of dreadful killers has Angus allied with? I hope they are killed on this mission, then I can get back to D.C. and blow the whistle on Angus and all of his conservative cronies to that lovely congressman and senator from Massachusetts. "Oh no, Mr. Volt, you can be assured we have in no way concealed anything or misled you in any way," he stammered. Mickey continued to scowl at what he considered a little turd until JD slowly nodded and reached over to accept the operations booklet.

Thirty minutes after the relief arrived JD crawled to a position offering a clear field of fire. He affixed the sound suppresser and then relaxed to wait for Mickey to get in position. Their plan, since it was essential they avoid alerting the compound of their presence was for him to take out two sentries with Mickey arriving at the position a second later to silence the last man with his knife.

He waited until he detected slight movement in the brush close to the outpost and knew Mickey was ready. The sentries, other than the one watching the compound appeared bored by the prospect of six hours on duty with nothing more to do than swat flies until their relief arrived at 12:00.

JD grunted in satisfaction as he saw one stand, stretch and stroll a few meters into the bush to relieve himself and then make the fatal mistake of stopping next to the underbrush where Mickey lay waiting like a coiled venomous snake. The man was oblivious to sudden violent death slowly rising behind as he unzipped and blithely aimed his stream at a nearby sapling. JD waited a few seconds until he heard a muffled grunt and thought, That's one , now it would be nice if one `a the others would get up to go see what happened.

"Thank you," he whispered, as one of the remaining sentries looked nervously around, called out twice and getting no reply elbowed the other to go see what was wrong. JD paused until the second man stepped out of the hole, then settled in the prone position, his left leg, firmly on the ground slightly bent at the knee, put the crosshairs on the base of the last mans brain stem which would result in instantaneous paralysis and death, inhaled slowly then exhaled as he exerted soft pressure on the trigger and sighed as the rifle fired and the sentry flopped face first, coming to rest in globs of brain matter and bone fragments at the edge of the hole.

The last man stopped as he heard the soft thud of the rifle and thunk of the round entering his amigos head, then turned and froze in fear as he saw the gore and death twitches of the man in the hole giving JD ample time to aim. The man squeaked a pitiful cry of horror struggling to get himself and his rifle under control as he desperately tried to bring it to bear on a terrifying unseen enemy.

JD regretted killing the horrified almost defenseless man but knew, if he didn't the sound of gunfire would alert the compound and the man would meet an even worse fate at the hands of Mickey. "You don't know it, Pedro but I'm doing you a favor," he whispered, squeezed, the rifle fired and a small hole blossomed in the precise center of the sentries forehead. They dragged the corpses in the bush. JD set the rifle up for the shot, then Mickey got fidgety as 0:800 approached and the target hadn't appeared.

"Will you keep still?" JD muttered. "You're gittin' on my nerves."

"Well, Dip-shit, what the hell are we gonna' do if the asshole don't oblige us by taking a fuckin' walk?" Mickey grumped. "If we'd gone in last night and cut his throat we could 'a been ten clicks closer to extraction by now." He had argued the night before that infiltrating the compound and cutting the targets throat was a better idea than taking a chance he would take his morning stroll. His main objection to waiting for the shot was, "what if he don't show and they get suspicious when the sentries don't answer a radio call or the relief can't find em? We'll end up running for our lives with a whole bunch 'a very pissed off heavily armed, mean mother-fuckin' Colombians hot on our ass."

JD had spent a half hour convincing him that since they didn't have a layout of the mansion's interior, the chances they could get in and out without getting killed were slim and none. Then he'd thoroughly irritated Mickey by adding his favorite adage.

"And Slims outta' fuckin' town."

To keep Mickey under control he'd proposed a plan he knew was probably doomed to failure, but was the best he could come up with on the spur of the moment. "How 'bout we wait until somebody squawks on the radio or the relief starts up the hill, lay a false trail back West, then ease back around to the East and infiltrate the compound from that direction. Most of the security force will be hauling ass the wrong direction and we won't have so many to contend with." To stall for time he was going back over that idea when Mickey put the spotting scope back on the compound.

"Will you shut the fuck up!" he growled. "It looks like they got company." JD swung his attention back and saw two military style Hum-vees roar down the rutted track and crash through the double-gated entry of the perimeter wall in the process ran down two sentries then slammed to a stop in the middle of the compound and eight heavily armed men erupted from each vehicle. They watched fascinated as the two teams systematically gunned down three guards stationed at the walls, six more as they erupted out the front door, then another two as they charged around the East side of the building.

"You reckon we'll get paid, if those guys kill our target and we get away without anybody knowing we were here?" Mickey grunted as the carnage ended.

A little awed by the raiders efficiency in dispatching their targets entire security force within a minute or so, JD slowly shook his head.

"If they kill him, he'll still be dead and we've spent a lot of time getting in position to do the job and in the process had to dispatch three that weren't in the contract. I figure we're entitled to the fee either way."

As the raiders finished off the target's security force JD and Mickey watched as four men entered the ridiculous mansion. They heard several muffled gunshots from the interior and then moments later the four raiders manhandled, pushed and shoved their target, another man, a gray haired old women and two beautiful young women outside at gunpoint and forced them to line up on their knees in the middle of the compound. The older women was pleading with the target and he was just shaking his head in resignation probably to let her know they were beyond help.

The first girl was a statuesque blond with a frightened but determined look about her. The other, a raven haired beauty was sobbing openly and both were scantily clad in filmy nightgowns barely covering the top of their thighs. Mickey readjusted the scope.

"Man, you ever seen a sexier lookin` couple `a broads?" JD spent a few seconds taking in the view.

"You got that right they're for sure Miz Smiths table grade appetizer, entrée and dessert all in one," he muttered. "Now, we know why the sentries were so interested in the house last night." At that moment, the target started raging at his captors. The apparent leader was a lean almost white headed man with a fair complexion. He absorbed the abuse for a few seconds, kicked the target over on his back, then turned, pulled a pistol and pumped a round in the back of the old women's head, killing her instantly.

Mickey emitted a low growl.

"Pop that mother-fucker, JD! killing old ladies just aint right."

"I feel the same way, but before we start a war with this outfit, it would be a good idea to wait and see what they're up to," JD replied thinking, we don't need to take on this small army. I didn't believe it when I heard some of these drug lords were paying ex British SAS and even American Special forces to train and run their security details. But watching this outfit operate, I aint so sure. That guy sure don't look like a Hispanic. They watched as the leader turned, grabbed a shotgun from a man standing next to him and blasted a hole in the target's back as he screamed a curse and tried to rise then turned and blew off half of the other man's head.

"You better not let that son-of-a-bitch shoot those girls," Mickey muttered. JD was in the process of building up a strong dislike for the bastard. As far as he was concerned killing the target was fine, but the deliberate murder of a defenseless old lady was beyond the pale. He aligned the crosshairs on the raiders left ear quietly murmuring "Calm down, I got the mother-fucker's ear in the crosshairs. He makes a move toward either one of them, I'll blow his brains out."

"If you'd been a little more alert you'd `a known, he was fixing to murder that old woman," Mickey grumped.

"Just how the hell was I supposed to know what the dick-head was fixing to do? I aint a `fucking mind reader, even if I can usually figure out what's moseying through that pea brain a yours," JD snapped. He knew there was no way he could have anticipated the old woman's murder, but still had a deep feeling of sadness and guilt at having been a witness to it. He kept the crosshairs lined up, then made an effort to calm Mickey down knowing if he couldn't get him under control there was a distinct possibility the crazy bastard would start a small war they didn't need to fight.

"Take it easy," he said in a quiet tone of voice. "I'm sorry for giving you a dose `a shit, but don't you think it would be smart for us to stay out of sight as long as possible?"

"You're probably right," Mickey grunted. "But I'll think about cuttin` you if you let that bastard shoot those women."

"What's the matter with you?" JD asked. "Since when did you decide to maim me over a couple of broads?"

"How many shit-heads have we sent to the great beyond or paradise in the last twenty years?" Mickey asked.

"Don't carve notches in the rifle, aside from using several different ones over the years it aint something I'd keep count of anyway," JD replied.

"I aint either but it's a whole bunch," Mickey said. "I reckon we better have a good story ready when we arrive at Saint Peter's gate."

"So what's so special about these women?" JD asked

"Outta` all the killin` we done, how many times have we had the chance to rescue two fine looking damsels in distress?" JD thought a moment.

" Can't recall rescuing any damsels."

"There you go," Mickey said. "Now's our chance to do it, so come up with a plan."

They watched for a few moments as the raiders seemed satisfied to just stand around, admiring the two women without making a move to molest or harm them. JD waited a few more seconds, then lowered the rifle and started to disassemble it for the trek back to their extraction point.

"It looks like they'll be alright," he said. "I recommend we start back to extraction post haste, Guy would wait until hell froze over but that little weasel, Mayer won't spend one extra minute before he'll be trying to talk Guy into buggin' out on us." Mickey lowered the binoculars, turned and glared at JD until he sighed in resignation.

"What the fucks the matter now?"

"How 'bout those girls?"

"Well, they're way too good looking to kill and considering the company they been keeping, they aint exactly vestal virgins. They might have to get a little friendly with a couple of those guys but more'n' likely that's what got them where they are in the first place, so it shouldn't be too much for 'em to handle."

Mickey thought a few moments, picked up the scope and trained it back on the compound. JD watched hoping he would see reason, then gave up. *Shit! I'm not gonna' get him to move until we do something stupid,* he thought, then reattached the scope for another look. He'd just got the blond in the sight picture when the same man who'd killed the old woman ripped her nightgown and shoved her on her back. Two men pinned her arms and another yanked her legs apart as two more wrestled the other women down and every man in the unit unzipped his fly and got in line. Mickey lowered the scope.

"You gonna' just sit there and watch those shit-heads gang-rape 'em?" he hissed.

"If we'd shagged our ass out of here when we should have," JD snapped. "We wouldn't have to watch, Asshole but since you've fucked around long enough to get us involved, you better grab your cock, lock and load cause we're fixing to start a war with some seriously mean sons-a-bitches." JD knew it wouldn't take a unit as well trained as they faced long to figure out where the opposition was so for better accuracy he removed the sound suppressor, aimed, and put a round in the side of the leader's head. And then dropped the two men holding the blonde's arms before the sound of the rifle registered, switched to the one holding her legs when he bolted and took him out in mid-stride. The rest started scrambling for cover and as they were in the middle of the compound it gave JD time to pop two more as they scrambled toward the perimeter wall, missing a third when the round caromed off one of the iron spikes on the wall. Mickey slapped him on the back.

"Great shooting!" he exclaimed, then chuckled. "You ever seen so many hard dicks wilt at one time?"

The women realizing what was in store when the whole unit started unzipping had been screaming and wailing like an entire Roman legion was about to ravish them. Then, as their captors started spraying gore and dropping all around them they came completely unglued, howled and pounded the ground until it finally sank in that nobody was holding them and maybe they could escape. They scrambled to their feet and dashed out the front gate screaming like the hounds of hell were in pursuit and started running up the hill directly toward JD and Mickey's position. The blonde, was almost naked with nothing on but panties and remnants of her nightgown. The other ones nightgown was intact but it wasn't designed for a lot of concealment in the first place and neither of them had any footwear on.

"What the fuck are we going to do with two demented women since it looks like, they're about to run right over us?" JD groused. "It's at least three or four days back to extraction without having to cope with a couple of deranged barefoot women. They'll probably scream and faint every time they see a snake or spider."

"Come up with something but you better not shoot 'em." Mickey muttered.

"Who the hell told you since I'm a better shot it automatically puts me in charge of all the fuck-ups!" JD exclaimed. "I reckon I'll think of something since I don't want you to slice me up," he added sourly. "Mickey ignored him.

"You finally figured out these two are definitely keepers," he said. "You gotta' admit that's a helluva' sight, two nearly naked beautiful women hauling ass up the hill like an army of horny Huns with rape and human sacrifice on their minds are after 'em.

★   # Chapter Ten   ★

April 17, 1993, 0:845
Highlands, 210 kilometers SW of Cali
Colombia, S.A.

"Nice shooting," Mickey said. Then focused the scope back on the two women. JD kept his on the compound hoping the raiders were foolish enough to mount an attack up the clear cut hill and give him a chance to eliminate a few more before they started the trek back to extraction.

"If you can stop admiring the view for a second," he muttered. "What the fuck are we `going to do with these broads? They'll probably have a heart attack when they get a look and a whiff `a us." They'd been slogging through dark, dank jungle for days. And the closest they'd come to a bath was wading across a few streams hoping there weren't any hungry critters in them. Their last shave was on the morning they'd embarked on the helicopter for insertion. To say they were a tad gamy was putting it mildly.

The women were still a hundred meters from their position, when one of the raiders peered over the wall, saw all of that desirable woman-hood galloping off and decided to recapture them. Three hopped over the wall to take up the chase and were rapidly gaining. Mickey watched for a few seconds and glanced back at JD.

"Well…Asshole, what you waitin' for? Pop those shit heads before they catch 'em and drag 'em back down there?"

"I can't!" JD exclaimed. "The women are in my line of fire and this rifle aint a mortar. It won't lob a round over their heads."

"Just calm down," Mickey ordered, stood, then moved to the edge of the jungle and yelled, "Hit the dirt ladies!!"

The blond having figured out that there was someone in their general direction that might be worse than who she was running from. But knowing what was behind, she was willing to gamble whoever it was might be a better deal than gang rape and probable murder. She heard Mickey and dove in the dirt like it was an Olympic pool. It was clear the other girl hadn't done any Olympic diving when she belly flopped directly behind her. Mickey glanced over his shoulder at JD.

"Go ahead before the dip-shits run up their ass," he snapped.

JD shot the leader of the looking-for-love sweepstakes in the forehead. Number two, trailing close behind, yelped in fear as he got sprayed with globs of his amigo's brains and threw on the brakes so hard he was tilting backwards as the next round arrived to take out his larynx. He went down making horrible gurgling noises until JD took pity and put another round under his chin to end his misery. He switched to number three, saw he was in full retreat and hesitated. Hell there aint any reason to kill this guy. he won't be any threat after seeing what happened to his buddies. His benevolent thought to spare the man, was rudely interrupted.

"Kill that mother-fucker!" Mickey snapped. He'll be one less we have to worry about comin' after us." JD aimed, fired, and number three dropped like a rock. He lowered the rifle.

"Right, any time I think it would be nice to avoid killing somebody who don't desperately need it, you're always here to straighten my silly ass out."

"Yeah, now the rest of 'em will stay behind that wall until dark." Mickey replied.

"They got any sense, they'll get in their vehicles and haul ass back to wherever they came from. We'll still get an eight hour head start either way."

"If anyone decides to get in a pursuit mode, we're definitely going to need it," JD groused. Set up some claymores with trip wires around this post, maybe that will discourage the rest of them since these girls don't look like they're ready to dance through the jungle on their tippy toes."

"Like I said, they're keepers," Mickey replied. "So think of something."

"I figured that out from the murderous look I got when you threatened to slice me up," JD mumbled.

Mickey ignored him and turned his attention back to the girls.

"Okay ladies, crawl until you get inside the trees," he ordered firmly. Susan crept into the underbrush, rose and looked around to locate her benefactor. Seeing Mickey and JD behind, she was jolted by their appearance and thought. *Oh my God! These are two the most dangerous looking men I've ever encountered. They are filthy and the one with a knife scar looks fully capable of our casual murder. Come to think about it, both of them do. They have already caused the untimely deaths of who knows how many of those men down there. They probably deserved it and their deaths saved Jo and I from gang rape and God knows what else. These men appear to be capable of rape and certainly are killers, but at least there aren't but two of them. Hopefully they won't subject us to the misery and indignities those slime balls, Jose and Juan put us through for the past week.* She looked at the man next to the tree lines hard bitten countenance then glanced past him at the man behind and noted the knife scar ran from his left sideburn down to the juncture of his lower jaw. Mickey could see both women were on the verge of flight as they froze and nervously started looking for an exit. He realized, he and JD were probably two of the nastiest, meanest looking individuals the women had ever run across. He also knew that two defenseless women could not survive in the jungle alone so they going to protect them whether they wanted them to or not. He waited a few moments, could see their indecision and growled, "I'll shoot both of you, if you don't get your butts in gear right now." As they came closer to the edge of the out- post, JD slowly devoured the blond with his eyes. *Jesus! I'll have to pat Mickey on the back for talkin' me into sticking around to meet this one.* He waited until Mickey followed them to the hole, then moved around to their right side and stood transfixed as he got his first close look at the women. They all froze for a few moments. The women feeling like a couple of lambs right before being thrown to a pack of starving wolves while JD was sure he and Mickey appeared to be anything but what they had hoped for when they decided to make their run for freedom. Tearing his gaze from the blond, he turned to Mickey.

"You reckon it might be a good idea to check the rear? The entire Colombian army could 'a showed up since the last time you looked."

Mickey snapped out of his trance, glared at JD and then turned to put the spotter scope back on the compound. "Those assholes aint gonna' move to take a leak before dark."

When she heard the men's deep southern accent, Susan relaxed and began to hope she and Jo might survive their ordeal without suffering rape and murder. I think we might have gotten lucky. These men are from the South. I've dealt with Southern men since I was sixteen and most of them believe in a proper code of conduct when dealing with women. Of course We've both led a sheltered life and haven't dealt with some of the less than desirable element. She spent a few moments studying the two men and thought, They are dressed like a lot of deer hunters except they are clad in black, I assume for operating at night. These men are hunters but they aren't hunting deer or turkey. They hunt men, other human beings!! They might be a God send, but how does one predict what cold efficient killers will do at any moment? Don't kid yourself that they are knights in shining armor. You just witnessed just how detached and dispassionate they were killing quite a number of other men at the Hacienda and then the three pursuing us. When the man with the scar broke the silence. She breathed a sigh of relief, realizing that despite the men's appearance they just might be the proverbial knights in shining armor.

"Ladies, I know we don't look very nice but we are Americans and if at all possible we are going to get you out of here alive and well." He paused. "You'll have a lot better chance of making it if both of you pay attention and do what you're told with no hesitation." He turned back to Mickey and nodded toward the three corpses concealed in the underbrush. "How about getting some boots and fatigues off a couple a' those bodies," he said. "We need to get some clothes for them or it's going to be hard to keep our mind clear and concentrate on any problems we might encounter."

Susan shuddered as she watched Mickey spend a few moments pulling three more corpses out of the underbrush, selected fatigues that weren't covered with blood and gore, stripped them from the bodies then returned and handed them along with boots to the She and Jo.

JD waited until they were dressed then searched his pack for clean socks and tossed them over.

"Put these and the boots on, we need to get moving," he ordered then waited while Mickey went back to retrieve an AK 47, several ammo clips and handed them to JD. Susan turned to JD as she and Jo finished lacing up their boots.

"Wouldn't it be a good idea for us to have a rifle?" JD paused, consternation flickering across his face. *No way Jose! I sure as hell don't want a couple 'a edgy females trailing us with loaded weapons. Chances of them hitting anything other than Mickey or me are slim and none and like the saying goes, Slims in jail.*

"No! we'll handle any shooting that's necessary," he stated flatly. Susan frowned. *Damn, with his typical Southern male mentality he'd never believe we frail women folk could handle a rifle. It would be a waste of time to tell him My dad taught me how to shoot and brought me on several deer hunts when I was sixteen.*

JD felt bad about barking at her and softened his tone. "Number one, you need to get your friend to stop shaking and moaning. She's making to much noise. Number two, I'm JD." He nodded at Mickey. "He's Mickey, and if we can prevent it, we're not going to let any harm come to either of you. Number three, you probably think we're ruthless killers but we don't usually terminate anybody who doesn't richly deserve it." She felt a sense of calm and, even considering the past week of horror they had endured, was beginning to get a glimmer of hope. She introduced Josephine and herself, then inquired, "are you United States Military?"

"No! And that's the first and last question you get," JD replied gruffly. "The less you and your friend know about us the safer it'll be for you in the long run." He realized, the idea he could shut her down with one question was stupid, when Mickey, displaying his usual diplomatic skills interrupted.

"You idiot, you think she's gonna' stop with one question, you might as well go on and shoot her, but remember what I said."

"Now she'll feel free to go into our entire history, Asshole," JD said frowning and turned back to Susan.

"Okay two more, but if you don't shut up then, I'm `going to gag you."

"What part of Alabama are you from?" Susan blurted.

"South of Huntsville," Mickey replied. Huntsville being fifty miles from the Tennessee border, left over four hundred miles she could guess about.

JD was fuming about him in effect admitting they were from Alabama, then his respect for her brains as well as her other assets increased when she said, "I'll hold the last question until later." She spent a few minutes explaining they had been in Panama City, Florida from the University of Alabama for Spring break when they were approached by what seemed to be two really nice guys at the hotel. After cocktails and dancing, they had agreed to fly to Nassau for some gaming and night life on a Lear jet.

"I guess owning a Lear probably makes you as handsome as pulling up to a dock in a large Motor yacht." JD said. "I've never owned one, but have a friend who does and we're sure prettier on that boat than off it."

Susan introduced herself and Josephine, then blushed as she continued, "We knew we were in big trouble when we landed in the middle of nowhere instead of Nassau and those two guys and their armed guards forcibly escorted us into that gauche mansion." She paused as her face turned red with rage. "I hate to admit it! But those two men have been raping us for the last six days," she said bitterly. "And I don't have any doubt that we were good as dead when the bastards got tired of us."

"You would `a been on social security before we'd have grown tired of you," JD said, smiling sympathetically. She returned his smile.

"We were relieved until we realized they were worse than Juan and Jose when those men showed up and killed that poor old woman and both of them out in the courtyard."

"You mean, the ones lined up in the courtyard were in Panama City, Florida?" JD asked in shocked disbelief. She nodded affirmatively and JD turned to Mickey.

"So much for Control's intelligence, I can't believe the guy was in Panama City while we were down here slogging through this friggin jungle."

Chapter Eleven

April 21, 1993, 13:45 hours
Highlands, 240 Kilometers S.W. of Cali
Colombia, South America

On the third day, JD and Mickey were exhausted from sharing the watch at night and pushing hard during the day. The women had almost dropped in their tracks as soon as he called a halt each night and he was surprised they hadn't complained about the pace. He slowed after Mickey, trailing as rear guard a half click back came forward to report no signs of pursuit. Susan noticing the relaxed tempo trotted up to JD's side.

"What's the matter?" she asked nervously. "Why are we slowing down?"

"I figured you and Josephine might be about to run out 'a gas," JD replied. "And it doesn't look like anybody is coming after us."

"I thought I heard Mickey say he was worried about some little twerp deciding to leave if you were late."

"Uh… that is a possibility," JD muttered. "But we've been going hard and I don't want to run y'all in the ground."

"Don't worry about us!" Susan snapped. "You go as fast as you like, we'll keep up," she added. This trek has been hell, but it's a walk in the park after what we've been through this past week.

The next day, JD was worried they would find the helicopter gone and muttered to Mickey, "Damn! We're ten hours behind schedule. I hope to hell Guy has been able to convince the little shit to wait. It's at least a couple 'a hundred kilometers to the closest town we might find some kind of plane and these women wouldn't be able to survive it.

They arrived at the landing zone mid-afternoon. Mickey charged forward when he saw the helicopter in the process of lifting off. He fired a burst just forward of the wind-screen to get Guy's attention, then was taking aim at the engine housing when Guy jerked the bird aloft, circled and then lined up the forward mounted 762's for a strafing run before he recognized them and slowly brought the bird back to earth.. JD trotted up to Mickey's side.

"What the fucks 'a matter with you?" he exclaimed. "If you'd hit the engines, all of us would 'a been walking!"

"Yeah, but if Mayer had survived the crash. I would have enjoyed disemboweling him" Mickey snapped.

"Well…that is the upside," JD mused.

After the helicopter had settled to earth the individual they'd been discussing, jumped out with his ever present briefcase and trotted over.

"I'm sorry gentlemen," he said. "I thought you had come to an unfortunate end." He had been frustrated by Guy's adamant refusal to let him near any communications equipment for the entire time JD and Mickey were gone. And had prayed the druggies would kill them during the attack. He paused when he saw the two women as they came out of the jungle to join JD and Mickey.

"Where did these women come from?"

JD started to reply and Mayer held his hand up to interrupt.

"I don't really care, they are not in the mission plan," he said. "I'm afraid it won't be possible to transport them." He flipped open his briefcase and pulled a map of the area out, scanned it, then marked a location and pointed it out to JD.

"There is a village twenty kilometers west of here," he said. "They can make their way there on foot and I'm sure the locals will see to their safety." JD knew the women couldn't survive in the jungle by themselves for three kilometers much less twenty. Then, if by some miracle they did make it, the village was probably controlled by the druggies and they'd be right back in the proverbial frying pan. He was beginning to get a real mad on when Mickey grabbed Mayer from behind and slid the knife up next to his jugular.

"You little piece a shit," he hissed. "Anybody's gonna' get left behind it'll be you.

And you won't have to worry about making it to a fucking village 'cause your head will be separated from your narrow little shoulders and jammed up your ass." JD was worried Mickey would take their prior conversation literally and was getting ready to intercede when Guy hopped out of the chopper, trotted over and shouted over the rotor noise.

Sorry about that, JD. I'd 'a stayed here till hell froze over but this asshole told me y'all were dead and we had orders to leave. I knew he was lying since he bitched and moaned because I wouldn't let him close to any radio equipment. I don't know who you're working for, but this guy aint trustworthy. Ya'll were late but I was planning to over-fly the area of operations and try an extraction there. "

"I figured as much, don't worry about it," JD yelled, then quickly turned back to check if Mickey had slit Mayer's throat. Shit! Smith will be super pissed if he kills the little twerp. He breathed a sigh of relief when he saw no harm other than a dark stain, indicating the prick had wet his pants and then nodded for Mickey to release him. Mickey flipped the blade to the dull edge and slowly drew it across Mayer's throat.

"We straight about the travel arrangements?" he asked quietly.

"Ya ya…yes," Mayer stammered as his knee's gave way. He remained kneeling, struggling to regain his composure for a few moments, then rose slowly while keeping a wary eye on Mickey then glanced nervously at JD.

"Mister. Volt, if you don't mind, I would like to make a suggestion."

"Go ahead," JD grunted.

"It would be wise for you and Mister Dix to escort these young ladies home via commercial airlines. Mr. Smith would be quite disturbed if we show up on a Navy ship with unidentified females."

"That's fine, but not from a Colombian airport," JD said, and then turned to Guy.

"Can you get us to Caracas without stirring up a lot of trouble?"

"No one will know we were ever in Colombia, if you don't mind clipping a few tree tops" Guy replied mildly. They climbed aboard and as night fell after a breathtaking low level flight to avoid radar, landed next to the Caracas terminal. JD gave the copilot cash to buy fuel for the trip back to the carrier while Guy stayed with the bird to oversee the refueling as he, Mickey and the women disembarked. Mayer minced in the terminal to contact the embassy and clear up any problems the local authorities might have about their unscheduled flight. JD and Mickey accompanied by the women ambled away from the Huey to escape the noise and Josephine grabbed Mickey's arm.

"Oh Mickey!" she exclaimed. "We won't feel safe unless you and JD escort us all the way back to the university!" With a look of sublime pleasure flitting across his face, Mickey disengaged himself and motioned for JD to accompany him off to the side.

"I can't see any reason why we shouldn't take 'em all the way back," he muttered. "If you come up with some dip-shit notion of security why we can't, I'll be permanently pissed." Mickey was always worried JD would come up with some reasonable sane thing to do instead of what he had in mind when females were involved.

"Hell, sticking with 'em for a few days to find out the depth of their gratitude sounds fine to me," JD replied. "Just think how they might feel after we clean some 'a this jungle rot off and shave." Mayer, had been very cooperative since he'd realized Mickey was deadly serious about relocating his head, hustled back out of the terminal and informed JD he had cleared them through the embassy. There were rooms reserved at the down- downtown Hilton and a rental car was waiting for them in the Avis parking lot.

"I have been in contact with Mr. Smith and he's looking forward to a full report within a day or so," he said. Then he paused looking at the array of weapons. "It would be wise to transport all of these other than side arms on the helicopter and please keep those concealed. JD nodded, he understood.

"That's fine, just tell him the target is dead, and we'll expect our fee to be deposited by tomorrow."

"It won't be a problem," Mayer replied, then handed him paperwork and keys to a Chevy Impala. JD and Mickey rejoined the girls and met immediate static from Susan as they started to leave.

"We're not going anywhere until we get a shower and change of clothes," she snapped. "There are bound to be some shops and facilities somewhere in this airport."

"Damn it!" JD exclaimed. "We'll be at the hotel in a half hour and you can wait. There's all kind a ladies shops there and you can take as long as you like bathing after we check in." Susan stomped her foot and looked at JD in disgust.

"It's bad enough being escorted by two disreputable, filthy, smelly men without looking like we're some kind of revolutionaries that belong with them" she hissed. JD was trying to think of a way to force her without getting physical when Mayer edged to his side and interrupted.

"Uh…if you'd like, while they are using the bathing facilities at American airlines VIP lounge, I can get the ladies sizes and pick up some clothing for them," he said proudly displaying an American airlines diplomatic card. Susan flashed a look of triumph at JD.

"See Grumpy, things aren't so difficult when you take the time to explore all avenues." JD gave Mayer a baleful look, then gave up and nodded agreement. They waited until the women were out of sight and then Mickey nudged JD.

"We better walk around the end of the terminal toting these pistols," he said.

"Yeah, you're right," JD mumbled jamming the pistol under his fatigue jacket. "God knows how long it's going to take 'em to bathe and dress. At least the little dork is buying the clothes and we won't have to listen to a dose 'a shit about our terrible taste in ladies attire." They found a relatively new Chevy Impala in the Avis lot and relaxed in air conditioned luxury for a half hour until Mickey elbowed JD out of a sound sleep.

"Hey, there's a car-wash over next to the rental office!" he exclaimed. JD jerked awake.

"Have you gone completely nuts?" He snapped. "You woke me up to tell me there was a fucking car-wash in the area! The damn car is clean, Asshole and even if it wasn't I wouldn't give a rat's ass."

"Don't get riled up, ya` grouchy old bastard," Mickey grumped. "I was thinking it would be a good idea for us to just walk through to get some stink and jungle rot off." JD thought about it a moment.

"Won't the water be too hot?"

"Naw, I went through one before I realized my window was stuck down, I got soaked but it wasn't that hot." JD drove to the side of the track leading into the car wash, parked and they got out. The attendant, looking confused motioned for them to get back in the car and line up with the track until Mickey walked over and handed him a ten-dollar bill. He turned to point at JD then himself and held his nose. The attendant goy a whiff of him nodded, bowed and waved them in with a flourish. It was a rough way to take a bath, but on arriving at the other end they were slightly parboiled from the hot water but smelled considerably better. JD handed the attendant waiting to wipe the car down another ten for some towels, then they walked back to the car to a loud crescendo of, "Loco Gringos!!"

JD drove to the arrivals exit and found the women, Mayer and Guy waiting. He got out and walked around to Guy.

"Call the Royal Sonesta in New Orleans in a week or so, Brother. We'll probably be there and would sure like to get together with you for a few drinks to remember some 'a the good guys, who got killed in that fucked up war." Guy glanced at the two women and grinned.

"Knowing you two, I figure it might take a little longer than a few days," he said chuckling. JD smiled and slapped him on the back fondly.

"I hope you're right, but make the call anyhow," he said and then turned back to Mayer.

"You be sure to remind Mr. Smith about our fee." Mayer sniffed and peered at him with a puzzled expression.

"You smell somewhat like a freshly waxed automobile."

"Yeah, I think the car-wash attendant was trying to be cute, and hot-waxed our ass," JD replied, then turned back to Guy and Mickey.

Susan and Josephine waited by the car while the three men recalled some of the ribald times they had shared during their service together and Josephine grew impatient.

"Men are so juvenile," she said with a touch of exasperation. "The way they're acting you'd think Guy was a long lost brother."

"In a sense, he is," Susan mused. "I think men who've been through war and combat together belong to a brotherhood other men who have never put their lives on the line for their comrades could never understand. JD and Mickey constantly bitch and gripe at each other but I'd hate to see what happened to anyone who posed a threat to either of them.

JD avoided Guys questions about who they were working for since their battle dress was completely void of any insignia until he finally gave up.

"Okay, I don't guess it makes a helluva' a lot 'a difference," he groused. "I'd a' had to haul your crusty butts anyhow." I did hear something on the Sat comm about somebody eliminating a big druggie and his entire security unit along with a bunch of another drug kingpins security and I'm pretty sure that operation had to be you two."

"How long you got to go for your thirty?" JD asked to avoid a reply.

"Eighty nine more days , that's why I was a tad upset about the order to take this mission until I saw who I was gonna' be hauling Guy replied.

"I heard you were divorced," JD said

"Yeah, about two years now,"

"How bout kids?'

" None, if I had to pay child support I'd have to stay in the army, if they would have me.

"Call me before making a decision to reenlist," JD said. "I'll know by then how this outfit we're with works out. They could probably use a pilot with your skill set and the pay is a lot better than the army." Mayer sidled to Guy's side and interrupted.

"Mister Dost," he said. "We need to take off immediately or we're not going to be able to rendezvous with the carrier." The three men turned as one and glared at the detestable little man. He met their malevolent looks and stepped back.

"Uh…if we don't leave now," he stuttered. "The ship will be out of range."

They ignored him, spent a few more moments bantering with each other, then JD and Mickey playfully pounded Guy on the back and he headed for the chopper and snapped at the little man as he strode by.

"What the hell you waiting on? You wanted to leave, so get your ass in gear."

Susan, seeing the men break up turned to open the front passenger door and nodded at Josephine. "You sit in back," she said.

"Kind 'a like JD, do you?" Josephine tittered. Susan ignored her, opened the door and sat down. I didn't realize it but she's right. If I had met him before suffering the horror we've been through, the aura of imminent violence would have scared me to death. I now know the safe secure feeling I've felt my entire protected life is nothing more than an artificial veneer. Deadly danger is just one slight mistake away. I'll never again be swayed by anti military Academicians and the liberal media when they blather their peace and love cures all spiel. If it weren't for men like JD and Mickey those idiots wouldn't be able to espouse their stupid opinions. I believe It would be a good idea to put them all in uniform in a war zone and see what it's like to serve the country in stead of themselves.

JD slid in the driver's seat and was pleased to see Susan sitting in front. He started the car then headed for the highway leading to downtown Caracas and then turned to her.

"In case you're wondering why we didn't leave on the helicopter, it seems the Navy aint real happy about moving a carrier out of its normal patrol area for over a week to drop a couple of operators they don't know beans about. If you ladies show up on the flight deck and they get the idea it wasn't anything but a damsel in distress mission. That might cause 'em to yell loud enough for the wrong ears to hear about it in Washington." He paused to see if he could read her reaction, couldn't and continued, "Anyway we've got rooms at the downtown Hilton tonight and I'll check on commercial flights in the morning."

She smiled at him sweetly. "After what you and Mickey have done to rescue us, we feel totally safe with you," she said. "There is one thing though."

"What?" Well shit! She's gonna` ask for a separate room.

"I thought you'd have been able to find a hotel with a little more local flavor."

"Having spent some time in out of the way and on occasion nasty places," JD said. "We've discovered, if you can find a Hilton, quit looking and settle in. There's enough local flavor around without having to sleep in it. You won't be bitten by any bugs or get sick eating at a Hilton. He parked the Impala in front of the hotel, got out and was starting around to open the door for Susan when Mickey stepped out to intercept, then pulled him a few meters away from the car.

"You planning on getting them a room of their own?" he whispered.

"No, the little twerp reserved two adjoining rooms and you sure aint invited to stay in mine," JD replied. "If they complain, I'll get 'em a separate room and we'll look up the two best looking whores in Caracas to help mend our broken hearts."

Chapter Twelve

April 21, 1993,19:35 hours
Hilton hotel
Caracas, Venezuela S.A.

Exiting the elevator and approaching the first of the adjoining rooms, JD used the entry card to open the door and almost jumped for joy when Susan brushed by him and blithely walked in the room. He still wasn't sure whether Beth would follow Susan until she passed by, snatched the other entry card out of his hand and then led Mickey down the hall to the next room. JD stood in the hall watching as she opened the door and preceded Mickey inside.

"Well, Silly," Susan said when she noticed JD hadn't entered the room. "Are you going to stay out there all night?" *My Lord, he's blushing. I can't believe this big hard man is unnerved by a little girl like me,* She thought. JD tripped slightly as he all but dove in the room.

"Why don't you take a long hot shower," Susan said. "I'd like to see, if there's a real human being under all that dirt and grime. There is a men's shop in the lobby, give me your sizes. While you bathe, Jo and I'll go buy some clean clothes for both of you."

"That's a good idea," JD replied. "My size in a polo shirt is extra extra large, pants are thirty four waist and thirty length. If they have 'em get a pair of size ten and a half loafers, socks, extra extra large vee neck tee shirts, boxer shorts, and don't buy any shirts without a pocket." He thought a moment. "Oh yeah, while you're at it go on and pick up anything you and Jo might need." She laughed lightly.

"My goodness, I wouldn't have dreamed you were so picky."

"I'm not, I just don't like tight clothes." JD replied. "And not being a card carrying member of the anti-smoking league I prefer shirts to have a pocket on the off chance I might want to put a pack 'a smokes or sunglasses in it. It irks me every time I buy one, then unwrap the damn thing and no pocket. I'd sure like to know who the hell told the shirt manufacturers since smoking is politically incorrect, they had to quit putting pockets on 'em. I'd permanently maim that asshole." She laughed at him.

"Don't get so upset JD, now that I've found out what a crusty old man you are I'll do my best to please you."

"I'm not crusty, it just cranks me off whenever I'm reminded of how the politically correct mavens have totally screwed up almost everything." She smiled and patted him on the cheek.

"Okay, have a leisurely bath. You know, it takes a little time for two girls to go shopping."

"Like it don't take time for one girl to go shopping?" he muttered, then handed her two thousand dollars.

He waited until she left, got undressed for a bath then cursed when the phone rang as he stepped in the shower. I know she couldn't have gotten in any trouble this fast so it's got to be Mickey. He strode back to the bedside table and snatched the receiver up.

"What the hell do you want, I was fixing to take a shower. No sound came forth for a moment then Mickey growled.

"You double barreled asshole, we were fixing to get in the bath tub together when Susan called and asked her to go shopping. She shut the bathroom door on me and took off for a shopping spree."

"Damn, I'm sorry but she'll be back in an hour or so," JD replied. "It won't hurt for you to clean up before you throw the girl in the sack. Take a bath and shave and she'll be a lot more receptive. JD hung up then went back in the bathroom and filled the tub with steaming hot water, luxuriating in it for a few minutes before standing to shower, soaping and rinsing off twice before he felt totally clean. He toweled off, shaved, then realized he had nothing to wear other than filthy fatigues. Damn! I'll just wrap a towel around my waist and wait until she gets back, He propped himself up on the bed, flipped on the television and swore when he discovered all programs were in Spanish. *I'll just take a little snooze* he thought, and was sound asleep within a minute.

An hour later Susan found him sleeping soundly. *He looks so peaceful and serene, one would never know he was capable of such deadly force,* she thought, quietly, stripped to her bra and panties, then slipped in bed and snuggled against his back.

"I thought you found me attractive," she murmured in his ear. It startled her when he snapped awake and snatched the three-fifty-seven off the night table before remembering where he was.

"Sorry," he muttered. "In my line 'a work you tend to be a little jumpy when you're as exposed as you are when you're asleep." Then he noticed her state of dress. "God, you aren't just attractive, you're unbelievable!" he exclaimed, then rolled completely over, gathered her in his arms and softly started a kiss that rapidly progressed to a deep, fully engaged probe of her mouth and breathless pressure against the entire length of her body. She pulled back for air and whispered, "You might not be completely awake but I can feel one part of you that is definitely...to use a military expression, at attention."

"Uh huh...I want to drink in every small inch of you," he murmured, then rolled between her legs and lifted himself up to take her entirety in. *If I get shot tomorrow I'll know I've had at least one dream come true.* He buried his face between her breasts then began a slow journey downward, absorbing every glorious inch. She raised her hips to help him remove her panties, then opened completely as he tasted the sweet nectar of her and began to lick her until she moaned softly in pleasure. He continued to lightly caress her orally until she began to move again then moved forward and thrust inside of her feeling a desperate need to bury himself totally in her wet velvety warmth. She met him stroke for stroke until he groaned and she yipped several times as they mutually exploded in unbelievably intense ecstasy. He disengaged and rolled off gasping for air. She leaned forward and smothered him with kisses.

"I don't know about you," she said. "But that will last me for a while and I'm hungry."

JD couldn't believe his ears. *Man, I better get away from this girl before I wind up married with a house in the suburbs and a bunch* of little assholes like Mickey and I were growing up to take care of. There aint the usual worry about how long I got to stay here pettin˜ her so she won't come up with something off the wall, like you don't really love me, you just want my body. I never have understood how some women think their body aint really them. If you can't tie up with your body you are none other than dead. I never been with a women before that after great sex knows it's normal for a man to want a smoke and something to eat. This girl is just to good to be true. "I could probably use a bite myself," he said chuckling. "Let's get dressed and head down to the coffee shop.

After ordering she posed a problem JD had been worrying about.

"How can you and Mickey get us back on campus without causing a big stink? By now, knowing my and Jo's father's the local police, FBI and CIA are looking for us," she said, then thought a few moments. "How about us calling and telling them the truth?

They'll be so happy we're safe they won't mind us spending a few days with you and Mickey on the way home." Recalling the incident that had launched him on his military career JD was painfully aware of the attitude most fathers would take about their daughter fooling around with a couple of hard cases like he and Mickey. Considering the obvious differences in age he was pretty sure she was reading her daddy wrong. While both women were college Seniors and had been around the block a few times. He and Mickey hadn't been on a campus since their junior college football days. Needing to be in shape to carry out the missions assigned for the past twenty years, knowing if they couldn't jog for miles over rough terrain with at times extremely unhappy individuals in hot pursuit.

The mental picture of being nailed to a tree with dicks jammed down their throats tended to inspire long hard workouts. All of which tended to make them appear younger than most men ten or fifteen years their junior. There was no doubt Susan and Jo's parents wouldn't be ecstatic about their daughters spending a week with them.

"It would be better if you tell them the truth about your kidnapping," he said. "Let them know you're being protected by imminently qualified people but it will take a few days to be sure there aren't any residual problems hanging around.

"You don't think those horrid beasts could possibly know where we are?" she asked nervously.

"No," JD replied. "But you impress on your folks that your and Jo's reputations will be ruined if word gets out about what you've been through. And Mickey and I sure as hell don't need our ugly mugs on the front page of any newspapers. To ease any fears they may have, give them the hotel and room numbers so they can call if they feel like it. I just won't answer the phone, nobody is going to be calling me anyhow." They agreed, it was the most sensible course to take, then JD asked the waiter for a phone, called Mickey's room and asked him to bring Jo down to eat. Mickey answered, and growled.

"JD, if you don't quit fuckin' with me, I'm gonna' come over there and kick your ass."

"Hey Dip-shit! Save some for later. I guarantee you it won't dry up and blow away," JD said. "Now drag your butt down to the coffee shop. It'll close in a few minutes and I don't want to listen to you bitch about being hungry and have to start looking for a late night restaurant to shut you up." He waited, knowing, it would take Mickey a minute to calm down, then heard a brief flurry of conversation in the background.

"How long before they close?" Mickey asked. "Now as I think about it, we are hungry."

"You got about fifteen minutes," JD replied. "I'll order steak and eggs if that's okay."

"Yeah, that's fine sorry for hollerin' at you."

"I'd a shot you years ago if I got upset every time you went to bitching and complaining," JD said. "Now get your ass in gear." Mickey and Jo arrived as the food was being served and Mickey sat down muttering something unintelligible.

"Thanks for ordering," Jo said, smiling at JD. "I appreciate it even if Mister Grouch doesn't have any manners."

"Don't worry your pretty head about it," JD replied. "The main reason I got ya'll down here was to get together and go over the story to explain how you girls turned up missing for the past week or so."

They spent the next half-hour eating and putting finishing touches on the tale, then adjourned back to their rooms for more lovemaking and rest.

JD arose the next morning at 10:00 and had to call repeatedly to get

Mickey and Jo moving. He was beginning to worry because Mickey hadn't cracked wise at him since the women had crawled in the firing pit. It was a sure sign he was in the first stages of love. Normally, he wouldn't let an hour go by without making some smart remark or bitch about how much gear and equipment they were toting. He just sat listening to Jo rattle on about anything and nod like her words were uttered by the second coming of the virgin. Jo was gorgeous but some of her dialogue didn't make a hell of a lot of sense to JD. He waited until Mickey got up during brunch to take a leak and followed him in the men's room.

"What the hells the matter with you?" he snapped as the door closed behind them.

"You're acting like a goggle-eyed teenager. We don't want...in fact, we can't get too involved with these women. Number one, we're over fifteen years older than them. Number two, they're going to graduate from the university in a few months, probably have a brief career in mind until the right doctor or lawyer shows up to ring the wedding bells. They'll be in junior league and in the Birmingham society pages within a couple of years. Hell! They'll probably be talkin' through their noses like the society broads in Mobile." He thought a moment and groused, "Every time I run into one 'a those Mobile debutantes, I feel like asking whether her mama taught her to sound that stupid or if they all had a sinus operation at a certain age to make sure they sound like they got a cob up their ass." Mickey glared at him.

"JD I've heard your thoughts on Mobile society broads before and agree with you," he growled. "Why don't you finish what you got to say so I can go on and kick your ass." JD paused for a moment to recall the next point he had planned. That's good when he gets mad enough to threaten me it means he's listening and is beginning to realize I'm probably right. "Number three and absolutely the most important is...our way of making a living sure as hell don't qualify for polite society," he said. "We're both from fairly well-off families but after what we've been doing for the past twenty years, by choice, I remind you, going back to join the family business aint an option. I can assure you no one at home will be ecstatic if either one of us shows up on a permanent basis.

Besides, we'd both go nuts inside of six months if we tried to settle down in our home town. And the last time I looked in the want ads there wasn't a big demand for sniper teams unless you want to re-up."

Mickey scowled, then grumped, "I'll figure something out, mind your own damn business."

Well we've progressed from getting my ass kicked to mind your business. Sanity is beginning to seep in that hard head of his. "Okay, I'll stay out of it but you're nuts if you think you will be able to put up with marriage, puttering around the yard on the weekends and raising a bunch of kids. The girl won't fall in love with Monroeville and aint either one 'a us will be able to support a family on our military retirement so you'll end up in Birmingham selling insurance or cars." He waited a moment to see if his arguments were having any effect and could tell Mickey was beginning to listen. "Maybe I'm wrong, but I don't think you got a sales type personality and both of you will be miserable and ready for divorce in short order. Now, we can keep working for Mister Smith for a few more years without getting outside the law in the United States. Then, if we aint dead, we'll have enough money to go with our government checks to live in comparative ease, buy a few toys and be able to afford women like these. Hell, if you want to we can go back out, lie like dogs and swear our undying love. Our only problem being a prior contract with our employer which is going to rule out any long term commitments for a couple 'a years. Both of them have enough sense to know the people we're working for aint exactly a bunch one would willingly get crosswise with and that ought to convince them to hold off on the wedding bells long enough for us to make some real money. Hell! I aint wantin' to get married in the first place." JD knew the spiel had worked, when Mickey stopped glaring and visibly relaxed as he began to think about married life. Good for the first time since we caught sight of the women, he's started thinking with his brain instead of his dick. It aint such a bad plan, I just failed to mention the idea that two beautiful women are going to wait around for a couple of old worn out operatives like us to stop by for an occasional visit is pretty far fetched. I don't know if he's ready to settle down but I'm damn sure I aint,

When they returned to the table, JD waited until they all finished eating and spoke to the girls.

"We need to get you ladies back in the states as soon as possible, so I've made reservations on a flight to Miami early this afternoon.

They arrived in Miami at 15:00, connected with a flight to Birmingham then rented a car for the fifty five mile drive south to the University in Tuscaloosa, Alabama.

The women excused themselves to freshen up after JD checked in a two-bedroom suite at the Sheraton the girls and Mickey braced him.

"When are you gonna' run the story by them?" he asked. "We probably won't see 'em for a while after tonight since we've got to head down to New Orleans for debriefing and they'll be going back to class tomorrow."

"I figured on going over the idea while we were eating,"

The girls finished dressing, then spent time making sure both men were groomed and clad to their specifications. I got a feeling we're going to be on display for somebody and I'm not to happy about it. JD thought.

"Why the hell have we got to get all spiffy?" he asked testily. "I was planning on eating in the hotel and getting back for some serious love making."

"Don't be such a grouch," Susan snapped. "It won't hurt you to eat somewhere besides a hotel restaurant for a change. And before I get through with you tonight you'll beg for mercy." After they were seated at Wings a restaurant operated by an ex Alabama and Miami Dolphin football player, a steady procession of the girls sorority sisters, stopped by the table to inquire why they were over a week late returning from Spring vacation and who the two hard looking men were. JD and Mickey dutifully rose to be introduced to each of them and JD began to get irritated. I knew it, they're showing us off. Come to think of it, this is the first time I can remember a women wanting to show me off to her friends. That is kind of nice. As they finished eating and ordered coffee. JD spent some time running the story he and Mickey had agreed on. It seemed to sell pretty well until Susan leaned over and whispered in his ear.

"You don't really think it will work that way, do you?"

"Probably not, but it would be great if it did," he replied, leaving them both an out with no regrets.

As the last couple of curious girls stopped by, JD was amazed at the yarn Susan spun to explain their absence and that the men escorting them were old family friends. He overheard one of the girls as she whispered in Susan's ear.

"Since when does your family need a couple of cut-throats for friends?"

"You never know when they might come in handy," Susan replied smiling as she glanced at JD and then nodded slightly to get her to move on.

"Girl, you are impressive," he said. "I sure hope you're still around in a couple of years."

"I will be but you better check in on a fairly regular basis," she replied smiling.

They dropped the women off at their sorority house the next morning and then JD called Mr. Smith from a gas station pay phone. He called back after the usual ten minute delay and JD told him, they would be in New Orleans that night.

"That's fine, I'll have rooms reserved at the Royal Sonesta under the names Wilson and Johnson. No one other than myself is aware of the names you are registered under or the room numbers other than a messenger and all he knows is your room number," Smith said. "You will find your fees have been deposited to your accounts if you check your bank." Yeah we need to wire transfer that money to our accounts at Barclays in the Bahamas this afternoon. JD thought. They had opened the Barclays accounts ten years previously after finding a sizable stash of cash in a briefcase one of their targets was transporting and had added to the accounts over the years whenever the opportunity arose. It wasn't exactly kosher but they reasoned it wasn't stealing because the targets were already dead and turning it in to the government didn't make a hell of a lot 'a sense to either of them.

He got back in the car and took the on-ramp to Interstate 59.

"Did he mention the women?" Mickey asked. "You reckon he knows we didn't actually kill the target?"

"No and that worries me," JD replied. "But, I think Mr. Smith aint stupid so we'll make a complete report and keep the money whether he likes it or not. We do need to wire transfer it down to Barclays before we report in the morning."

Chapter Thirteen

★   ★

April 25, 1993, 18:00 hours
Royal Sonesta hotel
New Orleans, Louisiana

They checked in the hotel and after a quick shower JD dressed, then walked through the connecting door to Mickey's room and plopped in an overstuffed chair.

"You want to go out to eat?"

"Naw, I'd rather order room service," Mickey replied.

"How 'bout heading over to Luckys for a drink after we eat?"

"Hell, I'll go if you want to," Mickey said. "But, I'd rather eat here, watch a little TV and get some shut eye."

"I hate to admit it but that sounds good to me," JD mumbled. "I reckon we're gittin' old."

"Aint no reckon about it," Mickey grunted.

The phone's ringing at 0:800 snapped JD awake. He snatched the receiver off the hook muttering, "who the fuck is this? It sure as hell aint Mickey, he'd sleep for two days if I didn't roust him out of the sack. I'm sure this is important since the desk knows not to disturb me," he snapped as he picked up the phone.

"Sorry to wake you, JD, I thought you and Mickey could join me for breakfast," Mr. Smith said.

Fuck! How the hell did the old bastard get here this fast, JD thought.

"Uh sorry, sir," he mumbled. "I didn't realize it was you."

"Take your time, I've got a table in the lobby restaurant and am enjoying a cup of marvelous New Orleans chicory coffee," Smith said.

"We'll be down in a few minutes," JD said, then walked over to Mickey's room and shook him awake. "Get your ass outta' that rack. Smiths downstairs."

The maitre de glanced up as they entered the restaurant. "Mr. Smith is seated at the rear to your right, gentlemen, enjoy your breakfast."

"How the fuck does he know who we are?" Mickey grumped as they headed for the table.

"I don't have any idea," JD replied. "Now shut the fuck up before the old man hears you." Mr. Smith rose as they approached.

"Have a seat gentlemen you both look fit and I presume well rested," Mr. Smith said, rising as they approached the table.

"Yes sir, we hit the sack early last night," JD replied. "If you don't mind, I'd like to get the report over before we eat."

His report included all pertinent details other than their carnal involvement with the women during the trip back to the States. Smith made a few notes and then paused for a moment.

"I appreciate your forthrightness and am gratified that you confirm my estimate of your integrity," he said. JD started to say something, stopped and thought, Big Jake always said, don't interrupt when someone is giving you a compliment. Maybe it's right that the truth will set you free, but I'll keep my lying skills intact in case they're needed.

"While you didn't actually eliminate the target you certainly would have if a rival cartel's forces hadn't intervened," Smith said. "Also, your action in almost wiping out that factions most trusted security force has shaken its leader and he has decided to negotiate a surrender with the Colombian government. We had no intention of becoming further involved but he was second on the target list. Your timely operation effectively killed two birds with one stone." He paused then continued, "There is another plus, the agency we had the contract with was so delighted by the additional good news they have increased our fee by an additional twenty-five percent. You will find a bonus in a like percentage has already been deposited to your accounts."

"Ah…now our faith in your integrity is confirmed," JD said. "Not that we ever doubted it," he added, smiling.

"It's not really integrity," Smith said chuckling. "I'm a firm believer in a basic rule of sound business practice. When a manager doesn't allow the sharing of added profits an employee provides, it inevitably spells doom for the enterprise." When they finished breakfast and were on their second cup of coffee, Smith pushed a thick manila envelope over to JD.

"This is another assignment, if you feel up to it." JD glanced at Mickey. He nodded imperceptibly.

"What the hell, we've had enough R and R to last awhile," Mickey said. "Anything we could come up with would pale in comparison anyhow."

"Fine by me," JD said, then pulled several eight-by-ten photographs out of the envelope.

The first photo was of a slim, bearded Arab man of average height with the intense eyes of an intelligent, zealous fanatic. There were ten more photos of larger men all appearing to be Arab thugs. JD flipped through the photos, then glanced up at Mr. Smith.

"I don't believe I've ever seen a nastier looking bunch 'a rag-heads," he muttered.

"The first man, is traveling under the name Saddam Bashra," Smith said. "That is a false identity. He is in fact a terrorist operating out of Libya, suspected of planning and executing attacks in Athens, Israel, Germany and England. And thought to be responsible for a high-profile airline bombing, all targeting American citizens. You can be assured, if he isn't guilty on all counts he is guilty of enough to warrant your full and undivided attention." He paused. "The other men in his entourage are all well trained security guards."

JD shoved the photos over to Mickey, then turned back to Smith.

"We all know who this dude is and killing him is going to be almost impossible. Hell, it probably is impossible or the Israelis would have offed him years ago. We'll need a heavy fee to even attempt it."

American Mercenaries

"There will be an additional fifty thousand dollars each, deposited to your accounts if you accept the mission," Smith said. "And another three hundred and fifty thousand upon its successful completion." JD glanced at Mickey and could see he was stunned at the amount. "There are a couple of other things we need," He said.

"What?" Smith asked guardedly.

"Number one, a complete get-outta-jail letter absolving us of any taxes on fees from assignments carried out on foreign soil."

"Everyone has to bear their fair share of the tax burden," Smith said grumpily.

"Yeah, aint everybody volunteering to try killing one of the most dangerous terrorists on the planet," JD replied mildly.

I wondered when he was going to figure that out, Smith thought. It shouldn't be to difficult since one of the founders of our enterprise is highly placed in the Treasury Department. "Okay, I'll have the letter delivered to you in a couple of days," he groused.

"You mean letters…one for both of us," JD said nodding at Mickey.

"Letters," Mr. Smith grumped. "What else?"

"You're about two hundred grand apiece light on the completion amount."

"That is ridiculous," Smith sputtered. "You are being entirely unreasonable."

JD waited for him to calm a little and looked him in the eye.

"Damn, the government spent fifty million trying to bomb Khadafi a few years ago and missed," he said. "I figure, you're getting a hell of a deal if we eliminate this dick-head without pissing off half of Europe and risking a bunch of military aircraft. Besides, there is a good chance we'll get killed trying and you won't have to pay anyhow." Smith spent a few moments glaring at JD, then relaxed.

"Okay, it's a deal," he muttered. "Is that all?"

"We're `going to need a couple of weeks here with a physical trainer to get back in shape," JD said. "I presume, you'll take care of the hotel bill until we leave for the assignment." He paused. "By the way, just how and where the fuck are we going to get close enough to pop this asshole?"

"Our Intelligence confirms he will be in Italy, outside the small coastal town of Sorrento on the point of land dividing the Bay of Naples

- 95 -

and the Mediterranean Sea in approximately twenty-eight days," Smith replied.

"Why don't you get word to the Israelis if you know where and when he will be there." JD asked. "They'd blow up the whole town to kill this particular mother-fucker, or better yet give the Intel to the Brits. The SAS would exterminate him without blowing up the town. They'd just blow up whatever building he's in… Personally, I'd go with the Israelis. You can be sure they'd wipe out an area large enough to leave no doubt the rag-head was dead.

"I'll answer your questions in order," Smith said. "I wasn't planning to foot the hotel bill and if successful you will have depleted our budget for the coming year; what the hell, why not," he grumped. "Our Intel source is an informant inside of CNN reports your target will be there to be interviewed in twenty eight days."

"Knowing them he'll probably be cast as a poor beset upon Arab, who was thrown out of his home by big bad America's Jewish friends," JD muttered. "That still don't answer, why us?"

"The simple reason is our government under the current administration hasn't the desire nor the will to take any aggressive action against anyone other than female secretaries or aides within arms reach. Certain members of congress and other agencies decided it was time to organize a black operations unit to handle problems that heretofore we've had to go hat-in-hand to our allies for satisfaction and it is about time the terrorists need to start worrying about us."

JD turned to Mickey.

"Sounds plausible to me," Mickey muttered. "You know what a draft dodger` our esteemed leader is." JD glanced back at Smith and nodded his agreement.

"I need to get going," Smith said. "I have an appointment with the head of one of our funding sources and after being severely fleeced this morning, I certainly can't afford to miss it," he added wryly, then rose, excused himself and walked out of the restaurant.

They waited until he was out of earshot and then Mickey muttered, "Man, you sure riled him up. You reckon he'll pay us all of that money?"

"He'll pay us if we survive," JD said. "But the odds against that are pretty good so he aint risking a whole lot. Shit! I should have asked for a hundred thousand up front."

Chapter Fourteen

April 26, 1993, 0:800 hours
Royal Sonesta Hotel
New Orleans, Louisiana

The phone's ringing woke JD to a huge throbbing hangover. They'd spent the prior evening at Luckys and JD had gotten thoroughly slammed. He slapped at the bedside table until he felt the receiver and snatched it out of its cradle.

"This better be life or death," he snarled. "I'm 'going look you up and rip your fuckin' head off if it aint."

"Er...I'm sorry to disturb you sir," a hesitant voice answered. "Mr. Smith told me to deliver a package to you before eight this morning."

"Yeah, it's okay, bring it on up. Sorry for giving you a hard time." JD replied in a calmer tone. He waited a few minutes until a timid knock alerted him the package had arrived and a manila envelope slid under the door with a note stating Mr. Smith's associate would meet them in the lobby at 10:00. JD pulled more photos of the terrorists and air surveillance of the villa they would be at out of the envelope, glanced at his watch then crossed to Mickey's room and found him sitting on the side of the bed with a dark expression on his face.

"What the fucks wrong with you?" he asked. "Get a move on, that little prick, Mayer will be here in a little over an hour and I don't want to talk to him here." Mickey looked at him dourly.

"We should 'a spent a little more time studying instead of following our dicks around when we were in school. Then we wouldn't have to hunt people somebody in Washington has a hard on for to make a living and we would a' been able to spend more time with Susan and Jo."

His mooning around missing Josephine, worried JD.

"That's probably true, but if we had done that we'd in all likelihood be married to a couple of women our age who'd be fat and mad at the world for having the bad luck to have hooked up with a couple of assholes like us," JD said. "Besides, we wouldn't have been there to rescue the Damsels. That being the case, both of them would have been raped by that small army and dead by now." Mickey, not being a deep thinker when JD spun one of his lines of bullshit bought it and brightened up.

"Yeah, I guess you're right," he said. "Why don't you want to meet Mayer here?"

"I don't trust the little shit and don't want him to know what names we're registered under or our room numbers. It'll be better to meet him in the lobby and take him over to Commanders Palace for brunch, its so loud and crowded there he won't be able to record anything we say." They dressed and descended to the lobby and then startled Mayer as he entered, grabbed him and yanked him outside to hail a taxi. He harumped a couple of times as they were seated in the restaurant.

"Jesus! what an asshole, Mickey groused." Mayer squirmed uncomfortably.

"Gentlemen, I sincerely regret the misunderstanding we had during your last mission and hope you will accept my apologies." JD looked at Mickey and saw him relax.

"Apology accepted," JD said. "With the proviso if we show up with extra baggage or people in the future…you will make sure there is adequate transportation."

They immediately got in a dispute when Mayer told them gear and weapons would be provided by a contact in Italy.

"That's not acceptable," JD snapped. "We want the same weapons we used in Colombia. I spent a lot of time balancing and sighting that rifle and don't want to take the risk of setting up another one on foreign soil. You're just going to have to figure out how to handle it." Mayer nodded slowly.

"I'll take care of it," he said and then continued, "Our intel sources have confirmed, your target will be located in a villa five kilometers West of Sorrento Italy. He will be there within twenty seven days and staying for approximately a week.

"How the hell, did you come across that little tidbit?" JD asked to check if smith really trusted the little man with all the facts.

"It's not necessary for you to know," Mayer replied.

"I don't give a big shit whether you think it's necessary or not." Mickey growled.

"You're starting to get on my nerves." Mayer glanced nervously at him.

"Mr. Smith, is going to be upset about revealing our source," he said. "But in the interest of cooperation he has been told the terrorist is being interviewed by some news organization during his stay."

"Which organization?" JD asked.

"That, I do not know," Mayer replied

That lets us know Smith don't entirely trust him or he would have known it was CNN, JD thought.

"You need to establish yourselves as tourists if you are to have time to plan the operation and your escape," Mayer said. "Do you need any other equipment other than what you needed in Colombia?"

"Yeah, ten claymores, six anti-tank mines and at least two dozen fragmentation grenades," JD said. "And you're going to have to get all of it to our contact in Italy for delivery when and where we're going to need it." Mayer started to object until Mickey stated flatly.

"If you can't handle that, how the hell can we rely on you to get us out if we get in a tight?"

"I'll take care of it," Mayer said. You won't just be in a tight, you'll be dead if I can get in touch with the right people. He thought then handed JD a manila envelope containing satellite photos of a villa and its surroundings. There were detailed plans of its interior and exterior along with topography and road maps of the area. Control lacks people with convivial personalities but they have sure improved their Intel. JD thought.

Mayer gave them fifteen thousand dollars for expense and bribe money, credit cards and a secure satellite comm. unit. Their new passports were genuine, using photo ID from their military days in used condition, showing entry and exit stamps for four years. Mayer got to his feet and pushed his chair back from the table.

"If those are satisfactory and you have no further requests, I'll be on my way." They nodded their agreement and waited for him to leave.

"These are for real," Mickey said, then continued sarcastically, "You reckon, we might need an M1 Abrams tank and a couple 'a Howitzers to go with that list? Damn! JD we're going to need bearers to tote all 'a that shit."

"Screw you, you tote your half and I'll tote mine," JD replied. "I just wish we could get through an hour without you bitching about something."

"Yeah, talking about bitching, we aint welcome in Luckys for a while," Mickey grumped. "Some guy got a little disturbed last night when you wandered your drunken ass over to his table and mistook his wife for one a the local whores and offered her fifty for a blow job. He was somewhere between real big and huge so I had to bust him up a little to keep him from stompin' your ass."

They'd found over the years that it was a good idea on the occasions when either of them decided to get blasted for the other to remain relatively sober to try and control any damage and injury to himself or innocent bystanders.

"Like you didn't get us barred from almost every bar on the causeway when you busted up with that girl in Mobile, then decided to whip anybody that said boo for the next month," JD snapped. "We can make peace and pay for any damages if we survive the mission."

"Aint no damages to anything but that big dude and he should be out a the hospital in a couple 'a weeks," Mickey grunted.

"Hospital!" JD exclaimed. What the fuck did you do to the poor bastard?"

"I told you, he was a big 'sumbitch. I had to get real serious about puttin' his ass away and probably broke his nose, jaw, an arm, a couple a ribs and fucked up his right knee."

"Shit! why didn't you just go on and kill his ass?"

"I reckon, 'cause I was madder at you than him. You should 'a known that woman wasn't no whore," Mickey snapped. "He'd have probably kicked your ass since you were too drunk to do anything but stumble around making a complete fool out of yourself. It's a miracle

I didn't have to fight half the people in the bar. You sure managed to rile up anybody you came in contact with." "

"I don't remember a lot but I guess I did get a little carried away," JD mumbled. "I'm going back to the hotel, take a steam bath and rest all day. We can head over to the gym first thing in the morning. You think the dude will sue us?"

"Naw, everybody in the joint heard him describe in great detail how he was fixin' to' take my butt outside and clean up the street with me before he came back inside to kill your dumb ass," Mickey replied.

Chapter Fifteen

★ ★

May 10, 1993, 22:00 hours
Da Vinci Airport
Rome, Italy

They caught a Delta flight to Atlanta and connected with a flight to Paris, then sat in the concourse lounge for two hours before boarding a Swissair jet for the final hop into Rome. JD called the contact number control had provided as they checked in the downtown Hilton after a hairy taxi ride in from the airport. He let the phone ring twice as instructed, cut the connection then redialed. A man with a heavy Italian accent answered on the second ring.

"Allo, thees iss Alphonce Gambino. Who mighta be callin pliss?"

"This is JD. Mr. Smith gave me your number," JD replied. "We just checked in the downtown Hilton."

"Oh yas, I ave beena axpacting you call. I willa meeta you ina lobby bistro in a hour and half, okey?"

"Fine," JD replied and hung up.

They took a quick shower to revive themselves. Then stationed themselves in the lounge with their backs to the wall at a table with a view of the entrance a half hour before Alphonce was scheduled to arrive. JD ordered a Scotch and water and Mickey asked for a cold beer; both were sipping their drinks when a man of average height with a thick barrel chest and the dark complexion of Southern Italy entered the lounge, scanned the room until he spotted them then approached their table. His garb of black slacks, dark gray silk shirt, matching alligator shoes and belt, along with a heavy gold necklace and diamond encrusted Rolex almost screamed Mafia. JD nudged Mickey as he approached the table.

"It looks like we got the paisans on our side," he muttered and nodded for the man to have a seat.

The man paused to shake hands with them before sitting down .

"I be Alphonse Gambino, isa nice to meeta you guys," he said. "Donna bother with intras, Mr. Smith he provide photos, so I alreada knew who you air." They had a drink and went over a few mission details with Alphonce until he asked JD for his room key, then waved another man hovering at the bar over and in rapid Italian told him to deliver two trunks in the back of his van to JD's room.

"I meeta you for breakfus at nina ina tha mornin thena take you to rental agencia for automobile," he said, then rose to leave. "Hava gooda night gennulmen, I see you in a mornin." They watched him leave, ordered another drink to settle their nerves and then turned down two fine looking ladies-of-the-night when they stopped by and asked if they wanted some company.

"Man, JD we are definitely gittin' old," Mickey said after the two call-girls excused themselves to join a boisterous group of German business men entering the lounge. "Or, you're right about Jo and Susan screwing up our minds."

"It's just the time-change that's got us fucked up," JD replied. "A couple a days and we'll be following our dicks around as usual." Mickey laughed.

"JD, you're full 'a shit.

"Stick it in your ear, I'm goin' to bed," JD snapped. Mickey followed him up to his room to check all of the requested gear in the trunks. After JD unlocked them and he saw the array, he groused.

"Damn! we're gonna' have to hire a team of bearers to tote all 'a this shit."

"We're probably going to need every bit of it so quit bitchin'," JD snapped. "Now get your ass over to your room, I'm so tired I could sleep a week."

Alphonce was waiting in the dining room the next morning. He dispatched two men to retrieve their luggage and the two trunks while they ate breakfast then drove them to a car rental agency that rented for cash and would lose the paper work when the car was picked up where-ever they left it. A large Mercedes sedan was fueled and ready to go when they arrived at the agency. Alphonce assured them that it would out-perform anything on the Iter other than a Porche or Ferrari and then shocked Mickey when he told them the rental fee was five thousand dollars American a week.

"Damn! Alphonce, we didn't want to buy the fucking thing!" Mickey exclaimed.

"The guy probably knows, if we get in a race with any Porches or Ferraris we'll more than likely dent it up running their ass off the road," JD snapped, hoping the rental agent didn't speak English.

"Yeah…but five thousand a fucking week?" Mickey grumped.

"Damn! Why don't we save a few bucks and rent a fuckin' Yugo if it upsets you so much," JD snapped sarcastically. "Shut the fuck up and let me pay for it before the man gets smart and refuses to let us have it." Mickey acquiesced grudgingly then stood by mumbling, as JD counted the money out and bought a road map for their route South through mountains to Cassino, Capua then skirting Naples to Castellamare where Alphonce had rooms reserved for them at a small inn. He said it was wholly owned by friends of his and they didn't have to worry about anyone getting into their rooms. JD drove as they both knew Mickey wasn't capable of handling anything with wheels and not have some type of catastrophe on a fairly regular basis. He enjoyed handling the big powerful machine around hairpin curves as they got into the mountains until he glanced over and saw Mickey go pale as he accelerated out of a steep curve. He wouldn't admit he was afraid of heights and had a death grip on the hand- hold over the glove compartment as JD powered around the curve.

"Will you slow the fuck down! You're gonna' kill us," he growled through gritted teeth.

"We can't crawl if we're going to get there with enough time to scout the objective," JD snapped. "How 'bout you shut up and let me concentrate on driving or I might miss one of these curves and fly over the side of a mountain." That shut Mickey up but he still went pale, cursed JD and took a deep breath as they neared each bend in the road.

When they pulled in front of the inn a two story very light tan stucco building with five arches supporting a covered sidewalk. The entrance was two heavy arched, burnished ornate doors located behind the center arch. There was a second floor balcony fronting on the street with eight panel French doors opening out to individual balconies from each of the rooms facing the street. JD was worn out and Mickey looked like he'd run the iron-man triathlon as they parked just past the entrance "We're not taking any more assignments in mountains," he rasped.

"It's a helluva' lot more comfortable tooling over mountains in a Mercedes than crawling through a stinking ass-jungle to reach our target." JD replied, then got out of the car and stretched. Mickey unfolded from the passenger side.

"How 'bout leaving the gear in the trunk?" he asked hopefully. "Alphonce said this place was secure."

"He said the rooms," JD replied "He didn't mention the street. There aint any way we're going to get separated from the weapons. I don't know what kind of car thieves they have in Italy, but it would be gone by the time we got to our rooms in New York." JD signed in and tipped the dual-purpose desk clerk bell-man a ten to carry their luggage up two flights of stairs while they lugged the trunks up. He tipped the clerk another ten and Mickey grabbed his lower back as the rooms door closed.

"I hope you're happy, Asshole," he groused. "My back feels like I been hit by a Mack truck."

"Fine, you want to leave 'em in here it's alright with me," JD replied. Mickey glowered at him, opened a trunk to retrieve his Glock and knife, then strode to the adjoining room and slammed the door. JD got his trusty six-shooter out, shoved the trunks in the closet, locked them and then walked in the bathroom for a shower. The inn wasn't a Hilton but was clean with firm mattresses, good locks and separate baths.

Chapter Sixteen

May 13, 1993, 12:00 hours
Castellammare, Italy

Arising at noon they dressed then descended to the small lobby and were directed by the desk clerk to a small ristorante a block away. After being seated in the dining room they felt lucky their waitress was fluent enough in English to take their order of pasta with an excellent sea scallop and shrimp marinara sauce, accompanied by hot bread and a good Chianti wine. Sated, they finished the wine then retired back to the inn to rest for a late night reconnaissance of their objective.

JD awoke at 17:30, donned slacks, a polo shirt and a windbreaker to conceal the shoulder-holstered Ruger. He walked over to get Mickey up and waited while he dressed, stuck the Glock in his shoulder holster and belted the knife's scabbard to his lower leg.

They selected black and gray camos, Nike running shoes and ski masks for that night and packed them in backpacks, then stacked the trunks in a closet and locked them before trotting down to the street to find the Mercedes unmolested. Mickey glanced at JD as he headed east for the short drive to Sorrento.

"How far, we gonna` have to hump it tonight?" JD scanned the map and reconnaissance photos of the villa.

"About five clicks both ways," he replied. "Alphonce gave me directions to a late night bar and restaurant catering to the upscale, looking for love set. A guy, named Marty Colucci runs it. He's supposed to be connected to the New York mob and knows we'll be parking the car there tonight." They spent an hour familiarizing themselves with the town's street layout, including the harbor and marina before driving to the outskirts to locate the bar facing a narrow paved road leading West toward their objective. Cruising the streets for another hour observing the local population to see if they could recognize any of their target's security force they realized most of the locals had dark complexions, brown eyes and black hair and they wouldn't be able to recognize any of the security men without staring to compare with their photos. To avoid being that obvious they gave up and drove to back to the bar. It was a two story masonry building with two large plate glass windows facing the street with an entry door in the middle between the two windows and two single windows on the top floor facing the front and two on each side of the structure toward the back. A high chain link fence surrounded the parking area behind the building with a gate on the East side that was open with a drop bolt and heavy lock for use during closing hours.

JD stopped a block up the street for a few minutes to get an idea of the bar and grills patronage and then pulled in the back. He locked the car and they walked around to the front entrance and went in to see if it was as good a place to look for short-term-love as Alphonce had described.

Mickey entered first immediately noticing the ratio of women to men was a whole lot better than most of the joints they were used to frequenting in the States. There were at least two women for every guy in the place and most of them looked to be a seven or better. Marty's bar and grill was a vast improvement over their usual hangouts. Most of those had three or four hard drinking women, two or three barmaids with a bunch of guys competing for 'em. By the time most of the men were drunk enough to hit on one of the drinkers or a barmaid, they were slobbering all over the poor women.

"Damn, we could get away with breakin' the number one rule for short term pussy, 'go ugly early'!" Mickey exclaimed. "We need to come back here for some R and R in a couple 'a days." JD remained silent, but was happy to see Mickey wasn't still mooning about Jo. It won't be long before we'll be back to normal. Get up, glance down and ask where we goin` and what we gonna` do today Richard?

On their fortieth birthday the prior year JD and Mickey had agreed they were getting a little old to drink a lot, chase women late at night and still be able to stay in shape. Quitting completely wasn't an option, but drastically slowing down was. Their having reached the age where drunk and after midnight, by the time a girl got undressed they'd be asleep anyhow. Marty's place was like all others in one respect. When the front door opened every man in the joint looked to see if new meat was coming on the market. They were quickly disappointed when JD and Mickey walked in and climbed on stools at the far end of the bar, and then realized everybody in the joint was speaking either Italian or some other foreign tongue.

"How the hell can we order anything?" Mickey mumbled as the bartender headed for them. "Aint either one of us knows a word in Italian besides amore."

"Just ask for a beer. He ought to be able to understand that," JD replied. "We have a ten or twelve kilometer hike tonight and don't need to drink any whiskey." The bartender overheard and grinned.

"You guys, American?" He was a big powerful looking man of obvious Italian descent, dressed very much like Alphonce. This has got to be Marty, JD thought. If you wanted to describe the perfect mob button man, he sure fit's the bill.

"Yeah," he replied. "And you'd be?"

"Marty Colucci. Alphonce told me to be on the lookout for you guys" the bar-keep replied and reached across the bar to shake hands with them. JD made the introductions then told him, they'd be parking the Mercedes in the back parking lot for a few hours.

"No problem, I live in an apartment over the bar," Marty said. "I'll keep an eye on it for you. By the way, did Alphonce tell you I was with a New York family till the fuckin` feds deported me?"

"He didn't tell us but I got an impression that was the case," JD replied.

"The mother-fuckers never proved a damn thing. They just decided I was an undesirable and kicked my ass out 'a the country anyhow. Since I was born and raised in Sorrento the Italian government won't let me travel out of the general area so I'm stuck here." Mickey nodded sympathetically

"There aint any doubt the feds can fuck up your program if they want to." Marty smiled at Mickey's sympathetic tone and continued, "The reason for bringing it up is I don't know what you guys are up to, but I can handle a pistol, rifle and on occasion have been known as a good demolition man. If you need any help I'd be real happy to get involved. After three years running this bar I'm all caught up on women and would sure like a little action."

"I appreciate the offer," JD said. "We'll keep it in mind and let you know." They sipped a beer and spent a few minutes talking about New York. Then, JD shoved away from the bar.

"Thanks, for the help," he said. "We got to get in gear. The car will be in back and we should be back a little before dawn."

"Don't worry, I got it covered. Just keep my offer in mind," Marty said, then showed them the back exit to the parking lot.

They changed into the camos, donned ski masks and then jogged for half an hour to the villa's outer perimeter. Mickey observed the building and its surroundings for a few minutes with night-vision binoculars to be sure it was uninhabited.

"All I see is one light in the kitchen, if there's anybody around they aint moving," he muttered.

The villa was a large one story what appeared to be adobe brick building at the end of the promontory separating the Bay of Naples and the Mediterranean Sea. It was in a small valley flanked by hills East and West, backing up to a cliff on the Mediterranean to the South with the front facing a gentle slope down to the Bay on the North side. The front entrance and main part of the building was at the end of an approximate four hundred meter drive leading in from a gated entrance off the road. There were El shaped wings on both sides of the back with a flagstone patio covering the area between the wings running back to the wall overlooking the cliff in back and what appeared to be an Olympic size pool in the center of the patio which came within a meter of a wall built out of the same brick as the villa extending across the back with ninety degree corners until coming even with the villa's wings then another ninety degree turn connecting back to the it's walls. There was a spiked gate in the middle of the back wall which exited to steps with one landing halfway down a steep cliff ending at a narrow rocky beach below.

Mickey scanned the cliff after they made a complete recon around the area and muttered,

"We aint mountain climbers and they'll definitely be covering the stairs so an approach from the sea is out."

"Uh huh," JD grunted, then spent a few seconds studying the hills to the East and West. "The hill on the West side has enough elevation to get a round over the wall," he muttered. "Range is a little long but it shouldn't be an impossible shot if the asshole decides to take a swim or get some sun around the pool." Easing back past the gate, they started a slow jog back to the bar.

"We'll come back and set charges on the beach and under the landing tomorrow night," JD grunted. "Then rent a plane to over-fly the place the next day. Security should be in place by then and we'll be able to get an idea of what we're up against."

Marty had just run the last lothario off as they arrived, closed the bar and had stepped in the shadows to wait on them. Mickey sensed his presence but couldn't tell who it was and had the knife at his throat in an instant, then pulled back.

"Sorry, couldn't see who it was" he muttered.

"You scared the piss outta' me," Marty mumbled and took a deep breath to regain his composure. "You boys, are into some serious shit. Right!?"

"You got it," JD said. "You'll be a lot better off if you don't get involved. The first place we're going to light is the United States, if we don't get killed. Since you've got to stay you'll have some deadly enemies who live right across the pond and you're connected to us."

"I don't give a shit," Marty said. "I've been in Sorrento for almost three years I'm tired of serving booze, running bar-girls at night and fishing during the day. I am going crazy for some action." JD thought a moment.

"We'll be back tomorrow afternoon, I'll let you know then."

Chapter Seventeen

0:400 May 14, 1993
Castellamare Inn
Castellamare, Italy

JD parked in front of the inn and shook Mickey awake.

"Come on, lets get a shower and some rest." Mickey stepped out of the car, stretched and yawned.

"Man, I'm fuckin' beat, how 'bout we sleep in tomorrow?"

"It is tomorrow, but you're right," JD said. "We need get as much rest as possible the next couple a' days. I doubt we'll be getting much after the rag-head arrives."

"What 'cha you think about Marty?"

"Don't know," JD replied. "He could be useful, I'll have Smith check him out and see what he thinks." Mickey trailed JD in his room and waited while he called control on the sat comm. He was told to stand by for ten minutes and Mr. Smith came on nine minutes later.

"Good evening JD," he said. "Do you need any help from this end?"

"Everything's fine so far," JD replied. "What do you think about us using some local talent that seems to be eminently qualified?" There was silence for a few moments then in a guarded tone of voice, Smith asked.

"Who and what do you have in mind?"

"Alphonce put us in touch with a guy named Marty Colucci. He says he was with one of the New York families until the INS deported him three years ago."

"I'll check him out and have an answer by 12:00 your time tomorrow."

"That's fine," JD said. "One more question?"

"Somehow I think it's going to entail money...right?" Smith grumped.

"Well...yeah, supposing he's an asset? Whose going to pay him and how much?" JD replied in an injured tone of voice.

"In the event he's found useful and reliable we'll handle his fee," Smith groused.

Mickey rose at 11:00 the next morning, crossed to JD's room and woke him up.

"Why the hell didn't you stop to eat last night?" he grumped. "I'm starvin' to death."

JD sat up and eased his feet to the floor.

"I was too charged up about the mission and didn't think about it," he snapped. "You, on the other hand would stop the world to feed your ugly face when something clicks in that pea brain 'a yours signaling it's time to eat. Besides, I don't recall you being a fuckin' mute. Why didn't you speak up if you were so hungry?"

"Sorry to be getting on your nerves, Ms. Volt," Mickey said sarcastically. "I wouldn't have riled you up if, I'd 'a known it was your time 'a the month and you hadn't changed your Kotex ."

"Screw you," JD said and glanced at his watch. "Since we're up and Smiths scheduled to call in less than an hour, you want to eat now or wait?"

"How 'bout I go on down to that restaurant and you take a warm bath to get outta' your grouchy ass mood?" Mickey replied caustically.

"I don't think it would be smart for us to get separated at this point," JD said. "We sure as hell can't be absolutely sure the opposition doesn't know about us and we need to be together if a bunch 'a rag-heads show up lookin' for trouble." Mickey hesitated a moment.

"Yeah, you're probably right, another forty five minutes won't kill me."

The sat.com buzzed at precisely 12:00 and JD picked up.

"Good day," Smith said. He paused until JD replied, then continued, "To answer your question about Mr. Colucci, our sources confirm he is connected to one of the New York families. The FBI credits him with at least six hits. They spent a year trying to uncover enough evidence to convict him, failed, and decided to deport him as an undesirable to his place of birth in Sorrento, Italy. From all reports, he is a quite talented operative and the government is happy to have him out of the country." He paused a moment.

"Have either of you been contacted by Don?"

" No, Why?

"It's nothing but I found the comm on his desk this morning and thought he might have been in touch."

"Is that unusual? JD asked a little twinge sparking in his mind.

"No, I'm from the dial phone era so he does all of the technology here and is always fiddling with the systems."

"You need to keep an eye on him," JD said.

"Not to worry, I keep an eye on anyone connected to the organization," Smith replied.

"Ask him why he had it," JD said. "Let us know if he doesn't have a good explanation." He decided to let it slide as there was already to much to worry about in the next few days. He cut the connection and relayed the news to Mickey omitting Mayer and the comm as Mickey pretty much detested him already.

"We aint paying him a dime outta' our cut," Mickey snapped when he heard about Marty.

"It's not going cost us anything Dummy," JD said. "Smith will handle his fee. Now, lets go eat before whatever brain cells you have left die of starvation." They donned light windbreakers over shoulder holsters, exited the inn and strolled a block to the ristorante. It was a bright sunshiny day, and a few tables arrayed under umbrellas between the sidewalk and the arched entry gave the eatery an even more pleasant atmosphere.

"It's a nice day, how bout we sit out here," Mickey suggested.

"To exposed," JD said as he led way into the interior dining area. "I sure as hell don't want a drive by shooter to blow our ass away."

Penelope Stuart couldn't seem to shake her feeling of melancholy as she sat with her cousin, Nigel West, her dearest friend Marlene and her husband Ian Bitner. Her sense of failure and sadness stemmed from her separation and recent messy divorce from Peter Smythe, her first lover and husband for the past three years. I was as wrong about this trip helping to get me out of my doldrums as I was when I convinced myself at the ripe old age of twenty that despite his obvious shortcomings, Peter was the perfect mate I could spend the rest of my days with, She thought morosely. She was trying, but doing a poor job of concealing her mood, barely able to keep a semblance of a smile as her companions prattled on about the weather and the long drive they faced returning to London in a few days. She felt a strong urge to scream when Nigel launched into another of his seemingly endless supply of inane witticisms when she glanced up and noticed two hard looking men as they entered the dining room. The first man turned from a conversation he was having with his companion and their eyes locked for a brief moment. Noticing the knife scar on the side of his face she thought. What a frightening pair, they both have an aura of violence and the one with the scar and brooding almost black eyes exudes imminent deadly danger. She observed the total vigilance of the men as they scanned the dining room. The man with the scar checked everything and every person to his left while the second checked the right, both seeming to take in every nook and cranny. Then she noticed the diners scattered among the other tables on catching sight of the men showed signs of alarm, dropping their gaze as the men's eyes flickered over them. The dark eyed man turned his attention back to her staring boldly until Nigel shook her arm.

"Earth to Penelope!" he said loudly. She blushed and brought her attention back to him.

"Sorry, I seem to have drifted off for a moment."

JD felt a little foolish as he almost tripped over a table staring at the beautiful young woman with what appeared to be a male companion and another couple. He tore his eyes from her and saw Mickey smiling as he sat down at a table backing up to the wall beyond the two couples.

"I reckon we need to get some warm bodies lined up," he muttered. "It looked like I might have to haul your ass off 'a that broad."

"Screw you," JD said distractedly, then glanced around looking for the waitress who had served them the day before and she didn't seem to be working. Immediate problems arose when they discovered her replacement spoke no English. JD was trying in vain to break the language barrier when the beautiful young woman rose and stepped over to their table. She was a little over average height, fair, with shoulder length lustrous black hair, deep sparkling sea-blue eyes, full sensuous lips and her softly delicate features bespoke of regal breeding with seemingly a depth of feeling and sensitivity that concealed a perceived sadness.

My lord! What has come over me? Penelope thought as she rose and stepped over to the men's table. I guess I am attracted to danger after living with Peter's infidelities for three years. These men are truly frightening in daylight, lord knows the terror one would feel meeting them on a dark street at night.

JD's first impression was she was slightly thin until he looked closer and saw firm breasts that seemed on the verge of bursting free of the light silk blouse she was wearing. A modestly tight dark-skirt, that almost, but didn't quite reach her knees revealed long shapely legs. She aint thin, he thought. I bet she would be exactly what Waylon Jennings had in mind when he wrote that song about old dogs, pickup trucks and firm feelin' wimmen. Completely forgetting about food, he and Mickey rose as the young women approached and lightly touched her elbow as he held a chair for her. She sat down and in a softly cultured voice with an English accent said, "Hi, I'm Penelope, you Yanks seem to be having a bit of trouble with the local dialect. I'm quite fluent and would be happy to help you order." JD glanced over at her table and saw what he supposed was her husband frowning, then sat back down and introduced Mickey and himself.

"Yes ma'am we'd sure appreciate it," he replied . Damn, I didn't think I'd ever run across a women as sexy as Susan and here one pops up in this little Italian burg a few days later. He snapped back to reality. She's obviously with one of those guys and even if she wasn't, I don't have time for romance right now. This job can sure fuck up a mans social life.

He sat entranced with her soft melodious voice as she explained each item on the menu then switched to Italian when the waitress arrived to order their selections. They got to their feet to thank her as she rose, then JD escorted her back to her table lightly touching her elbow again as he seated her.

"Man, I'd sure like to spend some time with her," JD said as he sat back down with Mickey.

"Yeah, and the other one is just as sexy," Mickey grunted. "But, you'd` a known we'd` a had a real problem snaking `em away from their boyfriends if you'd seen the look on their faces while you were talking to her."

Fuck em," JD grunted. "I reckon we'll give `em a pass. "We aint got time to get in a war over women right now anyhow."

Finishing lunch, JD stopped by Penelope's table as they were leaving and gently squeezed her shoulder.

"I sure appreciate your coming to the rescue, Penelope," he said softly. "I wish there was something we could do to return the favor."

A slight electric tingle ran down Penelope's spine at his touch. I wish I could have met this man under different circumstances. One wouldn't describe either them as handsome but the aura of danger and confident power gives an impression that they are both hunters and I don't think they hunt the four legged variety. She thought with a slight shiver and tried to think of a way to continue the conversation, but a glance at Ian confirmed he was on the verge of causing a scene. Damn! Why on Earth would the obstreperous fool think it was incumbent on him to protect me, she thought and turned back to JD.

"I'm quite pleased to help a couple of Yanks in distress," she said with an inviting smile.

"Well thanks again," JD said and returned Ian's glare. He nodded politely to the other couple, then followed Mickey outside. He was waiting on the sidewalk and slapped JD on the back.

"It sure don't look like you're so charged up about the mission that you've completely forgotten about Poon-tang," he said grinning.

"I told you we'd be following our dicks around inside `a few days,"

JD muttered. They walked a few paces back toward the inn and Mickey laughed.

"You're right, the job will eventually take a back seat to his stiff dick if a man don't get a little once in a while."

"We'll probably be up most of the night," JD said chuckling, "lets get some sleep."

They parked behind the bistro at 19:30 and found it deserted other than a couple of hard core drinkers sitting at the bar. Marty was sitting in a booth reading a newspaper until they slid in across the table from him.

"Evidently making a move for love don't happen before nine or ten o'clock around here," Mickey said.

"Nah, it's more like eleven or twelve," Marty replied, then continued in a pensive tone.

"You know, I was doing what I did to avoid working regular hours and here I am working the fucking graveyard shift every night, life's a bitch aint it?"

"Hell, I gave up trying to figure why we do anything," JD said. "Mickey and I just head down any road that's open and hope for the best." He paused, "We've been authorized to offer you a side job that might turn your crank and pays well if you're interested." Marty grinned broadly.

"You know damn well I'm interested," he said. "What kind of weapons do I need?"

"A side-arm and auto-rifle with sound suppressors," JD said. "And you'll need to find somebody who can be trusted to watch our wheels and handle the bar for at least one night."

"No problem, I have a Glock-nine hidden in the apartment and can get hold of an M-sixteen and silencers tomorrow morning," Marty said. "Oh yeah, I got a Bertram thirty one with twin Detroit six-fifty-one-tourbos down at the marina, it'll flat out fly"

"I hadn't thought about a boat but it might come in handy," JD said. "You know where we can rent a light plane and a pilot who can be trusted to keep his mouth shut?"

"Sure, a cousin of mine has one at the field just outside a` town he charters to tourists and he'd take the fifth in front 'a Saint Peter," Marty replied. "What you got in mind for tonight?"

"We need a little more recon and should be back by 23:00," JD replied not wanting to reveal they were placing charges

23:00, what the hell is that?" Marty asked quizzically.

"Eleven o'clock," JD replied. "I forgot you haven't been in the military."

"How 'bout after you get back?"

"Nothing, we're on R and R, which means rest and recreation tonight," Mickey said.

"You want me to line up a couple of our local beauties to help relax you?"

"That would be greatly appreciated," Mickey said grinning broadly.

"Welcome back to the world," JD said. "I wondered when old Richard would get control of you again." He turned his attention back to Marty and slid the photo of the target across the table. Marty spent a moment studying it, then whistled softly.

"Jeez, half the world is looking for this cock-sucker!" he exclaimed. "Is he supposed to be around here?"

"Well, he aint quite yet," JD replied. "But he is scheduled to be at a villa about five kilometers west of here tomorrow or the next day."

"Why the hell would he be coming here?" Marty asked puzzled.

"Our Intel says he'll be here for an interview with CNN and maybe they're afraid to do it in Libya. I don't care, we're just looking for a shot at eliminating him from the world scene before he blows up any more women and children; it'll be a pleasure and the pay aint bad."

"There's no doubt this guy needs killin'," Marty grunted. "What can I do besides setting you boys up with some warm bodies tonight?"

"Get that plane ready for a flight tomorrow morning at eleven hundred."

"No problem, I'll call my cousin tonight and we'll meet at the airport at ten forty five in the morning. Uh…I guess eleven hundred means eleven in the morning?"

"You got it," JD said. "How do we find this airport?"

"It's just east of town, if you look to your left on your way back to Castellammare, you'll see the beacon," Marty said. He thought for a moment. "Oh yeah, before I forget, Alphonce called and told me to let him know when you were headed back to the Inn, he's got some equipment for you." JD glanced at his watch, then rose.

"We'll be back in about three hours," he said. Changing into camos at the car they jogged to the villa's perimeter, skirted it, descended to plant charges at both ends of the beach and under the landing halfway up the steps to the patio. Arriving back at the parking lot they found Marty waiting by the car. He directed them to his apartment over the bar to shower and change then brought two local beauties by as they slid in a booth at 23:00. JD tried vainly to communicate with gestures until Mickey became edgy and turned to him.

"JD, the only way we're gonna' be able to tell if they're ready to jump in the sack is to dance with 'em. I know you think dancing your way to pussy is juvenile, but since we aint communicating well and asking them to screw in sign language is decidedly un-cool. Me, not being a smooth talker like you, I've found if a woman wants to screw she'll let you know on the dance floor." Five minutes elapsed and JD was still trying to communicate when Mickey strolled off the dance floor grinning as he walked by the booth and quipped, "We're headed up to the apartment, have fun JD." The young lady with JD frowned in exasperation as he continued trying to talk, got up, and grabbed his hand to follow Mickey and her friend.

They didn't get a lot of conversation going the next couple of hours, but everybody seemed to be on the same page about what went where, and they were back at the Inn by 02:30, pipes cleaned, and with a fresh outlook on life in general.

Chapter Eighteen

May 15, 1993, 10:45 hours
private aerodrome
Outskirts of Sorrento, Italy

JD was pleased to find Marty's cousin spoke good English when they arrived at the airport. He'd just started to discuss the flight plan when Mickey stalked by.

"JD, we gonna` stand around here with a thumb up our ass all day?" he rasped. "How `bout we get this over with."

Mickey wasn't keen about small airplanes since there was nowhere he could sit and not see the pilot and being afraid of heights didn't want to know if there was a problem since he couldn't do anything about it. He figured there was no sense in dying of fright before they crashed or whatever other horrible consequence befell them. JD turned his attention back to the pilot and told him they needed to fly past the villa on the north side at around fifteen hundred feet and continue west until they were well out of sight. Then, if possible land, spend a couple of hours on the ground before flying back for a view of the South side on the return flight.

"No problemo," the pilot said. "There is a ristorante on Isola Capri that has very good food. We can have lunch there and by the time we finish, it should be four o'clock before we arrive back over the villa." Mickey, overheard the conversation and motioned JD to the side.

"We need to talk," he muttered, then walked twenty paces away from the group. JD trailed after him.

"What the hell's 'a matter now?"

"Are you telling me we got to go up and down in that little piece 'a shit airplane twice?"

"It's either that or fly out over the water for three or four hours then come back, hoping we have enough fuel to make it." JD snapped. "You could catch a ferry back if the second flight scares you so much." Mickey frowned and thought for a few seconds.

"You know…it would be nice when I object to one a your grand plans if you could come up with an alternative that wasn't worse than the original." JD smiled"

"I'll try. Now how 'bout gittin' the camera out of the trunk and get on the fuckin' plane."

It took JD a few moments to convince the pilot he needed to sit in the left seat with binoculars so he could observe with Mickey in back using the long lens camera. The pilot finally nodded his agreement, grudgingly climbed in the right seat, took off and headed west. As they flew by the North side of the villa, JD put the binoculars on what appeared to be the target sitting with a skinny blond at a patio table. He wasn't sure it was their objective until he moved the glasses slightly and saw a video camera operator off to one side. There were three guards scattered around the patio, another at the front entrance, one at the head of the steps leading down to the beach and one positioned on top of each hill over-looking the villa from the east and west sides. JD scanned them closely.

"No one seems to be taking any notice of us maybe they aint as smart as we thought."

"Did you see, who that dirt-bag was sittin' with!?" Mickey exclaimed.

"How the hell would I know," JD snapped. "A skinny blond and a cameraman was all I could see."

"She sure as hell looked like that socialist liberal on the Clinton news network," Mickey said.

"Mentioning CNN and socialist liberals in the same phrase is being redundant," JD said. "It figures they'd want to interview a terrorist alleged to have casually murdered hundreds of innocent women and children, not to mention a lot of Americans. They'll probably put his story out with as much positive spin as possible. Hell, before they're through we'll hear, if it weren't for America's warlike policies and the mean-ass Israelis intractability this asshole would be a fine upstanding citizen."

"You been reading it pays to increase your word power again aint you?" Mickey growled. "What the fuck does redundant mean?" JD thought a second.

"It just means, it's not necessary to say liberal and socialist when you're talking about CNN. Anybody who aint got their head completely up their ass knows where they're comin' from. Did you get some good shots of her?"

"In living color," Mickey replied.

They landed on Isola Capri an hour later and the pilot prevailed on a local to drive them to the ristorante for a long lunch.

Mickey burped and pushed back from the table as they finished a delightful meal.

"Man, we're ruined JD," he said. "No way we'll ever find Italian food like this back in the states."

"You're right about that, we'd have to get golf carts to haul our fat butts around if this joint was convenient."

On the return flight they could see two guards on the beach and one on the landing halfway up the steps. All were stationed close enough to the charges they'd planted the night before to cease being a worry when the explosives went off. As they'd observed earlier, there was one on each hill, probably two more inside the villa, two on the patio and two at the front gate. Counting the two on the beach and one on the landing, that made ten.

"This don't look so bad," Mickey said. "We get any kind 'a break, we'll blow up the three on the beach and landing. You can terminate the one on your firing position first. I'll get the one on the other hill, then wait until the target shows and you take the shot before blowing the charges. You ought to be able to pop a couple standing around the patio before they figure out what hit 'em."

"I hope you're right, but we need to take a little fishing trip in the morning to see if they're still in the same position and the target is in the habit of sunning himself while he brags about his exploits," JD said

"Dammit! you didn't listen to the rest `a my plan," Mickey growled. "It wouldn't kill you to once in a while let me help with the planning."

"Sorry, please continue," JD said contritely. Mickey glowered at him for a moment.

"I'll help Marty take out the front gate and set the mines so nobody can escape in a car," he said. "Then eliminate the Western outpost while you're doing the one on your firing position. If we get just a little lucky and everything works right, we can take our time killin` the rest of `em." JD smiled and slapped him on the back.

"Well done; sounds good to me."

Alphonce was waiting when they climbed out of the plane and JD handed him a list of additional equipment they needed.

"How quick?" he asked.

"Tomorrow morning if we get final approval for the mission," JD replied.

"What the hell you mean final approval?" Mickey rasped. "I thought we got that before we left New Orleans."

"You're right, but, we didn't know there was going to be a nationally known newswoman in the target area," JD replied.

"The hell, we didn't," Mickey rasped. "Smith told us CNN was doing the interview and you know that broad wouldn't miss a chance to talk to a poor needy terrorist. Besides, you don't know for sure who she is and it don't make any difference anyhow," he snapped. "She, or the idiots she works for ought to know better than to hang out with a mass murderer of innocent women and children in the first place. It's unconscionable." JD grinned.

"Unconscionable? Talk about it pays to increase your word power Most of the time your vocabulary tends toward four or five letter words Where the hell did you pick up a word with that many syllables?" Mickey glared at him.

"Get to the fuckin` point!" he snapped. JD noticed Marty was nodding every time Mickey said something.

"Okay…if we get this fool newswoman killed, the shits going to hit the fan," he said.

Say we can do the job without killing or wounding her, it'll still hit the fan and splatter all over everybody involved. Those assholes at CNN will scream bloody murder when they find out somebody had the nerve to kill a son-of-a-bitch who richly deserved it. Knowing them, they'll be explaining how he really wasn't so bad, and he was probably abused during childhood. And after all, the Israelis have really been mean to the Palestinians for years, picking on poor people who by the way, drop in on occasion to murder their citizenry. They'll flush us all down the toilet and drop a grenade on our ass if that bunch of socialists ever figure out who initiated this operation. Control will make sure the buck stops with us and we'll be dead and harder to find than Jimmy Hoffa."

"Shit! I hadn't thought 'a that." Mickey grunted.

"That don't sound so good, "Marty muttered. JD couldn't help smiling at them.

"I'll tell Smith the good news and see what he has to say." After getting back in his room at the inn, JD put the call in and Smith called back after the usual ten minutes

"Good evening," he said. "The additional equipment you requested will be delivered by Alphonce before noon tomorrow."

"That's fine, but we got a problem," JD said.

"What's that?"

"We think, a well known newswoman is at the villa interviewing the target. There's a good chance she might get killed or wounded during the operation."

"Do you have photographs of her?"

"Yes, sir, Mickey got some shots with a long range lens." Smith paused for a few moments.

"I'll have someone at your hotel within an hour to pick up the negatives. We'll enhance them to see who we're dealing with. In the meantime, continue with the mission as planned.; I'll be in touch." They showered and changed, and then strolled down to the ristorante for another sumptuous meal. JD was disappointed when all he could get out of the waitress were shrugs when he tried to find out if she knew where the lovely English woman had gone. On arriving back at the inn, they found a young man waiting in the lobby. He identified himself as being from Control Associates. Mickey handed him the roll of film and he trotted to a parked car outside and was gone in a trice. Mickey glanced at JD.

"How much support you reckon they got in the area?"

"Probably more than we think," JD replied. "It is food for thought though, we'll be in deep shit if we fuck up. I aint got time to worry about it now so lets get some sleep. We are going to have a long day tomorrow.

Chapter Nineteen

May 16, 1993, 10:00 hours
Municipal marina
Sorrento, Italy

Marty ran the Bertram two kilometers out to sea at 10:00 the next morning then turned west and started to troll east to pass the villa's Mediterranean beachfront. Mickey was ensconced in the fighting chair drinking a beer with JD below using the camera with a long range lens. He could see the two men on the beach were sitting on a log but the one on the stairway was still in the same positions as the day before. Then he noticed the one on the landing had field glasses trained on the Bertram.

"Don't look in their direction," he called out. "Troll by and head South for a few hundred meters. Marty should be able to see up around the pool since he'll be facing that way without alerting anybody they're under observation." A fish hit as they turned.

Mickey started working it and Marty scrambled down from the Bertram's fly-bridge to help.

"I hope, you boys are enjoying yourselves while I sweat in this hot ass cabin," JD muttered to himself.

Marty gaffed the fish and brought it aboard and then held it up for JD to see. "This is the Italian equivalent of a trigger fish it's damn fine eating," he said. "I'll get the cook to fix it when we get back to the bar."

Marty throttled the Bertram back and idled into the marina and Mickey noticed two Arab hard-cases as they approached the slip. JD stayed out of sight below while Mickey and Marty tied up. He muttered curses in the sweltering cabin while Mickey stayed aft hosing the boat down to avoid alerting the Arabs that he wasn't a local. Marty jabbered with them in Italian until they left and got in a large black BMW with dark tinted windows. Mickey kept an eye on them as they drove two blocks up the street, made a u turn, then parked facing the marina. He continued watching until he was sure they weren't going anywhere, then leaned in the companionway hatch.

"JD, I hate to say it," he muttered. "You need to stay down there until those rag-heads leave or I could ease up there and eliminate 'em."

Mickey had had a permanent hard on for almost all Arabs since Jimmy Carter had fucked up most of the middle east kissing the Ayatollah's ass in the late seventies by terrorists sponsored in large by the Iranian regime causing an untold number deaths and unrest throughout the entire middle East.

"That's a peachy idea," JD snapped. "After you get through with those two drop by the villa and leave a message to let 'em know we're plotting to kill them all."

"Guess that's a negative on wastin' 'em," Mickey muttered.

"Sometimes you can be downright brilliant," JD said. "You and Marty leave and come back later to see if they're still around. I'll just have to stay put and try to slip by after dark." He laid down on the vee-berth after they secured the companionway hatch then dozed off as the cabin cooled after the sun slipped below the horizon. He awoke to sounds of someone fiddling with the hatch lock, pulled the Ruger and thought. Now, who the fuck is this? If it's those two Rag-heads I'll have to kill 'em and that will definitely alert the target. Whoever it was seemed determined to get in and after a few moments jammed a crowbar in the hatch to pry it open.

Deciding to forego using the pistol, JD stuck it back in his shoulder holster, then launched a classic head-back, forehead in the sternum tackle as the hatch opened, hoping there wasn't but one individual he had to contend with. In the process, he hit the left shoulder he had separated during his football days on the edge of the hatch. To say it smarted was an understatement. The tackle caught the man in the cockpit completely by surprise and he folded back to the deck gasping for air.

JD stood to check if it was one of the opposition and knew instantly it wasn't. He couldn't recall seeing anyone that even vaguely resembled the man lying in the cockpit.

This dude was huge and looked to be six seven or eight and three hundred plus pounds. JD was trying to decide whether or not to shoot him when the giant looking very unhappy cursed and started up. JD waited until he was halfway, then hit him with a solid right cross with all of his two hundred and ten pounds behind it. The blow shook him all the way up to his shoulder. He was admiring the punch just knowing the guy was out cold when the big bastard had the temerity to start up again. JD hit him a second time even harder and a jolt of pain stung his right hand. The gorilla went back down but was still struggling to get up until JD grabbed a fish club and pounded him on the head repeatedly. Now what the hell am I gonna' do if this monster wakes up again? He thought, then pounded his head until it was a bloody pulp. He quickly scanned up the street and was relieved to see the Mercedes was no where in sight. Checking for a pulse and finding none, JD cursed as he struggled to shove the huge mans body through the hatch to get it out of sight. He breathed a sigh of relief as he finally stuffed the monsters legs below, then replaced the broken hatch and started the approximate two kilometer jog up to the bar. Arriving, winded and blood spattered, he was glad he was clad in dark clothing that would hopefully keep anyone in the bar from noticing all of the blood. His shoulder and hand were throbbing as he finally entered the back entrance to the bar and found Marty and Mickey sitting in a booth dining on the fresh fish.

"Damn JD, you look like warmed-over shit. What the hell you been doing?" Mickey asked slightly alarmed as JD slid in the booth.

"You guys are now in charge of disposing of the biggest motherfucker I've ever seen outside an NFL dressing room," JD muttered. "He's in the cabin of the boat dead and you're going to need a back hoe if you decide to bury the bastard."

"What did he look like, other than big?" Marty asked.

"I aint real sure, by the time I had a chance to look close he was pretty bloody," JD replied. "But he was cursing me in Italian."

"I know who you're talking about!" Marty exclaimed. "He's a local shit-head that makes his living breaking and entering and generally terrorizing the local night spots. I thought about killing him when he caused a dust up in here but he hasn't been back. I guess someone gave him the word about who was running this place. How the fuck did you handle him without a gun?"

"It sure as hell wasn't easy," JD mumbled. "When you get through with him, see if you can find a medic to come work on my shoulder and hand."

"No problem," Marty said. "You want we should dispose 'a the body or get the Doc, first?"

"The body," JD grunted. After they were gone he took a few bites of the fish then struggled up to Marty's apartment and flopped on the sofa fervently hoping they arrived with the medic soon.

Pain jolted JDs entire upper body when Mickey and Marty showed with a doctor in a little under two hours. He shot JD's shoulder with Novacaine then yanked it back in socket. He waited a few moments for JD to recover from the jolt of pain, then examined his injured right hand.

"I'll need an x-ray to be sure," he said. "You might have cracked a knuckle, if it is, your hand should really be in a cast."

"No cast, Doc," JD grunted knowing he couldn't fire the rifle with a cast on his right hand. I'll pack it in ice for the time being and let you take another look in a couple 'a days." He took a hot shower and was grateful when Marty told him they had stolen anchors and chain off nearby boats and dropped the huge corpse about five miles out at sea.

"You destroyed the guy's head," Marty said. "It took us a while to wash all the blood out of the cockpit and cabin." He paused. "Take the bed and get some rest. Mickey and I will make do with the couch and the recliner." JD iced his hand for a few minutes, and then collapsed in the bed and was sound asleep within minutes.

Waking early the next morning JDs shoulder was still throbbing. His hand was bruised around the knuckles and palm but wasn't swollen. He popped a couple of pain pills the doctor had left for his shoulder then walked in the kitchen and found Marty and Mickey drinking coffee. They'd spent the night in an olive grove just east of the villa and had timed the guard rotation at eight hours: 0:200, 10:00 and 18:00. And they were sure the news-woman was still there as no one had entered or left. Then after discussing it for a few minutes they decided the assault had to be made the next morning as the woman was bound to run out of topics of discussion soon. JD figured the optimum time for the approach would be 0:400 as the sentries would be half asleep after a short night and two hours to get bored. The initial attack was to start with Mickey escorting Marty and Alphonce close to the front gate, take out the guard or guards there, leave Marty and Alphonce on guard then move to the Western hill to eliminate the sentry stationed there with JD taking out the one on the East and wait for the shot before he blew the charges.

JD had decided to have Mickey handle the gate as neither Marty or Alphonce had been trained in military special ops. He didn't doubt that they could handle the guards, bewasn't sure they could do it silently.

"I know you guys could handle it, but I also know Mickey can do it without making a sound," he said when both were a little miffed that JD didn't trust them. Both nodded their acceptance of his explanation.

After the gate was secured, Marty was to set the claymores and antitank mines, effectively sealing the target inside the killing zone while JD handled the sentry on his planned firing position and set up for the shot. He was worried Marty and Alphonce would set off WW 111 when the relief sentries arrived at the gate and prayed the target would come out before then. He instructed them to change jackets with the dead guards, hoping they could fool the relief long enough to be able to kill them quietly if they happened to show too early. They all hoped the target showed up on the patio before anybody realized the last shift hadn't arrived after being relieved.

JD got within a few meters of the guard on his position and was beginning to get real pissed at him. He, just like the idiots in Colombia was looking at the villa instead of the coastline he was supposed to be watching. JD crouched behind a rock silently cursing the idiot for half an hour waiting for him to turn so he could eliminate him and get the rifle set up for the shot. When the guard finally turned seaward, even Mickey would have been impressed with the way JD got to and silently slit his throat. He appropriated the guard's jacket then dragged the body down the hill toward the beach and buried it in a shallow grave. It wouldn't do for a bunch of sea gulls to show up and start feeding on the corpse at sunup.

He set the rifle up then relaxed, thinking, Wouldn't it be nice if the slimy son-of-a-bitch had a bout on insomnia and took a stroll. The moon is up and it's clear as day around the patio.

Chapter Twenty

★   ★

May 17, 1993, 09:45 hours
five kilometers west of
Sorrento, Italy

A relief sentry exited the villa at 0:945 and started up toward JD's position and the target hadn't showed. JD estimated he had no more then ten minutes before the relief arrived, forcing him to kill the man. He hoped the man had poor eyesight and would approach close enough so he could eliminate him without alerting anyone at the villa. The relief got within seventy-five meters, stopped and yelled something in Arabic. JD stood, held a hand to his ear and waved him forward. That got him moving again and JD desperately tried to think of a way to get rid of him with no one at the villa being aware of his demise. Then as the sentry came within fifty meters he spotted three men taking positions around the patio and then the terrorist accompanied by the newswomen strolled out and sat down at a patio table with the video man stationed off to the side. JD quickly glanced at the oncoming sentry and smiled when he estimated the distance at fifty meters. I don't think there are more than one out of ten rag-heads accurate at this range with an automatic weapon. I hope this aint the tenth. He realized there wasn't but one option, take the shot and hope the relief sentry missed. He dropped on the rifle, took a moment lining up, adjusted for a slight breeze over his right shoulder and the downhill trajectory, bent his left knee for a firm base, sighted on the target's upper torso, inhaled, then slowly exhaled as he exerted light pressure on the trigger.

The international terrorist, calling himself Saddam Bashra settled in his chair and looked across the patio table at the CNN newswoman thinking, Allah give me the strength to continue the charade with this stupid women. I wonder where they find such idiots to turn into media stars in America. She is like putty in my hands, ready to believe any tale I dream up to excuse past killings in the name of the cause. If she were to add a few kilos to her body it might be worth raping her but I would be destroying an ally and an enemy of the Capitalist in America. Allah be praised we could not survive without the American news media aiding us and helping to keep our stupid people stirred up. He was contemplating the rape of the woman anyhow just to let her know what it was like to be with a real man when he felt a sledge hammer blow to his upper abdomen, knocking him out of his chair.

"Allah save me," he screamed. "I have been shot!!" He looked desperately across at the woman and saw a look of abject fear on her face, then tried to crawl toward the villa as his heart seemed to explode and he vomited gouts of blood. he realized he was dying as his body refused to move other than to roll over on his back mewling, "Why now when there are so many Jews and Christians left to slay"

JD saw the target roll out of his chair and knew the shot was a good hit, but couldn't be sure how bad as the relief sentry finally figured out there was something terribly wrong And unloaded a full clip at him. It had always amazed JD how every Arab he had ever come in contact with never really bothered to aim an automatic weapon. They just pointed it in the general direction of the enemy and let fly with all it had. Either they figured on scaring the target to death or they couldn't possibly miss with thirty or forty rounds. This particular idiot not only missed, he didn't even come close enough to scare JD. And then, when he realized JD was swinging the rifle to bear on him he dropped the weapon and started running back toward the villa. JD didn't waste any time on the fleeing guard but swung the scope back to the terrorist lying on the patio deck to see if he needed further attention. It looked like a Chinese fire drill around the pool. Everyone but the target, newswoman and video cameraman were wasting enough ammo to last a platoon a week in Vietnam, all firing in the wrong direction. He realized Mickey had opened up to draw fire and had a fleeting thought. *Sometimes I need to tell Mickey what an asset he is.* Then had another thought, *Uh uh, he's hard enough to get along with without increasing his hat size.*

At that moment he set the charges off and after the ensuing chaos he could see the woman was the smartest one in the group. When her blouse got sprayed with blood from the man she was interviewing, and then the three explosions, one near enough to jolt the heavy flagstone, she screamed, took a running dive into the pool and proceeded to make like Flipper. The cameraman dropped to the patio deck and curled into a fetal position. JD noticed one of the guards trying to drag the terrorist to shelter so quickly switched to him, fired and the man dropped. He adjusted back to the target, saw slight movement and put two more rounds in his torso before seeking out the last two guards still visible outside of the villa. They obviously thought the missives of death were emanating from Mickey and were blazing away at his position from cover behind the far wall.

Knowing him, JD thought, *he's probably sitting behind a rock having a smoke waiting on me to finish up before coming down to help mop up.* He put a round into one before the second man realized there was someone on his backside dealing death and decided to make a run for the far wall. JD shot him in the chest before he made it around the end of the pool. There was still fire coming from the villa directed at Mickey and JD decided to make a run for the patio wall before somebody inside figured out he was doing all the killing. He swung the scope back to the guard fleeing down hill, saw he couldn't make up his mind which way to run, paused a moment to eliminate him then rose and started down to the villa at a dead run.

He was within thirty meters of the perimeter when another guard burst out of the living quarters through a sliding glass door and emptied a full clip in his direction. This one was just as stupid as the one before. All he had to do was wait at one of the windows on that side of the building and he could have picked JD off with one round. JD thanked the Lord for the mentality of Arabs with automatic weapons. The dolt missed, but did come close enough to scare hell out of JD. He dug a trench with his chin in the arid sand, brought the rifle to bear and could see the dumb-ass desperately trying to jam another clip in his weapon. He sighed in relief as he was still a sitting duck if the guard had sense enough to drop behind the perimeter wall for cover. The man's nervous hurry to reload caused him to drop the clip and JD could have approached close enough to kill him with the Ruger and that would have had to be real close since the pistol's accuracy was compromised by the notched dum dum loads he was using. He held his position and put a round in the man's forehead with the rifle, rose and scrambled the last thirty meters to cover behind the wall in record time, almost knocking himself out as he misjudged the last few meters and slid into the wall headfirst. He waited for his heart to drop below a panicky three hundred beats a minute and after what seemed like a half-hour but was probably more like ten seconds, took a quick peek over the wall and could see the terrorist hadn't moved. Ms. Newswoman was still making like Flipper. She'd come up every thirty seconds or so, scream like the hounds of hell were after her and dive back to the bottom. JD figured she was doing the most sensible thing she could. He waited a moment to see if any more guards were going to burst out of the villa thinking, If I was one ˜a those rag-heads I'd shoot her to shut her the fuck up. The cameraman was trying his best to dig a hole in the flagstone deck with his chin until JD pulled the Ruger, vaulted over the wall and pumped two dum-dums in the terrorist's head. He's dead, but after that, his mama won't be able to recognize him. The cameraman yelped and froze. The newswoman happened to be up for air at that moment, saw JD fire the two rounds and it sounded like 'Jaws' had taken a big bite out of her ass the way she screeched before heading back to the bottom. To allay his fear of another guard storming out of the villa JD pulled the pin and tossed a grenade through the conveniently opened glass door. That stopped the fire directed at Mickey. He scampered across the patio to the other wall and vaulted over it to cover Mickey's approach. He banged his shoulder again as he landed and groaned in pain and saw Mickey running hell-bent for leather down the hill. He scanned JD as he slid into the wall feet first.

"You hit?"

"No, why?"

"Your head is bleeding like a stuck hog. What did ya` do, butt the damn wall?"

"Pick a window we can negotiate without hitting my shoulder," JD said to avoid having to admit he had been dumb enough to slide into the wall head first. "Pop a grenade in and lets get through cleaning these rag-heads out and get the fuck outta' here."

Mickey peered at JD's head again. "You dumb shit, you ought to know better than to attack a stone wall head first without a helmet." He aint gonna` let it slide without gittin` in a few licks, JD thought.

"Screw you, what the hell were you doing charging down the fucking hill before I could get into position to cover your crazy ass

"Don't call me crazy to cover up the fact you did something stupid" Mickey grumped. "Besides, I was a tad worried about my partner gittin` his dumb ass killed."

"You goin` through the change 'a life or something?" JD snapped. "Since when do you give a shit what I say? Now...how 'bout poppin` a grenade in the fuckin` window!"

Mickey tossed a grenade, waited for the explosion, then dove through yelling,

"Try not to land on your head, JD" He aint gonna` let it rest until he does something just as stupid, JD thought.

He didn't land on his head but on the injured shoulder again, felt a stab of blazing pain, groaned and almost passed out. Mickey glanced at him, a touch of concern flashing across his face.

"You hurt?" he asked quietly.

"No, I'm severely hurt. Git your ass in gear before we start being attackees instead attackors," JD grunted.

They still had grenades so after checking all rooms in that wing and discovering two more bodies in a bedroom, alive or dead wasn't a question as Mickey pumped a nine-millimeter in both of their heads. Then they darted in the great room separating the East and West wings and found it deserted. Mickey tossed a grenade in the kitchen facing the drive down to the entry gate, then sprayed the dining room with a burst from his H&K. He waited, while JD popped grenades in the two bedrooms on west side and then pulled the Ruger. He checked the bedrooms and baths for hostiles and finding none, yelled at Mickey to check the front then ran back to the patio to see if any of the sentries on the beach or landing had survived and might be trying to scale the damaged stairway in an effort to protect the target. The one on the landing was blown to hell while the two on the beach had survived. He got a brief glimpse of them running west before they disappeared around a rock promontory

JD knelt by the video cameraman's side as he strolled back from the wall.

"You got any tape in the camera?" The cameraman blanched and nodded in the affirmative.

"Give it to me," JD snapped, then was distracted as the newswoman who was still making like a porpoise, glimpsed him on one of her trips to the surface and screamed loud enough to wake the dead.

"You might consider getting her outta` the pool before she drowns," JD said chuckling.

"Duh…do I have to?" the cameraman stuttered.

"I reckon the world could get along without her, but the Clinton news network would go ape shit if one `a their finest socialists happened to expire," JD said sarcastically.

The cameraman yanked the tape out and handed it to JD.

"I could care less if the network is upset. I'm independent, if she drowns it'll at least stop that god-awful racket," he said. "Uh…you mind if I keep a blank to get some footage of all this? It would be priceless on the open market." Not wanting to interfere with a true capitalist and in the process giving CNN a fucking, JD nodded.

"That's fine, but you even think about loading it before we're out of the area, you'll be dead and harder to find than Jimmy Hoffa." The cameraman showed him a tape still wrapped in cellophane.

"I won't unwrap it, if you're within a mile of here," he said. Mickey came out of the villa and strode over to JD.

"The front is clear. The guard evidently hauled ass down to the entry gate and the guys down there took care of him," he said, then trotted to the top of the stairs leading down to the beach. "The one on the landing, is blown to hell and the other two are gone."

They're running West," JD said.

"Why didn't you kill `em?" Mickey snapped. They'll probably get in touch with any connections they have to start looking for us."

"I just got a glimpse of them as they ran around those rocks and disappeared."

"Reckon we should go after `em?

"You want to, go right ahead. I feel like I been rode extremely hard and put up wet. I aint getting in a foot race with anybody," JD groused. Mickey nodded.

"You're right, it would take a platoon of naked zombie queers to make me break into a trot." He noticed the cameraman sitting up and moseyed back to his side.

"You try to get a shot of us," he growled. "I'll come back to slice your head off and jam it up your ass."

"Leave the guy alone," JD said. "I already had that conversation with him."

As they walked back through the villa to leave, JD glanced at Mickey.

"You're getting right attached to that head-up-the-ass threat, aint you?"

"I know you've had a nasty encounter with that wall," Mickey replied smiling. "But even a thick-headed asshole like you ought to be able to figure out it wasn't no idle threat. I was serious as a heart attack."
Shit! He aint gonna⌐ let it go JD thought.

★ Chapter Twenty One ★

May 18, 10:30 hours
five kilometers west of
Sorrento, Italy

"To bad Peter Allnuts wasn't doing the interview," Mickey muttered as they exited the villa, and started down the drive to link up with Marty and Alphonce. "I would 'a enjoyed puttin' a couple 'a nine-millimeters up his pompous ass." Mickey had placed Peter Allnuts second on his shit-list, right behind Hanoi Jane after he had spent the entire Gulf war along with CNN as Saddam's chief propagandist. Then he demoted him to third when the current draft-dodging Commander-in-Chief had decided to do everything in his power to completely fuck up the military. He reasoned Peter Arnett was more despicable but he wasn't capable of doing any real damage other than using his sewer mouth to pump up any identifiable enemy of the United States, while the craven liar currently residing in the White House had done real damage to both the military and general moral climate of the entire country.

Marty peered up at them, then he and Alphonce stepped behind the gate columns and brought their rifles to bear. JD and Mickey dropped to the ground and Mickey yelled, "it's us!" Marty stepped from behind the gate column and waved them forward.

"Damn, I'm sorry," he said as they approached. "We couldn't tell who it was, if you and Mickey take a look at each other you'll see why."

JD looked at Mickey closely for the first time and realized what Marty meant. He appeared to be a black devil from hell that had just finished roasting a few hundred Christians and assorted other sects. JD knew his blood-covered face and all the dirt and grime they had both collected, obscured any resemblance to the two men Marty and Alphonce remembered before the mission's onset. They were both bleeding from small cuts received while diving in the villa, JD's head was still oozing blood and he noticed Mickey was missing his left shoe.

Mickey returned JD's look.

"I would 'a took a shot at you myself," he grunted. "You look like you been in a fight with Cassius Clay." Mickey admired the ex-champion, but with his abiding dislike of all Arabs, he steadfastly refused to recognize his adopted name. He turned back to Marty and nodded at JD. "You're looking at the only man I know who's dumb enough to attack a wall head first without a helmet."

"You aint going to let it rest until you fuck up yourself, are you?" JD rasped, and glanced down at Mickey's left foot. "At least, I don't need to worry about some prince riding up on a white horse to see who a Nike fits." Mickey looked down and realized the shoe was gone.

"Shit! you think I ought to go back and get it?"

"Forget it," JD grumbled. "We need to have that doctor patch us up and work on this fucking shoulder again." Marty stood listening to their interchange. These guys never stop digging at each other, but I wouldn't want to be the one to threaten either of them. There aint any doubt the other would kill whoever it was in a New York minute.

"Why don't Alphonse and I strip to our pants then walk down the beach like a couple 'a tourists and get the car to pick you up." he said. Both of you look like a five kilometer hike might finish you off. You can hide in the olive grove until we get back. It's far enough from the scene that the cops shouldn't get around to searching it for a while."

JD and Mickey entered the grove down the road from the villa and then threaded deep enough in the grove to be sure they were out of sight and sat down with their backs resting against an olive tree. JD searched his pockets for a pack of cigarettes in vain, then tapped Mickey's arm.

"You got a smoke that aint a damn ultra-light?" Having become more health conscious with their advancing years. They had been struggling to quit. It wasn't an entirely failed effort. They had cut down considerably and were trying to stick to ultra-lights instead of the more robust brands. It was tough, considering the stress they were forced to endure during operations. The only time a smoke was better than after a successful mission was after sex. They had smoked before, during and after everything except in the Nam, but had found it tended to rile a girl if one sat up in the middle of love making, and said, "Hold on a minute honey, I got to have a cigarette."

"I have some," Mickey said and handed JD a pack of Pall Malls. "You might as well fire up a tampax for all the good an ultra-light does," he muttered. They lit up, sighed in contentment and laid back to contemplate the universe.

"Man, it's amazing how relaxed you get having a good smoke after you've been scared shitless for a while," JD mused.

"You're right," Mickey replied. "While I was sitting up on that outpost waiting for you to snuff that slime ball, I was trying to figure out why we got into this fucked-up way of makin' a living."

"That's a little scary," JD muttered. "I been thinking about it myself. I hope we aren't gettin' weird enough to start reading each others mind. I don't really want to be aware of what's going through that pea brain 'a yours."

"Screw you! How 'bout for once, you answer a question without a wise-ass remark," Mickey snapped.

The reason I'm not answering is because I don't know," JD said. "Thinking about it I figured it was because we were just too lazy to do anything legit. But looking back on all the blood, guts and sweat we've gone through…we can't be classified as lazy. How 'bout we just forget it until we're too old to do the job. Then, we'll retire with all the vast wealth we've accumulated and lie to everybody about how we got it. We're too damn old to try and figure out anything else to do anyhow."

JD used the comm to call Smith and he came on precisely ten minutes later.

"Do you have a problem?" he asked in an anxious tone.

"No, sir," JD replied. "You'll be happy to hear I put three rounds in the target's chest, then two dum-dums in his head. He is definitely either in paradise or hell. I'd go with hell." Smith hesitated a moment.

"How about the media personnel?" he asked quietly.

"The last time I looked the newswoman was making like Flipper in the pool and the cameraman was getting ready to record all a' the blood and gore."

"He didn't get a shot of either of you?" Smith asked alarmed.

"No sir, I got the tape out of the camera he was using in case he'd taped any of the action," JD replied. "But, I figured it would be a good idea to let him get some shots of the aftermath. And then maybe some rag-head will have second thoughts when he sees what can happen if he decides to take up terrorism as a career choice."

Smith was so happy, JD could visualize him gleefully rubbing his hands together.

"Since the news hasn't gotten out," Smith said. "And it doesn't seem that your and Mickey's identities have been compromised. I feel it would be wise for you to clean up, then get to the closest major airport and get the hell out of Italy. When this action hit's the news and it will be soon…the shit is going to hit the proverbial fan. As soon as you pick a point of departure, I'll have an agent meet you with any documents you need."

"Uh…there is one other thing," JD said.

"Is this about money?" Smith groused.

"No." JD replied quickly. "I assume you will deposit our money shortly but we need to do something for Marty, it's not going to take but a few days for somebody to put us together with him. He'll be deader than Jimmy Hoffa if we can't figure a way to get him out of the area. He's been a tremendous help and it aint right for us to leave him with his dick hanging out."

In the limited time JD and Mickey had been associated with Smith they'd found, other than prompt payment and providing requested gear and equipment needed that it didn't take a lot of time for him to make a decision. He pondered the problem for no more than thirty seconds.

"Okay, load him up and bring him with you. I'll have any necessary documents delivered to the airport by the agent and your fee's will be deposited tomorrow morning."

Alphonce drove up as JD finished the transmission and they got in for an uneventful ride to Marty's apartment and found him and a doctor waiting. Both of them plopped on the sofa exhausted. Mickey glanced at JD with a worried expression.

"You look like warmed-over shit go on and get treated first." JD sat up. The doctor popped him with a shot of morphine and waited a few minutes for it to take effect before he yanked his shoulder back in and prepared to sew up his head.

"Uh uh Doc, let me get a hot shower first," he said, then luxuriating in the streaming shower he thought, I know why people get addicted to that drug. The pain is still there but you just don't gave a shit. Clean with fresh skivvies on, a couple of butterfly bandages on his forehead explaining that head injuries usually bled so you thought the cut was worse than it really was then asked if he'd been hit? Before Mickey could chime in JD quickly replied, "No, I head-butted a wall," then rose to walk in the bedroomand fell in the bed and was sound asleep within moments.

Chapter Twenty Two

May, 21, 1993 0:600 hours
Marty's Bistro
Sorrento, Italy

Marty shook JD awake with bad news that there had been a couple of Arabs in the bar until closing time. They'd been asking anybody who would talk to them if they recalled seeing two Americans the past few days.

"Nobody around here particularly cares for Arabs in general," he said. "But, if they come back this afternoon and run into one of the matinee drunks, all 'a those guys have seen you. If they wave a little cash in front of them there aint a way hell one of 'em won't rat you out."

"Shit!" JD exclaimed. "Is Alphonce still around?"

"He's down in the bar sleeping in a booth," Marty replied. "I swear that guy is one cool dude. I was edgy as hell while those Arabs were hanging around. He just sat at the bar sippin' on a beer until they left. I asked him what he thought after I finished locking up and he said fuck em, then laid down and was asleep inside a few minutes." He paused and continued in an uneasy tone, "Can you talk to somebody about getting my ass out of here JD. It aint gonna' take long for even these dumb Arabs to put me, the bar and my boat together with you and Mickey, and I'll be dead."

"I was going to let you know the problem was handled when I woke up," JD said. "Pack a couple 'a changes of clothes and the weapons, then get back down to the bar and check to see if anyone has it under surveillance. You're coming with us and it looks like we might have a few problems gittin' out of the country."

Marty breathed a sigh of relief.

"Thanks, you tell whoever took care of it, they won't regret it."

"The outfit we're working for will probably contact you with a job offer in the near future," JD said. "And I guess you've already figured out what we do aint exactly what an insurance underwriter would classify as a safe occupation."

"Sounds fine to me," Marty said. "Hell working for the mob wasn't what could be called an insurable environment."

"Okay, go back down to the bar," JD said. "We'll pick you up at the side entrance in fifteen minutes." He waited until Marty grabbed a few things, then found Mickey sleeping on the couch and woke him up. While they were getting the weapons and gear together, Mickey turned the television on, flipped channels until he got CNN and there the skinny blonde newswoman, looking like a drowned rat was on the air describing the mornings horrible, unprovoked display of murder and mayhem. She paused to catch her breath and then said there would be video available as soon as the network came to terms with the independent cameraman on the scene. Mickey turned to JD grinning.

"That cameraman is a true capitalist aint he," he said chuckling. "He has any sense, he'll threaten to turn the tape over to Fox news and CNN will shovel money at him," They were enjoying the idea that they had helped to create additional heavy expenses for in their opinion, the most biased news network in America when the news woman came back on.

"We have obtained the video and will have it on the air within moments," she said, then continued, "I find it deeply disturbing to report that the two murderous thugs who perpetrated this horrendous massacre were almost certainly American military, but they had no insignia denoting they were so I can't be positive. There is one thing I am quite sure about. I overheard them talking to the cameraman and their accents place them as being from the deep south."

"Can you believe that!" Mickey exclaimed. "The silly twit makes it sound like we just murdered the second coming instead 'a one of the worst terrorists the world has ever known. I wonder if she realizes there are quite a few family members of the victims of that slime ball she was so happy to be having a discourse with who are enjoying every gory detail of his violent death."

"Don't tell me you're surprised CNN is taking the opportunity to slant a news story anti U.S. military." JD groused. "Shit, they're probably thrilled because they get to take a shot at the military and the South at the same time."

"Naw," Mickey said. "What really boils my balls about Hanoi Jane and comrade Ted is they think it's fine to tax every working stiff in the country to death to finance their socialist agenda, but don't want to give up all their mansions, ranches and billions to the cause. If they weren't such hypocrites, they'd give it all up and be satisfied with one big house in the suburbs, two cars a couple 'a television sets and no airplanes or yachts and turn the rest over to the government to be redistributed. Forget about it snowing in hell, there will be a full blown blizzard before they or any of their liberal friends in Hollywood give up their extra millions to the cause. " They were happy they had left a blank tape when the video came on. The woman prattled on describing the sequence of events as the tape panned all of the dead bodies inside and outside of the villa.

"I hope controls making copies of this," Mickey said. "It's a work of art as far as I'm concerned and I'd sure like a copy for my retirement years."

"Hell, there are probably millions of Americans tuning in to CNN for the first time in years. And half of Europe and all of Israel are using enough tape to keep Sony going for who knows how long. Getting a few copies isn't going to be a problem," JD said. Then, to hopefully get Mickey's mind off the head butt he added, "If you'd kept your yap shut she wouldn't have known we were a couple of Southern rednecks."

"I guess you aint realized it," Mickey groused. "You're just as big a redneck as I am and were running your mouth more than I was." He paused a moment and mused, "It would 'a sure been nice it had been Peter Allnuts instead of the woman. I would have enjoyed popping a cap in his ass, but he's probably still down in Baghdad kissing ass." If, there was anyone Mickey detested as much as Hanoi Jane and the current draft dodging commander in chief, it was Peter Arnett

They loaded the weapons and gear in the Mercedes, then pulled around to the side entrance to pick up Marty and Alphonce. While they were waiting for them to load their gear in the trunk. Mickey turned to JD.

What happens if we run into cops?" We got enough firepower to blow half 'a Sorrento away and I doubt any cop will be real happy about that. They've been flying back and forth to the villa all day and will sure be looking for any strangers leavin' town, especially toting a carload of weapons. This days event has got to be the most excitement they've had around here since the war. There are damn sure more dead bodies littering the landscape than anytime since then." Marty overheard him as he opened the door to get in the back seat.

"Don't worry," he said. "I know most of the local law and if worse comes to worse we might have to bribe a few of 'em."

"I guess it works the same over here as it does in the States" JD said. "Mob guys always know which cops can be bought."

As they finished loading their gear. Alphonce walked to the driver's side door, tapped on the glass and waited until JD ran the window down. "Why donna you letta me drove," he said. "I the best wheela man in Italia and you mighta be pretty busy witha Arabs somma time." JD stepped out of the car.

"You and I both know it could get real hairy Alphonce," he said quietly. "Mickey and I really appreciate what you've done for us. I'll damn sure see that you're rewarded but we don't want you to risk your life getting us out of the country." Alphonce grinned, hugged JD, then grasped his shoulders and held him at arms length.

"I didna have a this mucha fun sinz Lucky Luciano he died," he said. JD laughed acquieced and patted him on the back.

"I'm real happy to have an experienced wheel man driving."

He got in the back seat with Mickey to keep an eye on their rear and couldn't detect anyone following as they drove through Sorrento to head for Castellammare. As they approached the outskirts of Sorrento, they ran into a roadblock comprised of four Italian polizia and two Fiats.

"Stop about ten meters before you get to it Alphonce," Marty said. "Give me some cash JD. I'll see if I can pay 'em to let us by without having to shoot anybody." He waited until the car came to a full stop, got out and trotted forward, then jawed with the cop who appeared to be in charge for a few minutes, passed a wad of money, then trotted back to the car and got in. "Okay, drive through slowly," he said. "Keep the weapons out of sight until we're well past."

"How much did that cost?" JD asked.

"Two hundred American apiece for the three cops and four hundred for the sergeant," Marty replied. "They knew we were probably the guilty parties but the Italian police don't like Muslim terrorists any more than we do."

"Kind of expensive," JD muttered. "But, we sure as hell don't need the Italian police on our ass in addition to God know how many pissed off Arab terrorists." They spent another two thousand dollars in bribe money to get through Castellammare and Mickey got testy as Marty passed over the last bribe.

The next cop that holds his hand out is gonna' get shot!" he exclaimed.

"The tolls on this road are a mite excessive," JD said. "But, we'll keep paying 'em until I run out of cash. That's what the damn expense money is for and we'll get it all back and a whole lot more if we can make it out of this country alive. You stay cool, and try not to cause any trouble with the cops and we'll stand a lot better chance of makin' it."

Mickey continued to grumble about crooked cops.

"If there weren't crooked cops, we'd probably be dead or in jail," JD snapped.

"Amen to that," Marty said and paused. "I got to ask you something JD."

"What's that?"

"Why didn't the powers that be get you guys out with a submarine?"

"Because we aint really working for the government and our control didn't want a navy crew connecting us with the mission," JD replied.

As they left the outskirts of Castellammare and got into the mountains. Mickey forgot about how much they were paying cops and started cursing, Alphonce. He was handling the big Mercedes around hard mountain curves like a formula one race car until rounding a hairpin he almost rammed into the back of a Jaguar with British plates hogging the center line as it crawled around the curve. He squeezed by on the inside and JD scanned the occupants as they flashed by to see if they were Arabs and saw two couples as the Jag's driver tensed and rubbed the left rear quarter of the Mercedes.

"I bet they wet the leather front and back," Marty said nervously.

"I don't know whether they pissed their pants or not!" Mickey exclaimed , but I am if Alphonce don't slow the fuck down."

"I think I already did," JD said tensely. That calmed Mickey a little, it tended to calm him when he thought something scared JD more than it did him. The slight bump seemed to anger the jaguars driver and he got in a pursuit mode. Mickey glanced back and muttered.

"I wonder what this idiot thinks he'll do if he catches us."

"You don't need to worry about it," JD mumbled. "There aint any way he can unless he's Mario Andretti in disguise." Alphonce was negotiating the hairpin curves like they were on a flat highway in Kansas instead of a mountain road with thousand foot drops to eternity if he fucked up.

JD lost sight of the Jaguar after four or five twists. Then, after screaming around a hard turn, Alphonce locked the brakes and came to a screeching stop a hundred meters from what appeared to be another Italian police road block. They sat for a few seconds.

"They aint cops," Marty yelled. JD took a closer look and realized the cops were all armed with automatic weapons and the two cars they had blocking the road were large BMW's.

"Aint no cops in Italy driving Beamers," Marty yelped. JD had counted six men when another stepped from behind one of the cars with a rocket propelled grenade launcher and brought it to his shoulder preparing to fire. Alphonce saw the threat, jammed the Mercedes into reverse and burned rubber trying to back around the last curve.

They nearly made it until the idiot driving the Jaguar slammed into the left rear, lost control and almost flew over the edge of the precipice, coming to a stop with the car's front end hanging over the edge. The Jag's sudden appearance startled the Arab with the RPG enough to throw his aim off and he missed high by ten yards. They scrambled to get out and take cover behind the Mercedes and then started taking fire from someone on the cliff face between them and the roadblock. Marty and Alphonce started firing at that threat to provide cover and give JD enough time to take the RPG out.

"Mickey get up there and do something massive to that sumbitch" JD yelled. He propped the tripod on the trunk of the Mercedes and then took his time to aim and put a round in the forehead of the terrorist with the RPG before he could reload and fire again. All of the other Arabs were wasting enough ammunition on the Mercedes and cliff face to supply an entire platoon until JD dropped two more and they decided it was safer on the other side of the Beamers. He took a quick look at Mickey as he climbed up the cliff face, ducking for cover behind rock outcroppings as the terrorist on the cliff unloaded a full clip at him. I hope he don't look down and discover he's forgetting to worry about heights and have a heart attack. It would also be nice if he would shoot the bastard instead ˜a sneaking up to slit his throat. JD thought. Mickey did even better as he blew the rag-head off the cliff with a grenade, and then proceeded to deal death down on the remaining Arabs behind the two Beamers. Three of them fell before the last two dropped their weapons and stepped around the car with their hands over their heads.

" Fuck you" JD whispered, then dropped both of them before they had a chance to get back behind the Beamer. Marty glanced at JD, with a shocked expression flashing across his face.

"You're one mean mother fucker," he said. "Those guys were trying to surrender."

"Just what the fuck do you think we could do with a couple a rag-head prisoners?" JD snapped. "Besides the sons 'a bitches sure didn't ask for any ID before they decided to blow us all to hell." He waited for a moment to see Marty's reaction, and could see he understood ."Now…how 'bout trotting your ass up there to make sure they're all dead. And don't even think about coming back to tell me any of them are wounded. They all need to be stone cold dead for no other reason than to keep their mouths shut." JD covered Marty as he strolled up to the group of terrorists, shot one, checked to be sure he was dead and then gave the all clear. Feeling a little guilty about spoiling the four tourists European tour, JD decided to give them some help and strolled over to the Jaguar.

The woman sitting next to the back door locked up as he reached for it.

"You can stay in there if you want to," he said. "But there's a real good chance this thing is going over the edge any second and it's a hell of a long way to the bottom." The man on the far side back seat opened up and almost fell on wobbly legs. JD didn't blame him for being a little shaky. If he'd been in a car about to fall off a cliff while there was a minor war going on all around him, he'd have been a tad shaky himself.

The woman on his side stepped out and JD instantly recognized her as the beautiful Englishwoman who'd helped them in the restaurant back in Castellammare.

"Well hello Penelope," he said. "I sure didn't expect to see you again.

Penelope froze as she recognized him. I thought these men were dangerous in that restaurant, now my worst fears have been confirmed. She leaned against the car to catch her breath and jumped as JD abruptly said, "Penelope, you need to tell your friends in the front to crawl over in back before they get out. The car is rocking a little and I'm afraid it'll fall over if they open the front doors." She looked at him with a dazed expression, then shook herself and calmly leaned back inside.

"Marlene, you and Ian gingerly climb to the back and get out of the auto."

After they were all safely out. JD, using what he hoped would be a calming tone of voice quietly said, "We don't intend to harm any of you. Now...I'd appreciate it if you all will please move over to the cliff face behind the Mercedes, sit down and be quiet until we get sorted out." He escorted the four behind the Mercedes and made sure they were sitting quietly, then checked the car for damage and could see the radiator along with two tires and almost every window and door on the side facing the attack were shot to hell.

Marty arrived back from the road block carrying the RPG and projectiles and handed them to JD.

"I figured these might come in handy," he said. "And there aint anybody alive over there."

Mickey climbed down the cliff, jumped the last few feet and strolled over to JD, then froze as he heard an approaching helicopter.

"I kind 'a doubt that is friendly," he stated flatly. JD gave him the RPG and projectiles.

"Everybody needs to take cover behind the Mercedes," he shouted then turned his attention back to the Brits. "You people need to get flat as road kill." He barked, "It looks like more trouble is heading our way."

Chapter Twenty Three

May 17, 1993, 0:830 hours
Fifty kilometers north of
Castellammare, Italy

A Black Bell AH-1G Cobra gun-ship with no markings banked around the last bend they had traversed, leveled off and riddled the Mercedes with 7.62 mini-gun fire before continuing on to hover over the two Beamers. JD and Mickey lay prone behind the Mercedes trying to get thinner until the attack ceased. JD eased his head up and looked around to see if anyone had been hit and saw, other than expressions of stark terror by the four civilians, everyone seemed to be in good shape. These bastards are going to come back and blow us all to hell if we don't do something, he thought, then looked at Mickey to be sure he had the RPG, tapped him on the shoulder to get his attention and nodded at the Jaguar.

"Wait, until they hover on the next pass," he barked. "I'll take cover behind the Jag and draw their fire long enough for you to launch."

"Are you fucking nuts!?" Mickey exclaimed. "If they put a few rounds in that car, it'll fall over the cliff and you'll be standin' there with your dick in your hand."

"You won't have time to launch if I don't create a diversion, and it's the only thing I can think to do," JD muttered, grabbed an AK and trotted over to the Jaguar.

"You get yourself killed, I'm gonna` kick your ass" Mickey yelled. JD kept an eye on the gun-ship as it veered away from the Beamers and circled back for another run. He waited until it hovered and lined up on the Mercedes, then rose and cursed when the only available target was the gun-ship's armored under-body. He knew it was probably futile but still unloaded a full clip hoping the incoming would distract the pilot enough to give Mickey enough time to launch and then dove back behind the Jag. The pinging of the rounds ricocheting off of its underbody did seem to get the pilot's attention as he jigged to the side and brought the mini-gun back to bear on the Jaguar. Shit! I'm dead if Mickey don't hurry, JD thought desperately. The car literally disintegrated in front of him and slowly slid over the cliff's edge. When the next fusillade failed to arrive, JD cautiously raised his head and saw the pilot and copilot's expression of shear terror as they glimpsed a rocket a millisecond before it struck home, killing them instantly. Within a half second, the bird was consumed by a secondary explosion and the two side-gunners tumbled out and took the long fall to hell

"You are now officially in charge `a the RPG," JD muttered as Mickey walked over and they looked down at a pile of burning debris below. He shot a quick look at Mickey as the four Brits eased up and peered over the precipice to see what had become of their ride. The one Penelope had addressed as Ian, having decided JD was the leader turned to him angrily.

"We are quite perturbed you men almost ran us off the cliff," he said tersely. "And have involved us in some type of gang-land war."

"We wouldn't have hit you if you hadn't been hogging the centerline," JD snapped. "And what the hell were you doing chasing us with two women in the car?"

"That's the way anybody with a lick `a sense ought to` drive in these mountains," Mickey interjected.

Sensing strife in the ranks, Ian turned and introduced himself to Mickey along with the other man and woman. His name was Ian Bitner, the other woman was his wife Marlene and JD was pleased to hear the other man's name was Nigel West while Penelope's last name was Stuart. At least she aint married, he thought. He opted to ignore the irritating Englishman as Marty ambled across the road and peered over the cliff's edge.

"I'm glad I brought that grenade launcher back," he muttered.

"We'd have been in deep dodo without it," JD said. "How about checking to see if those Beamers are still drive-able."

They waited until Marty returned and told JD one car was still in good condition but the other ones radiator was ruined and a ricochet had evidently punctured its oil pan.

Ian, hearing there was only one available car turned to JD.

"Since you men initiated the incident causing us to be stranded I feel that it's only proper that we take the car and continue our journey. I will contact the authorities at the first opportunity. I'm quite sure they will arrive forthwith to transport you and your men."

Mickey, not being used to dealing with arrogant strangers realized he'd given Ian the wrong impression, glared at him and growled.

"No shit, Dick Tracy. I imagine the cops would bust their ass to come out here and round us up. You got as much chance 'a sprouting wings to fly out of here, as you have of gittin` that car."

JD watched as Ian seemed to deflate, but still couldn't believe the idiot had the gall to try and talk a group of men he'd just witnessed take down two carloads of heavily armed, as far as he knew, police and a gunship out of the only mode of transportation available.

Penelope seeing Ian wasn't going to be able to talk JD out of the car, decided to try another tack and edged to his side.

"Mister JD, the next town is at least thirty kilometers away and those men looked like Arabs," she said nervously. "I am afraid there might be others around, and if they find and interrogate us, I fear it would be quite unpleasant."

"You can bet your bippy on that," JD muttered. "The four of you'll have to pile in with us to get away from here post haste. We'll try to find a way to get you out of the country as soon as possible."

Ian regaining a bit of bravado accosted JD again.

"What will the seating arrangements be?" he snapped. JD, still feeling the surge of fear-induced adrenalin, paused to control a strong impulse to knock the pompous fool on his ass as Mickey prodded Ian with the H&K.

"Hey, Asshole! You'll sit wherever he tells you," he snapped. "We aint gonna` leave the women, but don't really give a big rats' ass about you and your buddy so shut the hell up." JD watched to be sure, Mickey didn't do anything drastic as he herded the Brits to the undamaged Beamer. He helped Marty transfer the rest of the weapons inside, then he punched the trunk lid open with the remote and motioned for Nigel and Ian to get in.

"Sorry, gentlemen," he said. "There's not but five seats in the car so I'm afraid you'll have to ride back here."

"That is ridiculous!" Ian sputtered, puffing his chest out and taking an aggressive stance. "You will have to shoot me before I get in that boot."

"Well...you don't have to get in," JD said mildly. "You do have another option."

"Just what might that be?" Ian asked in a bellicose tone of voice.

"It's either get in the trunk, or join your car down there," JD said nodding toward the edge of the precipice. "We aren't about to leave you here to start screaming at the first cop that comes by asking questions. Now get in the fucking trunk, or I'm going to blow your ass away and throw your carcass over the side. We don't have time to fuck around." Nigel climbed in the trunk and called to Ian.

"Ian please, quit acting an ass, there isn't enough room in the car for all of us."

Penelope stood while JD shut the lid then waited while Marlene crawled in the right side back seat and Mickey got in behind her. Then she got in the left thinking, *These men just killed ten or twelve human beings. If they are the bloody killers I know them to be our chances of surviving this horrid situation are remote.* JD squeezed in beside her, could see she was frightened and decided to try and ease her fears.

"Penelope, the people who attacked us were part of a terrorist organization," he said quietly. "We were lucky to find them exposed and had the good fortune to be in position to eliminate their leader. You and your friends just happened to be in the wrong place at a very bad time. I'm sorry all of you were caught in the crossfire, but since you were, the best chance you have of getting back to England in one piece is to stay with us until we can find a safe way to get you out of Italy." He paused and thought a moment.

"Was the Jaguar registered in Ian's name?"

"Yes," she replied.

"That being the case, the opposition will undoubtedly find his identity and start looking for him to find out who the hell we are."

"Are you the ones that killed that horrible terrorist?" she asked.

"Lets just say, we were there," he replied. It's nice to hear someone who appreciates what a miserable son-of-a-bitch that shit-head was and can read between the lines of tripe emanating from CNN.

"Would you have really have cast Ian into the abyss?" she asked quietly.

"Probably," he replied. "I would've hated to, but my first responsibility is to the safety of the team and the mission's security." She thought about his reply for a moment.

"I can see the sense of that and Ian was acting quite badly. I really shouldn't feel this way but it wouldn't have deeply disturbed me to watch the pompous fool go sailing over the edge. Seeing the way he has abused Marlene on this trip, I feel she wouldn't have been terribly upset either and I think it's wonderful that someone has finally sent that evil man to his just desserts," she said softly, then laid back in the plush leather seat and closed her eyes. My first impression that these men were lethally dangerous was correct, but to coin a phrase , they are the good guys. Fate has brought us together for a reason and I will get to know this man.

Alphonce drove north ten kilometers, then glanced back at JD. "I hava oncle who hava olive orchid fieteen kilo offa highway," he said. "He as beega house we stay untoll heata she blew ovair."

"Damn, I'd forgotten!" Marty exclaimed. "He's right, Alberto's place is perfect, it's well off the main road and the people around there are a lot like Sicilians. They don't trust anybody they don't know so there aint any Arab who'll have a snowballs chance in hell of getting any information out of the neighbors."

"It sounds great, Alphonce," JD said. "But, I don't want to put your family at risk."

"Donna you worry, my oncle Alberto he hatea terrorists and he be veery onhappy, ifa he fin out I didna aska fa halp." JD nodded his agreement but was surprised when Penelope opened her eyes, then glanced up at him and murmured,

That seems like a very good idea." Damn! It must have been a better selling job than I figured, JD thought, then tapped Alphonce on the shoulder.

"If you are sure it will be alright with your uncle it would be good for us to get out of sight for a day or so." Alphonce nodded, drove a few kilometers north, and then turned inland on a gravel road and continued for another few minutes before entering a driveway leading through an olive grove to a large house. The main house was a large two-story stone structure. There was an equipment shed and barn located behind what appeared to be twenty to thirty acres of pasture land leading up to steep tree covered hills.

An older larger version of Alphonce stepped out the front door armed with a double barreled shotgun as they ground to a stop then grinned broadly when he saw his nephew. He leaned the shotgun against the wall and gave Alphonse a bear hug as he stepped away from the car then scanned Marty, JD, Mickey and the women as they disembarked.

"Who are your fine friends?" he asked, speaking perfect English. JD watched, as the big man listened carefully to Alphonse's explanation in Italian, then a big grin appeared and he walked directly to JD and shook his hand vigorously.

"Signor, you and your compatriots are welcome in my home. It is yours for as long as you need," he said. "I had friends who were murdered by terrorists and the man you have killed was the one who planned and carried out the dastardly deed. The only thing that could have made me happier about the death of the bastard was to have been there to slay him myself."

"We sure appreciate your hospitality," JD said. "And we won't impose on you any longer than necessary. There is one question though."

"Yes?"

"Where did you learn to speak flawless American lingo?" Alberto smiled broadly.

"When I was a young boy I spent many months with General Patton's army as a guide on Sicily and learned all of the American accents. You for instance are from the South. There were a lot of Southerners serving with the general."

"You got it," JD replied chuckling. Mickey let Ian and Nigel out of the trunk then unloaded the weapons from the back seat. JD glanced around and saw Nigel and Penelope arguing off to the side and then overheard Nigel, as he raised his voice shrilly.

"I find it deeply disturbing the way you have become cozy with that killer!" he exclaimed.

JD was strongly considering kicking Nigel's ass then smiled, when Penelope hissed at him.

"You just bugger off, Nigel. I can and will decide who I'll be cozy with." He turned to locate Ian and Marlene and saw they were having a heated exchange on the other side of the car. Ian seemed on the verge of striking Marlene until he turned his back on her, and stalked around the car to join Nigel, whispered something to him and the two of them stormed out of earshot. It's gonna be almost impossible to keep those assholes under control without inflicting severe damage, JD thought. He edged over and nudged Alberto.

"Uh, is there a room or cellar in the house we can lock these men in where we won't have to worry about 'em getting out to do something stupid? None of us want to disrespect your home while we are here."

"There is a basement wine cellar," Alberto replied. "It's solid concrete and has windows for ventilation, but they are very small and barred to keep sneak thieves out. The door at the top of the stairs is solid oak and has a substantial lock and bolt."

"That sounds fine," JD said. " Is there a restaurant nearby that we can get some food? I'd like to get everybody fed before we lock 'em down."

"My wife Mirabella, would be most unhappy if she wasn't able to put a feast on for our honored guests," Alberto said. "Please don't mention sending out for food while you are here. You and your friends are welcome to stay until you feel it's safe to travel."

JD and Mickey humped the gear and weapons up to a second story room furnished with one double bed and an adjoining bath. Mickey turned to JD after the gear was secure.

"I aint sleeping with your crusty butt," he groused.

"We'll have to share the bed," JD replied. "But we won't be sleeping together.

Alphonce and Marty will sleep in an extra bedroom downstairs and will split up guarding the front gate. You and I will find an outpost inside the tree line and split up the watch for anybody coming in from the rear."

Alberto's wife, Mirabella showed the women to a room down the hall from Mickey and JD's with another adjoining bath. When they went back downstairs Ian heard about the sleeping arrangements and glared at JD.

"Nigel and I will sleep on the floor in Penelope-and Marlene's room, lest you men have designs on them," he said huffily.

"We'll finalize the sleeping arrangements after dinner," JD said to avoid a confrontation before everyone was fed.

Mirabella put a feast on and after they were seated she treated them like visiting royalty, repeatedly asking whether they had enough and if the meal was to their taste. She didn't speak English very well so JD turned to Alberto.

"Tell her it is delicious and if she will come home with me, we will marry and she can live out her life with a contented fat man." Alberto translated. Mirabella guffawed, rolled her eyes in merriment, then rattled off a reply in Italian and then waited for Alberto to translate.

"She say," Alberto said chuckling. "It wouldn't be a bad idea to trade in this worn out old man for a newer model."

After they finished the sumptuous meal, JD showed Ian and Nigel where they would be bunking and Ian immediately objected.

"If you weren't armed, I would give you a thrashing," he snapped.

To keep his end of the conversation up JD asked, "What the hell, is a thrashing?"

"What you Colonials refer to as an ass-flogging," Ian replied hotly Mickey overheard and interrupted.

"JD, this dude is in the dark ages when it comes to thinkin' up good insults," he grumped, then glanced to make sure the women were out of earshot. "I'd appreciate it if you'd let me take him outside and shut him the fuck up." JD knew better than to let Ian get anywhere near Mickey when he was in a bad mood. We aint paid to kill Englishmen, even a pompous ass like Ian, he thought.

"He aint pissed at you, Mickey," he replied. "But I will be, if you kill the silly son-of-a-bitch," he added and then turned back to Ian.

"In case you missed it, Ian that was a passably good insult." Ian turned red with rage.

"I will be in the front yard if you have the fortitude," he hissed and stormed through the door. JD felt like he was back in his twenties since that was the last time he'd been stupid enough to march his silly ass outside to prove his manhood in a fight. He started for the door until Penelope, sensing the imminent conflict tried to stop him.

"You men are all simply idiotic," she said. "I had hoped you could be more sensible, JD."

"Penelope, you are definitely right about this being dumb," JD replied, then walked through the door and got cold-cocked from the side. Ian was a big man, a couple of inches taller and outweighed JD by a good twenty pounds and he wasn't quite as stupid as JD thought. He'd pulled a trick that JD had used back in his bar fight days by going out first and getting the first lick in as his opponent stepped through the door. The blow knocked JD to his knees. He was counting stars, as Ian grabbed a handful of hair to line his jaw up for another blow and in the process pulled his head wound painfully.

That enraged JD. If this guy gets another lick in I'm going to lose this fight and have to put up with Mickey riding me for rest of my natural life. He reached up and got a vice grip on Ian's balls. Ian grunted in pain and hit him again, but the punch lacked any steam. JD held on to Ian's balls with his left hand, squeezed even harder and grabbed Ian's side to get up. The vise-like grip took Ian's breath away and he squealed until JD regained his feet, took a big breath, lined up, let go of Ian's balls, then smashed a thunderous left cross to avoid re-injuring his right hand to the same point of jaw, as he'd hit the monster back on Marty's boat. The results were much more satisfying, Ian dropped like a cold rock in winter. JD watched a moment to make sure he wasn't going to get up.

"I hope your nuts hurt worse than my head, Dip-shit," he grunted to himself, and then shook his head to clear the cobwebs and walked back inside.

"You won't ever change," Mickey said chuckling as JD entered the room. "You'll stroll right through a door and get sucker punched trying to come up with a snappy reply when a pretty woman says something to you." JD was trying to think of a smart retort then gave up when Penelope stepped over to inspect the bruise on his upper cheek.

"You should put an ice pack on that or you will have quite a black eye in the morning," she said sympathetically.

"Uh huh," JD grunted, then turned to Mickey and Nigel.

"How about hauling Ian down to the basement," he grunted. "He's not motivating very well at the moment. He waited until they went outside to retrieve Ian and then turned back to Penelope.

"I hope Nigel isn't in a fighting mood," he mused. "Mickey doesn't really know how to avoid doing extreme damage when someone attacks him."

"You don't need to fret about Nigel causing a fuss," Penelope said. "He is very mild mannered and I'm quite sure he won't create a problem." JD watched as Mickey and Nigel carried the still unconscious Ian down the basement steps.

"That might be true," he muttered. "But you can never be sure what a man will do if he thinks someone might be trying to fool around with his true love."

"Oh no! you have the wrong impression." she exclaimed. "Nigel is my first cousin. We are very fond of each other but he is not my lover. Quite the contrary, he doesn't care for the feminine gender in that way." What the hell, JD thought. Why would a beautiful women like this be tooling around the continent with a limp wrist. "I know it seems a trifle odd," she said blushing. "But I've just been through a rather devastating divorce and Nigel being the sensitive kind person he is volunteered to escort me on this tour to help me out of my doldrums."

"I'd like to meet the idiot who let a gorgeous lady like you get away!" JD exclaimed.

"Thank you kind, sir," she said smiling wistfully. "Sometimes the unknown foibles one discovers in the handsome-courtly-prince she expected wedded bliss with turns out to be something quite different after the heat of passion ebbs in a man."

"Uh...I see," JD mumbled, slightly embarrassed by her confession. "Whoever he is, he's still a double barreled dumb-ass as far as I'm concerned."

"I am sincerely grateful for your kind esteem," she replied softly. "The days events have exhausted me so I'll bid you goodnight," she added then started upstairs to join Marlene in their room. He was admiring her spectacular derriere when Mickey returned from locking Ian and Nigel in basement.

"Before you start thinkin' below the belt," he groused. "You need to remember, we have to figure out how to get outta' this country alive. You might recall the idea of gittin' nailed to a tree with our dicks jammed down our throat to help you concentrate on the problem." JD smiled as he noticed Mickey had gotten the whole soliloquy out with nary a fuck or any other expletive being used.

"Damn! you're gittin' right refined in your discourse," he said smiling. "Being in the company of the upper classes just might be rubbin` off on you."

"Stick it in yer` ear," Mickey growled. He still didn't tell me to go fuck myself, JD thought.

"Hell, we stay around these Englishwomen much longer you might eventually be able to rejoin polite society," he said chuckling.

"Go fuck `yerself," Mickey snapped.

Chapter Twenty Four

May 21, 1993, 11:30 hours
65 kilometers northwest of
Castellammare, Italy

Marty and Alphonce drove to a nearby village bistro in Alberto's pickup to spend a few hours schmoozing with the locals carefully seeking any information on any Arabs snooping around. JD told them to keep a low profile and try to find out where they were operating from if they happened to cross paths with any.

"Get back here by 22:00, you need to rotate a watch on the front gate.

"What the fuck is 22:00?" Marty asked looking confused.

"Sorry, I keep forgetting you've never been in the military," JD said. "It's a simple system to avoid confusion between AM and PM. A day is twenty-four hours long ending at midnight, or in military terms 24:00. The next day's first hour is 0:100 at 1 AM and progresses through 24:00 at midnight."

I'll still need a fuckin' calculator to figure out what the hell time you're talking about," Marty groused.

"Damn, just think and you'll figure it out," JD snapped. " The two of you need to get rid 'a the Beamer in the morning. We're asking for trouble using it and I sure as hell don't want to leave it here and have some rag-head connect Alberto with us.

Mickey and JD agreed on their rotation with JD standing the first watch beginning at 22:00 and Mickey relieving him at 0:200. He trudged up the slope behind the equipment shed and located a position inside the tree line East of the pasture affording a good view of both the front and back sides of the groves. The West was protected by fairly mountainous terrain and he hoped that Arabs not being noted climbers and the distance from the nearest road being double that from the East side. He figured it would probably be the direction a raiding party would choose. He didn't feel right about leaving the West exposed but they didn't have the manpower to cover it and if the past couple of days gave any indication of what they were facing the next forty eight hours, he felt uncomfortable about it but had to accept the risk.

It took him a few minutes to locate a natural declivity inside the tree line with good views of the house and surrounding area and settled down hoping for a boring four hours. Nothing stirred until a little after 24:00 when an owl flew past his right shoulder giving him quite a start. He cursed as the damn bird snatched a small mouse he'd been watching for the past half hour, then swiveled its head front to back and looked JD in the eye as if with the ability to speak, it would have growled, "Don't fuck with me, I'm eating." "Sentry duty would sure as hell be easier with the ability to swivel ones head like that," JD mused. I ought to blow the damn bird away for scaring the crap outta' me. He and the owl glared at one another for a few moments until it seemed to discard JD as an immediate threat and turned back to its well-earned meal. JD considered shooting it for a few seconds, then decided against it. Hell from the birds point of view, I'm just some asshole who might interrupt his tasty dinner. Turning his attention back to the house and surrounding grounds he noticed someone exit the front door. Using the starlight scope, he could see it was a woman but not which one. She walked up to the tree line and slowly began circling the edge. When she got fifty meters to the left side of the declivity, JD eased left an equal distance hoping anyone in the woods looking for his position would be fifty meters off making their approach.

As the woman neared he saw it was Penelope and stepped out of the trees to motion her forward.

"What are you doing out here?" he whispered after she had covered the distance separating them.

"Looking for you," she replied. Alberto told me you were somewhere in the trees. What are you doing out here?"

"I'm watching for irate terrorists in the area plotting to kill us," he muttered.

"Do you want me to leave?" she asked tremulously.

"No, follow me" he said as he turned back toward the declivity. "You can help me with the glasses but you'll have to stay completely quiet." He noted she was wearing the black skirt, dark hose and a black leather jacket over the light silk blouse. *I wonder if she knows how good her tits look in that blouse? She's gonna have to button the jacket or I'll have a hard time keeping my mind on business.* "I have to give you points for figuring out, black is the preferred garb for sneaking around at night," he said chuckling. "But button the jacket to cover your blouse. It's kind of bright and is definitely a distraction."

"Oh…I didn't think about that," she said, fumbling with the jacket buttons.

They settled in the hole, then he handed her the binoculars and told her how to scan the woods to their rear.

"Keep moving the glasses in ten to twenty degree segments through ninety degrees to the left rear," he said. "Don't stop for over a few seconds per segment unless you notice motion. I'll watch the right side."

"Why?" She asked quietly. "

"Stare at one place too long and you'll start imagining things, so don't lock in on something unless something moves. Be alert, anyone coming in behind will be moving very slowly" he replied. That satisfied her and with a look of serious resolution she started scanning the woods to their rear.

JD was slightly amused as he watched her dogged determination for a few moments. and realized he was failing to watch his side. He quickly scanned the house and grounds then swung back to the rear thinking, *I wonder what caused her to risk walking out here in the dead of night to find me?* "I'm sorry," he mumbled.

"Before I so rudely interrupted, you said you were looking for me." She lowered the glasses and turned to face him.

"I've never been around men like you and your friend before," she whispered.

He grunted in reply and waited to see where she was going. She turned back to concentrate on her assigned task for another ten minutes then lowered the glasses and faced him again. "How long have you and Mickey been involved in this type of activity?"

"For quite a spell," he replied. Five more minutes elapsed.

"Why?"

"It's what we do, and the pay aint bad." Another five minutes passed.

"It's not really the money, is it?" That one gave him pause. *Damn! She's right. We sure as hell didn't do it for the money during our Army careers, but the money is a prime factor working with control.*

"We were trained by the army," he said slowly. "And being used to the highs and lows of challenging the angel of death occasionally, we're probably to some degree addicted to it. We sure weren't doing it for the money while we were on active duty."

She looked at him with a confused expression.

"Are you saying you aren't with the armed forces?"

"Yes!' he snapped. "And you don't need to know any more than that." He felt slightly ashamed for speaking in such a forceful tone when he saw a flicker of fear flit across her face.

"I'm sorry, Penelope," he mumbled apologetically. "The organization we work for isn't an outfit you or anyone else needs to know a whole lot about."

"I understand," she whispered, thinking, *I'm sure he doesn't realize it, but if one asks the wrong question, he transforms from a seemingly warm caring gentleman to a terrifying killer in seconds. Should I even think about getting closer to this man. That thought scared her until she admitted to herself, I guess I might as well accept that, that is exactly what I want and set about making it happen soon as he could be killed or off on another mission in the near future.*

Those few questions were the only conversation between them until 01:30 rolled around and JD tapped Penelope on the shoulder.

"You better get back before Mickey shows up," he said. "He'll never believe I was doing anything besides trying to get in your pants."

"Alright," she said laughing lightly. "If you happen to be passing through England during your travels, I would very much like to see you again." She rose, handed him a gold-embossed card with her address, private and office phone numbers and then started back toward the house. He watched over her until she entered the house. It's a good thing I didn't have this view while she was here. A whole battalion could have shown up without me noticing. Those long perfect legs are attached to an absolutely spectacular ass.

Chapter Twenty Five

May 22, 1993, 0:200 hours
65 Kilometers west of
Castellammare, Italy

Mickey showed up at precisely 0:200. JD handed him the night vision glasses and was starting back to the house for some badly needed rest, when Mickey stopped him.

"You might think about calling Control for some ideas how to get our ass outta` here," he said. "But, I think, it would be a good idea to use a land line instead `a the comm. The damn terrorists don't seem to have much trouble finding us whenever we use the damn thing.

"I noticed that," JD said. "We are in deep shit if somebody at Control is giving our position away."

"Uh huh…but I got faith you'll figure a way to get us out," Mickey muttered. "We've been in a lot worse trouble before and you've always come up with something." After he got back to the house, JD decided to wait for Marty and Alphonce to return in the morning and have one of them drive him to a phone at least ten kilometers distant before he called control. Then he hit the sack thinking, *Shit! If Mickey's right about someone turning our location over to the terrorists, I don't have the faintest Idea how we can survive tomorrow, mush less long enough to get out of this country and back to the states.*

Mickey shook him awake at 0:630 the next morning with news that

Alphonce had called from a call box. He and Marty had been attacked on the road by another carload of Arabs as they were in the process of shoving the Beamer off a cliff. Marty was hit and had disappeared over the edge in the car. Alphonce had lost the Arabs, driving dirt roads and orchards in Alberto's truck and was holed up in the barn of a deserted farm about five kilometers Northeast of Alberto's olive grove. He was worried the terrorists would find him as another Bell Cobra gunship was searching the area and more Beamers loaded with rag-heads were roaring by the front gate every few minutes. He was anxious that they'd start checking each farm individually soon and there weren't that many in the area.

"You can get to this place over land," Alberto said excitedly after JD told him about the problem. The terrain provides good cover but it's rough so it will take some time."

JD hurriedly slung his rifle, grabbed an Ak-47, then passed the RPG and three projectiles to Mickey He voiced his usual complaint about the extra weight,

"You sure we don't need a Howitzer, JD?"

"No, but I'd like to have an M1-Abrams, if it was available," JD snapped back and then started for the door until Alberto grabbed his arm.

"I will lead to save time and help kill any terrorists we run into!" he exclaimed.

"No way!" JD exclaimed. "We already owe you more than we can ever repay, Alberto. You've probably got a truck and a nephew in dire circumstances and I'm sure as hell not going to risk making your wife a widow."

"Signor JD," Alberto said sternly. "You donna letta me lead, I willa follow and thassa stupido use 'a manpower." JD realized there was no way to dissuade him since Alberto took such pride in his mastery of American lingo and his lapse into broken English made it crystal clear he was extremely upset and was going with them whether JD approved or not.

"Okay, if you give me your word that you'll stay under cover and guard our rear when we get there," JD said nodding his agreement.

"I give my word as an Italian man," Alberto stated stiffly. I know he won't break that oath unless we're all dead and in that event I hope he's got enough sense to think about his family and head for home,

JD thought. They brought the Englishmen up to use the facilities, gave them food and drink then locked them back in the wine cellar. Alberto gave his wife the key and instructed her that under no circumstances was she to let them out before he returned. The three of them then spent two hours climbing up and down the small mountains Alberto had described as hills before arriving at the edge of a forest overlooking a valley surrounding an obviously deserted farmhouse and barn.

Mickey was carrying his rifle the RPG with three projectiles and his Glock. JD had his H&K, Ruger 357 and an AK. Alberto had the double barrel and the other AK they'd retrieved after the highway skirmish. JD felt comfortable that all was as it should be. If Mickey wasn't bitching about hauling gear and equipment something was wrong.

They left Alberto at the edge of the field then had almost reached the house and barn when the helicopter Alphonce had mentioned, thundered over the last hill they'd traversed and zeroed in on them. They dove in the dirt and prepared to get strafed when Alberto opened up at the chopper's underbelly with a full clip from the AK. It didn't do any appreciable damage to the armor plate, but did distract the pilot enough so he didn't have time to recover and fire before over-flying Mickey and JD.

Mickey scrambled in the barn as the chopper passed over and JD dove in the house. It was a two-story wooden structure on the verge of collapse from years of neglect and decay. He decided to go upstairs and try for a shot out of a window at the pilot, and then almost broke a leg and dropped the rifle when the stairs collapsed under him. The climb back down to retrieve the rifle saved his life. The chopper was armed with rockets and launched one that blew up the window he was heading for along with most of the top floor. Extricating himself from under the debris, he muttered, " I'm either going blind or my brain is slowing down. Failing to see those rockets should have gotten me killed. He heard the chopper circling for another run, and edged to the front door to try for a shot as it passed over. It dropped down to fifty feet and was lining up to fire when Mickey launched a projectile. As the pilot hovered to take better aim. Mickey, expecting him to over-fly had adjusted for forward motion and the projectile passed harmlessly a foot in front of the perplex. The pilot completely forgot about the man in the house he knew was armed with nothing but a rifle, panicked and almost put the tail-rotor in the dirt when he jerked back desperately trying to turn when he saw the projectile smoke by. Whether he was going for a shot at Mickey or simply haul ass out of range, JD didn't know. He'd have opted to get out of Dodge when that missile flew by.

Anticipating the pilot's reaction, JD stepped boldly out in the open and carefully aimed at the pilot's flight helmet. The chopper was still bouncing, but at a range of less than fifty meters and no sound suppressor he couldn't miss. The pilot took the round in the neck slightly below his ear and fell over the stick. The co-pilot desperately tried for control but with only fifty feet of altitude and the dead pilot's body lying over his controls, there just wasn't enough time. The chopper rolled on its right side and then collided with Mother Earth blowing up, scattering rotors, pieces of the chopper and bodies on impact.

JD was watching the ensuing blaze and Mickey was walking over to congratulate him when a carload of Arabs roared in the driveway and slammed to a stop fifty or sixty meters from where they stood. JD ducked back in the house. Mickey dove in the dirt as every man in the car jammed his weapon through a window firing at him. He calmly reloaded the RPG with bullets impacting all around him then launched and didn't miss this time. Two men recognized the RPG, bailed out and were hauling butt for tall timber as the missile struck, killing everyone left inside the car. Not wanting to hear Mickey bitch, or take a chance that the terrorists would spread the word about their location, JD shot one center mass in the back. The other one hit the ground, desperately crawling for the gate, got a round up his ass then jumped up trying to run as the next round arrived to sever his brain stem.

Mickey got up, dusted himself off and walked to JD's side.

"I think it would be a good idea to get our ass outta' here post haste," he grunted. JD glanced around as Alphonce roared out of the barn in Alberto's truck and slammed to a stop next to them.

"Get in!" he shouted.

"No, we've got to get Alberto," JD yelled. "You drive back alone. They'll be looking for a vehicle with more than one man, hopefully you won't have any trouble."

They watched the truck disappear through the gate, and then trotted back toward the last position they'd seen Alberto. When he saw them approaching, he charged forward

"Lets go back and kill some more of the bastards!" he shouted.

"There are probably an unlimited supply of 'em," JD said chuckling. "We don't have any compunctions about killing terrorist, but don't have time or ammo to take 'em all on."

The struggle back to Alberto's farm took over three hours. Adrenaline will keep a man going for many hours during combat. After the action is over the body sends a clear signal that it's time to for him to rest. They were exhausted when finally arriving at the farm they found Alphonce waiting with a dour expression on his face.

"I hatea to tella you," he said glumly. "They shoots Marty, as he was pulling the Beamer to the edge of the cliff and he wen over. They would 'a never known I wassa with him but it pissa me off and I squeezea a clip at 'em. Thassa why, they war chasin me."

"Anyway, Marty could have survived?" JD asked quietly.

"No, fity meter droppa to rock an he already shot in head," Alphonce replied.

"I hate to say it," JD said slowly. "But, if you do anything to retrieve the body the damn cops will nail you and we'll all end up in jail and on trial for murder. There aint a government in Europe including the Italian that isn't scared to death of OPEC shutting their oil off. Locking us up forever would be a small price to pay as far as they're concerned. Now…do you know where there is a public phone at least ten kilometers from here? I need to call Control before we clean our weapons and flake out."

Alphonce drove him to roadside call-box on the main highway. JD placed the call and waited the usual ten minutes. Mr. Smith came on the line and asked where they were and what problems they had encountered since their last transmission. He told JD, he was receiving advisories that seemed to indicate at least one other action besides the original operation and there was a major flap on at the State Department.

"I'm quite sure, you've been too busy to keep abreast of any news broadcasts," he said. "The media is going wild trying to figure out who is responsible for eliminating one of the most sought after terrorist in the world." He paused for a moment. "The news-woman on the scene who suggested the operation was carried out by two Americans has changed her description from horrid murdering thugs to probable U.S. military operatives. It seems their viewers were irate after her initial description of the action. The network got caught with their ass in the wind when they decided the death of that terrorist was unprovoked murder and their already low ratings dropped off a cliff."

"Once in a while, liberal zealots can't help showing their bias when they try to convince the public they don't slant news or compromise the facts," JD said. He thought a second then added, "We got in a little scrap you'll probably be hearing about in a day or so and lost Marty."

"By 'lost,' do you mean lost, lost?"

"Yes, sir."

"That is most regrettable," Smith said. "I know you had gotten close with him. I'll see to it that his family is well remunerated."

"I got a question," JD said.

"What would that be?"

"Why can't you send a helicopter in to extract us?"

"I fault myself for failing to do that after the operation," Smith said. "But sadly that option is no longer open. The Italian government is screaming to high heaven through the press and diplomatic channels, accusing our government of carrying out an unauthorized military operation within their borders. Any unidentified aircraft flying within a hundred kilometers of your location, I have no doubt the Italian Air-Force would shoot it down. The only good news is the authorities in Italy while not believing what our current Commander-in-Chief says about anything, which is good policy for any government or entity dealing with him," he muttered as an aside. "With our great leader's past record of taking proactive measures against anyone other than women, who had the temerity to admit their sexual encounters or attacks by him…I hear, they're having second thoughts and are turning the heat up on the British and Israelis.

"It's good to hear that CNN for once showed what a bunch whinny wimps they are,"

JD grumped. "But we still have the problem of how the hell we're going to get out of this country."

"If you feel it's safe…stay where you are for the time being," Smith said. "Things should cool down in a couple of days and I'll try to get some help to you."

"There is one other thing," JD said slowly.

"You're not going to ask for more money again?" Smith groused.

"Uh…no," JD replied. "Four British subjects got involved in our little skirmish, yesterday. We had to bring them with us and one of `em aint real happy."

"Do any of them know who you are, or, who you work for?" Smith asked sharply.

"No, sir," JD replied quickly.

"How about the three that aren't unhappy?"

"They don't know and don't care. They don't like terrorists any more'n we do

"They aren't by chance attractive women?"

"Uh…yes sir, two of them" JD replied then quickly continued, "we're not up to any hanky panky."

"Uh huh," Smith said doubtfully. "Try, to keep your distance. Sexual involvement inevitably leads to lax security,"

After JD and Alphonce returned to the farm, he woke Mickey up.

"I can't figure the old man out," he muttered. "If he's lying he's damn good at it. We need to stay alert until he gets us out or we're attacked then if he is trying to get us killed we'll just play it by ear and try to get back to the states and start huntin` his ass."

chapter Twenty Six

May 22, 1993, 15:00 hours
Alberto's olive groves 65 kilometers
west of Castellammare, Italy.

They set a guard-rotation of four hours, both day and night and Mickey volunteered for the first watch. He wanted JD to get some rest since the extra weight of having to make decisions affecting their chances of survival left him totally exhausted. JD watched until he entered the trees, then took a hot shower, donned clean shorts and tee-shirt and then fell in bed.

He jolted awake two hours later as he felt someone lightly massaging the back of his legs. He grabbed the Ruger, rolled over then lowered it quickly when he recognized Penelope. She was kneeling astride his legs, clad in the black skirt and light silk blouse. Seeing the business end of the Ruger pointed at her nose caused her to fall backwards off the end of the bed, giving JD a view of her gorgeous legs from perfectly turned ankles up inner thighs to sheer white lace panties. He quickly put the revolver back on the night table, scrambled to help her up hoping he hadn't scared her out of continuing the massage and found her spread-eagled, slightly dazed from bumping her head. Her skirt had slid up to her hips and he couldn't help pausing to drink in the sight of her long beautiful legs and the dark patch of hair revealed by her sheer panties. He gently helped her to her feet trying to conceal a tremendous erection.

"I'm sorry!" he exclaimed. "I had no idea it was you." She gave him her hand and lightly brushed against his cock.

"I didn't mean to startle you," she said huskily. "Why don't you lie back down, I think you will find a massage quite relaxing." He took her in his arms and kissed her deeply. "Just don't think about quitting," he whispered. She pushed him gently back on the bed. "Lie on your stomach," she murmured as she pulled his shorts off "I've not finished."

Starting at his feet she gradually worked up his legs to his back and shoulders pausing to inspect the many scars he had received over the years and kneading each muscle until she felt it relax then reached between his legs and lightly fondled his testes, causing him to start grinding the mattress. Not wanting him to climax, she stopped and moved up to his neck, gently worked back down to his buttocks and thoroughly kneaded them, occasionally reaching under to lightly tickle his testes and fondle the stone hard shaft of his penis.

"You don't let me turn over," he husked. "I'm `going to poke a hole in the mattress."

She gently tugged his hip, then glimpsed his engorged cock. My, you seem quite excited," she whispered.

"If you aren't careful, I will explode" he said breathlessly.

"We can't have that," she murmured. "You just need to control yourself."

"I have anything to say about what comes next?" he asked softly.

"No, but you seem to be enjoying it," she replied as she lightly fondled his erection A greater truth has never been spoken, he thought.

She massaged his abdomen accompanied by feather-light strokes of his cock. Then spent a few moments fondling it, stood, removed her panties and slowly lowered herself on him. He felt the wonderful sensation of sliding into a silky, glorious intense wet heat that seemed to suck at his very core and exploded within moments after she began to move. She pulled back to massage him back erect, then slipped him back inside and began to move again. She continued for a few moments then groaned, shuddered and fell forward onto his chest.

"Um, that was ever so nice," she whispered huskily.

"You are the master of understatement," he murmured. "I'll never forget it, now please lie on your back. I want to make love to you until we can't move." "He waited until she turned and opened for him, then plunged inside her silky warm, wetness, moving in and out with each thrust getting deeper until he pulled out for a moment to relive the incredible sensation of entering her once more. She waited until he plunged and started moving then began to moan, matching his every stroke until she shuddered and he exploded. He softly kissed her, murmured affectionately then rolled over and drifted into contented slumber. She smiled to herself as she watched him sleep thinking, there is nothing like great sex, to put a hard man to sleep and I believe he will remember this encounter to his last days. "She nudged him awake at 0:345.

"When are you supposed to relieve Mickey?" she asked. JD glanced at his watch and saw he had only fifteen minutes before he was due at the outpost. He got up and reached for his boots and fatigues, then turned back to Penelope.

"Penelope, I regret it," he said. "Things are liable to get hairy the next few days and I won't have any time to spend with you. We are going to find a way to get you and your friends out of danger. Mickey and I will get out of the world of hurt we're likely to encounter and I'd like to see you again. This afternoon has been the greatest and most memorable experience I've ever had and I'll never forget it."

"I rather enjoyed it myself," she murmured. "I know you're not in a position to begin a standard relationship even if you were so inclined." He started to interrupt and she gently put a finger to his lips and shushed him. "I realize you feel it necessary to express something other than desire contributed to our wonderful moment but please don't. Truthfully, you are so alien when compared to the only other man I've known, I can't tell you what my feelings are. Anyone with an ounce of sense knows, given the current dangerous state of affairs in our imperfect world, men like you and Mickey are necessary for the rest of us to exist in our rather insulated environment but it will take time for me to come to terms having a relationship with a man who is both a tender caring lover and also the total antipathy to my peace loving nature. It is hard for me not to wonder how many human beings you and Mickey have slain. My father served as an aide to General Montgomery during the war and I'm quite sure though not personally killing any of the enemy…He was surely responsible for many deaths during those campaigns but there is a vast difference between war casualties and the type of thing you and Mickey do. You both are so cold and detached about it. I don't know whether I could handle what I know about you and not be fearful if insulted or threatened-you might revert from the kind loving man you are now to the cold efficient killing machine I've seen." JD thought about her doubts for a few moments.

"You don't think we are at war with the terrorists?"

"It would certainly appear that we are," she replied, realizing for the first time that it was true.

" I'll admit, we are pretty capable at what we do," he said with a slight chill creeping into his voice. "You need to realize, we'd be dead if we weren't. If the terrorists you saw us kill had not attacked us they'd still be alive and the one we eliminated to begin with most assuredly earned it and a thousand other deaths."

"I'm sorry," she said quietly. "I'm well aware those men asked for and probably deserved their violent ends. Once we are free from danger and have time to think, I hope you will give me a chance to know you better."

"You can rely on it," he said, and handed her the card she had given him. I'm giving this back because Mickey and I are going to move out of this area and I don't want you to be connected to us if we're taken. We've been trained to memorize the smallest detail and you are anything but a small detail in my life so don't worry about me forgetting how to find you. I've got to get in gear now and relieve him. In case we don't see one another before we leave, I will be in touch."

"I hope so," she replied softly.

"I know so," he said walking out the door and softly pulling it closed behind.

Chapter Twenty Seven

May 23, 1993, 0:400 hours
65 Kilometers West of
Castellammare, Italy

JD thought. How the hell after all the years I've wasted whoring around the globe can the almighty put me in position to meet a beautiful women with character to match a few weeks ago and here I am with another who is even more beautiful with at least as much character. Either he is smiling on me or testing me to see if I'll fuck up on a grand scale and piss ˜em both off. He realized there wasn't a simple answer, gave up and headed up the hill to relieve Mickey.

Upon entering the trees he could see Mickey was out of position, crouched and slowly scanned the dark woods wondering where the hell he was. Easing down to the prone position he crawled quietly thirty yards behind and above for a better view of the terrain. No Mickey. Becoming more worried with each passing moment JD rose, decided to climb a tree for a better view then slung the rifle over his shoulder and reached for a low limb. A knife slid next to his jugular. Well shit! One great piece of ass and I walk up here with my mind outta˜ gear. Now I'm fucking dead. When nothing happened and he heard Mickey chuckle JD was torn between choking the asshole and hugging him. Mickey flipped the blade to the dull side and pulled it back.

"Where the hell's your mind?" he muttered. "You strolled up here like it was a walk on the beach. Half the knife-men in the world could `a slit your throat." JD took a deep breath waiting for his heart to drop out of his throat.

"You Dip-shit!" he exclaimed. "Why the hell are you practicing your stealth skills on me? I could `a had a fuckin` heart attack." That really tickled Mickey and he broke into laughter, then getting himself under control," asked.

"What you been up to JD?" You look almost as guilty as our esteemed great leader did when he was shaking his finger at and lying to the whole country swearin` he never got no blow job from that chubby little girl. You been messing around with one `a those women down at the house?"

JD didn't want to lie to him, absolute trust in one another was essential if a sniper team is to survive. Nothing undermines that trust more than lying and not wanting to lie caused consternation. Big Jake had drilled it into him from an early age that kissing and telling was a mortal sin for a decent man. Mickey saw his hesitation.

"Forget it," he muttered. "I don't give a shit whether you've been in a pile with both of `em, but you need to get your head outta` your ass before you come out here to watch for a bunch of rag heads bent on killing us."

"Okay," JD mumbled. "I'm properly chastised, gimme` the glasses and get your butt down to the house for some sleep." Mickey patted him on the shoulder.

"You'll do," he said. "But, we both need to stay alert if we're gonna` get out of this cluster fuck alive."

"I just said I would," JD snapped.

"Uh huh," Mickey grunted, and started for the house, then turned back. "I'll be back in four hours to relieve you. Try not to get killed and don't go attacking anything with your head." He aint gonna` ever let it go, JD thought disgustedly.

The next four hours passed quickly as JD silently moved around the entire perimeter of the groves looking for any signs of the opposition. He knew he wasn't as skilled and quiet as Mickey, but still felt there weren't any Arabs who could detect him before he found and got close enough to neutralize them.

He eased up to Alphonce's position at the front gate, then slipped behind him and whispered. "Hey, it's me." Alphonce jumped and almost dropped his rifle.

"Whatta the fuck are you doin' here?" he grunted. "You scareda the pess outta' me. I thoughta you were ina woods."

"Sorry," JD said chuckling. "I was checking the perimeter and wanted to see how alert you were."

"Wella you fine out and takea five years 'offa mina life," Alphonce replied huffily. JD patted him on the shoulder.

"Stay alert until daylight, then head on back to the house," he said smiling.

Getting back to his position twenty minutes before Mickey was scheduled to relieve him he spent the time trying to formulate a plan of escape without any help from Control. He was still thinking about a solution when Mickey showed up with Alberto in tow.

"Alberto wants to help," Mickey said. "He thinks we don't trust him and says to let you know he spent a lot of time on outpost duty during the war." JD clapped Alberto on the shoulder.

"It aint that we don't trust you Alberto," he said. "We appreciate the offer, but I for one don't want to take a chance with your life." Alberto patted the shotgun and the AK.

"Donna worry JD," he said. "I was with Lucky Luciano during the war and we killed many many Nazis. I can handle any damn Arabs that come thissa way" JD nodded his agreement.

"Okay," he said. "I appreciate the help. There have been a lot of changes since the war. You'll need to spend a few minutes with Mickey to update you."

"Don't need it, but that's okay with me," Alberto replied. JD nodded for Mickey to follow him a few meters back toward the house.

"You be damn sure he knows what he's doing before you leave," he whispered. "He's helped us more than anybody could hope for and we need to get the hell out of his house before the opposition figures out where we are."

"You got a plan how?"

"I'm working on it," JD muttered.

He found Mirabella waiting at the front door wringing her hands and pointing at the door leading down to the basement. He understood her consternation when he heard Ian pounding on the basement door screaming curses at the her. Shit! I'm gonna' have to quiet that fool down before Alberto gets back. He'll kill him if hears the language the dip-shit is using on his wife. He waited for Ian to catch his breath and start another outburst before snatching the door open, planting a foot in Ian's chest and kicking him down the stairs. He checked to see if Nigel was also in an aggressive mood as he followed Ian down and saw he was sitting trance-like on his bunk. Turning back to Ian he slammed a knee in his chest.

"Look, numb nuts," he snapped. "You're will stay down here until we think it's safe to move you. We'll truss you up and gag you and if that don't work, I'll let Alberto hear you cursing his wife, then you'll be fucking dead. Now...I'm going to let you up, then try to get some rest and I don't want to hear another peep outta' you." Ian gasped for breath for a few moments.

"I'll keep my peace until we are back in civilization," he said bitterly. "I will do everything in my power to bring the full force of law down on you then." JD carefully locked the basement door, wearily climbed upstairs to take a shower and get a little sleep. I wonder if Penelope will show up for a return engagement? I'll probably be a big disappointment if she does.

Mickey woke him up at 0:800 the next morning.

"Damn!" JD exclaimed. "Why the hell did ya' let me sleep so long?"

"I wasn't tired," Mickey said. "And thought it would be a good idea to let the only scheming conniving son-of-a-bitch we have get enough rest so he can figure out how to get us the fuck out of Italy."

"When you do something nice," JD grunted. "It'd be better if you did it without the insult."

"How the hell could I talk to your grouchy ass if I couldn't insult you occasionally," Mickey replied smiling. He waited while JD put a robe on, then they headed down to the kitchen and found Alberto waiting on them.

"Good morning," he said, "The night was uneventful other than an owl that flew down and snatched a mouse in front of me."

"I bet he turned around and glared at you while he did it," JD said. "I made his acquaintance early last night." JD had come to the conclusion during the night that they couldn't depend on Control. He told Mickey the best idea he could come up with over a cup of coffe was for them to move overland to Naples on foot. Then, either buy or steal a car for a dash to the frontier. He went back upstairs for a shower, and after getting dressed noticed Mickey was missing again. I wonder where the hell he is, we need to get some breakfast and get moving. He descended the stairs, walked in the kitchen and found Alberto at the table. He rose as JD entered. "Sit down, sit down," he said effusively. "Mirabella, she going to fix you a fine breakfast."

"Thank you, I'm famished," JD said. "But I need to find Mickey before I eat."

"That's not a good idea right now," Alberto mumbled.

"Why not?"

"Uh, from little noises I hear on my way down, I think he be visiting one of the young ladies."

Well shit! I wonder if it's Penelope, JD thought, and was immediately chastened by his salacious notion when Penelope walked in the kitchen.

"Good morning all," she said brightly. Alphonce trailed her in the kitchen and strode over to give Mirabella a big hug.

"Whassa, for breakfuss Aunta Mirabella?" Mirabella rattled off her reply in Italian and Alphonce held her at arms length stuttering, "You gotta bea kiddina me!" he exclaimed, then turned to JD.

"You, ainta gonna believa this," he said. "She makea scrambled ova, hama and hominia gritsa for honor you and Mickey."

"Where the hell did she find Hominy grits in Italy?" JD asked astounded.

"Mirabella, she make herself," Alberto said. "She know you and Mickey from the South and are supposed to eat grits."

"She's right about us liking grits," JD said. "But it aint like it's a law we got to them on a regular basis. I watched my old man make 'em when I was a kid and he boiled the corn in a big iron kettle for hours. She didn't need to go to that much trouble."

"She know that JD, but she want to make you and Mickey happy," Alberto said. "Mirabella, she think there should be more men like you, then there be less terrorists roaming around Italia kidnapping and murdering our people." Mirabella put a huge platter of scrambled eggs and ham on the table along with a big bowl of Hominy grits.

"Serva youself," she said smiling. "Fightin mana needa lotsa energia."

"Thank you Mirabella, I feel like I'm back home in Alabama." JD said, then turned back to Alberto. "I swear I'm going to try to talk her into coming home with me," he said grinning. "If she won't, and I ever decide to marry, I'm going to send my new bride over here for a six week training course." Alberto laughed.

"You better not leave a beautiful woman here for long, she be stolen by one of my nephews." They all turned as Mickey trailed Marlene in the kitchen. He held a chair for her then sat next to her. There was an uncomfortable silence until he glanced around the table and saw the bowl of grits.

"Where did you find Hominy grits?" he asked. "I didn't think they had 'em in Italy."

"It's a long story," JD grunted. "Just sit down and enjoy, it's probably going to be a while before we get any more. By the way, where have you been?" Mickey shot a quick look at Marlene and she blushed. "None 'a your business," he muttered.

"I hope you got a little rest," JD said. "I'm planning on calling Control to tell Smith we're going to get out on our own. It appears somebody in the organization is trying to get us killed. We need to get away from here before whoever it is locates us. I don't want to risk getting Alberto and Mirabella identified."

"Donna you worry about us!" Alberto exclaimed. "This house, she built like fort. We kill many Arabs, if they foolish enough to come here."

"We really appreciate it, Alberto," JD replied. "But, we really do need to get back to the States and start trying to find out who is betraying us."

"Okay," Alberto said. "That's probably true, still, you and Mickey know you are welcome here if things don't work out and you need a safe haven."

"Do you really believe there is a traitor in your organization?" Penelope asked concerned.

"I'm not positive, but it sure seems like it," JD replied. Mickey looked across the table at JD.

"There aint any doubt in my mind," he grunted, "what's the plan?"

"We're going to move overland at least ten kilometers before we use the comm," JD replied. "That shouldn't connect it to this place." He paused a moment and spoke to Alphonce.

"You need to stay here for at least two days in case worse comes to worse and the damn terrorists do mount some kind of attack." He turned back to Mickey. "You bring your H & K, Glock, the RPG and the remaining projectiles. I'll tote an AK, my rifle, the Ruger, the ammo, the claymores and we'll split up the grenades we have left "

"Why the hell we got to carry the RPG?" Mickey asked disgruntled. "That damn thing is heavy."

"I don't have any idea," JD replied. "We'd be dead if we hadn't had it on the highway and that abandoned farm. It would be nice if we could start without you bitching about what the gear weighs. I'll split the load as much as I can but you're going to have to tote the launcher and the projectiles. It don't make any sense for you have the launcher without the grenades."

"Alright," Mickey agreed resignedly. "When do you want to move out?" JD glanced at his watch.

"We'll get the gear together and leave in an hour," he replied.

"I shoulda go along asa you guide," Alphonce said.

"We'd love to have you, but it just wouldn't be right to leave Alberto alone until it's safe," JD replied and turned back to Alberto.

"You mentioned something about nephews before? It would be a good idea for you to round up a few of 'em with whatever weapons they have available to help you and Alphonce defend this place if necessary."

"Why don't you wait a few hours for me to get my nephews," Alberto said. "Then Alphonce will be able to lead you."

"Uh uh, we've got to get moving as soon as possible," JD said. He was unable to put off an action once a decision was made adding the stress of rethinking and added worry about whether it was the best possible course to take. He addressed Alphonce.

You can take the Englishmen to Naples so they can catch a flight home in three days, but you need to blindfold the men before you bring them up. They were in the trunk on the trip here and don't need to know exactly where it is. We ought to be out of the country by then. He touched Penelope lightly on her shoulder and in a soft tone of voice said, "can you tell Ian and Nigel we were extracted by a sub today. That might keep Ian from going to the closest Police station if he thinks we're already out of the country."

"Yes," Penelope replied quietly. "You know I'll do anything I can to help you ."

Alphonce interrupted their tender exchange. "Uh, I donna know whata you hava in mind JD," he said. "Ita mighta be good idee for me to calla my cousin. He livea in Napoli, and works ata Avianca factoria. They makea beeg luxuria yachts and deliver thema by sea all over world. I cana go seea heem thisa afternoon and he canna probablia getta you ona one ofa them." He wrote a phone number on a napkin and handed it to JD. "Ita isa about forty kilometers and ita probablia takea you two day by foota to geta there. He willa be axpaxting you call ina two days fromma now," he said. "Thassa hisa homa number, calla after eighta in evenia."

They finished the finest breakfast either of them could remember. Then, JD and Mickey trailed the girls upstairs and watched as they entered their room softly closeing the door without uttering a word to them.

"What the hell's the matter with them?" Mickey asked puzzled.

"Who knows?" JD grunted. "You got to remember they're `wimmen and subject to act weird at times. We aint got time to figure it out. I want to get started before 12:00 and be at least ten or fifteen kilometers Northwest before dark. As they finished packing the gear for travel, they heard someone tapping on the door. JD opened it and found Penelope standing outside.

"Do you have time to talk for a few minutes?" she asked softly. JD glanced back at Mickey and he didn't seem likely to leave and give them any privacy.

"Sure," he replied. "Is anyone in your room? Dummy here doesn't seem inclined to leave."

"Marlene is, but she wants to spend time with Mickey alone." JD glanced at Mickey.

"Have you been a bad boy?" Mickey glared at him.

"Mind your own damn business," he muttered.

"Don't get your panties in a wad," JD said chuckling. "I'm just yankin' your chain a little. At least I don't take a swan dive off the nearest cliff like you when you go to yankin' on mine."

He followed Penelope to her room and when Marlene left to join

Mickey. She shut, the door then turned and leaned against it facing JD.

"I don't know if we will see one another again," she said softly. " But, I do know I would like to spend more time with you."

"You mean you've decided your friends and relatives wouldn't be risking violent death if I was in the area?" JD asked lightly. He saw he had hurt her and quickly added, "I'm sorry, that came out wrong. I'm sure you know, neither Mickey nor I would ever do any harm to civilians over everyday disagreements."

"I know," she sighed, "I've come to understand over the past days, that the violence you both have displayed has been reserved for antagonists who richly deserved what they received."

"You got it," JD said. "We have never targeted anyone who wasn't either in the killing business or a legitimate military objective."

"Do you think we'll see one another again?" she asked, a sad smile wafting across her face.

"I'm sure planning on it," JD replied softly. "But, the first thing Mickey and I have to do is put some distance between ourselves and everyone else involved. We've put to many people in harms way for to long. I'll get in touch as soon as we cool off enough so we won't have to be worried about where the next ambush is coming from." She embraced him warmly.

"I hope it's not long," she said huskily. "I really do want to get to know you better." He held her tightly for a few moments. Damn! How is it possible for me to fall hard for two women in a few weeks. I haven't felt like this since falling for a girl in the ninth grade and making a complete fool of myself. He relaxed while she clung to him, then grasped her shoulders and held her at arms length. "Pay attention," he ordered. "I've told Alphonce to take the four of you to the nearest airport after we've had time to get out of the country. It shouldn't take more than three days. I'd tell him to do it as soon as we leave, but I don't trust Ian. The chance he wouldn't stop at the nearest police station are slim and none and we'd be dodging the cops in addition to an untold number of ticked-off terrorists. For safeties sake, pay close attention to Alphonce. He is the best chance you have to survive."

"You are probably right about Ian," Penelope said. "He is very unpredictable, and seems always on the edge of rage. I believe he has abused Marlene on several occasions. Their marriage is on the verge of collapse and I believe that is the reason." JD embraced her warmly again, "I'm going to miss you Penelope," he said tenderly.

"And I you," she replied softly.

Chapter Twenty Eight

May 24, 1993, 14:30 hours
Albertos Olive groves
65 kilometers west of
Castellammare, Italy

JD found Mickey in their room packing. "Did you pack the projectiles and grenades?" he asked, hefting his pack. Mickey waited until JD finished strapping his pack on then voiced his usual complaint.

"Why the hell, do we have to tote the claymores and grenades?" He groused. "They're heavy and all we'll be doin' is haulin' our butts through the woods."

"I don't have the foggiest," JD snapped. "But, figure, there's a real good chance we'll need 'em so quit bitching and lets get moving."

"What about the comm?" Mickey asked.

"We'll take it with us and call Control when we're at least ten kilometers from here," JD replied. "If someone is pinpointing the signal, they won't be able to connect us with this place." He slung the H&K G3 over his shoulder, reached for an AK, slipped the Ruger in his web-belt holster, checked his pack to be sure the Grenades and claymores were in it, then started out the door.

"I hope, you packed civilian clothes," he said over his shoulder. "We'll need some when we make contact with Alphonce's cousin. It damn sure, wouldn't look kosher for us to wander into town dressed in full combat gear."

There's a couple 'a shirts, slacks and some loafers. That's about all I could cram in since I knew you'd want to bring the damn grenades and projectiles," Mickey carped. He buckled his pack, picked up his MP-5, Glock, the RPG then followed JD downstairs to bid Alberto and Mirabella farewell.

The two of them were waiting in the kitchen and Mirabella gave both of them a big hug. She struggled with her emotions for a moment then blurted, "Ta Ta JeDe and Meekey, you comma back some a day." JD glanced at Alberto.

"Ta Ta?"

"English lady, teach her thassa way to say goodbye," Alberto said chuckling. "Ttake a care you havea any trouble come back here. We fight the damn Arabs to the death and they be really, really sorry they fool around with Alberto Gambini's friends."

"There isn't any way we can thank you and Mirabella," JD said with feeling. "You ever need a couple 'a half wore out warriors call Alphonce. He knows how to contact us and we'll be here quicker than jack rabbit."

"That be pretty quick?" Alberto said smiling.

"You got it," JD replied. "Thanks again, be careful and get those nephews over here today.

They trudged over the same craggy hills traversed on the rescue, of Alphonce before arriving at the edge of the forest bordering the deserted farm. Mickey scanned the area with his binoculars.

"Shit!" he exclaimed. "The fucking place is crawling with cops and Italian military."

"It figures," JD muttered. "We'll back off and go around. When we get five or six kilometers past we'll call Control."

Spending another two hours putting distance between themselves and the farm. JD called a halt just before sunset at the edge of an approximately fifty-meter oval shaped clearing. He glanced at his watch and saw it was 17:45, signaled Mickey to cover him then walked to the center of the clearing and punched the comm on to call Control. He waited the usual ten minutes for Smith to call back. I should 'a waited until it was completely dark I'm a sitting duck out here, but we don't have time if we're going to make contact with Alphonce's *cousin tomorrow night,* he thought, then breathed a sigh of relief when Smith called back.

"Is there a problem?" He asked. "Your instructions were to wait a couple of days so we could plan an extraction."

"Damn right, there's a problem!" JD exclaimed. "Every time we've used this gadget to contact you since we terminated the target, no more than a few minutes have gone by before a bunch 'a pissed off Arabs show up. It's enough to give us some real doubts about whether somebody at Control is trying to get us killed." There was dead silence for a few moments.

"JD…. all I want to do is get you and Mickey out safely," Smith said quietly. "Be assured that I have in no way tried to put either of you at risk."

"I truly want to believe that," JD said. "But, you have to admit these people aren't having a lot of trouble finding us when we use the damn thing."

"It does concern me that the attacks seem to be coming in conjunction with our communications," Smith said. "If, what you think is true…I will turn over any stone necessary to unmask the culprit."

"We would appreciate you doing that," JD said. " In the meantime we're going to do what we have to do to survive, so you probably won't be hearing from us for a while."

"I understand," Smith said slowly. "Is there anything I can do to help?"

"No sir, we'll take it from here. By the way, did you deposit our fee?"

"Yes, I have," Smith replied. " I've also wired transferred funds to Alphonce, to take care of expenses along with a healthy fee for him and his associates to handle the retrieval of Marty's body to be returned along with his fee to his family for burial." He paused then continued with a touch of irritation creeping into his voice.

"We have received a bill in the amount of forty-six thousand dollars for the complete destruction of a Mercedes automobile. Accounting has asked me to request that you use cheaper transport in the future."

"We would be dead if we hadn't been in that big hunk 'a German iron," JD said flatly.

"I understand," Smith said sighing in resignation. "Good luck and I'll be looking forward to your report when you get back in the country."

JD planted a claymore forward of the comm in the middle of the clearing and three more at the edge of the woods on the far side of the glade then moved back in the trees to join Mickey.

"Okay, I planted a claymore where I was standing and three more on the other side. That should be the direction they come from. We aren't but a few kilometers from the highway here and they won't want to run afoul of the Italian authorities behind us. We'll hunker down in the underbrush and split up the watch. I'll give you odds, a bunch of rag-heads show up before dawn." He paused to check the time. "It's 18:00, you take the first watch and I'll relieve you at 22:00."

"Why the fuck do I always have to take the first watch?" Mickey grumped.

"For some reason you can hit the dirt and be asleep in thirty seconds. It takes me at least an hour to unwind and even think about sleeping. It might have something to do with our relative intelligence," JD replied chuckling.

"Stick it in your ear," Mickey snapped and then unhooked his gear, sat back against a tree, propped his rifle up within easy reach and was sound asleep within moments. JD watched him nod off. It is amazing how he's been able to do that since military school. Even when we were on a cross country training exercise and had a ten minute break, he could sleep nine and a half. It would sure make life easier if I could do it. His watch was uneventful and Mickey was instantly alert when JD nudged him at 22:00

"I got it," he muttered. "I'll get you up at 24:00, get some sleep."

Two hours later an explosion followed quickly by three more, then agonized screams of dying men and the sound of Mickey firing, shocked JD awake. He grabbed the H&K, rolled over to the prone position, sighted forward with the starlight scope and saw two bodies where he'd planted the first claymore and more on the far side of the clearing. He quickly scanned each side of the clearing and saw two men on the left were trying to flank them. Mickey stopped firing to jam in a new clip and glanced at JD to make sure he was ready.

"Watch the left," he muttered, "There are a couple over there I lost track of, I'll take care of the right."

"I got 'em," JD muttered, what were the explosions?"

"Two were dumb enough to amble out to the comm.," Mickey muttered nodding toward the clearing. "I waited until they were right in front of the claymore to blow it, then punched off the three on the other side 'a the clearing. I figure the first two were lookin' for the damn comm and it sounds like there's a whole nest of 'em over there."

"You decided it was worth toting those heavy claymores now?" JD asked caustically.

"If you can take time outta' rubbin' it in, yeah," Mickey growled. "You want to check the left before those two flank us?" JD swung the scope a few yards forward of where he'd last seen movement and then waited for a few seconds for a target to appear, and a man crawled into the sight. Not wanting to take a chance the man was wearing body armor, he went for a head-shot then slowly exhaled as he exerted soft pressure on the trigger. The rifle fired, the man went limp and JD knew he was history. He swung the scope forward to make sure the second man wasn't leading the first, then back until he caught a glimpse of him retreating back to the other side of the clearing. He swung the scope further until he found a small opening in the underbrush and then waited for the target to appear. Arriving at the opening the man decided to jump and make a run for it, took two quick steps and died. Mickey crawled back and tapped him on the shoulder.

"Stay here and cover me," he whispered. "I'll circle the right side and see if I can get behind 'em."

"Be careful, there might be a fuckin' platoon over there," JD admonished him.

"Don't worry, I'll run over your ass on the way back if there is."

JD kept scanning the far side of the clearing and couldn't see anything other than an occasional muzzle flash and the sound of rounds striking nearby trees. The random nature of the firing confirmed the opposition hadn't pinpointed his location and he decided to wait for them to make a move when a blood-curdling scream shattered the black night. *What the fuck is Mickey doing over there? He's capable of having a man crawl right over him and killing him without anyone in the area having the slightest idea he's around. Why the hell did he let that son-of-a-bitch make all of that racket?*

The scream of agony silenced the firing from the West and eadly quiet descended for a few moments, then another horrible scream erupted followed by the grisly gurgling sound of a man choking on his own blood. JD swung the scope in the direction of the hideous noise and saw three men jump to their feet and sprint back toward the West. They were gone so quickly, he didn't have time to get a round in a one of them. He held his position, scanning the entire front for the next few minutes and was beginning to worry about Mickey, and then almost had heart failure when he tapped JD on the shoulder and whispered, "I've searched the entire perimeter and it looks like the rest of 'em hauled ass."

"Will you please quit sneakin' up on me!?" JD exclaimed. "You scared the piss outta' me and why the hell, did you let those two make enough racket to wake the dead?"

"Had the desired effect didn't it?" Mickey grunted. "It sure unnerved that group over there. It sounded like a herd 'a stampeding buffalo when they hauled ass."

"Right," JD grunted. "Let's get the fuck out of here before they come back with reinforcements and there's no doubt somebody is tracking the comm. We need to dump it on the first car or truck we run across and maybe that'll throw whoever it is off our ass for a while. I should have set it in front of the claymore and it would be history."

They spent the remainder of the night and next day covering the remaining distance to the main highway leading North to the seaside hamlet of Portici. After they hid the weapons other than side-arms in the woods outside of town, JD glanced at his watch and saw it was 19:00 hours.

"I figure it's about five kilometers to Portici," he said. "We need to get into town and phone Alphonce's cousin. They took cover next to a sharp curve in the small coastal road leading South from Portici and converging with the main highway at Torre. Mickey waited until a farmer in an old stake-body truck slowed to negotiate the curve, and then ducked behind, punched the send-button on the comm and tossed it the middle of the farmer's load of chickens.

"As soon as the damn thing starts transmitting, I bet they get a fix on it," he muttered. "You reckon they'll be able to hear those chickens cackling?"

"You're probably right about 'em being able to track it," JD replied. "But whoever it is won't have the sound on since it's office hours in the States."

"I hope a buncha' dumb-ass terrorists don't blow that poor farmer up," Mickey mumbled.

"Too late to do anything about it now," JD said. "We don't have but an hour and a half to call Alphonce's cousin so lets get into our civvies."

Chapter Twenty Nine

May 27, 1993, 20:30 hours
Portici, Italy on the southern
shore of the Bay of Naples

Entering the outskirts of the small seaside hamlet, they found a clapboard framed bar with a sign hanging from the front porch roof labeling it as the OK Corral. It was modeled on a Western saloon, including the swinging half doors at the entrance, a board porch and a hitching rail.

"I wonder if everybody is totin` a six shooter?" Mickey mumbled. "You ought to fit right in," he said, nodding at JD's Ruger. JD noticed a call-box by the front entrance. He peered in the front door and could see the bar was sparsely populated with no six shooters in evidence. He quietly shoved through the swinging doors and led Mickey by a few patrons sitting at the bar back to a small dance floor surrounded by booths in the rear.

To avoid any conversation and identifying themselves as Americans he held up two fingers as a waitress approached and said, "Heinekens." And then waited for her to return with the beer to hand her some lira.

"You know how much beer costs in lira?" Mickey asked as the waitress left.

"Aint got a clue," JD replied. "I just gave her enough to make sure she didn't ask for more." When she returned with his change, JD motioned for her to keep it. *I hope it isn't enough for her to remember us.* He checked the time, glanced at Mickey and rose. "Stay here, I'll make the call," he muttered

Alphonce's cousin picked up on the third ring and after JD identified himself said, "yes signor, I was hoping you would call tonight. There is a fifty-meter motor-yacht departing in the morning. The captain is a transplanted American who operates out of London. He delivers for 'Avianca' the manufacturer I work for and several other builders in Italy and the Netherlands to ports all over the world. He is a good friend of mine, a very capable seaman and is looking forward to having you on board for this trip to the river Thames."

"That's great!" JD exclaimed. "Alphonce told me your name was Ricardo, but failed to give me your last name."

"Gambini but all of my American and English friends call me Rich."

"Do you know where we can find an inn that isn't really concerned about passports and will take cash? It's been a couple of days since we've had a bath or any sleep to speak of."

"Oh yes," Rich replied. "I booked a room in the company name with two double beds and a private bath at a very nice inn near the harbor. We do that for customers who are in town to see their yacht under construction. You don't have to worry about checking in. I'll pick you up and get you situated."

After JD described the bar, Rich told him he knew the place and would be there in a few minutes. JD hung up, and then went to fetch Mickey and they decided to take their beer outside and wait in front.

When Rich pulled to a stop at the curb in a small pickup truck, Mickey muttered,

"Jeez! Between Alphonce, Alberto and this dude, it looks like they've already started cloning in Italy." They climbed in the cab and gave Rich directions to the location they'd stashed the weapons. After they loaded them in the bed of the truck, Rich concealed them with a tarp and then climbed back under the wheel next to JD and Mickey and headed for the inn.

"Alphonce told me you were carrying an arsenal," he said. "I guess, you guys are ready for anything."

"We try," JD replied, glanced at Mickey and chuckled. "Sometimes it takes a little convincing to get my partner here to agree to tote some 'a the gear we usually need."

"At least I got enough sense to avoid gittin' in a buttin' contest with a stone wall," Mickey snapped.

"Hell, aint no reason for you to worry about that," JD muttered. "There isn't anyway you could get hurt buttin' anything with that thick head 'a yours." Mickey noticed Rich glancing nervously at them.

"Don't worry about him, Rich," he quipped. "I think its his time 'a the month and he must 'a run out of Kotex." Rich shook his head laughing, then sobered.

"Do either of you know anything about boats?"

"I do," JD replied. "I was raised sailing on Mobile Bay and the Gulf of Mexico. I've sailed and operated all kinds of boats both power and sail. "But, I have to tell you Mickey isn't acquainted with anything that floats other than a rubber ducky he played with in the tub when he was a kid."

"That's good," Rich said, smiling at JD's remark about Mickey. "I told the captain he could save some money by going with two less crewman this trip since I was sure you were experienced boatmen."

"Kind 'a stretched the truth a little, didn't you?" JD said smiling.

"As it turns out…a little" Rich replied. "But, one must do what one must to get the job done, mustn't one?" he added chuckling.

"You related to an old man in Washington by the name 'a Smith?" Mickey asked dryly. "That's just the convoluted kind 'a thing he might say to explain why he decided to exaggerate a bit."

"Can't say I've ever made his acquaintance," Rich replied chuckling. "But he does sound like a man I would like to meet him. Rich helped them move the gear inside their room and then turned to JD.

"I'll pick you up at four-thirty in the morning," he said. "The yacht is moored alongside a quay a couple of kilometers from here. The captain and one crewman who is also the cook are already on board. She's been fueled and provisioned for the voyage. The local port captain is scheduled at eight to stamp the export papers and he shouldn't ask any questions since he's used to this captain using a varied mix of crewmen."

"Sounds fine," JD said. "Does the captain know anything about us?"

"He is aware that you've been on some type of covert operation,"

Rich replied. "And, as you Yanks would put it, 'he didn't just fall off a tomato truck.' I'm sure he has a pretty good idea what the operation was given the high media concentration for the past few days."

"You sure he isn't worried about having a couple 'a wanted men with probably high prices on their heads from certain quarters?" Mickey asked.

"He's quite a man and I would trust him with my life," Rich replied. "You'll understand when you meet him," he added smiling to himself.

JD thrust a thousand dollars at Rich.

"We appreciate the help. This is to cover any expenses you may have incurred and a little for the risks you've taken. I wish I could give you more but we're runnin' a little short at the moment." Rich glanced at the money and tried to hand it back.

You don't need to pay me," he exclaimed. "I feel, the whole of Italy if not the world owes you men a debt for eliminating that terrorist killer." JD folded the bills and jammed them in Rich's shirt pocket.

"It isn't our money, just consider it payment from the government," he muttered. Rich hesitated a moment then grudgingly accepted.

"It isn't necessary, but if you insist I'll take it." he said quietly

" I insist," JD said. Rich turned back to them as he was departing.

"I'm quite sure your presence here is unknown gentlemen, get some rest and I'll see you in the morning."

Their room had two double beds and an adjoining bath. Mickey jammed a chair under the doorknob with the two beer bottles from the bar' balanced on top of it to alert them if anyone tried to force the door, then turned to JD.

"You reckon we ought to split up the watch?"

"No, since there isn't a window, we don't have to worry about somebody tossing a grenade in. Anybody tries the door, we'll be able to blow hell out of it before they can get it open. You go on and take a shower. I'll stand watch, then get mine after you're through. I'm a light sleeper so I'll bunk in the bed closest to the door with the AK and a grenade."

JD finished his shower, propped the AK up within easy reach, placed a grenade on the night table, stuck the 357 under his pillow and then crawled under the covers for some badly needed sleep. Mickey reached to flip the light off, hesitated then sat up on the edge of his bed.

"What're we supposed to do on the boat?" he asked in a worried tone. "Rich said we were supposed to replace two 'a the crew and you know I aint real happy on anything that floats in the first place. Hell! I get seasick on an elevator."

"I'll check out the navigation gear to see if it's changed a lot since I was deepwater sailing," JD said. "I'll stand some relief watches for the captain and you'll be swabbing the decks and helping in the galley."

"Galley?" You mean this boat has oars?"

"No...Dummy it's what you call the food preparation area on a boat"

"Thanks a lot," Mickey groused. "I really appreciate you volunteering me for KP duty on my first ocean cruise."

"What the hell else can you do on a boat?"

"I can tie knots and shit like that, I was a Boy Scout."

"No shit! You were a fuckin' Boy Scout?"

"Yeah, an Eagle Scout," Mickey muttered, realizing JD was going to zing him.

"You're lying. The only way you could have made Eagle Scout was if your Daddy was scoutmaster and he don't look like one anymore than Big Jake does."

"You tellin' me you never joined the Boy Scouts?" Mickey snapped irritably.

"No, I aint sayin' I didn't join, but it didn't take long for me to figure out it wasn't a helluva' lot of fun wandering around the woods trying to make a fire by rubbin' sticks together."

"I don't recall you complaining about a nice fire on freezing cold nights during survival training at Fort Polk."

"Don't worry," JD said chuckling. "I won't tell anybody you were a itty bitty Boy Scout."

"Fuck you," Mickey snapped."

Book Three

Escape and Retribution

Chapter Thirty

May 28, 1993, 0:430 hours
Portici, Italy

Rich tapped on their door at 04:30 the next morning.

"You guys ready to go?" The captain wants to be sure you're on board before a lot of dock-workers are on the quay. He lugged a big wooden box in the room. I brought this along to pack your weapons and gear in," he grunted. "It wouldn't do for anybody to see any of them since none of them are legal in this country."

They packed the armaments and holstered their side arms under their windbreakers, loaded the box in the truck and then climbed in the cab next to Rich for the short ride to the quay. Mickey stared at the big yacht in awe as Rich parked.

"Shit! This aint a boat, it's a fuckin` ship!" he exclaimed. "When you said fifty-meters I didn't really stop to figure out what it was in feet."

"A meter is about thirty-nine inches and that makes this boat a tad over a hundred and sixty feet, we could probably get lost on it," JD said

"I think you'll find the accommodations to your liking," Rich said then chuckled.

"You're going to be a little surprised when you meet the captain." He helped them load their gear up the gangway and forward to the wing deck next to the pilothouse, then opened the door into the forward pilot house control and navigation area.

JD and Mickey were stunned as a large, completely bald black man with skin the color of dark rich teakwood with hulking shoulders and a thick neck and chest tapering to a hard midsection supported by massively strong legs turned from the chart table.

"Welcome aboard, gentlemen," he said in a deep stentorian tone. "I'm the delivery captain for this voyage and the name's Lawrence T Mulloy. He strode over and shook hands with JD. "You'd be, JD?" he said, then turned when JD nodded and shook with Mickey, "and you're Mickey. Rich here tells me you boys are from the South. It may surprise you to hear I'm originally from Loxley, Alabama; either one of you know where that is?"

"Hell, yes!" JD exclaimed. "I'm from the Eastern Shore and Mickey is from Monroeville."

"Well, I'll be god-dogged if this aint ole home week," Captain Mulloy said grinning, exposing perfect white teeth.

"It's a damn small world," JD said. "How the hell did a dude like you wind up in England running luxury yachts, Captain?"

"First off, forget the 'Captain,' my friends call me LT," Captain Mulloy replied. "It's a kind of long story. To make it short, I played strong safety for Ole Miss and got drafted by the Falcons in the fifth round. They put me on the taxi squad and then sent me to England to play in NFL Europe for a year. I tore up a knee halfway through the season and decided to spend rehad studying at the maritime school. The knee never came around and I got hooked on yachts when a friend of mine put me together with a crusty old retired Royal Navy Captain. He helped me get my masters ticket and the rest as they say, is history."

"Why don't you go back to the states and run 'em over there?" JD asked.

"For one thing, there aren't many really big yacht manufacturers in the states," LT replied. "For another, I aint seen any black captains running luxury yachts over there."

"You might be right," JD muttered. "I haven't been on any really big ones myself, but if I win the lottery and buy one, you'll be the man runnin' it."

"I'll keep that in mind," LT said jovially then slapped JD on the shoulder. "When you hit it, I'll be expecting a call," he added smiling.

He turned and rattled off instructions to a young Italian man as he entered the pilothouse from the main salon, then turned back to JD and Mickey.

"Aldo, will help you stow your gear in the lazarette and show you to your quarters," he said glancing at his watch. "The port captain is due in three hours, get settled in, have a nap and stay out of sight until Aldo comes down to get you. This particular port captain is a pretty good friend of mine and he won't do anything, but drink a cup of coffee and stamp the exit papers." He followed them outside the pilothouse as they were leaving and then glanced at the trunk. "You'll need to stow that case under the extra line and bumpers in the lazarette aft in case the port captain surprises me and wants to inspect the ship. If he does, try to avoid him and keep your mouths shut." Mickey grabbed one end of the trunk.

"LT, I got a good idea where aft is," he mumbled. "But, I aint got the faintest idea what the hell a lazarette is." LT swung around to Rich.

"I thought you said they were experienced seaman?" he snapped in an irritated tone of voice.

"JD is a very experienced seaman," Rich said nervously glancing at JD for confirmation. "Mickey don't know a lot, but he'll make a good deckhand with a little training." JD spoke up.

"I spent most of my boy-hood and leave-time for a lot of years racing one designs on closed courses and pretty good size sailboats offshore. I'll be able to stand some watches as soon as you update me on the navigation systems when we get on the open sea."

"That'll be fine," LT said relieved. "You'll be able to get up to snuff pretty quick. All these electronics are pretty idiot proof once you know how to operate 'em " he added nodding back at the control station. JD hefted his end of the trunk and they followed Aldo aft.

"Why do I always get the shit details?" Mickey groused as Aldo lowered the trunk down to them in the lazarette.

"like you said, I'm the shooter and smarter," JD replied grinning.

"I'm gonna' smart your ass one of these days," Mickey grumped.

"Don't get yer panties in a wad," JD said. "It aint my fault you never learned about boats during your boy-scout days." Mickey ground his teeth and glared balefully at him.

"You ever mention Boy Scout again," he hissed. "There will be consequences." They walked back to the pilothouse to see where LT wanted them to bunk and found him with Rich sitting at the chart table drinking coffee. They rose and then LT motioned for them to follow him back through a large galley with every appliance a gourmet cook could ever want or need to a beautifully furnished dining room with seating for twelve around a baroque, polished teakwood table with matching chairs. Aldo emerged from the galley carrying a platter of scrambled eggs, sausage and warm rolls, then went back and returned with a silver coffee pot. JD eyed the ornate silver cutlery and fine china settings.

"Whoever owns this boat sure likes to live right!" he exclaimed.

"The gentleman is an oilman and he do enjoy his comforts," LT replied smiling, then waved an arm to indicate their sumptuous surroundings. "Can't say, I aint lookin' forward to livin' like a king for the next week or ten days myself and people who own mega-yachts, don't mind paying a high price to make sure their new play toy arrives in good shape."

As they were finishing the meal, Rich glanced at his watch, then hastily pushed back from the table and rose.

I have to get moving," he said, "We're supposed to start laying up the hull on a 28 meter Sports fisherman early this morning. We build the smaller boats with fiberglass and I need to be there to make sure the laminates go in as specified."

JD and Mickey got up to shake hands and JD patted Rich on the shoulder as they moved aft through the main salon to the aft deck catwalk.

"You take care," he said. "I won't try to tell you how grateful we are for your help. You ever need a couple 'a old operators you just let Alphonce know and we'll be here."

"I'm happy I could do a small favor," Rich said. He trotted down to his truck, then waved and called back to them, "have a safe trip home. I hope we can get together again."

Aldo accompanied them below to two lavishly appointed staterooms, each with separate private baths equipped with gold plated fixtures. Mickey stowed his gear and then walked across the companionway to JD's stateroom. "I could get used to this in a hurry!" he exclaimed. "You got any idea what one 'a these things cost?"

"Don't even think about it," JD grunted. "We couldn't afford to park this bitch, much less buy fuel for it."

"Wasn't thinkin' about buyin' one," Mickey snapped. "I just figured with you being such a famous all wise yachtsman you might be able to answer the question."

"Sorry," JD said. "One as big and plush as this would cost ten to twenty million to buy and around a million a year to hire a crew and maintain it."

Aldo interrupted to ask their sizes, then disappeared for a few minutes before returning with deck shoes and casual yachting clothes. He made sure they were satisfied and then said in broken English, "Captain LT, he saya you takea shorta nap untila porta capitain he be gone."

JD took a long hot bath in the jaquzzi tub, rose to rinse off under the shower, dried off and put some boxer shorts and a T-shirt Aldo had provided and then laid down on the queen size bed and was asleep within moments.

★ **Chapter Thirty One** ★

May 28, 1993, 11:00 hours
Portici, Italy

JD awoke as the intercom on the bulkhead next to his berth came to life.

"Rise and shine," LT said. "The port captain just left and its time for us to get underway." He quickly donned deck shoes, shorts and a tee shirt with 'Avianca' emblazoned across the back then crossed to Mickey's stateroom and found a note on his berth.

"I got to feeling a little weird so decided to go on deck for some air." JD considered looking for him but decided he was probably just a little seasick and headed up to the pilothouse to join LT. He spent a few minutes with LT going over the control systems and navigation gear and was amazed at the amount of electronics, radar, navigation gear and redundant systems arrayed around and above the control station.

"Jeez, other than armaments, this thing is equipped for war!" he exclaimed.

"Except for deck-mounted guns we've got state-of-the-art hardware," LT said chuckling. "There are some small arms on board in case any uninvited modern-day pirates decide they want to come aboard."

"We've got some hardware that'll really fuck 'em up," JD said and then followed LT out to the wing deck on the starboard side and he nodded at Aldo standing on the dock by the bow line.

"How 'bout you take in the bow and spring lines, then go aft and help Mickey with the stern," he said then guffawed and went back in the pilot house chuckling, when JD snapped to attention, gave him a stiff military salute and barked, "Aye sir." JD felt a sense of serenity for the first time in what seemed years as he singled up the bow and spring lines then trotted aft to help Mickey. I don't know whether it's being aboard this fine yacht or I didn't realize how much I missed getting out on open water.

LT idled the powerful MTU diesels up slightly, reversed the starboard engine, put the port forward and the helm hard to starboard, engaged the bow thruster to hold the vessel along side the pier until Aldo climbed back aboard. Once, Aldo was on deck he put the helm hard to port, idled the starboard engine forward, reversed the thruster powered up the port engine aft, and slipped the large yacht away from the dock. When she was twenty meters away, he shut the thruster down, engaged both engines forward, put the helm amidships, powered up for headway and then headed for the sea buoy at the harbor's entrance. JD watched LT calmly handle the big yacht as they left the red buoy to port.

"Man, that was nice," he said. "I've run boats up to sixty feet, but wasn't sure how you did it on a big one like this."

"A boats' a boat," LT replied. "They all handle about the same. You just have to remember one this size has a lot more carry and it costs a helluva' lot more if you fuck up.

"What's our schedule?" JD asked.

"Cranked up, this lady will do twenty five knots," LT replied. "Since she's brand new we'll cruise at around fifteen or sixteen. That should put us at the mouth of the Thames in seven or eight days." He paused a moment then glanced at JD. "You think you'll be able to stand a watch now and then? Aldo aint really capable of making a decision in an emergency and there aint any doubt you can."

"Sure," JD replied. "I was raised near the Gulf of Mexico and raced the Southern ocean racing circuit several times, the Bermuda race twice and Cowes week once. The only piece of equipment I'm not familiar with is Sat nav. When I was sailing we used the Loran system in U.S. waters and the Decca system around England."

"That sounds fine," LT said. "After we get out on the open sea I'll spend a little time with you and you'll find Sat Nav. is a lot simpler than Loran. Why don't you relax and enjoy the view for a couple of hours?"

"I'll do that," JD replied. "We haven't had a helluva` lot of time for sight-seeing since we arrived in Italy."

"Don't reckon you have," LT grunted. "You mind answering one question?"

"Not a bit," JD replied. "Hell, LT if we didn't trust you we'd have been pretty stupid to get on this boat in the first place. Ask anything you like and I'll do my best to give you an honest answer." LT hesitated. I got a good idea what these two guys have been up to. I wonder if knowing for sure changes anything? Then again, they're already on board so I got to ask.

"You and Mickey aren't by chance the ones that popped a cap in that terrorist a few days ago?" JD could see his slight hesitation, I aint gonna` lie to this man, he's the first guy I've met since the Nam that I know I can trust.

"Yeah," he replied.

"Well...I don't think we got to worry about any pirates," LT muttered. "From the way the media described it, you shot that asshole from better than five hundred meters. Then, you and Mickey exterminated ten of his bodyguards and another dozen or so over the next couple of days."

"They exaggerated the range a little," JD muttered. "But, if we get in a long range shootin` contest with anybody there's a great chance we'll come out on top."

"I never thought I'd meet a couple of guys you read about in action books," LT said.

"I'm glad to have you on board and happy to call ya'll friends `a mine."

"We are your friends and our friendship is for good or bad times and life long," JD said. He nodded aft. "I'm going aft to see what Mickey's up to. Just give me a holler when you want me."

He found Mickey sitting on the aft deck lounge with his rifle and the RPG propped up beside him.

"What the fuck are you doin` sitting here with those things in plain sight?!" he exclaimed.

"Lookin` for rag-heads in helicopters," Mickey snapped back.

"It aint a bad idea, but you need to keep 'em under cover," JD said then noticed Mickey was a little green around the gills.

"How long is this trip gonna' take? I aint feelin' to red hot," Mickey groaned

"About seveor eight days," JD replied. "We aren't even in the Med. yet and it's a beautiful day. There aint any reason for you to be gittin' seasick."

"Why do you think I hate boats?!" Mickey rasped.

"You weren't sick on Marty's and this one's six times as big. What the hell's wrong with you?"

"A little boat that bounces around instead slow rolling like this one does, don't bother me," Mickey groused.

"I've heard it helps if you take deep breaths and concentrate on lookin' at the horizon," JD said sympathetically.

"I'll try it," Mickey said weakly. "I sure wish I hadn't eaten that big breakfast."

"You feel like you have to throw up?" JD asked, edging out of range. "Make sure you do it over the leeward rail or it'll blow back in your face."

"Shit! which one's leeward?" Mickey asked irritably.

"Engage your brain and you'll be able to figure out it's the one opposite from where the winds coming from."

"It's bad enough having to listen to your smart remarks when I feel good JD, how 'bout holdin' the wisecracks until I get better," Mickey muttered, rose, stumbled across to the rail and then proceeded to unload his breakfast over the side.

JD watched him for a moment, and was startled when he leaned further over the rail and heaved. The crazy bastard is going to fall overboard, he thought. He opened the lazarette hatch, climbed down to find a foul-weather harness then brought it back on deck and found Mickey sitting miserably by the rail. "Here, this'll keep you from going over the side," he said, then strapped it on Mickey and snapped the lifeline to a stanchion. "I'm going to get a little shut eye."

Each stateroom had its individual climate control system. JD set the thermostat to it's lowest temperature, then got undressed and took another steaming hot shower, put on fresh skivvies then flopped in the plush berth. Man it would be nice if we were going all the way across the Atlantic. This is the first time since the Royal Sonesta that I got control of the thermostat. I aint been this relaxed in years. Two hours later the intercom snapped him out of a deep dreamless sleep.

"Rise an shine, JD!" LT barked. "It's three forty-five, press the button on the side of the intercom, if you want to talk." JD shook himself awake and then punched the intercom.

"I'll be up in fifteen minutes." He got dressed, then went topside to check on Mickey and found him nodding in and out of sleep in an overstuffed leather lounge on the aft deck.

"Looks like you might survive," JD said chuckling.

"Aldo mixed up some kinda' iced lime drink with Vodka and it seemed to settle me down."

"I'm going forward to help LT. Just relax and get some rest, if you decide to go down to the stateroom, it might help to turn the air to freeze," he said then headed forward to the pilothouse. LT glanced at him as he entered and grinned.

"Evenin', looks like yachting just might agree with you."

"You got that right," JD replied chuckling. "I feel like a new man. There's nothing like a fine boat on the open sea for workin' the kinks out of ones psyche. Besides, this is the first time in weeks that we haven't had to worry about a bunch 'a pissed off terrorists showin' up with blood in their eyes. Barring submarines...I reckon we're about as safe as we've been in years."

"Submarines!" LT exclaimed, visibly alarmed

"Just kidding," JD said grinning. "That's one thing we don't need to worry about.

The U.S. Navy has the Med. covered like white on rice. That idiot in Libya is crazy as a run-over dog, but he don't want to tangle with Navy tom-cats again or any attack Subs or destroyers since they're cruising around hoping he does something stupid so they can take a few Libyan scalps."

"You do have a way of getting a man's attention," LT grunted. "Submarines, aint a damn bit funny."

"Figured that might wake you up," JD said laughing . "By the way, you got any plans for unloading us when we get to the Thames?"

"I'm supposed to deliver this lady to South Hampton and figured on dropping anchor off Cowes, then running you two ashore with the launch at night. Cowes race-week starts next week and the fleet's in. Launches, are running drunken yachtsmen back and forth all night so nobody is going to notice a couple more guys coming in. You've raced Cowes before, so you know how wild some 'a those dudes get."

"Yeah, that's where I learned what a peeler was," JD mused.

"A peeler? What the hell you talkin' 'bout?" LT asked puzzled.

"We were sailing a fast ultra light. I looked at a few British boats and asked one of the Brits why the hell they built 'em so heavy. He looked at me kind of funny and asked which boat I was on. When I told him he paused a moment and then asked if it was an ultra light. When I answered yes. He smiled.

"Good luck, chap. You're going to need it as you'll probably meet a few peelers out there." When I inquired what the hell that was, he replied that it was a fairly common wave one meets occasionally in the English channel or at Lands end in rough weather that doesn't just wash over the bow or stern. Rather it kind of stands up and slaps down on the deck to let one know one is not really quite as in charge as one thinks in these waters. They're called 'peelers' because they tend to peel the deck off of boats that aren't sturdily built. "I found out he was right two days after the race started. We were a lot faster than any boat in our class until we ran into foul weather at Lands end and were lucky to limp into Padstow over in Wales."

LT smiled. "There's no doubt the English channel can get rough," he grunted. "What do you think about my idea for getting you ashore?"

"Sounds fine to me," JD replied. "We've got some friends we met on a couple of joint operations with the SAS I know can be trusted. I'll get in touch with them for help as soon as we get ashore and here aint anything those guys can't do."

"Glad to hear you'll be in good hands," LT said sincerely then led JD to the chart table. We'll be leaving the Gulf and get into the Med. about ten tonight. I've got the Auto pilot on and we should be south of Corsica mid-afternoon tomorrow, then we'll set a course to pass seventy kilometers south of Majorca." He spent the next hour teaching JD how to operate the navigation systems then stepped forward, down a half flight of companionway steps to the captains quarters.

"If anything comes up, hit the intercom and sound off," he said over his shoulder.

"I've got it, go get some rest," JD said.

As they negotiated the strait the next afternoon, Mickey joined LT and JD in the pilot-house looking relaxed and happy.

"You seem to be feeling a lot better," JD said smiling.

"I had a couple more of Aldo's concoctions and went down to my room, turned the air down and slept for a good ten hours." Mickey said. "What does he mix in those things, LT?"

"Don't rightly know," LT replied chuckling. "Whatever it is, is probably illegal but it sure works."

They were well rested and completely relaxed as they arrived at the straits of Gibraltar a few days later. Other than two smaller yachts and a couple of tramp steamers encountered South of the Balearic islands which posed no threat, there had been no sign of opposition and they were sure that no one other than Rich and Alphonce were aware of their escape route. The voyage had been a pleasure cruise.

Two days later, LT dropped anchor a kilometer off Cowes harbor as the sun slipped below the horizon. They packed the gear and weapons in the trunk, but left the RPG. JD had decided to leave with LT and Mickey was relieved that he wouldn't have to tote it anymore.

"You might need this one day," JD said as he explained how to load and fire it. This will more than get their attention if any pirates decide to give you any trouble."

"Thanks," LT said. "It'll be quite a surprise for some enterprising buccaneer one of these days."

Chapter Thirty Two

June 5, 1993, 21:00 hours
The River Thames
United Kingdom

LT left Aldo on watch aboard the yacht, then launched a twenty-seven foot Boston Whaler off the boat deck with the starboard davit. He helped JD and Mickey lower the trunk down to the whaler then ferried them into the dock. They tied up, hailed a taxi and LT directed the driver to a small inn owned by a friend of his. JD and Mickey signed the register, using false passports Smith had provided and then trailed LT back outside.

"You've been a God-send," JD said. "You've helped a couple of old frayed around the edges operatives out of an extremely bad fix. Call this number if you ever have the type problem we're used to handling and we'll give you a hand," he said handing LT a card.

It's been a pleasure sailing with you," LT said. "I've always felt lucky and a tad guilty I came of age during a time, when there weren't any wars to be fought. I reckon, there aint any reason to be feeling that way anymore since I've helped a couple of guys that rid the world of a really evil terrorist."

"If it weren't for people like you, Rich, Alphonce and his family we'd probably be dead and CNN and the Democrats would be screaming about hard-right elements of the opposition using covert operatives in direct contravention of executive orders. We're going to get back over here for a get-together with our friends when things cool down and you'll damn sure be on the party list." They shook hands warmly then stood by the curb and waved farewell as LT climbed back in the taxi for the return to his ship.

"Were you serious?," Mickey asked. You've promised half the people in Europe we'd head over here to handle any trouble they might have. That could keep us busy for years."

"As a heart attack, JD replied. If it weren't for each an every one of them, we'd be dead.

Their room was on the second floor and after locking the weapons and gear up, they tucked their side arms under their jackets, then started walking the few blocks back to the harbor to see if there were as many Americans in town as LT had said. Finding it fairly quiet on the street, they decided to continue another block to a pub across the street from the Royal Yacht Squadron was stationed for the week. From the sound level it seemed to be the only place in town catering to the late night yachting crowd. JD preceded Mickey inside and found it jammed with sailors from all over the world, most of them well into their cups. He surveyed the boisterous crowd for a few moments and then nudged Mickey.

"We need to get the fuck out of here," he muttered. "It's too loud to use a public phone and with all of these drunks pushin' and shoving; Taking into account your short fuse, I smell trouble."

"You can leave, if you want to," Mickey said sharply. "We walked a mile to get here and I'm gonna' have at least one cold beer before I go anywhere."

Before JD could protest, he nudged his way to the bar and in the process offended a group of three boisterous Frenchmen. One, a particularly large young man, well over six feet tall and appearing to be two hundred-fifty or so pounds glared at Mickey. He, like most young men his size who had never been locked in mortal perilous conflict was used to intimidating men smaller in stature by puffing his chest out and cursing them. When Mickey ignored him completely and turned to the bar-keep, he became more irate.

"You got any beer on ice?" Mickey called over the noisy crowd.

"Sure, Yank," the barman replied. "What boat are you sailing on?"

"No boat, we're just passing through," Mickey replied. JD squeezed in next to him and nodded at the barman.

"We don't care what brand of beer you have as long as it's ice cold," he said glaring at Mickey. Mickey returned JD's look then muttered, "Don't get edgy, I aint gonna' start any trouble."

"It aint you I'm worried about," JD said quietly. "It's what this idiot behind us is going to do." He turned back to the bar as the barman slid two lagers across, hoping the fool would calm.

"You lads from the South?" the barman inquired.

"How'd you figure that out?" Mickey asked.

"I was stationed in Germany a few years back," The barman said smiling. "We went on joint maneuvers with the second armored division a couple of times. There were quite a few Southern Yanks in that outfit and it's not an accent one forgets." He reached across the bar to shake hands with them. "The name's Sean, it's nice to meet you, gentlemen," he said, then glanced at the big Frenchman, who was getting more agitated as Mickey continued to ignore him. "During race week it gets a little boisterous as the night wears on, but most of the chaps are decent enough." Mickey introduced JD and himself.

"Nice meeting you," Sean said. And then he had to turn to wait on customers at the other end of the bar.

JD glanced back at the Frenchman, noticed he was on the verge of making a very large mistake and nudged Mickey.

"If this big idiot starts something," he muttered. "Please try not to fuck him up real bad. We sure as hell don't need to get famous the first night we're in England." The Frenchman overheard, obviously couldn't understand exactly what was being said and turned to one of his companion's for a translation.

Mickey switched positions slightly to keep an eye on the man and then glanced at JD.

"You know I can't stand frogs. He fucks with me he will regret it."

"That's fine, you can spank him a little," JD muttered. "But, I'm serious, when I say it would not be wise to fuck him up bad."

After the big Frenchman's friend translated. He made the mistake of grabbing Mickey's left shoulder. Mickey spun on the ball of his right foot with blazing speed, grasped the man's arm in a vise-like grip, yanked his right shoulder down, then delivered a bone-breaking kick to the side of his right knee. The Frenchman yelped in pain and Mickey finished the move by ducking under the mans arm as he lost control of his leg and began to fall, and then rose behind and twisted the arm to the breaking point. He was preparing to cave in the big man's ribs with a knee when JD stepped in.

"Dammit don't do it" Mickey turned glaring at JD.

"You could fuck up a one-car funeral," he snapped. Still glaring at JD he twisted the Frenchman's arm just enough to pop his shoulder out of socket then released him and stepped back as the man screamed in pain and collapsed on the floor, groaning loudly. The big man's two friends stepped back, staring down in stunned disbelief at the goliath they had watched intimidate themselves and others for years until Mickey turned his attention to them.

"You boys lookin` for any more trouble?" he asked quietly.

"Uh no sir, no trouble!" the one who spoke English exclaimed as they backed away.

"Good." Mickey said relaxing. "No problem, but you need to drag this piece `a shit outta` here."

Mickey turned back to the bar ignoring them and JD watched as they helped the big man up yelping in pain and then stumbled out of the pub. JD swung back to Mickey.

"I hope you're satisfied," he snapped. "I asked you not to fuck the guy up."

"No, you didn't ask, you told me not to," Mickey replied mildly. "Besides I didn't do any permanent damage. His knee's a little fucked up but they can pop his shoulder back in easy."

"Don't tell me how easy it is to pop a shoulder in," JD rasped. "I know how that feels." He glanced up and noticed Sean standing behind the bar with a smile playing across his face.

"I'm real sorry about that, Sean," he said. "Mickey sometimes gets a little carried away when somebody he don't know tries to push him around." He paused to turn a baleful eye on Mickey, then continued. "We hope, it didn't upset you much." Sean smiled and shoved two more beers across the bar.

"On the house, that chap has been quite a pest for the past few days," he said. "I feel the same way Mickey does about loud obnoxious frogs." He hesitated a moment. "Don't take this wrong, both of you are more than welcome here at any time, but I fear that trio will lodge a complaint with the local constabulary and they will be here looking for the man who did so much damage to that big, bloody arsehole."

"You're probably right," JD said. "Thanks for your hospitality. We'll see you the next time we're in the neighborhood." He paused a few seconds then put a hundred dollar bill on the counter. "I'd appreciate it if anybody asks, you could forget we're Americans," he said. "The money is for the beer and any inconvenience we've caused." Sean accepted the hundred and smiled.

"You certainly appear to be a couple of Aussies to me," he said chuckling.

They left the pub and had strolled a block up the street toward the Inn when a police cruiser sped by, blue lights flashing, its ding-dong blasting and then came to a screeching halt in front of the pub. Two Bobbies got out and hustled inside.

"You think, Sean will stick to the story?" Mickey muttered.

"Don't know," JD replied. "I hope, he does, it aint any skin off his ass either way."

They waited in the shadows, ready to duck down a convenient alley until the Bobbies came out and got back in the cruiser, then switched the lights and ding-dong bells off and pulled slowly away to continue their patrol. JD waited until they were out of sight then turned to Mickey.

"looks like he stuck to it," he said. "There's a call-box up the street, I'll try to call Chris and ask him if he can come up with a way to get us transportation back to the States without anybody hearing about it."

Chapter Thirty Three

Three June 4, 1993, 0:500 hours
Arlington, Virginia
United States of America

The bedside phones insistent ringing jarred Don Mayer awake. He sat up and stepped in his slippers then minced around the king-size bed to unplug it. I should have roused the lovely boy and changed sides of the bed last night. I just didn't have the heart, he was so wonderfully receptive and I didn't realize sleeping on a different side of the bed would disturb my sleep pattern so much. That and the thought of facing another long arduous day with Angus Ewing, A.K.A. Mr. Smith to the covert team they had lost contact with ten days before had made for a very restless night. He had realized the two killers had disposed of the comm when he received word that the stupid Arabs had attacked some poor chicken farmer on the road to Salerno. The only thing they had accomplished was killing a truckload of chickens and further convincing Angus that the number one thug was right when he'd told him someone in Control was homing in on the comm to locate him and his malevolent sidekick for the terrorists.

On receiving the report of the attack on the chicken farmer from a contact in Italy, Angus got busy scouring the records trying to figure out who was leaking the information and how they were doing it. Don's heart had skipped a beat and he'd been in a constant state of fear and agitation since Angus had informed him as he was leaving the day before that he was bringing in outside electronics and computer experts to help apprehend the culprit.

He felt a shadow of doom pressing on his narrow shoulders. The thought of being arrested, disgraced and ultimately imprisoned appalled him. He knew, given his small, pudgy physique coupled with an overlarge cherubic face and round pinkish lips that he would quickly become the bitch for an uncounted number of horrible slavering convicts.

The seemingly endless night he'd spent after the lovely boy went to sleep worrying Angus and his minions might be able to trace the equipment he was using to track the sending unit until approaching the problem from every angle he couldn't see how they could trace the equipment to him even if they found the tracking equipment. The only link to him was the congressman who had provided it and he felt given their past amatory involvement, he would keep his word that nothing would be done to implicate Don. He fidgeted knowing the phone call had to have been Angus. No one else would be awake at this ungodly hour, he thought. I should have realized this day might come when Bernie called me at EPA and invited me to his apartment to tell me he and certain members of the Whitehouse staff had purged my FBI file of that ridiculous child molestation charge in Mobile. I thought he was doing it because he has the same proclivities for young boys as I do. If he hadn't told me the position he and certain members of the justice department had acquired for me at Control Associates would double my income. I would still be at EPA doing everything in my power to bring private enterprise to it's knees. God knows what is to become of me. My only hope is Bernie told the boy to let me know he was close to having enough evidence to be able to call for hearings and expose the whole murderous cabal and the right wing backers funding them. He thinks when those hearings take place that I will be a star witness and the President will undoubtedly award me a citizenship medal. He finished dressing and softly closed the front door of his condo to avoid waking the sleeping boy. He locked it then got in his VW bug for the short drive to Controls offices located in the business district of Arlington, Virginia.

Parking behind the office building and boarding the elevator up to the offices on the fourth floor a frightening thought hit him hard.

My lord what if Angus connects me to the leaks and passes the information to those malevolent thugs. As he entered the office suite which took up the entire floor of the four story building, consisting of an anteroom with an older woman who served as dual receptionist, secretary and file clerk. There were file cabinet along each wall backing up to Angus's office on the right and Don's on the left. There was a communications room behind reception that was manned by a six man crew on revolving shifts twenty four seven.

As Don entered, Angus barked, "The Italian authorities have an Englishman in custody and he's been screaming about two American operatives kidnapping him and three other British citizens. The one they have in custody gave the Italians the names of the other three Brits who were supposed to have been kidnapped and swore the killers who took them were Americans. The British authorities have confirmed that the three he named are safely on British soil and have strongly denied ever being kidnapped in the first place."

"That's quite puzzling," Don muttered, his mind racing at the possibilities.

"It is," Angus growled. "The State departments screaming and tearing their hair out trying to find who is responsible so they can be served up to the White House."

The secretary answered a call and said, "It's for you Don." Don shut the door to his office before picking up the phone.

"What's going on?" the lovely boy asked. "It's still dark outside and I was planning to fix you a delicious breakfast."

"Nothing for you to be concerned with," Don replied softly. "Why don't you hang around today love? There's plenty to eat and drink in the fridge. I should be home in time to fix us a wonderful dinner."

"That sounds marvelous," the lad purred. "I'll just make myself comfy andlook forward to what we're going to do tonight."

With lascivious thoughts of the boy and another night of debauchery, Don had to jerk himself back to reality.

The old bitch in reception was a constant source of irritation to him as she refused to unlock a file cabinet or turn over any files unless he signed for them and she watched the copy machine like a hawk if he had a file and always demanded that he return it to her before leaving.. On the one occasion he had approached Angus to ask for his own key to the office and file cabinets he'd been rebuffed.

"You don't need one," Angus had replied gruffly the first week Don had arrived on the job. "Nobody is allowed in the office but the communications staff unless I'm here. They don't have a key to the files and they know there is an alarm system if someone were to try to open them without my authorization and some rather unpleasant individuals would arrive shortly after the alarm went off."

That information had stopped any ideas Don had to get in the office and files at night to aid the congressman's effort to find enough information on the organization to hold hearings.

"The shits hit the fan over at State," Angus snapped.

"What's the status?" Don asked, desperately trying to remain calm.

"We have to figure out whether one of our contacts in Italy is betraying the team; you got any ideas?"

"No sir," Don replied. "I'll get my computer going and start checking our contacts right away."

"How long will that take?" Angus snapped.

"Two or three hours," Don replied. He excused himself then crossed to his office, quietly closed the door and then leaning back against it ,sighed in relief. *So far so good, I wonder where those thugs are. The fools in Libya think they are still in Italy. They are idiots and there is no way I can contact them to tell them to forget it with Angus charging around like a bull in a china shop. The chances they are still in Italy are beyond belief. If Angus gets the slightest whiff someone here is communicating with them. He'll be on the entire staff like stink on shit and if he decides to put me under surveillance, I'm in deep trouble.* He sat down to boot his computer up. Thinking about the boy back at the condo stirred the beginnings of an erection until he chided himself, *Don, Angus will keep you until all hours if you don't take care of things here.*

Chapter Thirty Four

★   **Chapter Thirty Four**   ★

June 6, 1993, 23:30 hours
Cowes harbor
United Kingdom.

JD punched the home number Captain Chris Washington had given him the prior year on a joint operation with the SAS fervently hoping he hadn't had a fight with his wife and she'd kicked him out. He fondly remembered Chris as a younger man of medium height, with a fair complexion and a short thatch of almost white hair. JD's first impression on meeting him during a joint forces briefing was that he didn't appear to be built for the brutal training and physical torture the SAS put its troops through. Any doubts he had were quickly proved wrong when he, Mickey and Chris stumbled across an Iraqi outpost during the Gulf war. While JD was waiting on Mickey to take the outpost out he noticed Chris had disappeared and then heard the muffled grunts of dying men. He spent the next few moments wondering where the hell Chris was until he and Mickey flopped back down beside him. Mickey wiped the blade of his knife on his desert camo trousers and then turned to JD.

"You aint gonna believe this," he muttered. "I think I've met a man that's faster with a knife than me." Thinking about that operation and the time they had spent with Chris on R & R after the war, JD recalled him as the most frenetic individual he had ever met.

The phone rang four times before an answering machine came on.

"Hello, you have reached Chris and Toni's call screening device. If you are selling something or have in mind changing our long distance service hang up immediately. Otherwise please state the time, your name and a good reason for interrupting our quiet solitude. Then, on the occasion that we are here we might decide to pick up. In the event we happen to be out and after hearing your message deem it worthwhile one of us will return your call. I presume whoever you are that you are of sound mind and know to wait for the beep, Ta Ta.' JD waited for the beep and barked.

"Chris, you bloody British snot, pick up the damn phone, this is JD!" He waited a moment then was getting ready to leave the Inns number and the name they were registered under when Chris answered.

"JD!" he exclaimed. "How the hell have you two scoundrels managed to stay out of the gaol since I last saw you?"

"It aint been easy," JD replied. "Especially being saddled with a loose cannon like Mickey." He paused for a moment then continued, "Uh...we're in Cowes and have a big problem and you're the only man in England I know we can trust."

"Say no more," Chris said. "I've been watching the Telly for the last week or so and knew it had to be the two of you. That operation was classic JD and Mickey for those of us who have seen you in action."

"Shit! I didn't know we were that transparent," JD groused.

"Just to those who are familiar with you and that's a very select few," Chris said.

"I knew there weren't but maybe two or three long shooters in the world who could put three in a target at that range with a sound suppressor after seeing the report on the number of adversaries and distances involved. I especially liked the coup-de-gras. Leonardo Da Vinci couldn't have put his head back together after three head shots with a 357 Magnum. That was another indication you were the guilty party as I know how much you rely on that idiotic six shooter of yours."

"How the hell did you find out I was using a sound suppressor?" JD asked puzzled.

"Had to have been," Chris stated flatly. "From the way the newswoman and her cameraman described the events, the whole cabal of terrorists never knew where you were firing from or even two murderous miscreants like you and Mickey might have found it difficult to eliminate all of them."

"The first shot was pretty good," JD said with a touch of pride. "And, I took 'em while one of the terrorists emptied a full clip at me."

"So much for the Arab penchant for wasting ammunition with an automatic weapon," Chris said chuckling. "I presume he paid dearly for the error of his ways."

"Oh yeah! He's wending his way to paradise or hell. You think anyone else has figured out who it was?"

"A few men in my company that know you," Chris replied. "But, you certainly don't need to worry about them. I don't imagine anyone will make the connection for a while as I wasn't completely sure until I saw the diagrams."

" What diagrams," JD asked alarmed.

"Guess you haven't had much time to watch the news," Chris muttered. "Fox , CNN, Sky news and BBC have diagrammed the location of everyone involved, alive or dead. Considering the number of bodies littering the landscape from the original operation and several other actions over the next few days I knew there weren't but two operatives in the world sneaky enough to create so much mayhem and then walk away unscathed. You are in decent shape chap?" he asked a note of concern in his voice.

"Other than a few nicks and bruises we're fine," JD replied.

"By the by…what ever did you do to get one of our citizens so disturbed?" Chris asked. "Don't answer that," he said chuckling. "I've met the ladies involved and have a pretty good idea." He waited for JD to reply for a moment, then when none was forth-coming continued, down to business. There is an old fighter base a few miles west of your location that ou shouldn't have a problem finding as any cabbie will know of it. Get some sleep and be there at 0:500 this morning, I'll be down in a light plane to pick you up and transport you to a safe house until we can come up with a way to quietly get you back to the States. He hesitated for a few moments. "I don't know whether you've figured it out, but considering the difficulties encountered since the operation I feel there is a traitor somewhere in your organization."

"No doubt," JD growled. "He is going to be one cold dead mother-fucker when we find him."

They checked out of the inn at 0:400, asked the night clerk to call a taxi and waited in front until it braked to a stop at the curb. After loading the gear and weapons in the boot Mickey slid in the front passenger seat and asked the grizzled cabby if he knew where the old airfield was.

"Sure Mate," the old man said. "It's abandoned but still used by small planes during daylight hours. There isn't anyone operating the tower so it's pretty well deserted at night." He pulled away from the curb and glanced over at Mickey. "Ye be meeting a plane, Yank?"

"Uh huh," Mickey muttered. "We're not sure about the time so I'd appreciate it if you would stay with us until it arrives."

"Don't mind at all, but I'll have to keep the meter running." JD passed a fifty-dollar bill to Mickey.

"Give him this, it ought to buy us an hour or so." The grizzled old man snatched the bill out of Mickey's hand.

"Righto Yank," he said.

When they arrived at the airport JD told the driver to back into an abandoned hangar. After they came to a stop inside he got out and retrieved his rifle out of the boot to assemble it and then turned as Mickey stepped out of the cab.

"I'll climb up in the control tower and keep an eye out until Chris gets here. You and the driver take cover somewhere outside."

Becoming curious, the cabbie got out to see what they were up to and saw the rifle.

"Hey mate!" he yelped. "I don't want to be involved in an assassination." Mickey snatched his MP-5 out of the trunk and turned to the old man.

"Just calm down," he said. "We aint gonna' kill anybody if they don't attack us. And, you won't come to any harm unless you're stupid enough to cause a problem."

"Er...oh no," the old man stuttered. "Ye just let me know where ye want me." JD watched until they took cover behind some pallets stacked next to the hangar, and then trotted to the tower's circular stairway.

As the Eastern sky turned pink, heralding the breaking dawn. A twin engine light plane with Royal Air force markings circled the field twice then made an approach from the South, touched down and taxied to the apron in front of the hangar. JD stayed in the tower covering the plane's exit hatch until Chris yanked it open and hopped down on the tarmac. Mickey stepped from behind the pallets and waved at him, then hustled back to the taxi with the driver to retrieve the trunk and gear. Chris scanning the area for, JD noticed him climbing down from the tower and then jogged over to let the cabbie know it was a military operation and warned him to keep his silence.

They waited until the cab was gone, then Chris turned to JD smiling.

"I suppose not trusting a soul is the reason you two have survived all these years, " he said chuckling.

"That's bullshit!" JD exclaimed. "You know damn well we trust you, but we couldn't be sure who was on the plane." Chris laughed.

"If, I were you, considering the trouble you've had for the past week or so I don't think I would trust the President."

"Shit! we'd trust that madman in Libya before puttin' any faith in that lying piece 'a crap!" Mickey exclaimed.

Two MI 'six agents were waiting as they taxied to a stop at a RAF airport between Staines and London an hour later. Chris helped them unload the weapons shaking his head at the array.

"We need to do something with these," he said. "My superiors will have my arse if they find I've turned loose the two knaves armed with an arsenal who have been creating such havoc on the continent."

"Thank the lord, somebody is finally gonna' take some 'a this gear off our hands," Mickey grunted. "You're lucky we didn't show up with an M1-Abrams tank. Every time we go on a mission, JD requests enough gear to equip a mechanized company. He don't want to swat a fly but would rather lob a grenade to be sure the pesky little critter's dead."

"We used all of these weapons and we'd more'n likely be dead if we hadn't had each and every one of 'em," JD snapped. He turned back to Chris. "No reflection on you Chris, but we need to keep the side arms, an AK, our H&Ks and a couple 'a grenades. The opposition has been dogging us since we completed the mission and I for one don't want to get caught with my dick in my hand."

"Okay," Chris said grudgingly. "I can see where you're coming from, but please, lord don't get in any pitched battles before you leave the British Isles."

"No problem," JD said. "We'll be so nice and quiet won't a soul know we were ever here."

"I bet," Chris muttered. "The good news is, I've got you tentatively lined up on a training flight to Bermuda tomorrow. You can hop a commercial flight to Canada from there, and getting across the U.S. border shouldn't be any trouble for two sneaky blokes like you." He paused and added, "I guess you know you can't carry those pistols on a commercial flight."

"We might look dumb, but we aint that stupid." JD muttered.

"Uh huh," Chris said, then continued, "You'll be staying at a small farm we use as a safe house until departure. You do understand that I've got the proverbial family jewels on the chopping block. The wrong ears hear about this and someone will undoubtedly lop them off."

"Don't worry," JD said. "We won't even breathe hard until we're out of here. And you know you can cash this check any time you want. Just call, wire or send up a smoke signal and we'll be here."

"I know," Chris said with feeling. "There isn't another Yank alive I'd crawl this far out on a limb for other than you or Mickey," he added, then shook hands with them. "I wish I could spend some time with you, but I'm scheduled to lead a mission over in grand old Erin against an unsavory lot of Provos tomorrow so I won't be able to see you before you leave. Good luck hunting the slimy turd that's betraying you."

Chris called at 0:630 the next morning. "Good news bad news," he said when JD answered. "First, I got lucky and was able to reroute a training flight to Nova Scotia leaving at 16:00 this afternoon. One of our people with MI six has been advised two Yanks will be on board and he'll meet you and transport you to Halifax. You'll be on your own from there."

"Sounds fine," JD grunted. "What's the bad news?"

"Two problems," Chris replied. "One, a contact of mine informs me there's a rumor making the rounds in Washington that there is a mole inside the covert organization responsible for the assassinations in Italy and the White House is desperately trying to find out about the organization. Be very careful who you contact when you get back in the States."

"I already figured that," JD muttered. "What's the real problem?"

"I hate to tell you this," Chris said hesitantly." Both, Ms. Bitner and Mr. West turned up missing day before yesterday then a reliable witness reported seeing another woman fitting Ms. Stuarts description being snatched yesterday. Also, the foreign office was informed that Mr. Bitner was abducted from the van transporting him to Rome last week. Why the bloody hell they waited a week to inform the home office, I don't know. But from the intercepts MI six has shared with us, it seems that he went rather willingly. JD we've got every available man scouring the countryside for them and have all exits buttoned up tight. Don't even dream of staying here and embarking on some type of vendetta. The best thing you can do to aid us in their recovery is to get back in the States, locate the traitor and find out who his contact is here. Besides, it won't do anything but slow the operation down if you two start tearing up the countryside, blowing hell out of every Arab you run across." JD was silent for a few moments.

"Okay, that makes sense," he said. "But, I'm trusting you to tell somebody to let us know what's going on while you're gone. And, if you find out they've been transported out of the country you'll let us know where. Those folks were innocent bystanders, who had the misfortune to wind up in the middle of a fire fight and we had to take 'em with us. Other than the asshole the Italians had, they're real nice people and we'll do whatever it takes to get 'em back."

"Just call my headquarters," Chris said. "Someone will be there twenty four hours a day and will know not to keep anything from you." He hesitated a moment. "Knowing Mickey's explosive nature, I feel it would be wise for you to wait until you're out of the country before informing him about these developments. It would be a disaster if he were to go charging around the country looking for these people."

"He'll probably kick my ass," JD grunted. "But you're right, he aint controllable when he's really pissed off."

Chapter Thirty Five

June 8, 1993, 0830 houra
RAF Brize Norton Station
United Kingdom

Command pilot, Captain Owen Wisenby eyed JD and Mickey as a sergeant from Chris's company dropped them off next to a Tri Star K1, C1. He continued his preflight checks of the aircraft thinking, I would like to know who the bloody hell decided to interrupt our regular training regimen to transport these two nefarious looking yanks to Canada. After the sergeant introduced them, Owen couldn't conceal his irritation at having two Americans armed with automatic weapons and side arms on his aircraft. He turned to his copilot and nodded toward the pilots lounge and locker room.

"leftenant, check the locker room for some fleece lined flight jackets for these men," he grumped. "At our planned altitude, they could freeze and we certainly wouldn't want them to get frost bite since someone over at Hereford holds them in high esteem." JD detected the irritation in the pilot's tone and made an effort to smooth his ruffled feathers.

"Uh...Captain, we're sorry to upset your routine," he said. "We didn't pick the mode of transport, but are mighty grateful for the ride."

"Not a problem, Yank," Captain Wisenby said curtly. "Orders are orders, it just seems I'm the tram driver today."

Mickey and JD stood as the pilot studiously ignored them until the copilot hustled back with the flight jackets. They accepted the jackets, mumbled their thanks, and then climbed through the aft fuselage hatch and belted themselves in. Mickey glanced down at the deck as Captain Wisenby taxied out to the runway and nudged JD.

"I hope there aint a bomb-bay that prick can open and dump our butts in the Atlantic."

"Just keep your mouth shut," JD snapped. " Don't even think about fuckin' with him after we land at Halifax. He might not be to happy about it, but he is helping us a great deal."

An MI six agent was waiting as they climbed down to the tarmac at Halifax Nova Scotia. They waited to thank the pilot, but weren't surprised when he strutted by with nose in the air.

"I'd sure like to kick that dip-shit's ass," Mickey growled.

"Yeah, I would too," JD said. We'd probably end up in the stockade if we go to maiming an RAF pilot on a Canadian airfield. Besides, we sure as hell don't want to` throw Chris under the bus."

"At least he didn't ask for the jackets," Mickey grunted. "It's colder'n` a witches tit here." They forgot the pilot as the agent walked up to introduce himself as James Hunt and looked askance at their weapons.

"I'd appreciate it, if you would keep the weaponry out of sight," he said. "And the government would look askance at your using them before crossing the border.

"Not to worry, Jim," JD said. "We'll be gone so fast, you won't be able to remember us."

Agent Hunt furnished them with fresh jeans, flannel shirts and wool sweaters. He waited for them to disassemble the weapons for concealed transport and to change in the pilots lounge before ushering them to a car for a two hour drive to New Brunswick and the town of Moncton.

He parked in front of a pub advertising spirits and fine eats at 22:30, and turned to JD sitting in the right front seat.

"I'm afraid, this is as far as I can go gentlemen," he said. then reached across to shake hands with JD.

"We appreciate the help Jim," JD said. "I Hope we can return the favor some day, thanks again and you take care."

"Not necessary, the best way you can show your appreciation is to get the hell out of Canada, forthwith," Jim replied as he put the car in gear, waited until they had stepped out and drove away.

"Damn! I'm gittin' the impression, we aint welcome in Canada," Mickey muttered.

"Who cares?" JD grunted. "We aint going to be here any longer than it takes to get to the border anyhow."

JD picked up a city map and apartment guide displayed on the front counter as they entered the pub, then followed Mickey to a booth next to the front window.

"Why the hell did you sit in front?" he asked.

" What's the one thing that you harp on the most?" Mickey grumped.

"You got me...What?"

"Don't trust anybody unless you absolutely have to and I want to be able to see any rag-heads that might show up.

A waitress approached to let them know, if they wanted to eat they needed to order right away as the kitchen closed at eleven. Mickey glanced across the table after she left with their order

"What the hells eating you JD?" he asked quietly. "You aint said much or cracked wise since we left the U.K."

"Uh... I hate to tell you," JD replied. "Chris called right before we left to tell me it appears that the opposition has grabbed Penelope, Marlene and Nigel. They've been missing for three days."

"Why didn't you tell me?" Mickey demanded.

"Chris asked me not to," JD said. "He didn't want to risk you going off the deep end and raging around the country looking for them. He thinks the best thing we can do is get back in the States to find the shit-head whose been feeding the terrorists information, then with a little persuasion, whoever it is might be able to give us the location of his contact."

"It aint right for you to hold back information like that," Mickey growled, at JD. "You know we got to trust each other if we're gonna' get outta' this cluster-fuck alive."

"You're right," JD grunted. "But you have to admit, you aint exactly clear headed when you get pissed off...I felt, Chris was probably right, besides, he asked and we'd still be in England with the British authorities looking for us if it weren't for him. I don't know how we would 'a been able to get this far without his help." Mickey calmed down and nodded his acceptance.

"Okay, what's the plan?"

"It's about two hundred miles down to a little town called St. Croix," JD replied.

"We ought to be able to steal a boat and cross the border there."

"How we gonna' get to St Croix?"

"We'll steal a car."

Mickey thought a moment.

"That shouldn't be a problem," he said. "The streets full of 'em."

"Uh uh, we can't use one of those," JD said. "They all probably belong to people in the pubs on this street. The owners will probably be heading home pretty soon and we don't want the one we're driving to make the hot sheet before we're through with it." He looked through the city map and apartment guide until he found an ad for a complex on the South side of town. "We'll take a cab to these apartments and pick one up there," he said. That should give us time to make the border before anyone wakes up and discovers their ride is gone."

They paid the cab off at the entrance to the complex, then strolled down the street and found a late model Camaro Z28 parked in front of a four-plex. Mickey checked to make sure there wasn't an alarm system, then picked up a brick to bust the window. JD grabbed his arm.

"Why don't we see if it's unlocked before you bust a window and we freeze all the way to the border?" He grabbed the door handle and opened it, then slid in the drivers seat. Mickey hot wired the ignition and JD sighed in satisfaction as the big V8 came to life. He drove as quietly as possible until they were a couple of miles from the complex, then checked the map and headed for the highway leading South Southwest toward their planned crossing point at St. Croix.

Chapter Thirty Six

June 10, 1993, 04:30 hours
St. Croix, New Brunswick
Canada.

They concealed the Camaro in underbrush a mile east of St. Croix, then walked to the banks of the St Croix river.

"Is that the States over there?" Mickey asked looking across the river.

"Uh huh," JD replied. "Lets head up the river bank toward St. Croix and see if we can find a boat." Mickey paused, gazing across the river for a few moments.

"Hey!" He exclaimed. "Are Niagara Falls around here? We sure as hell don't need to be paddling a small boat across that river if they are."

"No, Dumbass!" JD exclaimed. "The Falls are at least five hundred miles west of here and they aint even on this river."

"You sure?"

"Yeah...I'm positive."

"How?"

"What the fuck do you mean, how'?"

"I mean, have you been there and seen 'em yourself?" Mickey said flatly.

"No, Birdbrain," JD snapped. "I don't recall ever getting married and honeymooning at Niagara, but I have seen a map of the area and the falls are not on this river.

"Okay," Mickey said hesitantly. "But, I hear water roaring when we're halfway across that river, I'm gonna` choke you, JD."

"Damn it…Niagara is West of here and like I said, this aint even the same river so shut the fuck up and lets get moving," JD snapped.

They approached a small cabin after walking approximately a mile West. JD took cover behind a tree and motioned Mickey forward. He sidled to the cabin's near side then signaled JD to join him.

"There's a shed the other side of the cabin," he whispered as JD reached his side. "I figure there ought to be a boat in it." He peered around the corner of the cabin and then turned back. "There's a bridge about mile or so West of here," he muttered. "Why don't we just mosey up there and walk across?"

"I'm telling you, the Falls aren't anywhere around here," JD rasped. " And I don't want to use one of our passports and alert anyone we're back."

"Okay," Mickey mumbled grudgingly. "But it sure seems like it would be safer to walk across the bridge."

"Just go check out the fucking shed," JD hissed."

Mickey crouched and scuttled across the back yard then froze when he heard someone in the cabin cough. JD slowly peered around the corner of the cabin as he heard a screen door open and saw a large man, armed with a double barrel shotgun step out and start a slow scan of the back yard. His eyes passed over Mickey, still frozen in place and failed to register the dark mass as a man. He slowly swiveled his head back toward JD and tensed, as something clicked in his mind that something unusual was over by the shed. He slowly raised the shotgun and was starting to turn back toward Mickey as JD crept silently up behind and jabbed the barrel of the Ruger in the nape of his neck.

"Freeze! or I'll bow your brains all over the yard," he hissed The big man went rigid and JD felt him tremble slightly. "Take it easy," he said quietly, hoping to calm the man. "You'll be alright; just lay the scatter-gun down and don't move." The man dropped his shotgun abruptly.

"Please don't kill me," he pled. "I've got a wife and three kids."

"If you pay attention and don't try anything stupid, you'll be just fine" JD said. "Now, get down on your knees. I'm not going to hurt you unless I have to." He glanced up as Mickey walked over to his side.

"The damn shed is locked," he muttered.

"You got a boat in the shed mister?" JD asked.

"Yes sir, a bass boat and a canoe," the man replied.

"Is anyone else in the cabin?"

"No sir, my wife and kids are coming down from Moncton tomorrow afternoon for the weekend. I'm alone until they get here."

"Okay, get up and lets go inside," JD said. "Please, don't try anything...I really don't want to hurt you."

"I won't and you can have either one of the boats. I just need to get a key to unlock the shed."

JD kept the man on the back porch after he retrieved the key to the shed from a hook next to the back door while Mickey checked the rest of the cabin out.

"All clear," he yelled after a couple of minutes.

"Did you check the bathrooms?

"I said, all clear, Asshole?" Mickey grumped as he stepped back on the porch. JD nodded then prodded the man again.

"What's your name?"

"Gene Shillstone," the man replied. "You don't need to worry about me making no trouble, mister. Take whichever boat you want and I won't tell a soul."

"Don't lie to me Gene," JD said. "We don't expect you to keep quiet about a couple of outlaws holding you up in the middle of the night to steal your boat. Hell, I'd be screaming to every cop in a fifty mile radius."

"Er...maybe so," Gene said, a little nonplussed. "I worked hard to make a down payment on this cabin and them boats."

"We aint planning to keep your boat," JD said smiling. "We just need it for a couple of hours to cross the border. Give me your phone number and I'll call in a day or so to let you know where it is... okay?"

"That would be real nice, mister," Gene said, visibly relaxing. Mickey glanced at JD then turned to Gene.

"How far is it to Niagara Falls?"

"Niagara Falls?"

"Yeah...are they close?"

"No," Gene replied. "They're way over the other side of Buffalo, New York and that's a long way from here."

"You satisfied now?" JD growled.

"You can't blame me," Mickey muttered. "You been known to fuck up on more'n one occasion. I don't swim very well and you know I don't like boats.

"What the fucks swimming got to do with it, Dip-shit? A multiple Olympic gold medalist couldn't swim across the Niagara river anywhere close to the Falls."

Gene relaxed and smiled, as the two desperados he had feared were going to murder him a few moments before traded insults.

"I don't want to upset you, guys," he said smiling. "But you sound like a couple of old married folks."

JD and Mickey turned to glare at him and he stepped back startled until JD laughed.

"You're right," he said. "It would be easier if Dummy here knew a little geography North of Tennessee."

"You guys from down South?" Gene asked.

"The less you know about us, the safer you'll be," JD said. "I don't mean we'd come back to harm you. You might not believe it, but we are the good guys and there are some really evil sons-a-bitches hot on our ass. They wouldn't hesitate to murder you and your family and they get the idea you can give 'em any information about us. If you're smart you'll keep your mouth shut, pick up your boat when I call and pretend you never saw us. You do that and I guarantee you will be rewarded when we get out of the mess we're in. What did you pay for the boats?"

"Around fourteen thousand for the Bass boat and fifteen hundred for the canoe," Gene replied puzzled.

"Sounds about right to me," JD said. "After you get the one we use back, lock 'em both up and somebody will be by here in a few days to pay you more than enough for a couple of days rent."

Gene handed a key ring to JD.

"I believe you," he said. "The big key is to the shed's door and there's a light switch on the left side inside the door." He paused. "Good luck, mister. I hope you and your buddy can get out of trouble."

"Thanks," JD said. "I hate it, but we're going to have to tie and gag you when we leave. You know anybody nearby we can call to cut you free after we get clear?"

"Benny Cawarth has a cabin about a quarter mile from here. He's a contractor and is a good friend. I've got one of his cards," he said then pulled a card out of his wallet and handed it to JD. "The second number is his cabin and I know he's there because he called this afternoon to ask me to go fishing first thing in the morning."

"Okay," JD said. "Is there any rope in the shed?"

"There are bow and stern lines on the bass boat."

Mickey took the keys to the shed, opened it then returned a few minutes later with the rope. They tied Jim to a four poster bed in the cabins largest bedroom. He shook his head before JD gagged him.

"Be sure you shut all the windows and doors good mister," he said. "I don't want any critters to come in and start chewing on me."

"Don't worry," JD said. "We'll seal the cabin up tight and thanks for your cooperation." They finished locking up and opened the shed's door and JD looked the two boats over.

"Let's use the canoe," he said. "It'll be quieter."

"How did I know you'd pick the one we'd have to paddle," Mickey groused.

"Quit bitchin' and get that end," JD said, pointing at the end of the canoe closest to the door. "I'll take the other end and get the paddles."

They flipped the canoe right side up at the water's edge, then Mickey got in front and JD shoved off from the rear.

"You paddle on the right side," he said. "I'll help and steer back here."

"Okay," Mickey grunted. "You better not do anything cute like rocking this little fuckin' boat."

"I'm not going to scare such a brave Boy Scout," JD said chuckling. "I wish you weren't such a pussy around the water."

"One more Boy Scout remark and your ass is grass!" Mickey snapped.

Chapter Thirty Seven

June 11, 1993, 05:15 hours
Vanceboro, Maine
United States of America

The Eastern sky lightened, signaling the coming dawn as they landed a half mile West of Vanceboro, Maine. They hid the canoe in some underbrush a few yards from the river bank and JD stuck a note inside the gunwale giving Gene's name and number.

"You must be gittin' soft in your old age," Mickey muttered. "You never worried about requisitioning anything we needed before."

"Maybe...but, Gene was real agreeable for a man we held a gun on to steal his boat," JD said. "Besides, we aint in business to make life hard for a workin' stiff and we're going to do what we can to make it easy for him."

"You think havin' a gun on him just might have had a little something to do with him being so agreeable?" Mickey snorted. They walked into Vanceboro as dawn turned to day and found a small Café on main street, entered and slid in a booth. An attractive young girl in her very early twenties, slender with red hair and sparkling blue eyes came from behind the counter and handed them menus.

"You gents, new around here?" she asked flashing a big smile at Mickey.

"You might say that," Mickey replied. "What do you recommend for a couple a' real hungry dudes?"

"The Big Man's breakfast," she said, boldly gazing at Mickey. "It's a three-egg cheese omelet with Canadian bacon, hash browns, biscuits, orange juice and all the coffee you can drink."

"Sounds fine to me," Mickey said, "How 'bout you, JD?"

"I'll have the same," JD muttered.

The waitress scribbled their order on her pad then eyed Mickey again. "You must be from the South," she said warmly. "You sound like, you ought to be in that old movie, Gone with the Wind."

"Naw," JD said chuckling. "That flick was about Georgia and that's almost Yankee-land where we're from."

"I've never been south of Boston," she said to Mickey, ignoring JD. "You're the first real Southerner I've ever met. Do you still say 'ma'am' and things like that?"

"Yes, ma'am, we shore do. It's real nice to meet cha', ma'am," Mickey said, drawing the words out slow with a touch of nasal twang.

"Your order will be out in a few minutes," she said giggling. "How long are you going to be in town?"

"Sorry to say, we're just passing through," Mickey replied.

"That's a shame, stop by the next time," she said then wrote her phone number on the back sheet of her order pad and handed it to Mickey.

"My name is Jill Murphy, I'm here mornings Monday through Friday until after the Lunch crowd leaves. Give me a call and we'll get together."

"This will be my first stop," Mickey assured her.

JD waited until she left to turn their order in and got up.

"Where you going?" Mickey asked.

"I'm going to call Gene's buddy and tell him to release Gene and let him know where they can find the canoe."

"I thought you decided to wait until we were out of the area?"

"Fuck it, I'm doin' it now," JD said. "He was a nice guy and I hate we had to screw with him in the first place, that alright with you?"

"Fine by me," Mickey said. "You're the one in charge of plottin' and plannin, by the way, what is the plan?"

"If you can avoid jumpin' the waitress after we eat. We'll take a cab to the first truck stop South of here and try to hitch a ride."

"Screw you," Mickey snapped. "You're just pissed because she failed to notice what a Don Juan you are."

"The girl must be visually impaired," JD said smiling. "Why didn't you tell her that the chances you're ever going to make it back to Bangor Maine are slim and none."

"Yeah, and Slim's in jail," Mickey snapped. And I just might make the trip one a these days. Now cut the bullshit and tell me the rest 'a your grand plan."

"I'll call Sam and get him to wire me ten grand as soon as I figure out where we'll be tonight, we're down to our last few hundred of expense money."

"Who the fuck is Sam?"

"A lawyer in my hometown."

"You telling me a lawyer will wire you ten grand just because you call and ask?"

"No, I have an account in a little state bank there and he's got power-of-attorney to draw on it."

"Are you fuckin' nuts," Mickey exclaimed. "You trust a lawyer with your bank account?"

"Uh uh, I trust Sam. Him bein' a lawyer aint a plus, but Big Jake trusts him and that's good enough for me, besides I've known him since we were kids and we got the same low opinion about a few relatives we have in common."

"JD, I've met a few of your old friends and aint seen a one I'd trust with a used rubber."

"You're probably right, but Sam is different and since it aint your money quit bitchin' about it."

JD hung up after he told Gene's friend to go by the cabin to release him and where the canoe was, then slid back in the booth as their food arrived.

"Eat up, lets get out 'a here and walk up the street a few blocks to call a taxi," JD said. "It'll take 'em a while to connect us with the cab in case someone knows we're back."

They were browsing in a hardware store two blocks from the diner waiting for the taxi when two local police cars followed by an unmarked government sedan slammed by heading for the river.

"So much for trustin', Gene," Mickey grumped as the taxi pulled to a stop in front of the hardware store. Mickey got in back with the gear and JD slid in next to the driver.

"We're supposed to meet one of our drivers at a truck stop South of here and are running a little late," JD said, trying to disguise his accent.

"The Union seventy-six is twenty miles down the road. It's the only one South of here," the driver said. "That'll cost you forty bucks since I'll probably have to come back without a fare,"

"No problem," JD said and handed him the money. The driver thanked him, pulled into traffic then slowed as they cruised by the lane leading to the river.

"Looks like they might be having some trouble at the border," he said. "You boys seen anything?"

"Nope, but it sure seems like it," JD replied. "Could you step on it a little? We're running late."

They pulled to a stop in front of the truck stops main entrance a half hour later, JD got out then reached in the window to give the driver a five dollar tip.

"Thanks for hustling," he said

"Not a problem," the driver said. "You fellers have a nice day."

Mickey waited outside the drivers lounge while JD wandered around the restaurant until he heard a driver with a distinctly Southern accent ordering breakfast. *Maybe we're gittin' lucky, what are the odds against us finding a Southern redneck trucker in Maine?* He waited until the trucker finished his order, then approached his table.

"Mornin', friend," JD said. "I just happened to pass by when you ordered and there aint no doubt you're a rebel, mind if I sit?" The trucker glanced up and could tell from the accent that JD was from the South.

"Mornin'," he said. "Pull up a chair and set a spell. What can I do fer ya'?"

"My rig is broke down up in Vanceboro," JD said as he sat down. "The company is sendin' another driver to pick it up. My relief driver and I need to be in Baltimore in two days to pick up another load. I figured you might be headin' South and we could hitch a ride, help pay for your fuel and still put some of the expense money in our pocket."

"You're in luck," the trucker said. "I'm pickin' up a load 'a cranberries in Bangor this mornin` to haul down to Richmond." Mickey walked up as the trucker reached across the table to shake hands with JD.

"What's up?" he asked.

"This here's my relief driver, Mickey Dix," JD said. "I'm JD Volt and we will sure appreciate the ride."

The trucker nodded for Mickey to take an empty seat.

"Have a seat," he said. "Name's Willie Hansen. I'm independent so aint got anybody makin` rules about takin` on passengers. I'll be able to save a day of sleep-time on my log if ya'll help drive and fuel money is always welcome. You boys want to eat? He asked.

"Nope, we ate early," JD replied. We'll get on the road as soon as I finish breakfast," Willie said and paused a moment to ask where they were from.

"Nashville," JD replied hoping Willie wasn't from there.

"Well, I'll be dad-burned!" Willie exclaimed. "I'm from Chattanooga. How you reckon the Vols are gonna` do this year?"

"I figure they aint any doubt they'll kick ass," JD said.

"You got that right," Willie agreed. "This'll be the year they finally whup up on Alabama."

"Mickey was scheduled to drive this mornin` so as soon as you pick up your load he'll be glad to take the wheel for a while," JD said glancing at Mickey, hoping he could drive a semi and was relieved when he nodded.

Willie backed up to the loading dock of a cranberry processing plant two hours later, and was told by the dock foreman that the load should be finished in about an hour and a half. Mickey stayed with Willie watching the loading crew while JD spotted a pay phone at the other end of the dock and ambled over to call Sam.

"Where are you and how much trouble are you in?" Sam asked chuckling after he realized who it was.

"Damn Sam! Why do you immediately assume I've fucked up every time I call?" JD asked in an injured tone of voice.

"Because you usually have," Sam said flatly. "Now...who'd you rile up this time?"

"You don't want to know," JD replied.

"I'll accept that," Sam said. "What can I do to help?"

"We're in Bangor, Maine," JD replied. "You need to get over to the bank and wire ten grand to Western Union in Bangor right now."

"It would be easier to do a bank transfer," Sam said. "Besides, the closest Western Union office is in Mobile and it'll take me at least an hour and a half to cash a check and get over there."

"Sam just pick up the phone and call one of your lawyer buddies in Mobile," JD said exasperated. "They all know you got more money than God. One of 'em will handle it for you. Don't use a bank transfer because somebody in Washington is trackin' us and I don't want to use the federal system."

"Dammit!" Sam exclaimed. "How the hell did you get cross-wise with the Feds? Scratch that, don't tell me. I do know a good lawyer in Boston who handles outlaws like you. I'll call him if you think it'll do any good."

"Sam, it aint a lawyer type problem...I'll call you in a few days if we're healthy."

"You know I'll do anything I can to help," Sam said seriously. "In the event you get out of whatever the hell you're into, how about stopping by the next time you're in town. We'll drop by Gambinos for happy hour one afternoon. My reputation's getting a little stodgy and it would help my criminal practice to be seen with you."

"Yeah, your sense 'a humor's gettin' a little stodgy too," JD said. "Uh...don't let anybody know you've been in contact with me. It's a little dangerous to be connected to us right now."

"Now, you're really beginning to worry me," Sam said. "But, I know you aren't going to take my advice or change any plans you have in mind anyhow."

"Okay," JD said. "Now get on the phone and send the money."

"Don't worry, it'll be there in a few minutes," Sam said. "One question."

"What?" JD asked, knowing he couldn't avoid one of Sam's lectures.

"I know you think we don't worry about what's going on in the world here on the serene Eastern shore but I do watch the Fox news channel with some passing interest and I think you ought to remember your age and consider retiring if you were involved in the latest fracas over in Europe."

"Yeah Sam," JD said slightly miffed. "You get out of that three-piece-lawyer suit and work out occasionally you'd know, I aint to old to do anything I could do ten years ago."

"Uh huh," Sam said doubtfully. "When was the last time you made some lady scream with delight after midnight?"

"Damn! You are gittin' stodgy," JD said. "Just, cause you're an old completely tamed married man don't mean, we've all given up on sampling the variety of blooming, young lasses available."

"I give up," Sam said. "You take care, and keep me informed."

"You got it. I'll call in a few days," JD said. "Bye."

Chapter Thirty Eight

June 11, 1993, 10:30 hours
Bangor, Maine
United States of America

After JD finished the conversation with Sam he called a taxi and told the driver to take him to the Western union office. When the cab pulled to a stop in front of the office. He asked the driver to wait, entered the office, showed his ID and watched while a clerk counted out the money, and then stuffed the cash in his jacket pocket, reentered the cab and told the driver to take him back to the cranberry plant.

The truck was loaded and ready to leave with Mickey in the driver's seat and Willie in the passenger seat waiting as he exited the cab.

"Take the sleeper," Mickey said as JD climbed in. "You need to be alert and rested the next day or so."

"Why do he need to be rested?" Willie inquired curiously. "Hell, far as I know, except for the damn log, aint no trucker ever been worried about how much sleep he got."

"Uh...he does all the negotiating with our boss," Mickey said to cover his mistake. "The company we work for is run by a sneaky sum-bitch, name 'a Myers and he stays up at night tryin' to figure out new and more inventive ways to fuck us outta' our pay."

"Know what you mean," Willie said. "I used to work for a' asshole too until I got my own rig and went independent."

JD climbed in the sleeper as they pulled away from the plant and slept soundly until Mickey pulled into a truck stop on I-95 South of Boston for fuel and shook him awake.

"Get outta' that rack, I got to get some shut-eye. Willie's gonna' drive until we get on the Jersey turnpike."

Willie took an off-ramp and stopped at a diner south of Bridgeport, Connecticut for a late lunch. He started to wake Mickey and JD reached across to stop him.

"Uh uh, let him sleep," he said. "He's a real grouch when he wakes up and I'd like to eat without listening to him bitch."

While they were eating JD ordered two cheeseburgers and a coke to go for Mickey, then found him still sleeping soundly as they climbed back in the cab. He gave Willie three hundred dollars for fuel, put the burgers on the console and the coke in a built-in-cooler back in the sleeper.

"Them burgers are gonna git cold," Willie said.

"Don't matter," JD replied. "He'll eat 'em anyhow."

Mickey woke up when they stopped at the first toll booth on the Jersey Turnpike and then complained as he munched on the burgers. "Aint nothing like cold cheese-burgers," he groused.

"I'd rather listen to you gripe about cold burgers than have to put up with you bitchin' about not getting' enough sleep," JD said.

"You aint the one has to eat the damn things," Mickey carped.

"We'll stop at the next truck stop and get some hot ones if they're that bad," JD said.

You need to relieve Willie anyhow." Mickey finished wolfing the burgers down as Willie pulled in a rest stop. They used the facilities and he told Willie to get some sleep as he climbed in the cab.

Willie woke up as they parked in a truck stop east of the Baltimore-Washington thruway. Mickey jumped down from the cab and JD waited until Willie took the driver's seat, then thanked him profusely and promised to get in touch the next time they passed through Chattanooga.

"What's the plan?" Mickey asked as they watched Willie run through the gears on the thruway on-ramp.

"You remember Billy Mandino? He was the spook with us on the mission in Peru when we were detached to the company."

"Yeah, I remember he was called the Rainmaker. Every one said he would rather climb a tree to tell a lie instead 'a standing on the ground to tell the truth. He's one of your old friends I was thinking about. You know you can't ever tell about a spook anyhow," Mickey said. "You reckon we can trust him?"

"I aint positive," JD muttered. "Spooks all lie, but he's the only guy we know in Washington that might be able to help us find the shit-head trying to get us killed." He bought a paper as they entered the truck stop's diner, then glanced through the used car ads until he found a ninety model Oldsmobile eighty eight for sale by owner.

Mickey waited in the diner with the gear while JD called and was assured by the owner that the car was in good running condition. He took a cab to the address the owner gave him, then drove the car for a few blocks to make sure it was in decent shape and its headlights, taillights and turn signals were in working order. He figured, since the local police had been accompanied by what was almost certainly the FBI back in Vanceboro, someone had obviously put an all points bulletin out. And the worst thing that could happen would be for them to get pulled over by the State patrol or the local police for some minor safety infraction. He haggled with the owner enough to avoid any suspicion, then paid him about five hundred dollars more than the car was worth, collected the title, bill of sale and last tag receipt and then drove back to pick Mickey and the gear up. They loaded the gear in the trunk, then Mickey slid in the front passenger seat as JD started for the on-ramp to the thruway and looked over as they built up speed to merge with traffic.

"Why'd you buy this piece 'a shit instead of rentin' a decent car?" he grumped. "The fuckin' air is barely working." JD punched the recirculate button and glanced back at him as the air began to cool.

"Because, we aint going to be sending any paper work to the DMV and it can't be traced to us," he snapped.

He exited the thruway as they approached the beltway around Washington, then pulled in an Exxon station and parked next to a phone booth to call the number Billy had given him after the Peru operation. A woman answered on the second ring and when JD asked if Billy was in she told him he wasn't expected until a little after nine.

"I'd appreciate it if you'd tell him, JD called and I'll call back at eleven if that's not too late?" JD said.

"Oh no, he never gets to bed before midnight or so, I'm his wife, Anne. He has mentioned you and I think another man named Mickey fondly and I'm sure he'll be glad to hear from you."

"Thanks, Anne, I hope we can meet you sometime," JD said. From the warm reception, Billy evidently kept his mouth shut about what we do.

They picked a Holiday Inn right off the beltway on the north side of Washington and paid cash for two adjoining rooms. JD left a wake-up call for 22:00 hours to give him an hour to drive a safe distance from the hotel before calling Billy in case he proved to be untrustworthy. He figured the distance should throw anyone off that might trace the call long enough to give them time to get some rest before having to come up with plan B.

He woke up at 21:45 hours, took a quick shower to get the cobwebs out then was getting dressed when the desk called and Mickey walked through the room's connecting door. They drove around the beltway until they were on the South side of Washington. JD exited on to I-95 South then took the first off ramp, and pulled into a service station with a phone booth on the side of its parking lot to call Billy and he picked up immediately.

"Damn, I can't believe it's you JD," he said. "Where are you?"

"A few miles south of Washington," JD replied and paused. I hope we can trust this guy. "Uh…Mickey and I have a little problem and hoped you might be able to help us."

"What is it?"

"Are you aware of the operation in Italy a few days ago?"

"Hell, the whole world has heard about it," Billy said. "I thought it might be you and Mickey when that liberal broad on CNN said the two men involved sounded like they were from the south.

"Yeah," JD said. " The problem is somebody has been trying to get us killed since the mission by feeding information to the opposition. I thought you might be able to poke around quietly and let us know who we need to make an unscheduled call on."

"I know exactly who is causing the problem," Billy said. "As luck would have it, an old retired controller of mine is running a covert operations group out of an office in Arlington. He asked me to put a surveillance team on his top aide."

"What's the old man's name and the address of the office?"

"I'll give them to you," Billy said. "But, you got to promise me you won't harm that old man. He was my field controller for years and I'd stake my life on him being straight with you. Hell!...I did stake my life on him for years."

"I promise," JD said. "Who do you think the traitor is?"

"There isn't any doubt, it's his aide," Billy said. "His name is Don Mayer. You might have run across him if you're working for Angus."

"We've met," JD said. "What evidence do you have?"

"It didn't take but one day for my guys to discover him eating lunch with a limp-wrist congressman from Massachusetts. He's been supplying Mayer with young boys from his stable and I hear he's trying to get enough evidence to open hearings on Angus and his backers."

"Angus?"

"The old man's name is Angus Ewing and he'd never betray an agent!" Billy exclaimed.

"I told you we wouldn't harm him," JD said flatly. "Will you please give me the location of the office and the fruitcakes address?" Billy gave him the requested information then paused.

"I wouldn't have given it to you if I didn't know I could trust you," he said. "You owe me one, JD."

You can book it," JD replied and then hung up and got back in the Olds and told Mickey what he'd learned as they headed back North.

"I'm pretty sure Billy is straight," he said. "But, I sure felt exposed staying on the phone that long in a parking lot since he was forewarned about the call. Spooks have got state-of-the-art tracing equipment."

"Uh huh," Mickey mumbled, glancing at the rearview mirrors to see if they'd picked up a tail. Do some double backs to see if we have anybody following us."

"Not a bad idea," JD grunted as he jerked across two lanes to speed down an off ramp and then crossed over and jumped back on the highway in the opposite direction.

They jumped on and off the beltway twice, back tracked and circled several blocks before driving behind Georgetown university since it was impossible for a tail to follow them on streets running parallel to the one they were on. When it was obvious they were clean, he got back on the on the beltway to the North-side and they arrived back at the hotel at 23:55 hours.

"What's the plan?" Mickey asked as they got in JD's room.

"We'll drive down to Arlington in the morning and stake out that office," JD replied.

"Lets get some sleep, tomorrow's liable to be a long day."

Chapter Thirty Nine

June 13, 1993, 0:945 hours
Arlington, Virginia,
U.S.A.

They stopped the next morning to buy warm up suits with hoods at an athletic store and changed in the fitting room before driving down to Arlington. Control associates offices were in a four story innocuous brick office building at the address Billy had given them. JD parked in front and waited while Mickey went in to check the lobby directory. He returned a few minutes later and informed, JD the office occupied the entire fourth floor of the building. JD pulled back in traffic to circle the block, then parked a half block up the street and checked the time.

"It's 11:00, We'll probably have to wait a half hour or an hour before Mayer goes to lunch."

"How you know he don't brown-bag it?" Mickey asked.

"Would you, if you were on a government expense account?" JD replied and sat back for a nap. Mickey shook him as Don Mayer walked out of the building's entrance at 11:30.

"There's our boy," he said and started to get out of the Olds. JD pulled him back.

"Uh uh, you stay out of sight," he said. " He'll cause a stir, since the last time he saw you he was scared to death you were going to slice his head off and jam it up his ass."

"That is exactly what I'm planning to do!" Mickey snapped.

"I don't think the Arlington cops would be real happy about you lopping the faggot's head off in broad daylight," JD said chuckling. He waited a moment to be sure Mickey was under control then stuffed some napkins in his cheeks to alter his appearance, flipped the hood over his head and then followed Mayer two blocks up the street to a small upscale restaurant.

He paused outside until he saw the maitre de lead Mayer to a booth in the rear of the dining area and then stepped inside a few moments later, quickly glanced back at the booths and saw Mayer slide in one across the table from a prissy looking young boy.

"He's in there with a real cute young lad," JD muttered when he got back in the Olds. "They're doing everything but kissing each other. He'll be in there for an hour before he heads back to the office so lets go have a talk with the old man."

He parked in front of the building, they changed into the flight jackets to conceal their weapons, then entered the lobby. JD located an elevator to his left and nudged Mickey.

"You take the stairs in case the old dude is an exercise freak," he muttered.

"Why don't you," Mickey groused.

"Because he probably isn't, and I don't want you to fuck with him," JD snapped, walked to the elevator and followed a cantankerous looking old woman inside. She sniffed her displeasure at being trapped on the elevator with a disreputable looking roughneck dressed in warm-up pants and a leather flight jacket.

JD stepped back to let her exit first as they reached the fourth floor and was startled as Angus Ewing a.k.a. Mr. Smith stepped in and spoke to the old woman.

"Maggie, I'm going to get a bite to eat," he said and glanced at his watch. "I should be back by one o'clock."

"Yes sir," Maggie replied. "Did you remember to take your comm unit?" Angus rummaged through his jacket and located the unit in one of the inside pockets.

"Uh...yes I've got the infernal thing," he grumped. "I think God was punishing mankind when he let some damn Asian invent these things. There isn't a place on earth one can escape the hellish things."

"Mr. Ewing," Maggie said primly. "You know wireless phones are the coming thing and they were invented in America."

"Maybe so," he grumped. "But the Japs will be the ones manufacturing the damnable things."

"You are going to be forced to join the twenty-first century one of these days," Maggie remonstrated him then turning a baleful eye on JD once more before stepping out of the elevator. *I hate to admit it, but I'm beginning to like this old man. He feels the same way I do about the information age,* JD thought as the elevator door closed, then tapped Angus on his shoulder.

"Yes," Angus said, as he turned to face JD puzzled and stepped back as recognition dawned.

"My lord! I didn't believe it when Don told me he thought you and Mickey were back in the country," he exclaimed. "How on earth did you manage it?"

"Never mind that," JD snapped. "How 'bout telling me whose been trying to get us killed since we completed the mission."

"I guess, considering that you've found me we, can forget the 'Mr. Smith'," Angus said. "The name is Angus Ewing but I imagine you already know that."

"Uh huh," JD muttered, "Lets get back to whose been fucking with us."

"I'm not sure…but I've started a thorough investigation," Angus said. "Don seems to think it's Alphonce, or one of his associates in Italy."

"That's bullshit," JD snapped. "How the hell did somebody know when and where we were going to cross the Canadian border? Hell, we didn't know ourselves until we made the crossing."

"That is a good question," Angus replied. "How do you know someone had that information?"

"Somebody had the FBI waiting on us in Vanceboro, Maine it might have been the owner of a canoe we borrowed to cross but the cops and the FBI showed up. I don't think the Feds would be interested in a stolen canoe unless someone told them there were a couple of terrorists coming in. It had to be somebody connected to your organization." JD said flatly, paused and then posed a question he knew the answer to. "What about Mayer, have you checked him out thoroughly?"

"He came over from EPA and there's nothing in his FBI file

to suggest he's anything but a loyal federal employee," Angus said guardedly and continued slowly. "He along with every one on the staff is a target of the investigation I mentioned. And I'm expecting a report within a matter of hours. I certainly hope he isn't culpable as he's been a huge asset handling our financial and communications arrangements."

"Communications?"

"I has been a long time since I was active and I'm quite the dinosaur when it comes to computers and communications equipment," Angus replied. "Our principals pulled me out of retirement for the simple reason that I was the only one they felt they could trust not to divulge information under any circumstances. The Washington establishment has become infested with save-my-ass types for years. With the current administration in power it has become all too clear that the President and his party backers will say, or do anything legal and skate right up to the edges of the law for the sole purpose of staying in power."

"Did you know Mayer was a homosexual?" JD asked bluntly.

"It never crossed my mind. Are you sure?"

"Well, he's having lunch with a youngster you'd have to yank the pants down to certify its gender."

"I don't know what to say," Angus muttered. "Although the politically correct thing would be to say, it doesn't make any difference."

"We both know that's horseshit!" JD snapped. " Think about it, who in Washington would he be socializing with? How about a limp wrist Congressman from Massachusetts who has one of his pages running a gay connection service? Who also, by the way is doing everything in his power to expose Control associates with a congressional hearing. If he succeeds, we are all going to get flushed down the toilet."

" My lord," Angus gasped as he realized the gravity of the situation. He paused for a few moments…"I should have some answers for you by tomorrow morning. The people who are investigating him are old associates of mine and are very good."

"I've already talked with them. They are going to give you their report sometime tomorrow. You wait for the report and we'll have a little talk with Ms Mayer tonight."

"I'm not sure that's necessary," Angus said. "The solutions that you and Mickey use to solve a problem are usually fatal."

"I give you my word we won't do anything massive before checking with you. Time is of the essence as the three British citizens involved have been kidnapped by a the terrorist collaborating with the Brit the Italians had in custody," JD said, then punched the lobby button to get the elevator moving.

"I don't suppose there's much I can do to deter you," Angus said.

I'm sure you could, but I'd appreciate it if you wouldn't," JD said as the elevator door slid open at the lobby revealing Mickey, standing with a hand on his Glock-nine.

"Good morning, Mickey," Angus said, then walked blithely past him and out of the building.

"What the fucks goin' on!?" Mickey snapped as JD stepped out of the elevator. "I was fixing to get the rest of the C-4 and blow hell out of the office."

"That would a' been a big help," JD said sarcastically as they got back to the car.. "At least, nobody could have identified my body." They drove to a bar a few blocks away to have a sandwich then located Mayer's address in a Condo development on the outskirts of Arlington.

JD parked in an empty space a block from the condo then walked back to the unit's front door. There was a security company sign posted next to the door and he heard a television on inside. He punched the doorbell and waited until the intercom next to the door came to life.

"Who is it?" a voice with a decided lisp asked.

"Mr. Mayer? I'm from the security company," JD said. "We're having a problem with some units and I need to check your system."

"He's not in, but he's usually home by five thirty. You'll have to come back then."

"Thanks, I'll call back," JD said and walked back to the car. Mickey waited until JD slid back in the driver's seat and shut the door.

"Was anybody in there?"

"Yeah, it sounded like the sissy he was having lunch with," JD replied. "Lets go back to the office and follow Mayer. The boy said he should be home by 17:30."

They parked a block up the street from the office and waited until 17:00 when a canary yellow VW bug with an imitation flower vase behind the back seat pulled out of the rear parking lot.

"The windows are deep tinted so I can't be positive, but I think it's him" Mickey muttered. "Nobody but a woman or a fruitcake would drive a car like that." JD pulled away from the curb to follow and crept to within a car length of the VW.

"I can't see who's driving," he complained. He dropped a block back and followed until the VW parked in front of a wine and cheese shop. Mayer got out and walked in the shop as they drove by.

"That's our boy," Mickey muttered. "He's probably buying some fancy goodies for a little love-fest tonight."

"Yep," JD said. "We'll go back to the condo and wait. There aint a chance in hell he's goin' anywhere but home with the boy waiting."

He parked a block up the street from the Condo, then pulled out as the VW passed and pulled into a parking slot. Mayer stepped out of the car holding a grocery sack. He yelped in fright and dropped the bag as Mickey jumped out of the Olds, reached him in two strides and then slammed him face first against the side of the VW.

"Shut your mouth, or I'll cut your tongue out and make you eat it" he hissed. JD reached to open the back door as Mickey shoved Mayer's arm up to his shoulder blade and then quick stepped him into the back seat of the Olds'.

JD kept an eye on the rearview mirror as he drove out of the development to check for anyone that might be following and noticed an obvious unmarked black Ford Crown Vic with multiple antennas entering the complex as it passed them and muttered to himself, "Why would a surveillance team drive a vehicle like that? If they were tailing us I would have spotted it in a block." He glanced to the back seat to make sure Mickey didn't peremptorily kill the limp wrist before they had a chance to interrogate him and heard him squeal as Mickey grabbed his hair and yanked his head back to expose his throat. Mayer groaned as he felt the knife slide up to his throat.

"Don't cut him before I get a chance to ask him a few questions!" JD snapped before turning back to concentrate on the late afternoon traffic. He drove for a few minutes and became worried when he heard no more sounds emanating from the back.

"You haven't killed him have you?"

"Naw, the little shit pissed his pants and fainted," Mickey grumped.

Chapter Forty

June 12, 1993, 17:45 hours
Arlington, Virginia
U.S.A.

JD took I-95, South for twenty miles to an exit to a secondary road and then drove west until he saw a lane into an opening in the woods. He pulled off the road until they were out of sight and parked next to a big Elm tree. He got out to keep an eye out for anyone passing by while Mickey yanked Mayer out of the back seat and propped him against the tree. JD strode over and slapped him until his eyes fluttered open. Mickey pressed the knife point under his chin.

"You lie once, or fail to answer one question," he hissed. "I'm gonna` stick this blade up in your brain."

Mayer squeaked.

"I won't...please don't kill me."

"You won't, what?" Mickey growled.

"La la...lie!" Mayer stammered.

"I think, he might be ready to confess his sins," Mickey said nodding at JD. And he stepped up to face the little pipsqueak.

"Where are your terrorist friends keeping the three British citizens?" he asked in a quiet mild tone of voice.

"Wha...what British?

"Do you really think it's worth a slow painful death to protect a bunch of terrorist?"

Mickey hissed then pushed the blade a millimeter into the soft skin under Mayer's chin.

He rolled his eye's toward JD.

"Pu, pu…please," he begged pitifully as he felt blood trickle down his neck, saw no sympathy and then desperately looked back at Mickey only to meet the implacable face of death. He shuddered, then sighed and shrank further back against the tree.

"They are being held in Northern Ireland on the outskirts of Whitehead at a small sheep ranch " he whimpered.

"Are they still alive and why did they take 'em there?" JD snapped.

"Fa fa…friends…They have friends in the IRA who are planning to smuggle them out of Ireland on a Libyan sub."

"Why are they still there?"

Uh…one of the ladies involved is the daughter of a ranking member of Parliament.

The British Navy has been put on alert and they are patrolling around Northern Ireland and the Libyans are afraid to approach the area."

"What's their plan?"

"Wha…What?" Mayer said tremulously. I don't understand."

"I mean, when are they planning on moving them?" JD barked then glanced at Mickey.

"The next time this piece of shit tries to be cute or says something stupid, jam that fucking knife up to his brain…and make it slow so he'll be able to feel every millimeter of it," he hissed.

"Oh God," Mayer murmured, quivering.

"I…uh talked to them two days ago and they have a source inside of Parliament, who informed them that the British labor party is preparing to raise a stink about the patrols in an effort to get them withdrawn. They are confident the Navy will pull out in a week." JD backed up a step and slapped him.

"Don, you piece of worthless dog shit," he said quietly. "I promised Angus we would avoid killing you, but I got to tell you it's real tempting." Mickey applied pressure to sink the knife a millimeter deeper.

"What about Marty?" he growled. "This fuckin' faggot got him killed."

"I want to slice the mother-fucker up as bad, as you," JD said shaking his head. "We gave Angus our word we wouldn't do anything massive."

"You think killin' this cocksucker is massive? That's bullshit! He aint worth the price of a small caliber bullet and it would be a lot safer to permanently shut him the fuck up. I would have already cut his throat but he aint worth the time it would take to clean the blood off 'a my knife," Mickey rasped, glowering at JD.

"We don't have to worry about him talking to anybody," JD said flatly. "Angus will tend to him."

"What makes you think he won't turn the little pud-fucker loose?"

"Because, he was a spook for over thirty years. I guarantee, he is just as cold-blooded as you are when it comes to eliminating a traitor," JD said. "I'd rather get to Ireland and eradicate the sons-a-bitches who killed Marty and are holding our friends instead of wasting any time disposing of this scumbag's body." Mickey relaxed and slowly nodded his agreement.

"Okay, what will we do with it?" he inquired, using the pejorative 'it' to indicate, he felt their captive was sub-human.

They bound and gagged Mayer and dumped him in the trunk and then stopped at the same service station phone box to call Angus.

"What is your situation?" Angus asked when he answered on the first ring.

"We have the problem in the trunk," JD replied.

"Is it moving?"

"Oh yeah," JD said. "We didn't have to rough the little faggot up much before he popped his cookie's."

"What are you planning to do with him?"

"Turn him over to you," JD said. "You know, if he gets loose he'll call that fruitcake congressman and then get word to the terrorists holding the British citizens and they'll be dead."

"Meet me in the office parking lot in an hour," Angus said briskly.

"No problem," JD replied. "One other thing."

"Yes."

"Mickey and I are going to England to help some SAS people we know extract our British friends," he said firmly. "We're going to need new documents. Mayer has got the FBI and INS looking for the ones we've been using."

"Bring the treasonous cur to me Angus said. "You can be assured that he won't survive to have a conversation with the congressman nor anyone else. I'll have new passports available by 0:600 hours tomorrow and the FBI and INS problem will be handled immediately; Now I have a question."

"What?"

"You haven't mentioned money."

"Angus, this one's on the house, just get us transportation to England. We'll take it from there," JD replied.

They pulled into the parking lot an hour later and found Angus waiting in the back seat of a black Crown Vic accompanied by two large, capable looking men in front.. He got out as they pulled in to meet JD and Mickey as they exited the Olds.

"Is there any visible damage to him?"

"Nothing that won't pass for a shaving accident," Mickey grunted.

"I feel like such an old fool for not recognizing Don's obvious character flaws and am dreadfully sorry that he caused so much grief," Angus said.

"You know the chances of operating in this business without casualties, are slim and none," JD said.

"Yeah, and the last time we checked, 'Slim was outta' town,'" Mickey said irritably. Angus smiled for the first time then nodded to the men in the car.

One of them turned to JD and said, "Keys." JD tossed them, then he and Mickey stood back as they as they unloaded a large case out of the trunk and put it in the trunk of the Olds and then yanked Mayer out and tossed him in the Crown Vic's trunk, slammed it shut and got back in the front seat.

"What's in the case?" JD inquired.

"I had the forethought to collect the weapons and gear you will need when you meet your contacts in Hereford," Angus replied. "Meet me here at 0:800 hours tomorrow. There is a Lear Jet scheduled to leave from a small private airport at 12:00 which should put you in Britain by 20:00 hours their time."

"You never cease to amaze me," JD said, but we need to change our destination to Belfast. The hostages are at a little sheep ranch outside of Whitehead."

"Can you get to your contact in England?" Angus asked.

"Yes sir," JD replied. His team is already in Ireland and we'll contact him to set the extraction up."

"Will you please try not to create a major international incident?"

"If you make sure that piece of dog-shit doesn't get loose to open his yap, it should go down without a lot of noise," JD replied.

"Don't fret yourself," Angus stated. "He's not going to be talking to anyone other than Saint Peter at the Pearly Gates and I imagine, he'll lock them firmly and boot Don's ass to hell." He paused a moment to shake hands with them. "Good hunting," he said smiling. "I'll be looking forward to your report when the mission is successfully concluded."

As JD pulled out of the parking lot Mickey glanced over at him.

"The way those two gorillas were gruntin' with that case," he groused. "It must 'a been heavy, so there's probably enough weaponry in there to make you happy."

"Uh huh," JD grunted then yawned. "Man, I feel like I could sleep a week," he said. "Let's find a good steak house and eat the biggest slab of meat they have and then hit the sack. We need to get up at 0:630 to get back here and meet Angus in the morning.

Chapter Forty One

June 14, 1993, 0:115 hours
N.E. Washington, D.C.
U.S.A.

JD called Chris after they arrived back at the Holiday Inn and waited impatiently as the answering machine ran through the rather long message, then barked, "Chris, it's JD pick up the phone or call me at area 202 878 5500, Room 436 as soon as possible. He was preparing to add that they knew the whereabouts of Penelope, Marlene and Nigel when, Chris answered.

"Bloody hell, JD!" he exclaimed. "Do you know what time it is here? I just got back from our unsuccessful patrol. It seems the provos are getting smarter about where they hide."

"Aint got the foggiest," JD replied. "Sorry to interrupt your beauty sleep, but I thought you might like to know where your three British subjects are."

"You know the location?" Chris asked doubtfully.

"Uh huh...Northern Ireland at a small sheep ranch outside the town of Whitehead," JD replied. "You got any Intel on the area?"

"Oh yes, that sector has been quite the hot bed of activity for years. We've run several missions in the region."

"Very good," JD said. "Can you get a team together by 20:00 hours your time tomorrow and meet us at the Belfast airport?

"I don't suppose I can dissuade you and Mickey from sticking your rather large noses in this affair," Chris grumped.

"You got a long shooter as good as me?"

"Come to think of it…no," Chris replied. "Maybe having a bloodthirsty dead-eye on hand could be useful, so… yes. I'll meet you with some of my chaps."

JD hung up and glanced at Mickey.

"Looks like we'll be playing with the first team," he muttered.

"The SAS?"

"Yep."

"That always makes things easier."

"Uh huh."

They met Angus at 0:800 hours the next morning and he drove them to a private airport where the Lear was waiting to take off. The pilot lifted off, as they buckled their seat belts, then crossed the coast of Maryland within a few minutes and set a course for a fuel stop at Newfoundland. Mickey reclined his seat and was asleep almost immediately while JD tried and failed to concentrate on a crossword puzzle in the morning paper until they landed, refueled and then took off again for the Trans-Atlantic flight to Belfast. He gave up on the crossword shortly after take off, tried to sleep and finally nodded into restless slumber until the copilot came back to tell him an SAS unit commander had been in contact as they crossed the northwestern coast of Ireland. They would be landing in thirty minutes and would be directed to a RAF hangar after touch-down.

After the pilot taxied in to the hangar, Chris and six well armed hard bitten SAS veterans clad in black assault gear were waiting by two Land Rovers as they debarked and unloaded their weaponry. Chris introduced them to the other members of the team then nodded at one of the vehicles.

"JD, you ride in the command car with me and my second," he said. "Mickey needs to ride in the other with the entry team to go over points of ingress." He glanced at the case and smiled.

"I suppose those are your weapons?"

"Yep, is the hangar secure?" JD asked. "We need to check 'em out."

"Quite," Chris said then turned to his XO. "Rustle up a couple of helmet mikes for them Leftenant."

Getting in the secure hangar, they opened the case and found the same weaponry they had used on the prior two missions along with black fatigues, jump boots, flak vests, helmets and a note from Angus.

"Both rifles have been rebalanced and sight adjusted by a very experienced army sharp-shooter. He assures me that you will find them satisfactory. I would say good-luck, but have noted that you and Mickey seem to make your own, so good hunting lads bring back their scalps.'

After they changed and assembled their weapons, JD got in the back seat of the Land rover with Chris's XO and reached across to shake hands with him.

"It's an honor to be serving with the best," JD said, then reached up to get Chris's attention. " How did you find the ranch?

" There aren't any Sheep ranchers with a large Mercedes parked in back and Arab sentries front and back," Chris replied.. There are quite a few in the area but that pretty well confirmed it. We've had surveillance on a knoll three hundred meters south of the main house since we found them. We have seen the women tied down in two bedrooms downstairs. Mrs. Bitner has been repeatedly assaulted by the Arabs seemingly with Mr. Bitners connivance."

"How about Ms. Stuart." JD asked.

"I don't know why, but as yet she is unharmed," Chris replied. " I had to give the surveillance team strict orders to keep their position until we got the whole team in when the assault on Mrs. Bitner ensued. They wanted to attack after seeing the rape of that poor women."

"It would be a good idea to keep that information from Mickey until we get the operation underway," JD said. "There is no way to tell what he will do. He is rather fond of that lady."

"I am well aware of Mickey's proclivities for abrupt violent action when something deeply disturbs him and have instructed the entry team to keep quiet about it until the operation is over," Chris replied. JD turned his attention back to the XO.

"What's you name Leftenant," JD asked.

"Ian Smythe," the XO replied. "Some say that we are the best, but if half the tales Chris has been telling us about you and your mate's exploits on the continent are true, we could use a few lessons."

"You tellin' me, you didn't know Chris was a pathological liar?" JD said lightly.

"There is a rumor to that effect," Ian said grinning.

"Both of you can bloody well bugger off!" Chris snapped.

Chapter Forty Two

★   ★

June 13, 1993, 22:30 hours
Holyhoke sheep ranch, five kilometers
North of Whitehead, Northern Ireland.

The sound of Marlene's groaning again woke Penelope in the room
next to the dingy bedroom Marlene was in. She had been tied hand
and foot to a shabby iron bed for two days and had struggled with the
leather restraints binding her wrists to the rusting headboard until
burning pain and blood trickling down her arms convinced her that
any further exertion was futile. She heard Marlene cry out again. Oh
my God! That vile wretched man has turned those animals loose
on her again. The buoyant spirit she had felt on surviving the peril and
passion experienced with JD in Italy were all lost when she stepped into
a taxi after a shopping spree at Harrods.

She hadn't felt at all threatened by the driver being an Arab as over
the past few years middle-east immigrants seemed to be driving almost
every other taxi on the streets of London. The first inkling she got that
something was amiss was when she realized the trip was taking longer
than usual and glanced up from the latest copy of Elle and noticed they
were pulling into a rundown warehouse district that certainly wasn't
on the normal route to her upscale condominium in Soho. She became
alarmed when the driver pulled inside a deserted building and two Arab

thugs hauled her out of the taxi, bound, gagged her and then threw her into the boot of a Mercedes and she knew she was in terrible trouble.

The next hours were horribly uncomfortable. She didn't have the faintest idea where they were bound until she felt the big car lurch onto some type of ramp then park. The rumble of big diesel engines and gentle roll of the sea let her know they were on a ferry and probably headed for Northern Ireland. She was on the verge of becoming seasick in the stifling boot until she felt the car drive off of the ferry, then endured more hours of discomfort as it bumped and bounced over rough tarmac before coming to a stop. She was roughly pulled out and carried into a fairly large clapboard house to be deposited on a sofa next to a distraught Marlene and Nigel. She didn't have any idea how long her friends had been held captive as one of the Arabs struck her hard enough for her to black out when she tried speaking to Marlene. On regaining her senses, she'd had to control a terrible urge to scream as her lifelong friend and companion began to sob uncontrollably. Nigel sat rigid, almost comatose with fear, seemingly unaware of Penelope's arrival while five Arabs and Ian ogled her. *God forbid, it's Ian, I've always felt he was an IRA sympathizer but would never have dreamed he would give aid to and consort with terrorists!* The Arabs stood ogling Marlene, displaying brownish tobacco stained, rotting teeth while Ian raved, gloating about how he had given the band of terrorists detailed information about all of their usual habits and movements which had made their kidnappings and transport to Ireland quite simple. "I'm well aware of how you behaved with that American murderer while you were in Italy my dear," he'd said, spitting in Marlene's face. "Since you acted the harlot with him...I think it only fitting that you serve to entertain my friends while we wait for the accursed British Navy to grow bored with their futile exercise and leave." He had savored Marlene's expression of horror a few moments then turned to Penelope.

"And you...you little trollop are no better," he'd hissed. "But...I've always wanted to show you how it felt like to get a thorough fucking by a real man, so I'll reserve you for my personal pleasure."

"If you consider yourself to be a real man she'd blazed. "You more than flatter yourself. You are nothing more than a contemptible, miserable piece of excrement and would not have the faintest idea what a real man is." Ian had turned red with rage, then slammed his fist into her jaw and everything turned black.

Coming to her senses, she found her hands and feet were bound to the corners of an old four poster bed. I don't know how long I was in a stupor but I seem to remember it has been two days. I haven't seen anyone other than that red-haired Irish witch who has fed and escorted me to the loo. She dimly recalled her abject horror and fear as she heard the sounds of the Arabs animal pleasure and Marlene's screams as they had repeatedly violated her for the past two days. She knew Ian was biding his time in anticipation of the utter subjugation he planned for her, and was probably thoroughly enjoying the horror she felt hearing the degradation being visited upon Marlene.

Feeling the utter futility of not being able to do or take any positive action, her greatest fear wasn't the promised rape and probable murder. It was the horrible thought that Ian stood an excellent chance of avoiding the consequences of his terrible collusion with the terrorists. God, please bring JD and Mickey to us, She prayed, then thought, Penelope you are being a fool, they are surely back within the safe confines of America by now. I know they have not forgotten us but it is sheer folly to hope that they will arrive in this God forsaken place to rescue us. Even if they have been informed of our plight there is no way they could possibly find us here. Jesus make me strong, She prayed as the door swung open.

Chapter Forty Three

June 13, 1993, 22:30 hours
Holyhoke sheep ranch, five kilometers
North of Whitehead, Northern Ireland

Chris and JD jogged up a hill three hundred meters west of the terrorist's lair, then found a position offering a good view of the front, North, South and back sides of the main building. It was a story and a half clapboard house with a front porch covered by the roof extending the entire width of the front. The backyard appeared to be almost an acre in size surrounded by a rail fence which connected to a sheep cote or barn in back.

JD set the H&K's Bipod firmly in the turf then slowly began to scan the house with the starlight scope. He immediately noticed a darkened window above the two first floor bedroom windows on the South side, indicating a second floor.

"Shit!" he exclaimed. "I didn't see a second floor on the plans you showed us."

"Bloody hell," Chris swore. "There wasn't one, hopefully it's just an attic" JD watched through the scope as Mickey, accompanied by the front and back entry teams took their positions, preparing for their assault in the darkness surrounding the house. He picked up a sentry on the left side of the front porch and another walking a post in the backyard. He tapped Chris on the shoulder.

"There's a sentry on the porch and another in the back yard," he muttered. "The one on the porch seems to be half asleep but the man in back appears to be alert."

"I got 'em," Chris muttered then spoke into his helmet mounted comm. "Night hawk two…be aware that there might be a second floor, so look for stairs when you make your entry. There is a target on the front porch and one more in the backyard."

"One…do you want us to eliminate them?" Sean, Night hawk two asked.

"Hold position, Two," Chris replied then nudged JD. "Can you take them out at this range?" he muttered. "Neither the front or back yard offers any cover and it's going to be difficult for the teams to make their entry without one of them raising an alarm."

"No problem," JD said as he attached the sound suppressor. "Let Two know I'm going to drop the one in back first and they need to keep an eye on the porch in case that one hears him hit the ground."

JD waited until the front sentry moved out of the shadows to light a cigarette, then stepped to the side of the porch and unzipped his trousers to take a piss.

"Wait until he's got a good stream going," Chris whispered. "I've never seen an Arab with his dick in his hand that could focus on anything else."

"Didn't know you spent time watching rag-heads play with themselves," JD said chuckling.

"Stick it in your bloody ear," Chris hissed.

"Sorry…couldn't resist," JD whispered suppressing a smile.

Back to business, he thought then moved the scope to the back corner of the house and waited for the sentry to walk into the sight picture. He didn't want to risk the Arab was wearing body-armor so aimed for a head shot as the man strolled into view, inhaled and slowly exhaled as he exerted pressure on the trigger, then sighed as the rifle fired and the target dropped in place. He swung the scope back to the front porch and saw that sentry in the process of shaking off, seemingly oblivious to his comrade's sudden death. He moved the cross-hairs to the sentries head, slowly began to squeeze, then stopped. There aint any way that rag-head can get his dick back in and zip up holding his rifle. Why take the chance of him firing it by accident when he falls? All I need to do is wait for him to prop it against the house or porch rail. His thought was quickly rewarded as the sentry propped his rifle against the front wall. He calmly went through the firing process again, the rifle fired and the sentry toppled off the porch.

Chris patted JD on the shoulder "Excellent," he whispered then spoke into his comm. "The backyard and porch are clear Two, get into position for entry."

"Hold!" JD snapped, as a light came on in one of the bedroom windows. He moved the scope over and could see Penelope bound spread eagled on an iron bed. Ian Bitner was standing at the foot of the bed leering at her as he unbuckled preparing to drop his trousers.

"What's the problem?" Chris hissed, "We have to get this operation underway before someone inside discovers they have two dead sentries in the yard."

"Just fuckin' hold," JD barked, then calmly waited until the would-be-rapist stepped out of his pants and moved toward the bed to mount Penelope.

Maybe I can belittle his manhood enough for him to settle for beating me senseless. Penelope thought as she watched Ian fondling his erection.

"I hope you weren't planning to impress me with that insignificant little wee wee," she spat at him. "Why don't you go back to the ewes cote. Maybe you can find a young lamb small enough to actually feel the little thing."

Ian's face mottled with rage and he was starting to step forward when the window tinkled and the member he had been so proudly fondling seemed to explode in his hand. JD is here! She thought joyously.

"You can cut 'em loose," JD muttered to Chris. "But tell 'em to stay out of the front bedroom on the South side, I got it under control," he said as he moved the cross hairs, waited a moment for Ian to appreciate the condition of the member he had been so proudly displaying then squeezed off another round and saw a small hole appear in Ian's forehead a second before he folded like a wet paper doll. I knew that mother-fucker was trouble the first time I met him. It's a shame I didn't pop a cap in his ass and throw him off the cliff when I had a chance. He probably engineered the kidnappings. He heard Mickey and the entry team as they lobbed stun grenades and flash-bangs through windows on both sides of the house then in the front and back doors as they kicked them open. He pulled the Ruger and started to rise to go free Penelope until Chris grabbed his shoulder.

"No!" he barked. "Stay here and cover the area in case any of them get out and try to escape."

JD eased back to the prone position and had just put the scope back on the bedroom window when two figures came crashing through. He leveled the cross hairs on them as one jerked the other erect, and saw a terrorist holding a knife to Penelope's throat as he started dragging her toward the cote. Two SAS troopers dropped out behind them and the terrorist yanked Penelope around to place her between himself and the troopers, then started screaming epithets at them in Arabic. JD kept the terrorist in his sights and nudged Chris.

"Tell them to keep their distance," he muttered. "Have them move to his left side toward us and stay out of the line of fire. I need his head on this side to get a clear shot." Chris relayed the message. Then, as the SAS men slowly moved to the Arab's side, he jerked Penelope further around to keep her between himself and the troopers, renewed his tirade and then jerked his head around to keep an eye on them.

Penelope had almost laughed out loud when she saw the befuddled expression on Ian's face as his penis literally disintegrated in his hand. He had a look of agony and utter confusion when he glanced down, then screamed in abject fear as he met her eyes waiting for the sure death he knew was eminent as it dawned on him who was concealed somewhere outside.

She watched fascinated as the scream of excruciating pain and apprehensive horror built deep within his thorax until it was cut short as the glass tinkled again, then a neat hole appeared in his forehead and he dropped from her sight. She laid back relaxing for the first time since her abduction as she heard the front and back doors crash open, then several loud explosions and what was surely a team of commandos begin a methodical extermination of the terrorists. Her torpor suddenly ended when one of the Arabs crawled into the room, reached up to flip the lights off, sidled to the side of the bed, quickly cut her loose then dragged her out of the bed. *JD is here, but it's to late,* she thought, then fainted as the terrorist held a knife to her throat and dove through the window.

JD inhaled as he waited for the two heads in his sight picture to separate. Time seemed to drag as the Arab continued mouthing obscenities at the SAS troopers. The heads finally separated slightly and he exhaled as he softly squeezed the trigger. The rifle fired and his heart stopped as both figures toppled to the ground in a heap. Fuck! I,ve killed her, he thought desperately then jumped up and started running toward the two bodies. He was halfway down the hill when he heard Chris over the comm.

"Slow down, JD. Night hawk Two says she's bleeding from a nick to her throat but it's not life threatening." He slowed his mad dash and was startled to see Mickey bracing himself against a porch pillar vomiting, then continued to the trooper kneeling beside Penelope and could see the cut wasn't serious as the SAS trooper slapped a dressing on the wound and glanced up at him. "That was one bloody hell of a shot, Yank!" he exclaimed. "The next time we need a long shooter I'm going to see if Captain Washington can convince you to join us."

"Thanks," JD muttered. "You sure she's okay?"

"I've nicked myself worse shaving," the trooper replied.

"Take care of her," JD mumbled. "I need to see what the hell's the matter with my partner." He walked back to the porch and found Mickey still heaving.

"What the hell's the matter with you? As many bodies as we've left lying around the world, I don't recall you ever gittin' sick about it. It aint like I don't know," he muttered to himelf.

"Those slimy Cocksuckers!" Mickey grunted as tears rolled down his cheeks.

"What the hell did they do?!"

"They been using her like a Shanghai dockside whore for two days," Mickey choked as two troopers carried Marlene out on a stretcher. "I wish we could have kept the greasy bastards alive so I'd 'a had time to spend at least a week killin' 'em slow," he added bitterly. JD grabbed his lifelong friend and brother-in-arms around his shoulders and helped him across the yard as two ambulances Chris had standing by a kilometer up the road slammed to a stop in the front yard. "You got something to help my brother?" he muttered as a medic, thinking Mickey was wounded trotted up.

"Is he hit?" the medic asked.

"No but I'd really appreciate it if you'd pop him with something to knock him out," JD pled.

The medic met JD's eyes and could see he was deadly serious.

"What would you suggest, sir?" he asked hesitantly.

"Fuck! Just knock his ass out," JD exclaimed as he glanced at Mickey and could tell he was almost overcome by grief and rage.

The medic rummaged through his kit, selected an ampoule then shot Mickey in his upper thigh as another trotted up with a stretcher.

"Lower him on the stretcher, sir," he said as Mickey went limp. "He'll be asleep for at least eight hours."

JD watched as the medics loaded Mickey in the first ambulance then walked over to Penelope's side and waited for her to be loaded in the second. He knelt beside her as a medic popped some ammonia under her nose. Her eyes fluttered and she gazed up at JD. He smiled as a look of relief and euphoria crossed her face.

"I knew it was you when Ian glanced down and found himself missing a body part he was so proud of," she said giggling, then a dark cloud crossed her features as she quietly sobbed, "how is Marlene? Those barbaric animals have abused her for days." JD glanced at Marlene as she was loaded on the ambulance and then turned back to Penelope.

"Physically, she's pretty beat up but she'll recover from those injuries in a couple of weeks," he said. "The question is how long will it take to heal the psychological wounds she's suffered. That is going to take time and a lot of help from those closest to her." He paused as the medics lifted Penelope. "I'll see you at the hospital," he said. "You'll be fine and I think with your help, Marlene will also."

Chris strolled to JD's side as the ambulances pulled away. "That was an unbelievable shot," he said. "I didn't think you could peel that bloody Arab off of her without a scratch." JD gazed at the scene of the recent carnage and turned back to Chris.

"What about the people who own this place?

"They were found locked in a root cellar scared witless," Chris replied. "We'll check to see if they have any IRA connections, but it appears that a woman sympathizer living in Whitehead picked this place for it's remote location."

"Any casualties on the team?"

"No, we almost lost one man when he decided to avoid killing the woman. She pulled a Makarov and would have blown him away if Mickey hadn't been quite as soft hearted and stitched her buttocks against the wall."

"Any rag-heads survive?"

"Nary a one," Chris replied. "Whoever was controlling this cell will hopefully decide the cost might be a tad steep to pursue this little escapade any further."

"Why the hell do you think the bastards snatched 'em?" JD asked puzzled.

"I don't really have the foggiest," Chris replied. "The only thing that makes any sense to me is, Mr. Bitner convinced them to do it for the sole purpose of taking his revenge on the two women."

"He was for sure a piece of shit," JD said "You got any overseas communications handy?" Chris pulled a sending unit out of the nearest Rover.

"What number? JD gave him the number and waited while he punched it in then was surprised when Angus answered on the first ring instead of the usual ten minute delay.

"How are things coming along?" Angus asked, bypassing any pleasantries.

"Okay…I'll bite," JD snapped. "How the hell did you know it was me?"

"It's no big secret," Angus replied. "All of our operatives of which there are few, have been issued an individual contact number. I always know who is calling." He paused a moment then continued, "I take it, the mission was successful?"

"For the most part," JD replied.

"What do you mean by most part?"

"Uh…Mickey is pretty tore up about a woman he was pretty attached to, the damn terrorists fucked her up pretty bad.

"That's a shame," Angus mused. "There is another assignment I was holding in abeyance hoping that you and Mickey would be available soon."

"Uh uh," JD muttered. "Mickey won't be ready for anything for a good while and to tell you the truth, I'm not either. You can keep us on your list, but consider us on R& R for at least a couple of months."

"I understand, but I feel that given the way our current chief of state picks out any target that is convenient to get the media's attention off his sexual and criminal misdeeds and refuses to take any pro-active measures against terrorism. And those ineffective little pinpricks only serve to invite more and bolder attacks in the future. I truly believe terrorism will take center stage in the near future and the nation needs men like you and Mickey to eliminate at least some of the ungodly number of extreme Islamic Jihadists embedded in every part of the world. I doubt that you, Mickey nor the citizenry is aware of how many are currently residing in the United States alone. The numbers would boggle your mind. Please keep in touch as I fear terrorism will come to our shores in the very near future."

"Uh huh," JD muttered, not really believing anyone would be crazy enough to commit major acts of terrorism within the borders of the United States. "We'll keep in contact, but don't plan on us going active real soon. It's been a pleasure working for you, Angus you're the best controller we've ever been associated with."

"You and Mickey are a great team," Angus said. " I'll be looking forward to hearing from you soon."

"When Mickey is better I'll see if he's up to it and call you," JD said. " You take care."

"Tell Mickey, I wish him all the best and that goes for you too," Angus said with a sigh of resignation. JD hung up.